An Accidental Affair

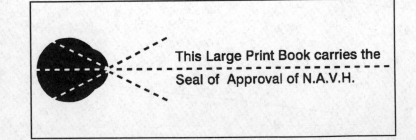

AN ACCIDENTAL AFFAIR

ERIC JEROME DICKEY

THORNDIKE PRESS
A part of Gale, Cengage Learning

GALE
CENGAGE Learning®

Detroit • New York • San Francisco • New Haven, Conn • Waterville, Maine • London

GALE
CENGAGE Learning®

LIBRARY OF CONGRESS CATALOGING-IN-PUBLICATION DATA

Dickey, Eric Jerome.
    An accidental affair / by Eric Jerome Dickey.
      pages ; cm. — (Thorndike Press large print
African-American)
    ISBN-13: 978-1-4104-4472-1 (hardcover)
    ISBN-10: 1-4104-4472-4 (hardcover)
    1. Married people—Fiction. 2. Screenwriters—Fiction. 3. Motion
picture actors and actresses—Fiction. 4. Large type books. I. Title.
PS3554.I319A65 2012b
813'.54—dc23   2012006668

Published in 2012 by arrangement with Dutton, a member of Penguin Group (USA) Inc.

Printed in the United States of America
1 2 3 4 5 6 7 16 15 14 13 12

For Dominique

Regina Baptiste interview. *Vanity Fair.*

"Attack every role, whether you're playing fragile or fearless, good or evil, you
attack it, you let go, you live it, or you
walk away and let a better actor have the
part. I know that sounds silly and childish, because after all we're in the business of make-believe. We have to sell it
to ourselves first, then, as in make-
believe, we make you believe. How does
it feel when the camera is on? The
camera is on and you're a tool. A tool of
the writer. A tool of the director. A tool
of the cameraman. A tool of the guy who
is in charge of lighting. And a tool of
your own needs as an actor. We have to
make it real. The competition? Many
want you to succeed, but more than a
few want you to fail. The pressure is
ridiculous and every great acting career

comes to an end, and for the performer oftentimes too soon. Norma Desmond? Well, yeah. A lot of us end up like Norma Desmond. You move from being a working actress to a celebrity who used to work. You move from being a grand movie star who has steady work to barely being able to secure a special guest spot on television. You have a star on the Walk of Fame, which to me is funny . . . a star on the ground . . . no one should be able to step on a star and leave it all dull and smudgy. Oh, don't get me wrong. I want one. And this girl from Montana wants one badly. But, as I was saying. It's strange. The Hollywood Walk of Fame. You're walked all over by the public, all shapes and sizes of shoes stepping on your name, most of the public never looking down, so many names, so many people forgotten and yet trampled on daily, which I guess is symbolic, for some, not all, of the way most feel that they are treated in Hollywood. Women, we sacrifice our unborn babies, give up motherhood to become stars. Does having to compete for so few roles and being a woman in Hollywood scare me? It terrifies me. Norma Desmond was washed up before she was fifty. Time is not on a woman's side in Hollywood. It's our enemy. Clint Eastwood, Cary Grant, Peter Sellers, Morgan Freeman, all are or were in demand way beyond their half-century mark, and always paired up with female leads pretty much half or a third of their ages. Women have to do twice as much as men in half as much time."

"That's one thing I like about Hollywood. The writer is there revealed in his ultimate corruption. He asks no praise, because his praise comes to him in the form of a salary check. In Hollywood the average writer is not young, not honest, not brave, and a bit overdressed. But he is darn good company, which book writers as a rule are not. He is better than what he writes. Most book writers are not as good."

— Raymond Chandler

"Audiences don't know somebody sits down and writes a picture. They think the actors make it up as it they go along."

— *Sunset Boulevard,* 1950

"Its [Hollywood's] big men are mostly little men with fancy offices and a lot of money. A great many of them are stupid little men, with reach-me-down brains, small-town arrogance and a sort of animal knack of smelling out the taste of the stupidest part of the public. They have played in luck so long that they have come to mistake luck for enlightenment."

— Raymond Chandler

"A celebrity is one who is known to many

persons [that] he is glad he doesn't know."
— H. L. Mencken, *US* editor (1880–1956)

Superstar Johnny "Handsome" Bergs
8 hours ago

Rumors are circulating that actor Johnny Bergs has joined the Celebrity Sex Tape Club. But this is not a normal homemade sex tape with an unknown woman as his costar. Details are sketchy at this moment but the sex tape is said to be hotter than Japan's nuclear reactor and involves Golden Globe–nominated actress Regina Baptiste. Apparently the tape was professionally filmed during production of their up-and-coming movie, and the clip is said to show how up-and-coming Johnny Bergs was on set. Regina Baptiste was only coming. Baptiste is married to writer James Thicke. Johnny Bergs is married to the business of Hollywood.

CLICK HERE FOR OTHER CELEBRITY SEX TAPES

Los Angeles Times (blog) — (500) related articles.

CHAPTER 1

I dropped the .38 on the passenger seat, then sped down a damp Sunset Boulevard. Johnny Handsome was bleeding, limping, running, fleeing, his trek looking like a scene from a horror film. He saw my car coming and stumbled out of the street before I could mow him down.

My anger wanted to chase him. But I was done with Johnny Handsome. For now, I was done with him. I had to get to my home in Los Feliz and kill Regina Baptiste. As I changed lanes like a madman, as I ran traffic lights, as I passed by the proliferation of homoerotic male pinups advertising every product from Calvin Klein underwear to aftershave, as I passed by ads touting female models with bodies so perfect as to make ordinary women feel inferior, I knew that by the end of the night my wife would be dead and I'd be holding a smoking gun and trembling.

13

Soon I would have to speed-dial a dream team of well-dressed and overpriced attorneys.

Traffic became as brutal as the beating that I had given America's favorite actor. Rain came from the dark sky so fast that my windshield wipers lost the battle with the storm. Most of the surface streets that led into the homes below Griffith Park had a poor drainage system, so by the time I made it back to my zip code, the roads that flowed into 90027 were flooded and it looked like traffic was backed up for miles. Angry brake lights screamed in my face.

But the driving conditions were no match for the paparazzi. Like flies drawn to shit, they had come to my estate, were buzzing around my property, the residence that I shared with Regina Baptiste, the stunning actress who was willing to do anything to make herself famous. If she had been ugly the streets would be empty and the cameras pointed in a different direction. Stunning Hollywood actress fucks up. The pack salivates and attacks like hungry wolves. She had sold her soul. She had destroyed our marriage. She had earned herself the bright lights of fame and infamy. America loved it when people fell. Hollywood loved it more. TMZ loved it the most.

Regina Baptiste's face stared at me from a billboard, an advert for her new perfume.

Heavenly, mysterious, the naked fragrance he will want to embrace for an eternity.

Baptize your senses in a touch of heavenly elegance.

MAPONA by REGINA BAPTISTE.

Face flawless, wearing diamonds and her smoldering grin, she spied down on me from the land of soy lattés, macrobiotic baby food, tofu, and Xanax. Her goddess-like image was very powerful, yet very accessible, very womanly, unremorsefully and lethally womanly.

MAPONA by REGINA BAPTISTE.

Also on that billboard was a male model, his face unseen, holding her as if she was the woman all men desired. My cellular rang. I looked down and thought that I would see my wife's name on the display. But it was one of Hollywood's power brokers calling me. The cellular was connected to the car's hands-free system and answered automatically. I didn't say anything. I sat in

15

the car, in the rain, watching the press as they stalked my once peaceful home.

Two police cars were parked outside the gate. The long arm of the law had arrived.

"James."

"Hazel Tamana Bijou."

"Where are you?"

"Two minutes away from my estate with a gun in my hand."

"Please don't do anything else stupid."

"You heard about my little meeting with Johnny Handsome?"

"What did you do to Johnny? You have set Twitter and Facebook on fire."

"I beat his ass."

"You attacked Johnny Bergstein?"

"Where are you, Hazel?"

"I'm in Atlanta. Good Lord, James. You don't mess with Johnny Bergs. Not that family."

"I have to find Regina. It's her turn now."

"Do not do anything to Regina. Do you hear me?"

"Atlanta. You're missing all the fun, Hazel."

"I left LAX eight hours ago . . . made it to Hartsfield ahead of severe thunderstorms, damn tornadoes, and winds at sixty-miles-per-hour. I'm trapped here in this god-awful place. Otherwise I'd be on a plane back to

16

Los Angeles at this very moment. I'd come help."

"I should've left a bullet in his fucking face."

"Wait, you have a gun?"

"It's America. We all have guns. Robert Blake, Phil Spector, the kids at Columbine, the D. C. sniper, cops, drug dealers, and angry husbands. God bless the Republicans and the NRA."

"Please, James. Think before you do something that will have you in jail forever."

"O. J. got off. Blake got off. Spector got off the first time. Why not me?"

"James. Tell me that you're joking about the gun."

"Which side of this line are you standing on?"

"I am on your side. Your wife, well, that ambitious actress is a vindictive piece of work to say the least, but I still have to work with her on this issue as well. And you. The former gives me no pleasure and the latter is where my professional effort remains."

"The film? Someone forwarded that clip to my phone."

"It was sent to my phone too, James. Sent from an unknown number."

"It was sent to mine unknown as well. It's all over the Internet."

"It's gone viral."

"How many hits?"

"You don't want to know. I'm working on getting it shut down."

"*The damage is done.* It's probably been bootlegged and is being sold on every corner."

"James, I saw it. It was shocking, to say the least. I'm already fighting for that part of the film to be removed and shelved permanently, even for the release of the DVD. My lawyers are on it. I have to get ahead of the game. But for now, I'm in a battle on your behalf so we can keep it rated at R, not at NC-17 or X. If it goes NC-17 or X, those parts will still be in the film."

"Do you ever leave work mode, Hazel? Do you? I don't care about NC-17 or X at this moment in my life. In the morning, the next day, maybe. Now, I don't care about a movie rating."

"Sorry, James. Forgive me for sounding insensitive, but I'm in your corner and I'm already on the phone and online looking out for you."

"It's posted on Facebook. It's posted on Twitter and being retweeted."

"Calm down, James."

"What the hell happened? And don't ask me to accept this shit because of its artistic value. He fucked my wife on camera. My wife fucked him on camera. I saw the fucking money shot. I saw it, Hazel. How in the fuck did Regina Baptiste . . . what the hell happened on set?"

"James, I have no idea. Last I heard they were having problems with that scene. They improvised. They took liberties with the script. And with that one improvised sex scene, this production changed into an out-of-control version of *Nine Songs* meets *Lie to Me.*"

"Was Regina coerced into fucking her costar on camera in front of everybody?"

"James, you saw as much as I saw. I have no idea what happened on set. *Nine Songs* set a precedent, showed the actors having real sex, and maybe this director felt as if he had to follow that controversy, if only for the sake of generating buzz about his next film. Mr. Director would sacrifice us all and write his name in the blood of others in order to make his reputation."

"That is what Alan Smithee does best."

"And he does it well. Alan Smithee cares only about Alan Smithee."

"This is a nightmare. He took my script . . . and my wife . . . this is a nightmare."

"This project has been a nightmare for

19

me and everyone involved. And as a co-producer I know that somewhere along the line, even if unbeknownst to me due to my ambitions and the way I drive people to be successful, maybe I was the spark that lit this fire, as I did want more, want better, want perfection, but this was too much, even for me."

"I have my gun, Hazel. I can create a climactic chapter with a few bullets."

"James, no. Just meet me and we can talk this thing through."

"I'm so fucking done."

"I swear, what happened on set that last day of shooting was out of my immediate jurisdiction and beyond my control. And I can't make choices for actors. I can't control directors any more than a man can control the choices that an ambitious woman makes."

"Yeah, I know. No man can control a woman's choices; good, bad, or otherwise."

"What she has done, in the end, will do as much for her career as being in *The Lover* did for Jane March. Once you do a part like that, you're the chick who fucks in movies, nothing more. Men don't suffer from having sex on camera. Women do. Regina Baptiste will be done in Hollywood. In this matter I can speak my mind and make threats and phone calls, but despite my roar I am powerless. You, me, no one in production, we didn't see this coming."

"Nice choice of words."

"James —"

"This is unreal."

"I'm so glad you answered your cell. I'm so glad."

"The car answered. Just when I thought it respected me."

"Either way, intentional or accidental, I've been trying to reach you since everyone started blowing up my BlackBerry. You've deleted your Facebook account."

"Suspended. Those information-stealing fucks don't actually let you delete Face-book."

"All of your AOL, Gmail, and Yahoo! accounts have vanished."

"When I need you, I'll e-mail you from a phone. More than likely I will have to send you a message to come and post a multimillion-dollar bail, or help me escape the country."

My cellular rang again. This time the caller ID read DRIVER. I told Hazel to hold on and then I clicked over and talked with one of my loyal employees. He was paid to be loyal.

In the deep voice of a strong man Driver

said, "You didn't wait for me."

"Some things a man has to do on his own, Driver."

"I know that. We all have to fight our own battles at some point."

I looked at the blood on my fist, then opened and closed my hand.

He said, "Miss Baptiste isn't at the estate. All the workers have been calling each other, so I know that for a fact. One of your cars is gone, so they assumed she left in the Bentley."

I held my gun, gritted my teeth. "So she's not there."

He asked, "What can I do?"

"It's done. The first half of it is done. The second half, in due time."

"I wanted to stop you before you did something that couldn't be fixed."

"Drive by Sunset and La Brea."

"Sunset and La Brea. I'll head that way."

"At the intersection."

"Oh. Bobby Holland dropped off flowers and a package at the estate."

"That bastard came to my house? Bobby Holland came to my house?"

"Saw him when I was there looking for you. Miss Baptiste's ex came to your estate."

"In this world he's nothing but an animal-cule that jacks off to the misery of others.

Tell the guards to kick his Norwegian ass if he comes back. If you do it I'll double your pay."

I let Driver go and clicked back over to Hazel Tamana Bijou.

She asked, "Was that Regina?"

"No. She's not answering my calls. Calls are going to voice mail."

"Don't do anything crazy. Sit on it for a moment. You're enraged. Running on emotions. Think. Call me back at this number. Call anytime. Send up a smoke signal before you do something foolish. James, I pulled you into this business, fought for you and the first screenplay you wrote, and your work pushed my career to where it is now. Back then I told you about the crossroads where many came to sell their souls to the devil. It cost me my marriage. We're standing here together now, and I'll fight with you. I'm a warrior. But I am also your friend."

"I guess what she did is part of the feminist movement."

"Bullshit. I am a woman. And as a woman what transpired on set is an embarrassment. It has cheapened every woman in the business and I no longer want my name associated with the wretched project, but I still must see this catastrophe through until the end."

I paused. "You heard the applause."

"I heard it, James. I heard the applause."

As anger made it impossible to breathe, I fell silent. Watched traffic and rain.

For the first time since birth I was speechless. Absolutely without words.

The phone buzzed again. Driver was calling back. I didn't answer.

Hazel asked, "What are you going to do, James? Talk to me."

My head ached and as I looked at my loaded .38, I hung up my phone.

My quandary had me nonplused.

The phone rang again and the car answered without my permission.

"Driver. What's up?"

"The Porsche is still sitting in traffic, window broken, engine running."

"That's the way I left it. No sign of Bergs?"

"No sign. Raining hard. A tow truck is pulling up. Police are already here."

"Then it won't do me any good to come back that way and finish what I started."

I couldn't go home. Not now. Not for a while. I told Driver what I needed.

"Everything." I said that, then grimaced and repeated, "Everything in a U-Haul."

I killed the call the way I wanted to kill Johnny Handsome and Regina Baptiste.

If a man has never wanted to kill a woman, a man has never really been in love.

I looked down at my wet T-shirt. SUCK IT EASY. Spots of pink were on its golden front. It was his blood mixed with rainwater. It was Johnny Handsome's blood splattered all over my clothing. The knuckles on my right hand were raw, blood dripping back into my palm.

Not far away, in the hills above my home stood the iconic HOLLYWOOD sign.

Hollywood was where a man could have everything, and still have nothing.

It was my home. But I had to leave the land of lights, camera, and action.

I had to get out of here; I had to make myself disappear.

The billboard with my wife's sensual smile stared down on me as I made a U-turn.

Her image remained in my rearview mirror as if she was following my retreat.

Anyone who didn't know about Regina Baptiste before, did now. I wouldn't be able to walk down the street without seeing her face on a newspaper or up high on a billboard. She was everywhere. The problem was being James Thicke. I didn't want to be James Thicke anymore.

The phone rang again, a roaring monster that refused to sleep.

My eyes were closed, head throbbing, breathing curt, and the car answered.

He said, "James Thicke. I know you're there. I can hear you breathing."

"Bobby Holland. The only man I know whose voice sounds better on mute."

"I've been trying to reach you and Regina Baptiste to talk about this prop—"

"You know we return calls up here, not by the squeaky wheel, but from most important to least. I was going to get around to you, hopefully before I turned eighty, ninety at the latest. I hadn't called you, but you were on the list. The problem is not that you were at the bottom of mine, but that I was at the top of yours. That's the source of your angst, bad prioritizing."

"We sat next to each other in class at USC."

"We were in the same room. I never sat next to you."

"And we did a movie together."

"A project that I want to forget. I had to sue you to get paid. We had a contract. It took me four years to get paid. And then you had the audacity to demote me in the credits, from 'screenplay by' to 'story by', so I had to sue you again. So fuck you, you

26

piece of talentless shit."

"You betrayed me and took my woman. She betrayed me and went to you."

"Fate. You couldn't handle her. I'm the better man. Take your pick."

A pause rested between us, as comfortable as a bed made of rocks and bad memories.

"I need to see you right away, Thicke. Not on the phone. Face-to-face. I had hoped that we could be civilized long enough to sit down for dinner tomorrow night at Crustacean."

"A bottom-feeder wants to meet at a place named after bottom-feeders."

"I need investors. I need your money. And I need a hot script. I want your script."

"Here's a script that you can write yourself. It'll be autobiographical. Down-and-out film director coping with a myriad of crises, personal and professional, from alimony to child support to IRS to being jilted by beautiful women, lies and cheats as he struggles to misdirect another mediocre film as he deals with fights and all the drama associated with the cast and crew."

He raged, *"Bet you're glad that you married her now, you prick. How does it feel to see your wife on camera fucking another man? That whore is the new Paris goddamn Hilton."*

27

I hung up on him. The sky puked rain from the blackness over my head.

I drove like a man leaving the scene of a deadly crime. Woebegone, I sped toward restless nights. My heart ached. Blood dripped from my right hand. Demons rose around me.

Regina Baptiste had brought humiliation to my gates, had shame at my front door.

In this town, everybody got fucked over.

It just took me a while to make it to the front of the line.

News for Johnny Bergs

msnbc.com

Superstar Johnny "Handsome" Bergs beaten

8 hours ago

A deranged fan attacked Johnny Bergs as he sat in traffic. No details have surfaced. Witnesses claim that they saw a man pull Johnny Bergs from his Porsche and pummel the superstar. Johnny Bergs fled in the rain. Rumors have swirled that the attack may be related to what happened on the set of his latest movie. His costar is Golden Globe–nominated actress Regina Baptiste. Apparently . . .

Los Angeles Times (blog) — (6000) related articles.

News for Johnny Bergs

msnbc.com

4 hours ago

Witnesses said that superstar Johnny Bergs was pulled from his 1955 Porsche 550 Spyder and assaulted in rush-hour traffic. A witness driving in the next lane likened the brawl to Danny "Partridge" Bonaduce pounding Barry "Greg Brady"

Williams, with Johnny Handsome Berg being Greg Brady in that one-sided fight.
Reps for Johnny Bergs said, "Johnny is
no f**king Greg Brady. Johnny Bergs is a
black belt. He's Moses Bergs's son and
Moses raised his five boys to be bona fide
shit kickers. Johnny Bergs is tougher than
John Wayne's old boots and could take
down three Marines, Schwarzenegger in
his prime, Stallone in his prime, and Bruce
Lee without breaking a sweat. So all of
that bullshit is a lie."

Los Angeles Times (blog) — (4700) related
articles.

Johnny Bergs Tweeted that no one had pulled him from his Porsche, and no one would dare. Moments later, he told his followers on Twitter and Facebook that his Porsche had been stolen since he left the country. His missing Porsche was the same model as the one James Dean was driving when he died. The man who had stolen Johnny Bergs's prized automobile, rumor has it, was tracked down by his bodyguard/stuntman/lookalike brother then pulled from Johnny Bergs's car and beaten on the corner of Sunset and La Brea. No video was posted. Johnny Bergs's publicist verified that the superstar (and member of the Hollywood A-List women's club) wasn't in Los Angeles at the time of the alleged incident and has been relaxing with one (or more) of his many women in the Recloeta area of Buenos Aires since finishing his project with his latest conquest, the very married Regina Baptiste, who engaged in real sex on camera. The torrid scene from that untitled movie was leaked online and immediately went viral. Johnny Bergs's climactic performance has made him the talk of the town and three quarters of a million new fans are following him on Twitter, his sex-on-film second only to the headlines created by Charlie Sheen's meltdown. Insiders present on the set deny speculation that the sex is CGI created as a publicity stunt. The usually vocal Regina Baptiste has made no comment.

(CLICK HERE FOR PHOTOS OF THE WOMEN JOHNNY HAS ~~SHAGGED~~ DATED)

Los Angeles Times (blog) — (9700) related articles.

Johnny Bergs was captured on camera phone today, his face beaten and nearly unrecognizable. A photo of his badly broken nose, broken jaw, and severely bruised face was just posted at MEDIA TAKEOUT.COM. A porn star-goddess-girlfriend whom Johnny Bergs was spending time with snapped the photos and took video with her iPhone as he slept, allegedly drugged up on her prescribed Vicodin as well as her medicinal weed and cocaine — a combination that he has been on for months. She also stated that Johnny Bergs never went to Brazil. (Bergs's porn goddess thought that Buenos Aires was in Brazil.) She said that Johnny Bergs had called her to come rescue him after he was attacked on Sunset Boulevard. He had abandoned his car and locked himself inside a bathroom at an Arco gas station, too terrified to come out because he feared that his attacker was chasing him. She said that Bergs was battered, bleeding, screaming that his face was ruined, and crying like a two-year-old. Video has surfaced, but the quality is too poor to make out faces. However, the car is indeed the same make and model of the Porsche owned by Johnny Bergs, but there was no clear shot of the license plates. The porn star said that she came forward after seeing the video of him having sex with Regina Baptiste. She said that the film is real. She knows Johnny's penis by sight and says that if she were blindfolded and given ten penises she could feel and taste the difference. Bergs eats a lot of asparagus. She said that Johnny Bergs was ranting that he is planning to sue James Thicke for all that he is worth. After reviewing the video she also said that she was better in bed than Regina Baptiste and recommended that Regina stick to acting. See the porn goddess at work on sites including youporn.com.

James Thicke, the man who allegedly attacked Johnny Bergs, was the writer of the screenplay for the movie starring his wife and Johnny Bergs. He has not issued a statement or been seen since the alleged incident.

Los Angeles Times (blog) — (9700) related articles.

CHAPTER 2

Facebook, MySpace, Bebo, Friendster, hi5, Orkut, PerfSpot, Zorpia, Netlog, Habbo, LinkedIn, Ning, Tagged, Flixster, Xanga, Badoo, MiGente, StudiVZ, and Twitter were all ablaze.

Less than twenty-four hours later, with eyes sunken and hollow and a body that was sleep deprived, I parked on a side street in Hollywood and stepped away from my car and slid behind the wheel of a U-Haul. Driver had left the U-Haul where I had instructed. I took to the streets and made it to the freeways and exited the 605 at Imperial Highway. Downey, California. Southeast of Los Angeles. An area that, before the arrival of conquering Europeans, was formerly populated by the Native Americans known as the Tongva.

Rambunctious music came from every apartment and every car that passed by, angry, vulgar songs that cycled the same

35

five notes to express about as much emotion and intelligence as a dial tone. The place seemed to prove that the gods ignored the weak and aided the strong. It was a good place for me to get lost until the media found new prey.

I started to unload my furniture and drag boxes to the second floor, only to find the elevator deceased. One of the neighbors saw me struggling with the mattress. He was well-built, a man with pale green eyes, dark brown wavy hair, a cleft in his chin and dimples in his cheeks, a blue-collar man who probably had women galore in these worn out buildings.

He introduced himself and said, "Chet Holder."

A dozen names went through my head. Curt Cannon, Hunt Collins, Richard Marsten, Richard Bachman. But my mind remained with my wife and one name had stuck.

I bypassed all of those and said, "Varg Veum."

"Interesting name. Where you from?"

I paused to remember. "Bergen, on the west coast of Norway."

"You're a long way from home."

After the mattress was inside my apartment, I thanked him. I thought that he'd go on about his way, but he followed me back down to the truck and unloaded more furniture. We made it back just in time to watch a Spanish family curse at a Muslim family because they had parked in their assigned parking spot. The Spanish man called the Muslim man a terrorist just as many times as the Muslim man shouted that his neighbor was an illegal wetback. Mr. Holder went over and diffused the verbal war before it became another Sunset and La Brea moment.

I opened and closed my aching hand and said, "They were vicious."

"Get used to it. Pointless battles are waged at this complex at least once a week."

"Has anybody been killed down here?"

"Not in a couple of years. Stabbings mostly. Weekends. Alcohol related."

Mr. Holder scratched his head and looked over what was left, then settled on the dresser. There were blankets and mats inside the truck. He covered the dresser with the blankets. Then we carried it down the ramp and walked it into the stairwell, the turns severe.

He said, "You got a good grip on your end of the dresser?"

"I've got a good grip."

"Looks like the furniture at Italy 2000. I

go down to the store in Hawthorne from time to time and walk around and dream about being able to sit and sleep on furniture as nice as this."

I said, "Don't hit the wall. It's padded, but the pad might be too thin."

"I can handle the weight on my end."

I said, "I'll pay you for helping me move this heavy stuff."

"I'm not doing this for money. When a man sees another man who needs help, he should help that man. That would make the world a much better place. A man never knows when the tides will turn and he'll be the one who will need help."

My arms and legs ached. My right hand was still swollen, weak from the attack. Mr. Holder helped me unload one of the bookcases. Moving up the concrete stairs made enough noise to cause insults to fly out of the windows at the midnight hour. We were being rained on by profanity from men, women, and children, yells that sounded like the outcries from a many-headed beast, roars and bellows and rudeness and ignorance that Mr. Holder told me to ignore.

I said, "I have a mattress that I can sleep on."

"That's a nice mattress too. I bet it cost a mint."

"Overstock.com had a sale."

"Must've been some sale."

"The people upstairs are still screaming at us."

"Ignore them."

"You sure about that?"

He said, "The wolf attacks with its fang, the bull with its horn, the asshole with curses."

When we made it back down to the truck, a woman with a very nice figure was standing in the darkness, stationed at the rear of the rental, peeping inside at my belongings, her back to us. She had on a light blue Nike tracksuit. Her hair was long, hung to the middle of her back and was colored as bright as the noonday sun.

Mr. Holder said, "Sweet Isabel, you looking for something to steal?"

"This is lovely furniture. I should steal the entire lorry and make a mint."

Her accent told me that she was British. She turned and faced us, her smile broad and welcoming, her physical build as delicious as her mild California tan. She was a mature, beautiful woman. Just like a woman I had dated and fallen in love with before I married.

Isabel said, "You have all of this nice stuff and you're going to just leave it unguarded while you march up and down the stairs in this crummy place? What kind of berk are you?"

Mr. Holder said, "Isabel, this is Varg Veum. Varg, that is the lovely Isabel Beaupierre."

I said, "Nice to meet you, Isabel Beaupierre. I'm the berk in question."

She possessed cobalt eyes and a face that reminded me of blue-blooded Helena Bonham Carter. Isabel made strong eye contact and gave me a firm handshake.

She said, "Varg Veum?"

I nodded and felt a combination of guilt and frustration taking control of my expression. She looked me up and down, as if she had come from a long line of barons and baronesses, diplomats and people in power. She, like me, didn't fit in with the surroundings.

She hesitated. "Varg Veum, where are you moving all of this lovely furniture?"

"E-213."

"Well, Varg, if you and Chet don't mind, I'm going to keep my eyes on the lorry. There are a lot of sticky fingers around here and they'll burgle you without a moment's notice. I've lost more things than I care to remember here, my sweet virginity not being one of them."

She was curious about my furniture and regarded me with undisguised suspicion.

Cars passed. Neighbors walked by speaking in vulgar slang.

From the third floor, a television screamed loud and clear. I heard Regina Baptiste's name and I looked up, my heart beating fast, and was bombarded by what I was avoiding. A neighbor was in her window, entertaining a man in an intimate way, her radio obnoxious.

Sex tapes are important these days, and she has one. Thirty years ago they shut down an actor's career and they'd be lucky to get a job working at a Dairy Queen along a barren stretch of I-10 in the middle of Texas. Now they are goldmines. Sex tapes are profitable for those who want exposure but have no real talent, other than spitting or swallowing. But Baptiste has talent and now we will see that in more ways than one. Make that money and congrats to Baptiste. And in the meantime, will somebody please find us a Scarlett Johansson or Halle Berry sex tape? Beckinsale, Alba, Lopez, Natalie Portman, Keira Knightley, Camilla Belle, time to up your games.

A horn blew and pulled me away from that broadcast. A new black Lincoln Town Car crept down the side of the building and pulled over. The man at the wheel turned his lights off and eased out. He was six foot two and dark as an open road. That was his description of himself. I'd steal a line from a Janis Ian song, "Society's Child," and say that his face was clean and shining black as night. He was bald, wore frameless glasses, expensive black suit.

I excused myself and went to Driver.

He said, "This isn't the place I recommended. I said the Park Regency Club."

"Well, I saw this one first and its beauty caught my eye."

"We're going to have to get your eyes checked, Thicke. Your mind too."

"It's not as nice as Park Regency Club Apartments. They have a nicer gate. But this will do. Five freeways are nearby. Food Lion and Target and Starbucks and a lot of other shopping are right up Imperial. If I decide to leave or need to clear my head, the Metro station is within walking distance. Downtown L.A. in about twenty minutes. Long Beach in about the same time."

"Yeah. It's not for me to question, Thicke."

"Reminds me of my childhood."

He repeated, "Not for me to question."

"I know that it makes no sense to you. But at the moment it does to me. I need the world to stop. I need the off button. I just want some time. I just want to rest and be by myself. If I can't make it stop, maybe I'll just go back to the days I used to sell gum and sodas on the streets."

"No need to explain. I just follow orders and collect my check."

I said, "You packed the whole damn cottage."

"That one-bedroom cottage is your office. And you said to pack your office."

"You overdid it."

"What were your instructions?"

"To pack everything in my office."

"Well, leave what you don't want inside the truck and I'll take it back."

"It's here now. I'll make it work out."

"I'm done for the day. Let me take off my coat and help."

"One of the neighbors is helping. Looks like he's going to see it through."

Driver said, "Regina Baptiste didn't return to the house."

"I called her publicist's office and no one would talk to me. Same for her management team. Her mom and dad haven't heard from her and had the nerve to ask me what I had done."

"Johnny Handsome?"

"I messed him up pretty bad."

"Yeah. His daddy, Moses Bergstein, was being interviewed. Daddy is outraged. Word is he was a gangster when he was back east, decades ago. Johnny is the only one he sent to college. Then this acting thing jumped off and made that family like a thugged-out royal family."

"If you hear something about Johnny, let me know. If you find him, call me. I don't care if his old man was John Gotti or Al Capone, I would love to pick up where we left off."

"With legerity."

Driver took in the worn complex, then eased back inside the town car and drove away.

Mr. Holder had continued moving boxes to the edge of the truck in my short absence. Isabel watched the town car as it left the complex, then she regarded me in search of answers.

Mr. Holder asked, "Who was that?"

"He was lost. Gave him directions."

Ten minutes later another one of the neighbors had stopped and spied inside the truck. She was in her late-twenties, breathing hard, very sweaty. She wore black workout gear, low-rise sweats, the jacket opened over her soaking-wet sports bra. She was five-ten, her hair in a ponytail that hit the middle of her back, and she held a half-empty water bottle in her left hand.

She said, "After sixteen years you're finally moving out of this dump, Mr. Holder?"

"No, helping this young man with his belongings. Elevator is out."

She looked at me with familiarity, and then she smiled. "Oh, hi."

Mr. Holder said, "Varg, this is Mrs. Patrice Evans. Mrs. Evans, this is Varg Veum."

She swallowed before she asked, "What do you do, Varg?"

I paused, thought, and then gave her eye contact. "Photographer."

"Praise the Lord. My husband and I need a photographer. You have a card?"

"Not at the moment. My hands are full at present. Maybe I'll see you around."

"Where's your apartment?"

She had cornered me, and Mr. Holder knew, so I had to tell her the truth.

Then her cellular rang.

Isabel was there observing and evaluating my goods, but hadn't said a word since Patrice had arrived. Not until then did Isabel open her mouth. She said, "Your husband is calling you, young lady. You'd best run along because you know Ted hates for you to be gone too long."

Patrice looked back at me. "I'll get your card some other time, Varg."

Mr. Holder and Isabel didn't say anything. But they both wore frowns of disapproval.

Two hours later, when we were done, when the natives had finished shouting their threats at us, after the truck was locked up, Isabel shook my hand again. She held onto my hand, bit her lower lip then regarded me with a kind smile formed underneath suspicious eyes.

She said, "Chet tells me that you have roots abroad. In Norway, he said."

I nodded. "Bergen."

She backed away, told Mr. Holder good-night and waved good-bye.

Mr. Holder stayed with me, was in no hurry to go home. We jumped in the U-Haul and I took him down to Marina del Rey to grab a middle-of-the-night bite to eat at Jerry's Deli.

Mr. Holder told me that he was fifty, was married in his twenties, had an adult daughter. He was divorced and estranged from his only child for the last fifteen years, laid off three times, bankrupted once, and now he was trying to get back on his feet and get his life in order.

He showed me a photo of his daughter. It was a picture from fifteen years ago when she was around ten or eleven years old. She was a pretty girl in pigtails, with a wholesome face.

He said, "We've finally gotten back in contact with each other after over twenty years."

"That's great."

"She's getting married, so she tells me. She said she's going to come out here to meet me so we can get reacquainted. Said she wants me to be in her wedding and walk with her."

Two police officers came inside the diner and sat next to two beautiful Central American girls who were seated in the rear of the place. I tensed and lowered my head.

Mr. Holder asked, "You scared of the police? What's going on?"

Again enraged, I massaged my temples. "You have time for a long conversation?"

He nodded.

While we ate, I told him who I was. I told Mr. Holder my real name. It had only been a few hours, but being Varg Veum was already too hard. I told him more about my wife. About the situation. About the screenplay. Mr. Holder sat across from me mouth open, speechless.

He nodded. "Can you sue?"

"I'll probably get sued for attacking Johnny Handsome."

"Johnny Handsome?"

"Johnny Bergs. You probably know him as Johnny Bergs."

"I own a lot of his movies. You serious? That's who your wife had an affair with?"

He had called it an affair. I didn't know what to call what had happened. It was ridicule.

I didn't say anything. I wished that I could have taken back what I had already said.

He said, "So you're running."

"I'm not running. Only the guilty run. And my wife has run. She's logged on to our Expedia account and booked a one-way ticket to the Netherlands, to Amsterdam. She went someplace where not many would recognize her face."

"Hell, go on the talk shows. That's what you Hollywood people do. Go on the attack. Tell them what your wife did. Get that political spin and make it work in your favor."

"It does a man no good to attack a woman, no matter how wrong she is."

"You left without saying a word in your own defense. They're going to say that you ran."

"They're going to say all kinds of things. That's what the tabloids do. I'm sure that Johnny Handsome will have a great spin for this. Regina is probably working on hers too."

Mr. Holder's cellular rang. He took the call, said that he was out with a friend and he'd be back home in a couple of hours. Then he closed his phone and sipped his coffee.

I asked, "That was your wife?"

He smiled. "No, I have a girlfriend. She lives with me."

"Didn't mean to pull you away."

"I needed a break."

Outside, the darkness was losing its edge, sunrise impending, and I shifted in my seat.

He asked, "How are you feeling?"

"I'm numb one moment, like now, and the next I'm out of control."

"In too much pain to feel, then you feel too much pain to think straight."

I nodded. "Sounds like you can relate."

"Living with Kerri-Anne did have its good moments, but those moments of quiet were like the one-minute rest between three-minute rounds."

"Kerri-Anne?"

"My daughter's mother's name was Kerri-Anne. Now I'm shacking up with a Vera-Anne."

Another moment slipped by. He told me that when he was young, around my age, he

49

had been very arrogant, but confessed that he had been chastened by life's hardships and was now more cognizant of his own failings and weaknesses. Over the last few hours, I had been humbled too.

Misery loved company. Mr. Chetwyn Holder was a good man and good company.

I said, "Mrs. Evans said that you've been living at The Apartments for sixteen years."

"A lion has to be in the jungle in order to exist. A lion understands the jungle. It understands the hunt. You take a lion and drop him off in the suburbs, away from his wilderness, and he has no idea how to survive. Most of the people in this complex, this is their jungle."

"There's only one world, Mr. Holder. Only one jungle."

Mr. Holder said, "The guy in the suit, who was he?"

"An employee of mine. He's my driver."

"Your chauffeur?"

"You could call him that, yeah. But I just call him my driver. It's not that serious."

He nodded and had an expression on his face that was hard to read.

I said, "I need another favor, if I'm not asking too much."

"What you need?"

"I need to take the U-Haul back up by

50

Hollywood and Vermont, then pick up my car."

"You sound nervous about that. What kind of car you drive?"

I smiled a thin smile. "The kind I don't want anyone seeing me drive."

Televisions were on in the diner. It was the late-night recap of all of the late shows. My humiliation was a running joke on *TMZ, Letterman,* Leno, Kimmel, *The Colbert Report, The Daily Show,* and a dozen other shows that chastised the ups and mocked the downs of those living in Hollywoodland. Regina Baptiste was getting her fifteen minutes of fame, was being talked about, laughed about, was being made infamous and lauded in one punch line. Johnny Handsome was called a stud muffin. It would do wonders for his image. When a man looked that good, they all wanted to fuck him and reproduce. That was the joke that women on shows like *The View* told. Fucking the handsome man. Trading up and finding a better spot in the DNA pool. Pretty babies. My wife was sullied and I was the Jennifer Aniston of this joke. I was the also-ran in this nightmare. My life's pain was being played out by others, the fodder of jokes and punch lines. Anger rising, I looked around the sparsely populated diner to see if anyone recognized me.

Again, on the television a comedienne was being spotlighted for her crass wittiness.

Could you see that in a prison scene? Johnny Bergs confronting Greg Brady in the prison yard; next scene, Greg Brady making sweet love to Johnny Bergs like he's on the bottoms end of Brokeback Mountain?

The audience exploded with laughter then applauded the mean-spirited joke.

She had cleaned her act up for television. Yesterday I had heard the uncensored version of the same routine. It pissed me off. At least I wasn't seen as Greg Brady in that joke.

I took care of the bill. Mr. Holder insisted on leaving the tip. And then we headed back for the U-Haul. The air was brisk. The dark skies were struggling to become a brand new day.

Once inside the U-Haul Mr. Holder looked up at the ominous sky and said, "Good thing you moved in tonight. The storm break is ending. It's supposed to rain again all day tomorrow."

"Yeah. Another storm is on the way."

I said that, and then I looked at the swollen knuckles and my scarred hand.

CHAPTER 3

I wish that I could've recorded the priceless look on Johnny's face when the crowbar shattered his driver side window. By the time he realized what was going on, by the time he'd recovered from that surprise, I'd already pulled him out of his sports car. If his seatbelt had been on, then I wouldn't have been able to get to him. But Bad Boy Johnny never buckled up.

I dragged him to the pavement, grunted and as cars blew their horns, and as a cold, cold rain fell on us, I pummeled his face. I pounded him until I had to stop for air. Then I took a deep breath and left him doubled over and bleeding as I picked up the crowbar. Johnny had scampered and made it to his feet and took off running blindly through late-night traffic.

As I stood fuming, in a state of high indignation, I should've shot him right then. We were surrounded by two-story electronic billboards that lit up the night advertising for Johnny's next movie with Lionsgate. JOHNNY BERGS. JOHNNY BERGS. JOHNNY BERGS. Everywhere I looked, on the sides of buses, on movie marquees, and on billboards I saw the face and name JOHNNY BERGS. As traffic stacked up on Sunset, as horns blew, as people held up cellular phones and recorded, I rushed inside my Maybach and sped away.

That film was sent to my cellular. It fucked me up beyond repair. As I stood frozen inside of my shopworn apartment, as I became a statue surrounded by boxes and furniture that was placed haphazardly, I saw the images from that film clip in my mind. It had been on loop for endless hours. It was like I was on set, sitting in a twenty-foot-high director's chair, script in hand.

I heard Alan Smithee yell, *"Action."*

There, in a room with lights and a crew, heat enveloped Johnny Handsome. The camera moved across his beloved face. He tongue kissed my wife and my wife tongue kissed him in return, gave him tongue followed by a puckish smile, an impish grin that made her look like a seductress, an expression that was worthy of a movie poster, and the camera panned across their passion, as his legs tensed, as her buttocks tensed, as waves of insanity roared through their camera perfect bodies, as his pace quickened, as skin slapped against skin. Their collaboration was as intense as honeymoon lovemaking. Her plangent moans said that she was in a state of connubial felicity. It sounded like he was punishing her, beating her the way that I had beaten him. She pulled him closer, took him of her own volition, and as her rhythm responded in kind, the jitters attacked him and he held my wife so tight it looked like he was about to break her in half. Johnny Handsome's own plangent moans rose as he grimaced and slavered.

Then Johnny Handsome trembled and removed himself from being inside of my wife, as if that were his right. His face was ugly and orgasmic, his breath coming in short spurts and his moans loud. In a loving tone he whispered *Sasha,* the name of Regina's character from the film. The camera pulled back, gave a view of the penis that droves of women would form groups to rush and see. Johnny Handsome pulled out and there was that five-second shot that showed how real the moment was. Even then it didn't look like porn. Porn wasn't personal. Porn was pain and action, not tender. This looked personal and emotional, like an amateur couple with the camera accidentally left on them. Then, as Johnny Handsome grunted, as Regina Baptiste sang an orgasmic song and begged him to not take his big dick away from her, she reached up and masturbated him. The camera stayed with them, showed his orgasm. Then after he had come, the camera panned across their sweaty faces, across eyes that looked deep into each other's faces, captured the intensity of reddened faces still in the heat of the moment.

Regina Baptiste looked at her hand, at the come sliding between her fingers, and the lustful smile, the expression of satisfaction left her face in small increments. She was no longer in character. Sasha was gone, sent back to the script, and Regina Baptiste had returned.

Her head turned and she looked directly into the camera. Her eyes widened.

Then, in the background, I heard applause. That applause filled my ears.

The approbation and praise publicly expressed by the clapping hands echoed.

Applause was the clamor and bellow of acceptance.

To me that applause had sounded like

publicly approved ridicule.

My wife. Fucked right in front of my face. Fucked in front of the world.

In high dudgeon, as I watched that travesty, tears ran down my face and burned like fire.

News for Regina Baptiste

msnbc.com

Regina Baptiste flees after completing role in pornographic movie

32 hours ago

A video sex scene involving the popular actress from Montana and Johnny Bergs was widely circulated on the Internet. The lovers engaged in sex while filming on camera and spectators said that the couple was completely naked and appeared to have enjoyed their performance. An anonymous source close to the Hollywood film industry said that the sex was spectacular — like watching gods fornicate.

Regina Baptiste is married to screenwriter James Thicke, the writer of the screenplay.

Hollywood. Where if you're not sinning, you're not winning.

Los Angeles Times (blog) — (1300) related articles.

News for Regina Baptiste

msnbc.com

Fleeing Regina Baptiste kicked off flight

12 hours ago

Actress Regina Baptiste and her publicist were thrown off a flight from LAX to Amsterdam as it sat at the gate at LAX. Regina Baptiste threw her drink at the flight attendant after she was asked what was it like to "have sex" with "well-endowed" Johnny Bergs, the man that many say was harder than an Oscar statue. We hope that sex with Johnny Bergs was worth the felony charges.

Just hours since the release of the explicit sex-clip from her upcoming movie with Johnny Bergs, things have continued to fall apart for the once-lauded Regina Baptiste, a Golden Globe nominee whom many movie watchers have described as a woman with talent to be reckoned with, but who, as of late, is behaving like an also-ran who would do anything in the name of money without any modicum of dignity. The court of public opinion is in session.

Los Angeles Times (blog) — (4300) related articles.

CHAPTER 4

Around six the next evening, there was a rapid, urgent knock at my door. Sirens pierced the night air and raced up and down Imperial Highway, and that already had me on edge. The knock made my heart race. There was no reason for anyone to knock on my door.

I looked through the peephole and saw Mrs. Patrice Evans. I pushed my lips up into a thin smile to hide my anger and opened the door. She had a small brown paper bag in one hand and a colorful Domino's Pizza door hanger in the other. She rocked from foot to foot and grinned.

I took a breath and said, "Hello, neighbor."

She stood before me wearing a gentle smile. "Hello."

I rubbed my eyes. "What can I do for you, Mrs. Evans?"

She hesitated. "Wanted to look at your

portfolio. Might want to hire you in the future."

"Sorry. Everything is packed up. And I might have left my portfolio behind."

She smiled. "I was about to go for my daily jog and decided to stop by and bring you some cookies. Homemade. Oatmeal raisin and chocolate. I hope you like one or the other."

"Actually, I like both. Thanks."

"Where is the wife or girlfriend? I want to say hello."

"No wife. No girlfriend. No cat. No dog. No parrot."

"I assumed that you were moving in with your wife or girlfriend. The stuff you have, it's so classy and I know a man couldn't pick out this kind of stuff. Well, not a man's man like you."

"My wife had an affair with this guy at her job."

"Aw. Lot of that going around."

"Ever since women have had jobs."

"That's so sad. That it happened to you, not that women have jobs. How long ago?"

"Recently."

Patrice took to the sofa and I sat on a red leather chair. She looked at the Domino's Pizza door hanger decidedly, then set it down on the coffee table and nodded.

I asked, "Was that on my door?"

"I brought it for you. Hopefully you can use it."

I offered her tea and she accepted. I had hoped for the opposite. While I heated water she told me the *Reader's Digest* version of her life's story. I nodded a lot and three minutes later I handed her tea and honey. She was twenty-five with a degree in something useless and said that she was stressed out about her irrelevant job, a job that she both hated and was afraid to lose, a job that burdened her with the drudgery of repetition, doing the same menial task eight hours a day. Mrs. Patrice Evans was married to a thirty-two-year-old guy who worked his fingers to the bone doing something that was as profitable as selling ice during a deep freeze in Alaska.

We sipped teas and I chewed on cookies and she smiled at me a lot. She would smile at me, look away, look down at her feet, check her watch, and suck on her bottom lip, thinking.

I smiled and said, "These cookies are very good."

She smiled. "I used my mother's recipe."

Before she could question me, I decided to question her. "Where are you from?"

"Pensacola. I was working at the Seville

Diner when I met Ted and moved here."

Patrice walked to one of my vitrines and stared through its glass at my novels. I had unpacked hundreds of books and DVDs before I had unpacked any of my clothing. I still had some clothing in the living room, across dining room chairs. Patrice looked at those and nodded.

She said, "Versace. Ferragamo. Carlo Milano. You have good taste."

She strolled into my kitchen and looked at the GNC bottles I had on the counter. Arginine 5000. Force Factor Ramp Up. Nitro Muscle Mass and Mojo Blast. 8-Hour Sex.

She smiled, picked up the RockHard Weekend and read the package. "All natural. Works in thirty minutes. The seventy-two-hour sexual performance enhancer for men."

She said that her husband couldn't please her the way she needed to be pleased. I didn't say anything. Then she corrected herself and shook her head, gritted her teeth, and said that her diabetic husband didn't please her the way that she *deserved* to be pleased.

She looked at me, checked me for a reaction.

I offered her a small smile.

She grinned. "I don't have a lot of time."

"To work out."

"No, I don't have a lot of time to get my cardio in. But other than that, I'm very business-minded. I like to get to the point. Do you mind if I show you something?"

"Sure."

With that, she stepped away and went inside the bathroom.

In that moment flashes of Johnny Handsome being inside my wife corrupted my smile.

Mrs. Patrice Evans came back out naked.

After I adjusted to the surprise I said, "Looks like your clothes fell off."

"Lot of gravity in your bathroom. Pulled everything right off me."

I evaluated her and nodded. "You've kept yourself in shape."

"Basketball and track and tennis. So. Yes or no?"

Revenge, the need for revenge grabbed me, squeezed my heart until it wanted to burst.

I said, "Yes."

Mrs. Patrice Evans came to me and we kissed. She sucked my tongue as if it were her vagina tightened around my penis, sucked and pulled at my clothing, took off my T-shirt.

She took my hand and hurried me into my bedroom, led me as if I were inside her home.

She said, "I'm not big on chitchatting. Actually chitchatting bores me to tears."

I rubbed her breasts, her belly, and her shoulders. Her skin was beautiful, its texture smooth. She was not as stunning as Regina Baptiste, but her body, the skin and flesh that people judged as being more beautiful than the eternal soul that the aging tissue housed, was nice. I pulled the bedspread back and she hopped on the bed. I crawled in with her and she kissed me again, kissed me and pulled me to her as she opened her legs for me.

She whispered, "You're bigger than I had expected."

She held onto my erection and moved it back and forth across her vagina as we kissed, moved it back and forth then began to work me inside. She was tight. I wanted to hurt her. I wanted to hurt her good. But she hadn't done me any wrong. She hadn't betrayed me.

I whispered, "Relax."

"My husband is bigger than you but you're a lot bigger than my husband."

"Slow your breathing down."

"Okay."

"I'm not going to put it all in."

"I would hope not. That's a helluva coochie stretcher you have."

She moaned and held onto my back, her nails raking my skin.

I sank inside her a little more, just beyond the hat. She made a face like she was in severe pain. The same face Johnny Handsome had made. I paused right there. Held it right there until she nodded for me to continue. I worked her slowly, worked her until she opened up, and worked her until most of me fit inside her. I put a hand around her neck and slid all of me inside of her. Her eyes and mouth widened. I took her the same way Johnny Handsome had taken my wife. I relived that scene in my angered mind. I made her crazy. I made her scream. I called Patrice a whore. I called her a slut. I called her all the things that I'd called my wife when I had left a message on her cellular. Again her eyes opened wide, then rolled back in her head. We fornicated in the shadows of Odysseus, had sex in the breath of Prometheus, fucked in the presence of all of the mighty adulterers and sinners. I didn't care anymore. Outrage possessed me. I moved like I was trying to force this umbrage out of my body. She looked in my eyes and I went deeper, stroked her faster and harder. My toes curled and hands became fists, one fist pulling her hair as if I wanted to yank a fistful out by the roots. Agony left me with a force, a powerful force that made me feel like liquid fire, as if I were melting into the fabric of the universe, and that overwhelming sensation stole me from this level of existence and took me close to one thousand little deaths. I couldn't see anything. I could barely hear anything. I couldn't move.

Patrice wailed and cried and moaned, "That's it that's it come with me come with me."

My orgasm was fugacious, brief, but it was a juggernaut, crippling. Just like that I was weak. My head was spinning. The room was humming and it felt like the ceiling was ready to fly away. The world remained out of focus. She moved against my body, her orgasm dragging out the moment, and when she let me go I rolled away from her. She struggled to breathe for a few moments, then turned on her stomach, pulled her tangled hair away from her dank face.

Another man's wife smiled. She looked guilt-free. She rested her hand on my chest.

In my mind, I heard applause.

I turned toward her, looked at her body in the light, saw her body unclothed. Being in

Hollywood made one look at things that were perfect as-is and see fault. In my mind I imagined the areas where a plastic surgeon would draw black marks showing what needed to be nipped and tucked and given a round of liposuction. Fifteen years from now, if she didn't keep hitting the gym hard as hard as life was hitting her, if she didn't actually walk and do squats and stay on a decent diet, all of that softness would become fat and would end up being in need of liposuction.

If any of that narcissism and bullshit sold by commercials and magazines mattered to her.

This was the real world. I'd been around shallow people. I'd been around people who sold the shallowness that they despised as if it were a religion. I worked where those deemed too fat were hung on a cross until Jenny Craig took them down and made them household names.

I massaged the bridge of my nose and whispered, "That was unexpected."

"Not for me," she answered. "I've wanted to get to know you all day."

Then arrived the awkwardness that came after the first time strangers had stolen sex.

She coughed, caught her breath, and said, "Glad I did this. So glad that I did this."

We stopped moving, our breathing thick and labored, like we had hiked Mt. Fuji.

I asked Patrice, "How do you feel?"

"Alive. I've been feeling dead a long time."

"You're married and you feel dead. Better than being married and feeling like killing."

"Marriage can start to feel like a slow death. I had no idea it would be like that."

"Not for everybody. Marriage is supposed to be about a new life, a new beginning."

"Look at divorce rates. We really need to start learning from other people's mistakes."

"I stand corrected, statistically, but still I don't think that it's a slow death."

"Your marriage did you a lot of good, Varg. It is Varg, right?"

"You forgot my name."

She hadn't forgotten my name. I had forgotten my name. I was James Thicke. Being Varg was new. She had come here for Varg Veum, not to welcome James Thicke to the area.

She laughed. "Okay. What did you say your name was?"

"Yeah, it's Varg."

"Your name got my attention too. It's different. Makes you seem exotic."

"A name is just a name is just a name is just a name."

She took another deep breath then pulled

herself to me. We kissed again.

"The woman or women that you go out with, do you like to see them in makeup, in heels and jeans, in business suits, in soft pants and heels, or in a nice fitted skirt and heels?"

"I can't date you, Mrs. Evans. I need you to know that right now."

"That's fine. Just let me come by for an hour at a time, like I'm on vacation."

"This isn't Club Med. It's Club Cuckold."

She asked, "Was your wife pretty?"

"Like a movie star."

Then my mind was gone, felt like it was a billion miles away from this room.

Patrice was next to me, but I was with Regina Baptiste, holding my wife's hand as we walked through the circus of tourists at Hollywood and Vine. Out-of-work thespians were dressed up in superhero costumes. They were taking snapshots with tourists while other travelers searched the Walk of Fame for names of their favorite stars. We walked the strip and held hands. We were across from where they filmed *Jimmy Kimmel Live!* And that night Regina Baptiste was scheduled to appear on the show, her face on the electronic billboards that lit up the strip.

I asked Regina Baptiste, "Are you excited?

70

In four hours you're taping his show."

"Very excited. I hope I do a good job. I hope he's as funny as Letterman."

"You will do great. They love you in New York and L.A. Everyone loves you."

She paused, removed her sunglasses, put on her trademark smile, and I used my Nikon to take a dozen photos. Tourists recognized her, Asians, Blacks, Whites, women, men, even the thespians in superhero costumes flocked to her. She posed for a few photos, posed with tourists, Spider-Man, The Hulk, and Catwoman. The crowd became crazy fast and I had to play bad cop and pull her away from her public. I never grew accustomed to the part of her that I had to share with the world. We'd never be able to take a peaceful walk through any part of town until her fame had diminished. And she loved the rise to the top. Fame was very profitable.

It took a strong man to be with a beautiful actress who would go to work and kiss other men, handsome men, rich men, men who were on the front of the magazines. It took a strong man to be able to watch her have pretend sex and share her real tongue with other pretend lovers over and over as many watched. A man had to be secure to be able to watch his wife bare her body in front of many, a body that she worked hard to keep looking like a work of art. A man had to be trusting to watch her topless or naked in scenes that the world would see, then still feel as if her kisses and nakedness was special and, somehow, just for him.

We ran away from the crowd, ran away laughing as cameras and cell phones flashed in our wake, took to a side street and resumed walking hand in hand, arms swinging like children.

She said, "I wish that I could turn this fame on and off. You can go to the bathroom without people following you and yelling through the door while you sit and do your business. You don't have people taking your picture or shoving cell phones in your face because they want you to talk to their momma or listen to their dog bark 'The Star Spangled Banner.' "

"Yeah. But the people love you. They're just showing you their love."

"Who teaches their dog to bark 'The Star Spangled Banner'?"

In some ways I was as envious of Regina Baptiste as she was envious of me.

I wondered what it would be like for that many people to demand to touch me, to demand a piece of me because I had written the words that actors had regurgitated with style and flair.

Someone yelled, "Hey, look over there, *it's Regina Baptiste.*"

Laughing, we held hands and took off running again. Driver was there that day, shadowing us as he drove one of my cars. That day I think it was the Bentley. Might have been the Double-R. We ran to the car and fell into the backseat laughing like we owned the world.

I said, "Sing that Janis Ian song you like."

"Driver, please pop in the Janis Ian CD. Play 'At Seventeen.' Volume at thirteen."

Then she sang and gave me kisses.

It felt like she was here with me now, her warm tongue inside my mouth, her sweet lies inside my ear. Her hand moved across my chest, touched my nipples and I licked my lips.

I snapped out of that trance when Mrs. Patrice Evans rubbed my chest again.

She said, "Did you hear me?"

"What did you say?"

She caught her breath and said, "Today is my fifth wedding anniversary."

I blinked marital memories from my eyes.

She sighed, moved her hair from her face, and said, "Five years with Ted."

I opened and closed my damaged hand.

"Even mistakes have anniversaries."

"I doubt if he remembers that today is our anniversary. He didn't mention it all week, said nothing this morning. No card, no flowers, no hugs and kisses. So I decided to have sex. I just didn't know if I was going to have it by myself or with you."

"He forgot your anniversary."

"Or worse. He remembers and just doesn't care."

We listened to cars racing over speed bumps two stories below, to loud conversations that came from open windows, to music, to crying babies. The noises were unending. Even words of kindness were loud. It was a world where no one spoke, but everyone yelled like they were in a kitchen shouting orders. It was evening and everyone was returning home.

A tense moment passed before I asked, "How much time is left for us to share?"

"Enough time to make me come again."

"Is there?"

"Put your finger here; make me come with your fingers."

I was about to, then I saw blood on the sheets. Not much. Just a couple of streaks of red. Just enough to remind me of the blood that had covered me after I'd beaten Johnny Bergs.

I said, "You're bleeding."

She sat up, saw the results from our war, from our round of vengeance, and cursed.

She asked for a towel then hurried to the bathroom and washed herself.

When she came back she asked, "Can we do this again?"

"Sure. On your sixth wedding anniversary."

"Don't tease me like that."

I asked, "Did your husband do something else to deserve being fucked over like this?"

"He fucked me over first. He broke the Eleventh Commandment."

"Which is what, exactly?"

"Thou Shalt Keep Patrice Happy."

"Your unhappiness is his failure?"

"All I know is that I hate California and I was very happy in Pensacola."

"Nobody is happy in Pensacola."

"There are plenty of happy people in Pensacola."

"Why you're straying, why you're unhappy, it has to be deeper than that."

"I told you."

"The child's version. Tell me the adult version."

She paused. "I like sex. I need to feel a man get hard inside of me, and I mean real hard, not weak like Ted, and I need to feel a man the way he's different sizes inside of me, need to feel a man grow inside me and lose his mind and come for me. I'm addicted to that sensation."

"Hundreds of men are in this complex."

"All losers with the same street address."

"Tens of thousands of men live in this city."

"When I first saw you at the U-Haul truck, I lost it. Yesterday I didn't even know you existed. Now, I'm excited about you. I tossed and turned all night thinking about you. Yeah, it might seem like coming here was easy, but I played this out in my head all day. I'd imagined that you'd take me as soon as you opened the door. That you'd throw the cookies across the room and manhandle me, take this Pensacola pussy like you wanted it as bad as it wanted you."

I didn't say anything, just lay in silence and took in my claustrophobic surroundings.

She asked, "Was I okay in bed?"

"Mrs. Evans. You were very good. But I wouldn't quit my day job."

She chuckled. "You're older and you keep calling me Mrs. Evans."

"That's who you are. Mrs. Evans. Mrs. Patrice Evans."

"Can we do this again tomorrow

evening?"

"You want to have a daily vespertine affair."

"And you sound smart. Very smart. Where are you from?"

"Norway."

"Wow. That's hot. I did it with a guy from Norway."

"I'm tired. I need rest. Have to unpack. Day after tomorrow might be good."

"And get condoms. We rode bareback this time. Felt good, but can't do that again."

While I pulled on my pants and T-shirt, she said that she'd leave a blank Post-it on my door. Nothing would be written on the Post-it. She would return later. If I was available, the Post-it would be removed and the Domino's Pizza ad would be left on the door handle.

I said, "That's why you brought the Domino's door hanger."

"Guilty."

"Nice meeting you, Mrs. Patrice Evans."

"We did just have sex, you know. You should call me Patrice."

"Okay. Patrice. And thanks for the cookies."

"Welcome to the neighborhood, Varg. I'm going to be glad that you moved here."

Her cellular rang and she jumped like she

had been hit with a stun gun.

She tightened her lips for a moment then said, "I have to go."

When I opened the door, someone was waiting.

CHAPTER 5

Driver was in the hallway. He was one door down, looking in the opposite direction. He stood motionless. Patrice saw him, saw his back to her, and started walking, a quick and nervous walk that changed into a jog. She didn't want her face seen. Driver didn't look at her.

Driver came up to me and handed me three bags, all from the Apple Store at the Grove.

He said, "New iPad 2. New MacBook Pro. Disposable phone with four SIM cards. Don't use your old computer. Or the other iPad. GPS is tied to your MobileMe. Shut it down."

Another box was on the floor. A box that weighed twenty-eight pounds.

He said, "I brought Underwood separately."

I nodded. And took a step back so he could come inside. He picked up the weighty box that held Underwood and made his way to the kitchen counter, found a clear spot, and put it there; then he saw the cookies that Patrice Evans had left behind and helped himself to one.

He asked, "Want me to send somebody over to help you unpack and clean?"

"I can manage. It will give me something to keep my mind occupied."

"Typewriter paper, ribbons?"

"No hurry to work. No hurry to reconnect with anything concerning Hollywood."

"I'll drop some off anyway. I'll expense you for it, if you're not in jail, plus gas."

"Just when I thought we were friends."

"You pay me on time, I am your friend. Stop paying on time, end friendship."

I motioned at a stack of magazines that had been taken out of a box. British magazines that were more literary than entertainment-driven with Regina Baptiste's beautifully made-up face on the covers. She was on the *Yorkshire Post.* And on the cover of *The Week: The Best of British and Foreign Media.* "Regina Baptiste on the Perils of Stardom." A year ago, she had appeared on BBC on the *Graham Norton Show* and admitted her love for the Swedish pop singer Robyn, saying that she loved her style and the song "Who's That Girl" so much that she sang almost every morning in the shower, like a rock star. Graham Norton dared her to take her inner rock star to the stage and show his audience her little shower act, and to outrageous laughter and huge applause, Regina Baptiste accepted the dare, let it all hang out, and the girl from Livingston covered that UK hit, covered it and set the UK on fire with her singing and dancing, two hidden talents that the world hadn't seen, talents that would land her in musicals, and that day we escaped London, six thousand fanatics followed her. *The Week* called her performance "The American Invasion." A simple magazine brought back images so strong. Next to them were American magazines that reflected the frivolity of a nation at war, articles proclaiming that Regina Baptiste had the prettiest thighs, prettiest face, prettiest and nicest shaped buttocks, female-driven magazines that dissected and evaluated her existence body part by body part.

They were surgeons then and they were surgeons now, cutting us to shreds.

Driver said, "Word on the street is that Johnny Bergs abandoned his car that night."

"I was there. He ran away from his car like Cinderella escaping the ball at midnight."

"Bergs has four brothers and a junkyard dog for a father."

"I've seen them before. Johnny's clan can do some damage. Looking for trouble?"

Driver shrugged and picked up a bottle of water. "He might be with them. Hiding out."

I had a flashback from the Bergs; then I asked, "How's the staff?"

"Shocked. Worried. Gossiping. Speculating. Hoping they don't lose their jobs."

"Who are they blaming?"

"Some blame you. Some blame her. Some don't care one way or the other."

"Who is blaming Johnny Handsome?"

He shrugged. "Should I fire the ones that blame you?"

"Don't fire anyone yet."

"Instructions?"

"At the house?"

"Yeah. Instructions."

"Tell them to sign for nothing in my absence. Accept no packages."

"Okay. The police have been by there twice. You can only hide so long, Thicke."

News for Regina Baptiste
msnbc.com
Actress Regina Baptiste
30 minutes ago

The controversial producers of the XXX films *Back Shots* and *Nutts to Butts* have offered Regina Baptiste 3 million dollars to make a thirty-minute sex flick.

No response from Regina Baptiste or her publicist.

Los Angeles Times (blog) — (500) related articles.

News for James Thicke
msnbc.com
Writer/Producer James Thicke
30 minutes ago

A photo was just placed on Sharon Mackey's Facebook. James Thicke was spotted at Jerry's Deli at three A.M. He was with another man who was at least fifty years of age. Rumors are that since he allegedly attacked Johnny Bergs, writer and newly crowned Bad Boy, James Thicke, now travels with a bodyguard. The waiter said that James Thicke looked violent and enraged, and his body appeared to be exhausted. James Thicke had a salad and left a five-dollar tip.

Los Angeles Times (blog) — (500) related articles.

News for Baptiste/Bergs

msnbc.com
10 minutes ago

MORALITY CLAUSE INVOKED; THE STUDIO will cancel engagements of Regina Baptiste and Johnny Bergs. Alan Smithee, the director, has offered no comment as to exactly what happened during shooting and his part in the matter.

Los Angeles Times (blog) — (100) related articles.

CHAPTER 6

The moment Driver left, I showered and put on the same jeans that I had worn the last three days along with a severely wrinkled T-shirt. I grabbed my sullied sheets and headed downstairs. The elevator was still out, so I went down two flights of concrete stairs. The musty and badly painted laundry room was barely big enough for the three washers and three dryers, each a different color and model, each ancient and dented and marked with vulgar graffiti scratches. Only one washer and one dryer worked.

Someone had loaded their dark clothes in the only working dryer, then had been rude enough to abandon their belongings. My washing was done in twenty-five minutes and they still hadn't returned. I yanked out the clothing and saw that it was the earthy apparel of a woman. I pulled out wrinkled, colorful T-shirts that had comical and incendiary sayings across the front:

ALL WOMEN MASTURBATE. GIVING BLOWJOBS IS AN ART. BUKKAKE QUEEN.

Reading her T-shirts distracted me. As did her lingerie. She had a ton of lingerie. Twenty minutes later I was taking out the last of her lingerie, folding and putting each item in her light blue plastic basket when she staggered in yawning and wearing Mickey Mouse pajama bottoms, a beat-up and severely wrinkled T-shirt that read NO-BODY DIES A VIRGIN: LIFE FUCKS ALL, SO DO ME DOGGIE, and no makeup. Looked like she was living on very little sleep. She came my way and I still offered her no sound, no expression. She was tall enough to be a runway model, with keen features and clear skin. Eyebrows severely arched. Her dreadlocks were long, light brown waves that framed her face and cascaded over her shoulders like a cape.

She snapped, *"Vell, mudda sic."*

She snatched up her clothing, yelled some vulgar pieces of her mind, then pushed me out of her way, and stormed out like she was going to get a gun to come back and shoot me.

After I finished drying my sheets, I returned to my hideout and made the bed.

There was another knock at my door.

The confrontation from earlier came to mind. Laundry Room Girl had probably tracked me down and had come seeking vengeance. But it wasn't Laundry Room Girl. It was Sweet Isabel. Like an actor, I began to play the role of another character. *The Life of Varg Veum.* Isabel had on black pants and a short casual jacket, flat ballet-style shoes. She brought me a small fruit basket. Bringing food to a neighbor was the *Desperate Housewives* way of getting invited inside to snoop. Discomfort took root, but I remained cordial. I thanked her and carried the fruit to the kitchen, set everything on a circular cherry wood table that was bar height.

Isabel said, "Blimey. Look at all of these wonderful books you have."

"Blimey? Did you just say *blimey?*"

She said, "This is a Hemingway. *In Our Time.* First edition of his second book."

She handled the novels with care, then returned them as she had found them.

She said, "This is like being in a quaint library. Hope you don't mind my browsing."

Isabel picked up *The Pregnant Widow,* then sat at my kitchen table and started to read.

She said, "So you're a book collector and

screenwriter, *Varg Veum.*"

The way she said my name made me pause. Isabel had come here for a reason.

She asked, "From where did you matriculate?"

"USC."

"From Norway and went to USC?"

"Exchange student."

"With no accent."

"I still have it packed in one of these boxes. I'll take it out and wear it later."

"Varg Veum. USC. I'm a UCLA girl. I matriculated from Sarah Lawrence back east, had left London to go to school in Yonkers. But when I came out West, I never left. Loved the weather. I went back to UCLA for my master's. So, on this coast, I'm a UCLA girl."

Isabel looked around, again took in my leather-bound books, my furniture, my bruised right hand, curious, but too cultured and polite to ask the questions inside her head.

Then she said, "I'll tell you this, Varg Veum, just so you'll know."

"Okay. I'm listening."

"I've read all of the long-dead authors like Fitzgerald, Faulkner, Steinbeck, and Joyce. But I also read crime novels written by Norwegian author Gunnar Staalesen."

I nodded in return. She had me cornered. And she knew that she had me cornered.

She said, "You're a bad liar. A very bad liar."

"I'm a damn good liar. I'm just a bad actor."

She asked, "Married?"

"I just left my wife."

"You left abruptly."

"What brings you to that accurate conclusion, my dear Sherlock."

"No one would move in during the middle of the night in the rain."

She motioned in a kind yet firm way and I sat down at the dining room table across from her. Isabel reached across the table and took my right hand. She pulled her lips in and looked at my bruised knuckles, stared at each one, read each bruise as if it was a horrific chapter in my life.

"The wife?"

"Not the wife. Didn't touch her."

"With whom did you have a row?"

"The guy she slept with."

"She had an affair. Not you."

"Her. Not me."

She patted my bruised knuckles, and then she let my wounded hand go.

She said, "No matter what you do, or what she did, Varg, don't put your hands on her."

I nodded. She said that like she'd been through more pain than I'd ever imagine.

She asked, "Mind if I sit here and read for a while?"

"Sure. Have a seat."

She read while I unpacked. I opened my iPad 2 and MacBook Pro. I unpacked the screenplay that I was working on. *Boy Meets Girl.* That was the next film, the one that I was writing for Regina Baptiste. It was a love story. And now it felt like I'd constructed a well-written lie. Not long after, there was another knock at my door. It was Mr. Holder. He was coming to check on me too. When I invited him inside, he was surprised to see Isabel reading.

He told Isabel, "You're cheating on me already?"

"Tell that to that child who lives with you, Chet. You have three babies in your home."

"Sweet Isabel." Mr. Holder chuckled. "Where are you coming from looking that fresh?"

"Changing the subject, are we? Are we being polite in front of Varg Veum?"

"Yes, we are."

Moments later, there was another knock at my door. Again my nerves were on edge.

I'd left my estate in search of solitude and landed in the middle of Union Station. This was why people lived behind gates and had bodyguards and Dobermans. Not for protection, just to keep people from ringing their fucking doorbell and dropping by whenever they felt like it.

I opened the door and it was a smiling young woman who looked like she was old enough to be in college, but her face still belonged in high school. She had two kids with her, one walking and the other in a stroller. The one walking looked about three and the one in the stroller a little over a year old. The young girl had the body of an exotic dancer and a church-going smile. There were two plates of food resting on top of the stroller.

She said, "Varg, right?"

She had shoulder-length hair dyed shocking pink, same hue as her nails.

"Yeah. I'm Varg."

Mr. Holder stood up when he heard her and her kids outside my door.

Mr. Holder was surprised to see them. He smiled, but his eyes told the truth.

She said, "I'm Vera-Anne Trotman. Guess he didn't tell you about me."

"He was just talking about you."

The giggling had ended and she set free a smoky, mature voice that sounder older and wiser than she appeared. Before me stood a dozen wonderful, sensual contradictions.

I stepped back and she and her children came inside. She spoke to Isabel. No hugs.

She told Mr. Holder, "I didn't know how long you'd be up here, and you haven't eaten since breakfast, so I cooked and brought you some dinner. I brought you a plate too, Varg. Miss Isabel, I can go back and get you one. I didn't know that you were up here too."

She had brought food so she could come in and spy on Mr. Holder.

And just like that, I knew that I was sitting in a room filled with dishonesty and liars.

It was the same feeling I had whenever I had a meeting with studio executives.

Vera-Anne froze, her eyes wide. She trembled.

I said, "What's wrong? Are you all right?"

"Your art. He told me that you had nice furniture, but he didn't mention anything about your art. Am I dreaming? Oh my god. Is that glass sculpture a Chihuly? Can I look at your art?"

It was too late because she had already moved across the room.

"You have art by Frida Kahlo. She is my inspiration, believe it or not. Love it. Colorful, but depressing, in my opinion. Whoa. Is that Van Gogh? And Elizabeth Catlett Mora. Are you serious? Hirschfeld did a celebrity caricature of you? Get out. You have the Austrian artist Gustav Klimt too? You have at least one piece by everyone that I study and admire."

A few steps later she was in front of my bedroom. The door was closed, but she pushed it open without asking. Vera-Anne clicked the lights on and looked at my furniture, ran her hand over the smoothness and richness of my dresser, then gazed at my bed like she was in awe.

Her mouth fell open. A moment passed before she whispered, "Wow. Nice as hell."

I smelled Patrice in the room. Her scent was still there, moving in circles, fading.

And I smelled Regina Baptiste. Everything that I owned possessed her energy.

Vera-Anne said, "Have you known Poppa long?"

"Poppa?"

"Mr. Holder. Chet. I call him Poppa."

"We met yesterday when I was moving in, just like he said."

"So you and my old man aren't really friends then."

"We're friends."

"Where did you get all of this nice art?"

"It fell off a truck."

"What do you do for a living?"

"Unemployed."

"What did you use to do?"

"As little as possible."

She stared at my face, at my chin, at my lips, her head tilted; then she licked her lips and proffered me an erubescent smile. Her heated smile was the harbinger of danger.

I offered a cautious smile. "We'd better move this party back to the living room."

"Oh. I'm in your bedroom. Yeah. Good idea. Very, very nice bed, by the way."

"It fell off of the same truck."

"Must've been a truck that was heading to Rodeo Drive."

I directed her back into the communal area and her family.

We ate dinner followed by cookies and sipped water and Vita Malts, then fell into a forgettable conversation until I moved on toward the kitchen area to throw things into the garbage. Vera-Anne Trotman remained ecstatic. When Isabel and Mr. Holder weren't looking, she made envious faces as she evaluated the art again and again, her eyes moving around the room. Her smile was broad. She was young and owned the generous beauty that came with youth. But there was something about her that the camera wouldn't like and that would leave her on the cutting room floor. Mr. Holder and Isabel were talking as Vera-Anne made her way into the kitchen and stood near me with her youngest baby on her hip.

She asked, "Can I get a cup of water for Reyonce Beyhanna? She's thirsty."

"Yes, you may."

"I don't think Junkanoo wants any. He's always up under Poppa."

While she gave her baby water, she told me that more than a few women in the complex had taken notice, especially with me being the mysterious new guy on the block, the nice dressing man who was rumored to be single and who had expensive Italian furniture, the man with more books than a library, and how many had said they would love to meet me.

I asked, "How old are you, if you don't mind me asking?"

"Twenty-one."

"You look younger."

"It's the hair."

"Of course."

She said, "Poppa didn't talk about your art. He told me about the books, the furniture mostly, but he made it all sound boring. Like he was up here moving a lot of junk for free."

"I took him to breakfast afterward."

"When he was gone all that night I was a little pissed off. Actually, a lot. He just left me and helped you moved in and stayed out all night with some guy that I had never heard of, and then he comes back at sunrise with this fishy story. I wanted to see everything myself."

Mr. Holder said, "What y'all talking about over there?"

Isabel said, "Let the woman enjoy talking to someone her own age for a change."

Mr. Holder threw his hands up. "Isabel, must you get in my business all the time?"

"I don't have to, but I take pleasure in making you sweat."

Everyone except me laughed. I was the outsider in this verbal war.

Baby on her hip, she went back to Mr. Holder. He loved her. I could tell.

Music kicked on next door. Loud music. Jennifer Lopez and Pitbull were on the floor, but in the background, from other parts of the building I heard Lady Gaga and Dr. Dre.

Isabel read my expression and said, "Get used to it. But the people who live over you are the ones with whom you are going to be the most intimate. Late night is when you will be entertained the most. At least that's when the lovely uphill gardeners who live

97

above me are the friskiest. Their crude music is never loud enough to mask the sounds that come from their weights on their cheap bed as their fornication enters the assertive last moments of its final act."

Mr. Holder said, "Isabel, you remember what fornication is?"

"And I still practice it every chance I get."

"With who?"

"No one as old as you, that's for sure."

Again we laughed. Her British accent and blunt humor were enchanting.

"People from my side of the pond invented fornication, you bloody wanker. Where do you think the bloody Yanks came from? They came from dumping the results of our fornication over here with the bloody natives so they could fornicate and destroy their culture."

I said, "God bless the queen."

Vera-Anne laughed, laughed harder for me than she did for Isabel, did that as if to be rebellious and prove a point, but by the darkness of her eyes I could tell that she wasn't amused.

Her laugh was as fabricated as Sweet Isabel's lovely smile.

Not long after that, Mr. Holder walked his ready-made family back home. He left with his young queen like a king leading his imperial family to their castle.

Isabel stayed. She was as sharp and as clever as she was kind and patient. A riddle sat before her, a misleading man, a mystifying man who owned leather-bound books and she wanted this enigma solved, wanted to conquer the conundrum before her. She was like water and I was stone. Over time, drops of water would wear down the toughest of stones, would erode all.

I asked, "A round of tea?"

"I never turn down a spot of tea with a gent, even if he's a liar."

"Earl Grey?"

"Especially Earl Grey."

"What shall we talk about?"

"You can be the gentleman and choose the topic."

"The complexities of life and the immorality of slavery leading up to the Civil War."

"I was a history teacher. History and literature. I'm much smarter than you."

"Again, the truth. You are full of the truth."

"And you, my charming neighbor and gracious host, are quite the opposite."

"Vera-Anne."

"What about her?"

"I detect that you don't care for her."

"If only she would get out and try to a get a job. Chet pays for everything and she's real comfortable not working. She uses those children as an excuse not to do any better. She hides behind those kids. And that's not fair to them. When I'm up in the morning running, I see men and women leaving here. But I notice the women, some in McDonald's uniforms, some in nice businesses clothes. Food Lion, Target, Starbucks, there are a million places to look for a job on Imperial Highway, from the bottom of Palos Verdes all the way down to where it ends at the beach by LAX. Vera-Anne's babies have become crutches, one for each arm."

I didn't respond.

Mr. Holder returned with a worn box of dominoes. The energy shifted when he came back. Intellectualism and gossip went away. That quiet energy Isabel and I had shared was over, and Isabel lost the inquisitive, hawk-like expression. We cleared the kitchen table.

Isabel surprised me. The beautiful Brit owned a very gritty side as well.

She played dominoes better than both of us.

An hour later, a little past midnight, the

neighbor over my head started having loud, obnoxious sex. When that moaning kicked in, we decided that it was time to shut it down.

Sweet Isabel left first. Mr. Holder stayed.

He shook his head and said, "Your wife. Regina Baptiste. You married a movie star."

I changed the subject, told him that Vera-Anne was as nice as she was beautiful.

He chuckled. "She's the same age my wife was when my first marriage went bad."

I nodded. And in that pause, he took the reins and turned the conversation again.

He said, "I think that I'm looking for redemption. Leaving my daughter haunts me. Maybe since I failed back then, when my daughter's mom was Vera-Anne's age . . . I don't know."

His words were so heavy that they made my plight seem like a feather in the breeze.

He readjusted and said, "Well, no one around here has recognized you."

"Someone will connect me with Regina Baptiste. If Johnny Bergs has filed assault charges, I'll be found. Anybody can find anybody, when they have money, given enough time. And since I have money, I'm sure that Bergs won't hesitate to sue for ten to twenty million."

Mr. Holder paused for a moment. "How

much do you have?"

I smiled. "It's not polite to talk money."

"It's not polite for people with money to talk money with people who don't have money."

I sensed that he was offended. Still I said, "However you interpret that is fine by me."

"I'm still blown away. Your wife is getting paid to have sex with another man on camera."

"That's not what happened."

"You said she had sex on camera. And she's getting paid for that acting."

"She is."

"So she was getting paid to have sex with another man on camera."

His logical progression was flawless. I swallowed as much discomfort as I could.

He added, "And that man she was with was getting paid to do the same."

Again I swallowed. Those images that had been sent to me put fire in my eyes.

He said, "You brought a lot of nice stuff with you. You brought a whole house with you."

I looked around. "I could've gotten by with a mattress, a table, and a chair."

"Still, if this is what you brought by accident, what are you leaving behind on purpose?"

I didn't say. Mr. Holder was grabbing pieces of my life, constructing a puzzle.

I faked a yawn, looked at my watch and said, "We'd better call it a night, Mr. Holder."

"Yeah, you're right. Holla if you need anything. You need me to run out and get anything for you, because I know you're not driving around in that smancy car of yours, just let me know."

Then he glanced at my Italian furniture, shook his head with envy, and left.

He had a beautiful young woman in his apartment, sharing his bed, sharing her gifts, and he didn't want to leave until I put him out. I had lived in eight thousand square feet with one woman. He lived inside of eight hundred square feet with an un-industrious woman and two children.

Every man needed a cave. Every man needed his own toilet.

A newspaper was on the table. Entertainment section. Mr. Holder had brought that with him when he came back with the dominoes. I picked it up to see what he had been reading.

It was an article about Johnny Handsome and Regina Baptiste. Johnny Handsome was officially Hollywood's stud of the year and my wife was regarded as a conquest on film.

Mr. Holder had been studying my agony. He'd been researching my misery.

He'd circled my wife's name with a red pen in a second article.

Regina Baptiste, Angelina Jolie, Sarah Jessica Parker in three-way tie for Forbes highest paid actresses list at $30M

I was richer than Mr. Holder, but he wanted to feel smarter than me, better than me. Ridicule was fueled by envy. Jealousy was fueled by hate. I knew people like him. They competed on all levels; small, meaningless victories validated self. He'd won that round.

I took my .38, tucked it inside the small of my back, put on a USC jacket, picked up my Nikon, and went for a stroll. Outside, I took random photos of the beautiful ugliness.

I was a stranger in a strange land, as foreign as the accents around me.

After a twenty-minute stroll around no man's land, I went back to my apartment and put my camera down next to Underwood. Then I put a sheet of paper in Underwood and started typing. Fell into a lull, the rapid *click click click click click* of the old-fashioned keys calming my nerves, but not enough. My mind was on fire and I wanted that fire put out.

Soon I was in my zone. The writer in me was the inner Chandler inside of me. Chandler was a master communicator. I'd run into a lot of self-proclaimed writers, screenwriters, and novelists, but not many effective communicators and wordsmiths. Most had never taken a typing class and I doubt if many had ever even owned a typewriter. Typewriters were heavy machinery and in the old days were good at keeping a lot of the hacks out of the business. Computers had invited everyone in and now the market was flooded with mediocrity.

I was stirred from my reverie by a soft knock at my front door.

I picked up the gun and moved across the carpet, easy steps, like I was a burglar.

When I opened the door, on the other side stood Mrs. Patrice Evans.

Her hair was down. She smelled freshly showered, and she wore a smile, a short black skirt, a dark CSULB hoodie with nothing underneath, sandals, and she held a box of condoms.

CHAPTER 7

Mrs. Patrice Evans took fast breaths, eyes closed tight and mouth opened in the letter O. With each exhale she released powerful *ahhhhs*. Her approaching orgasm was strong. Five minutes removed from that moment, as heart rates slowed down and breathing smoothed out, Patrice frowned like she was upset, but her leg bounced like she was living in joy.

"Ted had an allergy attack. I drove him to the emergency room at the Kaiser on Cadillac; got there around ten, and the doctor gave him a Benadryl shot in his ass. It knocked him the hell out. He looked like he had been hit by Tyson, a train, and a bill from the IRS. So I crept back."

"I needed this. But we're going to have to talk about this Post-it thing."

"Turn the ceiling fan on and open a window. I'm suffocating. Never mind, I'll do it."

She did, then pulled off her hoodie and kicked off her sandals before she took off her skirt. That was all she wore. She took a pillow and crawled inside my bed like she was settling in for a long stay. I went to the bathroom and took the condom off, then eased back in the bed.

We rested in silence, fan blowing, our heads at opposite ends of the bed.

I picked up my camera before turning on a small lamp that had a low wattage bulb.

She was tipsy and naked. Breasts showing. I took photos of her as she trembled. She was in silhouette, her face impossible to make out, the act of sex apparent, this sin documented.

I told her, "Chin down. Eyes up. Like you're giving a blowjob. Yeah. Like that."

She did what I asked her to do. I snapped a few more shots of her angst before I put the camera away. Her expression remained troubled, a riled Doberman on a leash of barbed wire.

She handed me a condom then laid back, her legs open like the doors of a church.

Minutes later, orgasms had been shared again and we were both out of breath.

Patrice panted. "Now that's what I'm talking about. That's what it's all about."

She took the condom off me, staggered to

the bathroom and flushed it, then came back.

She said, "You have a lot of nice magazines. Were those your wife's?"

"Packed them accidentally."

"She must be a big Regina Baptiste fan."

I said, "She's her number one fan. That's who matters to her the most."

"People tell me that I look like her. Pisses me off. I don't really care for her. Her singing is horrible and I can't watch her movies. I can't stand looking at her for some reason."

"I can't stand looking at her either."

She fell asleep within a minute. I was wide awake and heard her heavy breathing.

The timer on her watch went off and she jerked awake, yawned, and gathered her clothes. Above me, the neighbors started back to having sex, hard relentless sex.

Patrice said, "Whoever is up there, they make love like they're newlyweds."

Skirt and hoodie on, sandals in hand, she walked to the door, each step slow and heavy like she didn't want to leave. Mrs. Patrice Evans bounced her sandals against her leg and waited for me. I went to the door and peeped out into the hallway. She was afraid to walk out without me checking first. I nodded that all was clear. She dropped the sandals then slipped them on.

We kissed. She smiled like this wrongness gave her a thrill.

I said, "Post-it Girl, use the Post-it plan."

"Okay, baby. Okay. I'll stick to the Post-it system."

Then she left, her stroll casual, empowered, confident, very brazen, and dangerous.

She was going to be a problem. I knew that. I just didn't know to what extent.

CHAPTER 8

I stripped, showered, and sat on my bed naked, covers pulled back, fan circulating Patrice's scent as I went online. Obsessed with pain, I used my iPad, searched for more news.

REGINA BAPTISTE went ballistic when a reporter from *Hollywood Scoops* and another reporter from *The Hollywood Daily News* asked her questions she didn't like. Just after her meltdown at LAX, she was spotted near Manhattan Beach, where her publicist lives, her publicist and personal assistant at her side. The sweet, Christian-raised girl from Montana set free the bitch inside her and unleashed on both reporters and unsuspecting victims.

"You know, as a woman, I really find your questions very fucked up and the way you're assaulting me very fucking offensive. As a woman, I find it really embarrassing and terrifying when packs of pricks follow me all over the goddamn city . . . and get off on asking me bullshit like that without any regard for how my family feels at this fucking time. Do you have to ask that shit over and fucking over?"

CLICK HERE FOR PHOTOS OF REGINA BAPTISTE ENRAGED

In a phone interview from an undisclosed location, her costar Johnny Handsome told the reporters that in between takes, as he did with all of his stunning costars, he'd watch porn, masturbate, and talk about sex with Baptiste. When confronted, Baptiste denied all that Bergs said and then delivered a swift and brutal roundhouse kick to the reporter's nose. Seems as if her six weeks of hardcore training with Bill "Superfoot" Wallace has made her take her ability to be an action heroine to her head.

I sent Driver a text. Immediately he called and told me that the police had come back thrice. And late this evening, a representative from Johnny Bergs had come by the gates.

I asked, "An attorney? Or a process

server?"

"Only said that they were there on behalf of Bergs."

We left it at that. That meant a storm was brewing. If there had been an attorney or a process server, that would mean that this was now a legal matter.

He said, "Also, someone named Steve Martin has been sending messages."

"Where did he send the messages?"

"They came to my phone. Somehow they got my personal cellular number."

"They're going down my friends' list."

"Short list."

"You're the only one on it."

"I didn't know it was that long."

I thanked Driver, apologized for waking him at four A.M., then ended the call.

I went and stood before my magical Underwood. Next to that magical machine was the script that had torn my world apart. I had been proud of that script when I had finished. Now it was my black beast. Regina Baptiste was the actress in the dark, erotic, suburban thriller. A movie that was like a Richard Yates's novel, dialogue quick and as rich as the words of Chandler, but, like *Body Heat,* it was also as intense as it was sensual.

Hollywood had wanted it as hot as it was Kaufman-brilliant.

Once Johnny Handsome had signed on, my wife fought to get the part of the lead actress. She demanded a hit movie. Her last film had opened at number three, trounced by a lousy motion picture with a contrived gospel theme and an over-the-top comedy. She wanted to be number one. I wanted her to be number one. I wanted that association. I was married to Hollywood too. The brilliant were needed, talent was demanded, but only the hardnosed survived. The brilliant lived in soup lines and homeless shelters and told stories of how they *coulda woulda shoulda* been rich and famous. Fame had no ceiling. No matter how well people did, they wanted bigger and they wanted better. Everyone wanted a *Titanic*. An *Avatar*. An *Inception*.

I inhaled the staleness of my eight-hundred-dollars-a-month prison.

Above me, my neighbors returned to the art of copulation, the squeaks from a much cheaper bed screaming in my ears. They had a different rhythm this time. It was like listening to a different song. Like listening to different people engaging in sex. The rhythm was different, but her moans sounded the same. When Holder and Isabel were here, it was like salsa. Two hours hour ago was like jazz. Now it was like hard-core rock. I stared at the ceiling and all I could see was Johnny Bergs pumping himself inside my wife. I went into the kitchen, made a cup of Jack Daniels, sweetened it with a little tea, bit on a cookie, bit on fruit, ate some of Vera-Anne's cooking. Buzzed and naked, I looked around me, took in what had been an impulsive move.

When I was done, I made another cup of Jack, sans the tea. I wanted a glass big enough to dive into so I could swim to the bottom and come back to the top and tread in my misery. I kept my angst to myself. Nobody wanted tea and empathy, even when they bought the tea. So I did like most men when something pissed them off, I attacked my innocent liver.

In a bitter, inebriated tone, I whispered, "Regina Baptiste. Damn you."

Everywhere, in every corner, she surrounded me, a dozen beautiful wraiths dancing in pure cocaine. Then I was more worried about her than I was angered with her. I turned on my iPhone and tried to call her numbers. They all went to voice mail and her message box was full.

Before I could shut the iPhone off, it rang.

I looked at the caller ID: UNKNOWN.

I answered in a voice filled with anger and concern; "Regina, where the fuck are you?"

"You sound like a broken man, James Thicke. I know what that feels like."

"Who is this?"

"This is not Regina Baptiste, you back-stabbing bastard."

"Then this is somebody less important."

"We need a face-to-face. Personal issues aside. We can be professional about this."

"It wouldn't be mutually beneficial."

"How do you know?"

"Your record makes the Timberwolves look like world champions."

"Things are about to change. Pull your head out of your ass. I need a meeting."

"You've gone off the deep end."

"Almost as deep as Johnny Bergs was inside your wife."

"Fuck you, Bobby Holland. Fuck you."

CHAPTER 9

Bobby Holland's foreign voice made my bowels itch. We had a history as kind as the final days of Dean Martin and Jerry Lewis. We'd crossed paths for years. In this business, we all crossed paths over and over. I knew his ugly, bitter, cynical attitude. And he knew mine.

"How did you get my number, Bobby? Meant to ask you that the last time."

"I'm parked near a Mediterranean Villa on North Catalina Street, walled and gated."

"You're at my home?"

"Why don't you open up and let an old friend come inside for a drink?"

"I'm not there. And if I were at home, I wouldn't let you inside of my gates."

"I need a meeting."

"Like I told you before, I'm busy. And keep away from my property."

"No time for the people that you have shat

on as you ascended to the top."

"I never shat on you."

"Regina Baptiste."

"You weren't man enough to keep her, Holland."

"Now you're sliding down that same shit like it's a ride at Raging Waters."

"Don't call this number again, Holland."

"Tell her that my kids still ask about her. They're asking what happened to her."

"Tell them that I saved her before you destroyed her."

"I saw the film. Excellent."

"Fuck you."

"No, Johnny Handsome fucked her. He did her damn well. He fucks Regina Baptiste for a few seconds and shifts the Earth on its axis. Every day opinion is changing in Johnny Bergs's favor. After all you've done, the public wants her to leave you and go to him. They want her to take her money; they want her to take your home and cars, and go fuck Prince Charming and make pretty Hollywood bastard babies. Don't you love this business, James? Don't you? They need a new Brad Pitt and Angelina Jolie. A new Liz Taylor and Eddie Fisher."

"Are you finished? I don't want to be rude and hang up on you like so many others have."

"So kind of you. You've always been a thoughtful man, always a true gentleman."

"It's a character fault."

"Now the world sees her true character. Not the made-over image."

"At least she has character, Holland."

"Did she ever tell you about the time that we were pulled over and fined for having sex while speeding on the motorway in Norway? That was a hefty fine. She was on my lap and I was doing thirty miles over the speed limit. Have to admit that I was driving pretty erratically at that point. I couldn't see much. Her back was in the way. The police followed us and filmed us. Luckily, in Norway I'm respected. I'm the Krzysztof Kieslowski of Norway. My work there is more popular than his *Three Colors* trilogy and I have clout. I have clout and respect and they do what I ask because of that. I have the tape, James. I have that tape of me and Regina, and more."

"That tape was before I was with her. That tape is four years old."

"Today, in this climate, during this scandal, that tape would be priceless."

"From a man struggling to find work, strapped by child support, and in debt to the IRS."

"I settled with the IRS."

"Which means you owe them a fortune and payment is due in installments. And, oh yeah. You're kicking down what, about one hundred grand for private schools. How's work?"

I held the phone, rubbed my nose, and took a thousand deep breaths.

On the other end, based on his breathing, Bobby Holland was doing the same.

He said, "You'll call me to meet. And we will meet face-to-face. Like men."

"Keep away from my wife."

"She was mine first. Johnny Handsome had her last, but I had her first. You got sloppy seconds and he got sloppy thirds. This is what happens when you marry a whore."

"Keep away from her and keep the hell away from me."

"Enjoy the rest of your night. Tomorrow will only be worse. As will the day after."

"Things can only get better for me, Holland. It will get worse for you if you call again."

"Afraid not. In the meantime, take my advice. Do like all of the other losers in Hollywood do when it gets bad, run out and attach yourself to a worthless cause, donate a lot of tax-deductible money to a group that has benefits and telethons for the

119

deformed and the diseased, take photos with the terminally ill, send money to a society that collects donations on behalf of an illness that they will never cure, adopt a baby from a small AIDS-ridden village in Africa, do something pointless and humanitarian and get positive press to raise your diminishing stature."

I hung up on that cockroach. Or he hung up on me. In the end it didn't fucking matter.

The moment I hung up, the iPhone rang again and I exploded with rage.

Area code 419.

I had no idea where that was in the United States of America.

This time I didn't answer. The Jack Daniels pulled at me and the room moved in circles.

I turned the phone off and let it fall to the floor, kicked it across the room.

Above me, as the sun rose, my neighbors started another round of sex.

I screamed, "How much fucking can you do in one fucking day? Give it a rest already."

Now the rhythm sounded like a Russian revolutionary march.

Tonight, everybody was getting fucked. And everybody was getting fucked well.

But no one was being fucked deeper, harder, and longer than me.

CHAPTER 10

Two years ago.

Regina Baptiste entered the dimly lit bar, the glow from her confidence astounding. Her build very slim in the middle, then easing back out, upper body lean, particularly the arms and shoulders. She was a hard one to not notice, especially inside of a practically empty bar room.

I think that Driver had felt the heat rise too. He was in a back corner, under a sliver of light, sipping on a ginger ale and doing a crossword puzzle. But he looked up when she entered.

With the diamond earrings and matching diamond bracelet, all that and a face by M•A•C, she looked like an A-list movie star. Even if she wasn't, she was dressed for the part.

Then Driver went back to his crossword puzzle. He went back to being unseen.

That night had been busy.

I'd vacated the celebrities, men in trendy dark suits and women in colorful meat dresses and taped nipples, and crept away to the bar. My patient moment of solitude was now over. I checked my cellular again. Zero text messages. My attention returned to Regina Baptiste. She held onto her camera-ready smile and I held onto my liquid comfort. We were at the back end of a boring industry event that was held at a five-star hotel in the shadows of L.A. proper. The red-carpet fashion show and photo-op had long ended, most of the people already back inside their limos and Ferraris and Lamborghinis and gone home long before last call, because Hollywood loved to sleep and sleep with each other. Long legs taking short steps, Regina Baptiste sashayed over, her skyscraper heels clicking on the tile, and took the barstool next to mine.

"James Thicke."

"Why, Regina Baptiste, you actually remembered my name."

Her remembering my face along with my name was an honest surprise. Writers tended to be known by their names, not by their faces. Actors, their faces and bodies were their calling cards and many people forgot their names. I was two days unshaven, the look of a man who worked in Hollywood and rejected the place that he worked. The look of an unknown man who resented all who used his words to reach fame then forgot his name in the process.

She said, "You're always so incredibly dapper."

"Thanks. And likewise."

The bartender came and Regina Baptiste ordered a Johnny Walker Blue, no ice.

A moment later she sipped and smiled. "You always duck out of the industry functions."

"My tolerance for narcissism is low these days."

"It's not that bad once you get used to it."

"I'd rather go planking in the center lane on the 405."

"Mind if I . . . ? Drinking alone is a sign of alcoholism. Two drinking is a party."

"Sure. You've already parked your pretty dress on the barstool. Go right ahead."

In her intoxicating timbre she asked, "Waiting on someone?"

"Did everyone leave?"

"Everybody and the paparazzi. We're all that's left."

"Then, no. I'm not waiting on anyone."

She asked, "What are you sitting here in the dark drinking and thinking about?"

"The imperfections of the universe."

She said, "We were designed to be un-happy for life, make love while we could, and reproduce whether or not we liked children, to have children whether or not we could afford children, and live miserably ever after. We have to constantly replenish the overpopulated and jobless world with more unnecessary people who won't be able to find jobs and will be unhappy for life, making love while they can, and reproduc-ing whether they like children or not."

"Geesh. You're actually quoting part of a scene from *Toto Against Hercules*."

"Loved it. It was a nice political thriller. I had auditioned for the part of the female lead."

"Thanks. Sorry you didn't get the part. But Hathaway gets what Hathaway wants."

"You're intelligent and it shows in your work. Brilliant. I'd love to pick your brain."

"Everyone I meet tells me that they want to pick my brain. I don't like having my brain picked. Sounds too painful. I don't need fools on an expedition inside of my head."

"Don't you teach as well?"

"I just finished a series of three-day story and screenwriting master classes."

"L.A. Dallas. New York. That was two

weeks ago."

"So you already know. Feel free to sign up for the series in three months."

She said, "I heard that your next script is pretty hot. I heard it's very A-list."

"There is a rumor."

"Everyone was talking about it at the party tonight. Who's attached?"

"Too early to say. But that's not my department. I'm just the writer."

"Your last one was brilliant."

"So they said. But I have to give the actors credit for bringing it to life."

"I've studied you. Your mother was British. She had you in San Francisco, then raised you and your brothers in Hackney and in Tottenham, and moved to some European place with an atrocious name, then brought you back here to America when you were a teenager."

"I know a little about you too, Golden Globe nominee from Livingston, Montana."

"Do you?"

"Nice Golden Globes, by the way. Hiding them in that dress, brilliant move."

She laughed and her breasts jiggled. Electricity moved between my legs.

I said, "Well, physically, you're in the eight percent of women with that much-desired build. I read that in a magazine. Five-nine

126

and size 34-23-36. I read that in the same magazine."

"You read magazines? You're a top-shelf guy. You don't seem like the magazine type."

"I keep a few in the bathroom. In case of emergency."

"That was *Cosmo*. Well, you'll have to blame those imperfections on my mother."

"You went to university at sixteen. B.A. at nineteen. M.F.A. at twenty-one."

"Broke at twenty-one. Student loans up to my neck. Don't leave that part out."

"Intelligent with a strong imagination. You like the Stanislavski method of acting."

"I came from theater. I have been acting since I was six years old. Everything, every moment, every step across the room, every action, every reaction, which is one of the keys to being a great actor; reacting is about motivation. The most important goal of Stanislavski is to have complete understanding of the motivations and intentions of your character in each moment."

She told me that she had arrived in California big in talent but lacking in social graces, in second-hand clothing, wearing the wrong makeup. She came here penniless and busted her butt as a singing waitress in Beverly Hills and used that money to pay rent and study her craft. She had done everything from community theater to student films to indie projects, union and non-union, and had endured countless auditions. For a while she had been part of an improv group.

Like everyone else in town she had been trained, taught how to stand, how to sit, how to get out of a car without giving a revealing vagina shot, how to smile and wave and laugh in the proper tone. The Montana girl had scored movie roles and was photographed on the arms of handsome men in no time. Being photographed with the right people increased net worth.

Her cellular rang. Bobby Holland's face popped up on the caller ID. She answered.

"Hey. Just about to leave the event. Boring. Heading toward my car."

I heard his voice, his North Germanic cadence that sounded like a cross between Swedish and Dutch.

Regina Baptiste told him, "We'll have to talk about it. My publicist is concerned. Not if what you're saying is true. Yeah, I trust you. I'll be home soon. You too. Bye."

She hung up. And in that moment she looked stressed. Very pissed. She tapped her glass with her nails and bounced her leg before shaking her head and taking a deep breath. She sipped her whiskey twice. In the

meantime, I checked my cellular again. I had a message from another employee, a tall and thin Latin man we called Flaco. His message said that superstar Johnny Bergs had called. He wanted free admission to Club Mapona. I approved the request.

I asked her, "You need to leave?"

"No rush tonight. Never know when I'll get a chance to chat with you again."

"How are you and your favorite director Bobby Holland doing?"

"Come on now. You've heard the rumors. The women. Everyone in Hollywood talks."

Then I did an unflattering imitation of Bobby Holland, put on a thick Norwegian accent and said a few very vulgar things. Regina Baptiste's eyes widened and she howled with laughter.

She said, "My, God. You sounded just like Bobby. That was scary."

She sipped her whiskey. A lot of women in Hollywood bypassed Jenny Craig and used alcohol to stay thin. She had on a silky beige dress that was inspired by the barely-there dress that had made J. Lo famous in the 90s, and heels that cost at least three grand.

I said, "Nice dress. I assume that it was designed by either Viagra or Cialis."

"Actually they collaborated on this one."

"The part you have on is very nice. Where's the rest of it?"

"They charged two grand to rent this much. Couldn't afford to lease the rest."

"You rented that number?"

"Same for the jewelry and purse. Rentals. I pay a monthly fee and belong to a club."

"Sounds like it's as easy as renting DVDs from Netflix."

"Comes in a box and you mail it back by UPS or FedEx. You can rent a two thousand dollar Escada for two hundred bucks, or find a Halston for a C-note. Shoes too. I rented these Jimmy Choos for three days. I must be tipsy as hell. Don't believe that I'm telling you my secret."

That night I had on a British-made Ozwald Boateng suit over a twelve-dollar T-shirt that I had bought on Vermont Avenue. It was a deep red T-shirt with golden lettering that said: I THINK THAT I JUST FELL IN LOVE WITH A PORN STAR AND GOT MARRIED IN THE BATHROOM HAD A HONEYMOON ON THE DANCEFLOOR AND GOT DIVORCED AT THE END OF THE NIGHT AND THAT'S ONE HELL OF A LIFE.

She read my T-shirt and laughed. "Yeah, that would be one hell of a life."

I sipped my drink. Back then it was Jack and Coke, more Coke than Jack.

She said, "You look at me. You act like you're not looking. Am I wrong on that one?"

"I have looked at you a time or two hundred thousand."

"Almost as many times as I've looked at you."

"I've seen you. You come into a room and all eyes are on you."

She said, "You don't come on to me. Actually, you don't even speak to me."

"The trades said that you and Bobby Holland were engaged."

She waggled her left hand. "No ring on my finger."

"But you're sleeping together on the same mattress."

"Sleeping is about all we're doing. On opposite sides of the bed. It's a big mattress."

"You're too beautiful to nap with. Some women you sleep with, others you stay awake with. You're definitely one a man would want to stay awake with. Well, for at least an hour."

"Would be nice to have a man who would stay awake with me for at least an hour."

"Most women don't last thirty minutes."

"I'm not *most* women. And don't try and threaten me with a good time."

"You and Bobby Holland are on the cov-

131

ers and on almost every entertainment-driven magazine. The good-looking, controversial director from Norway and the hot actress from Montana. You looked great."

"Yeah, they love me in Montana. Well, now that I've left and I'm famous, they love me."

"You came to Hollywood and left your boyfriend behind."

"How did you know? Was that on a Web site or something?"

"Calm down. Every actress out here left a boyfriend behind."

"Most of the actors left good-looking boyfriends behind too."

"Now who's making the jokes?"

"I was serious."

"I stand corrected and will calibrate my humor to meet your level of entertainment."

"Those with no dreams and without ambition have to get left behind. Same for out here. They teach us all the same thing: Drop a guy for a film, but never drop a film for a guy."

"How did your family end up in Livingston?"

"My mother grew up there. She's a schoolteacher. Music."

"Dad?"

"Laborer. My father is a tall, handsome,

curly haired, hardworking Conky Joe from Spanish Wells. Small, quiet island. Only a half mile wide and two miles long."

"Guess they won't be having a marathon there."

She laughed. "His father was a fisherman. Dad grew up in Spanish Wells then went to work for the government in Nassau. He worked at BEC. He's a career electrician."

"Baptiste. From a former British territory called Spanish Wells to Montana to Hollywood. Saw you in *Vogue, Allure,* few others. You're taking up all of the eye-level shelf space at the newsstands."

"Doing my best to over-saturate the market with my face before the next It Girl shows up."

"I think the interview I liked most was the one with you in *Elle.*"

"In which I was happy sitting out by the swimming pool with the three dogs."

"Yep. The one with you and Bobby Holland and his rug rats and pedigreed mutts."

"Hate dogs. I have allergies. But posing with animals makes a statement. Says you're kind. People like people who like animals. I think that it's a nurturing thing. His kids are the worst behaving kids I've ever met. But since I don't have kids, posing with his regrets was a way to reach out to all of the

133

mothers and stepmothers of the world and say, 'Hey, I'm just like you.' "

"Only with nicer ankles. Nicer knees. Nicer buttocks. Nicer breasts."

She looked toward the entrance. "Felt like I was being watched."

I asked, "Where's Bobby Holland's spread?"

She laughed.

I asked her what was so funny.

"I thought that you were about to ask me where Bobby Holland is spreading my legs."

"I guess one response can answer two questions."

"Thousand Oaks. Where do you spread legs at night?"

"Los Feliz. Just moved into a small home right below Griffith Park."

She said, "You have no idea how cold and uncomfortable I am in this outfit right now."

"I would offer you my coat, but I don't want you to put it on and spoil my view."

"Glad someone appreciates the mountains and valleys."

"You look like that and Bobby Holland isn't being a caveman every night?"

"Yeah, I look like I should be getting ridden hard and put up wet, but I'm not."

"My mistake was assuming you were the happy couple."

"And the *professional* drama is the killer. He doesn't want me to work with certain directors. People whom he considers his competition, he doesn't want me to do their projects, but I refuse to wait on him to come up with work for me. He doesn't want me to work with certain actors."

"Really? Sounds like he's a jealous fuck and controlling your career."

"Or with a certain a writer named James Thicke."

"I've heard of that guy."

"If Bobby saw me chatting you up he'd go ballistic."

"Is that why you keep looking toward the door?"

"I thought somebody was watching us. Only takes one fool with a camera."

"No one is there."

Not until then did she look across the room and see Driver.

She shifted away from me and asked, "The guy in the corner?"

"It's okay. He's with me. He's on my payroll."

"You have a confidentiality agreement with him?"

"Of course. And at this moment, you're underneath my umbrella."

A moment went by with no conversation

between us. My eyes were on the movie. But my mind was somewhere else. With someone else. Wishing my phone would vibrate with a text.

Regina Baptiste sighed. "I can tell you how many times we had sex in a month."

"So we're back to talking about sex."

She stared at her whiskey. "When living with a man becomes worse than a marriage and that marriage becomes business and sex goes out the window, that's when a woman starts looking for a place of comfort. But in Hollywood, you have to be careful what and who you do."

"So you're ready to take things into your own hands."

"I'd rather be in the hands of a capable man."

"You have needs."

"I am a woman with the needs of a woman, and those needs require a man."

"I'm a man with the needs of a man, and those needs require a woman."

"What a coincidence."

"So you're looking for someone to take care of your needs tonight?"

She smiled. "Got my eye on somebody."

"And?"

"I've had my eye on him a while. Especially tonight. Too nervous to approach him."

"Too nervous to approach him because you don't want to damage your brand."

"No. He's just a hard one to read. One moment joking, the next brooding and serious. Hard to tell if he's interested or if he's just being polite and enjoying the view from his barstool."

"All of a sudden you're nervous."

"Because of what I'm thinking."

"Which is?"

"I think you know. By now, I think you know what I'm imagining."

I asked, "Where is Bobby Holland?"

"Filming an indie in Oslo for the next ten days."

"So you don't have to rush home."

"No, I don't have to rush home."

Her hand moved across the edge of the bar and touched mine. Our fingers danced over one another's for a moment. Then we made eye contact. Her face was in a curious rapture, the smell of her perfume soft and inviting. Her nipples were hard.

I reached over and traced my finger around her left nipple, then did the same to the right.

She leaned in and eased her tongue inside my mouth. It was a gentle kiss and just like that I was sober. We ended that first kiss, stared at each other, and then we kissed again.

I was a man who appreciated a woman who knew how to kiss. Most women had tongues, but not many had the skills to use them properly. Too many were either timid or sloppy kissers. Or kissed like they didn't like kissing, but did it because it was expected, because it was a prelude to getting naked. Regina Baptiste's tongue was sweet and did a slow dance inside my mouth. She jerked and moaned as we tasted each other, her body sensitive to my touch.

For a moment I kissed her like I was engaged in cunnilingus. She reciprocated by sucking my tongue like she was practicing fellatio. We stopped tasting each other, stopped arousing each other and, gradually let each other go. The sensual kiss ended, her lip gloss making our lips stick for a second, and she smiled like she was surprised, aroused, and anxious.

She whispered, "That handsel was a preview."

"Nice trailer."

"The movie is better. Has action, romance, and more than a few happy endings for all."

"You want to follow me home? Want me

to ride with you? Ride with my driver and me? Should I call you a cab? Or should I call us a cab and we move this party to my house?"

"You know that in this town, none of those are the right answers."

I touched her nose, wiped away a speck of happy powder. She took that as a sign of affection. I was trying to protect her even then. One snapshot of her inebriated and with blow on her nose, one photo online posted at *The Judiciary Report* could damage her career.

She chewed her bottom lip. "This night has to be between us."

"Understood. Being with a woman as unattractive as you could damage my brand."

"I had my assistant rent a room under her name and with her charge card. Your secret is safe with me, James Thicke. When I go upstairs, she'll leave. So give me thirty minutes."

She whispered her suite number, slid me a room key so I could have access to her private floor, told me to knock when I arrived, winked, stood, adjusted her barely-there dress, picked up her small purse, and walked away, high on cocaine and alcohol, but not one step gave it away. When a woman had on a dress like that, no one cared how she walked. Her breasts jiggled. The dress made it look as if she were naked. That was what men and women noticed. Well, women noticed the shoes. Men didn't care, not at the onset, not when the blood was being forced into a direction that made lust rise. The only thing out of place was the nervous smile on her face. She left the bar without waving good-bye, taking confidence, energy, and heat with her. Still I waved, took a breath, sat and held my drink and stared at the clock.

A woman that beautiful was nervous because of me. I felt powerful.

I motioned and Driver came over, stood next to me, crossword in hand.

He put his empty glass on the bar and asked, "Ten-letter word for frenzied or agitated."

"Unrestrained."

"Not unrestrained. It's corybantic. You're a wordsmith and should know that one."

"That was my next guess."

He sat where Regina Baptiste had been and we both looked at the classic movie. It was the end of *Sunset Boulevard.* The writer was gunned down then fell into the pool.

As the credits rolled I told Driver, "You can go. I'll take a cab home from here."

"Taxi companies keep records."

"Good point."

"Taxi drivers love to talk to the press."

"That they do." Driver was protecting Regina Baptiste back then too. "Good looking out."

"I'll be in the lobby no later than seven A.M. If anything goes wrong tonight, call and I'll be back within twenty minutes. Otherwise, have a good night and I will see you when I see you."

Then he folded his crossword in half and left, long quick strides, always looking alert, even when he had been on the clock for over twelve hours and counting.

I paid my tab and left a tip large enough for the bartender to have two hours of amnesia.

I adjusted my suit coat and, once again, I became a rake, a man in search of pleasure.

At the elevator, I checked my cellular. Still no text message from my first choice.

CHAPTER 11

I'd expected Regina Baptiste to change her mind by the time I had arrived.

Thirty minutes was enough time for a hot woman to cool off or a tipsy woman to have passed out. Or simply come to her senses. Or for Bobby Holland to have magically shown up.

When she opened the door, she looked refreshed; soft music was on the CD player; the lights were down low; and most importantly, she was naked except for her leased high heels and rented diamonds. She was astonishing. I admired her hard work. The public never realized how hard actors worked, how they worked out for hours, trained like athletes to stay in shape, worked sick or well, starved to stay fit, were paranoid about weight, paranoid over looking too human. No one saw how an actress freaked out over gaining two pounds. I knew. I had dated more than a few.

But I don't think that any could touch what stood before me.

Regina had worked very hard.

She closed the door and stared at me, a wildness in her eyes, her cheekbones prominent, her eyes dark, her breathing heavy, her chest expanding and contracting, causing her breasts to rise and fall. She came to me, her face flushed, craning her neck as her beautiful lips moved toward mine. Her lips touched mine and we were one aroused creature with no beginning and no end. It was a touch that redirected my blood flow as it changed my future.

She said, "Hope you don't mind the birthday suit. I don't have any lingerie with me."

"The birthday suit is nice. It's easy to take off when the time is right."

She smiled. "I showered and was about to put on lotion."

"I can do that for you."

"Will you do it naked?"

"Sure. I brought my birthday suit with me. But don't expect me to wear high heels too."

"You disappoint me, Thicke. I like my men in high heels."

"In that case, I'll consult Prince's shoemaker first thing in the morning."

She smiled. "You have no idea how nervous I am."

We reconnected at the lips, then with our tongues, then again with soft kisses. Her nose teased around mine, her breathing erratic, like she was drowning. Her hand rubbed across my crotch and I exhaled fire. Her hand massaged my growing penis and I sucked her lower lip; then I sucked her tongue and kissed her. She moaned. Her soft breasts pressed against my chest. She moved her hand and my erection moved back and forth across the valley between her legs, my body feeling like it had gone mad with passion, and I knew that if I kept it up that I would come in my pants, knew by the way she moaned and took deep breaths and held on that she would eventually come too. We kept grinding, my mouth moving from hers and finding her ear, sucking on her lobe. That was her spot. She couldn't stand that for long.

We stopped and stared at each other, both of us panting. We were on that road now.

I picked her up and carried her to the king-size bed, laid her down, pulled her high heels away from her feet. She watched me undress. I took in the suite; the wood furnishings bathed in soft tones of peach, mauve, sage, yellow, and beige. There was a spacious living room with a large work area with desk, marble bathrooms, a Jacuzzi tub, and most importantly of all, Regina Baptiste, naked in my honor. Then I went to the bathroom and took a quick shower, came back to her with my skin damp, and lotioned her from her feet to her neck, lotioned her back, her butt, her breasts, stayed with her breasts as she stared into my eyes, put my nervous hands on her naked body, touched each part of her as if they were separate works of art, not connected into one sculpture. Then I leaned in and kissed her neck, my breathing deep, each exhale a plea for her to not change her mind, a sweet begging for her to not rush me to be inside her.

I looked at her body, looked at every part and whispered, "You're pulchritudinous."

"What does that mean, James?"

"It's a compliment. It's a compliment that is as deep as I want to be inside you."

"What are you waiting on?"

"Be patient with me, Regina Baptiste. Be patient and enjoy the moment."

Her vagina was beautiful. Genteel. Like a subtle kerf on smooth, unblemished skin, and just beyond that moist kerf, just beyond that opening was the most beautiful flower in the world.

She shivered as if she were afraid of me. I put my hand between her legs and felt how damp she was. Her eyes weren't closed. She stared into my eyes the entire time. I wasn't just another man in her bed. She wanted me. She claimed that she was my groupie. I needed that. I licked her breasts and her breathing deepened. I sucked one breast and squeezed the other while I massaged her clit, then slid two fingers inside of her. She was arching her back again, panting, squirming, losing it. Then I backed off, kissed her stomach. She shivered. I slipped my tongue inside her navel, took my tongue to her thighs, sucked her inner thighs, moved my tongue across her vagina, a vagina as wet as a ripe Asian pear, and I paused. This was what a beautiful woman was supposed to taste like. Like mangos and cherries, sugar apples and sweet dilly. My tongue teased her lips. She sang for me. I dragged my tongue across her vagina again, and again, and again, made her release a soft desperate cry as her back arched, and as I swallowed another taste. I sucked her. She trembled and set free a heated moan, the first sign of her losing control. She held my head, pushed my face deeper, rolled her hips and rode my tongue. Sensuality escaped from her lips as I sucked and licked

146

her inner thigh again. As I licked her, my hands cupped an ass rumored insured by Lloyd's of London, an ass that looked perfect on screen, and savored her as if she was the sweetest forbidden fruit. I tasted her and she lost control, trembled. Her legs shook like earthquakes were coursing through her body. That time I felt the power of Regina Baptiste's orgasm. She jerked, sang, and cursed as her legs trembled.

She struggled to breathe and whispered, "What are you doing to me?"

"You want me to stop?"

She tugged at my arms and I eased on top of her, and the legs of a movie star opened for me like it was a gate to my vacation home. I kissed her and she welcomed me inside a brand-new paradise.

She moaned and I did the same. I looked into her eyes and she looked into mine.

She smiled. I smiled too.

She whispered, "Oh my God. I'm with James Thicke. I'm actually with you."

She was tight. Soft. Wet. I rose and fell, measured her, made circles and stirred her, and she moved against me. Her movements were slow, intense, and exquisite. When she had adjusted to me, she became forceful, losing control, then regaining control, her orgasm rising.

"Your strokes . . . the way you move . . . so delicious . . . this doesn't feel like sex."

"What does it feel like?"

"Heaven."

She turned me over on my back, mounted me, and her body became a storm of varying temperaments. She could move like a gentle rain or become a hurricane. She had me rising and falling on her waves. I wondered if she had made all men feel that way.

"Jesus, Jesus. Jesus, James. I'm about to come again."

Eyes closed tight, mouth opened wide, she moved her head side to side, in pain, in pleasure, in Heaven, sweating as if she were in Hell's mezzanine, overwhelmed, weighed down by the length of her own orgasm. When she was done, when her body became so sensitive she couldn't stand to be touched, to be stroked, she panted and eased away from me. I followed her and slid back inside of her, not done, not finished, became intense with her again. She caressed my ass; every time I rose and fell she sang. She hooked her ankles around my calves and moans sounded like we were burning in the sweetest flames. Regina Baptiste cursed and begged for me to come. She said that she wanted to feel me, the man she admired, orgasm.

I worked hard and she struggled, but she kept up with my every stroke.

She whispered, "Look at me, James. I want to look in your eyes while you come."

Regina Baptiste sweated as if she was suffering. Her body tensed. Her toes curled. Her nails raked my flesh. She trembled. Pulsated. Bit my flesh. I was about to come too. I became rough with her, as man did when he was in those final moments of madness; then I slowed down.

But it felt too good. I was beyond the point of no return. I moved faster, made skin slap. And when I started to pull away, as my heart rate increased, breathing became ragged, muscles tensing, when I had swollen and become engorged and pleasure was about to spew, she held onto me, wailed and kept me deep inside her, pulsating as I thrusted, thrusted, thrusted.

Chapter 12

Regina Baptiste kissed my dank neck, licked my skin, and said, "Jesus, Mary, and Joseph."

"You okay over there?"

"Could you feel my insides trembling when I came?"

"Like seismic tremors running along a penile fault line."

"You're really good. You're a Vagina Whisperer."

"I've trained a few."

"It feels like all of the muscles in my body are contracting. I get this huge rush of blood that makes me feel lightheaded. And then my body trembles. I feel like I'm going to pass out and then it hits me, the best feeling in the world. And when it dies down, I can feel the blood flowing back through the rest of my body. Your sexy ass took care of business. Damn, James Thicke made me come. I mean, could you feel me pulsating like I was going crazy?"

"You pulsated a long time."

"You know why a woman does that? It's in order to suck sperm toward the egg. And it massages the man. Makes him want to give a woman his sperm and let them go on a journey."

"A journey to the Land of Child Support and Misery."

She laughed. "You and your jokes."

"I was serious."

"So true. Bobby Holland pays through the nose. That's why he calls his kids his 'regrets.' "

"I heard."

"No regrets?"

"None that I know of. None that I care to hear about."

"I meant with sleeping with me."

"Definitely no regrets. The way I feel right now, if we made a regret, I wouldn't regret it."

She laughed harder. "I had no idea that you were this funny."

I leaned in and kissed her. Licked her breasts. Focused on the nipples.

She whispered, " 'In the end we are all victims, not of each other, but of nature.' "

"I'm giving you titty-head and you're

151

quoting my screenplay. This is getting scary."

"Hush. I loved that line. I posted that one on my Facebook page."

"Really?"

She moaned. "You really know how to suck a breast, you know that?"

A moment later I set her nipple free from my lips and I eased out of the bed, stretched, and staggered to the bathroom.

She whispered. "Is my hour of sexual healing with the legendary James Thicke up?"

"Only if you're kicking me out in the middle of the night."

"If someone is expecting you, if you have another appointment, I'll understand."

"I don't have to leave. No one is expecting me."

"Don't want to mess up anything you have going on back at your spread in Los Feliz."

"I live alone. No live-in lover. No dogs. No regrets."

"Stay, James Thicke. I want you and that thick dick from Brit to stay a few hours."

"That made no sense."

"Whatever. I think you rattled my brain when you came in for a landing."

"Sorry about that. But you kicked up a lot of turbulence yourself."

"I have to be out of here by nine. I have

an audition and a lunch engagement."

"Then set the alarm for six thirty. I can be out of here before everyone gets up."

"Okay. I'll call in a wake-up for six thirty. Wow. I have you for four more hours."

I ran hot water and grabbed a hand towel. I made it soapy and cleaned myself. My reflection showed a man with a grin. A man who had just been in bed with Regina Baptiste. I wondered if men who had slept with goddesses like Gina Lollobrigida or Dita Von Teese or Mayra Veronica or Monica Bellucci or Diana Dors had felt the same way after. I grabbed another hand towel and made it wet with hot water and wiped myself. Then I made a soapy towel and a wet towel and went back in the bedroom. I stood and watched her in her postorgasmic nakedness. I took in a view of her body, of her stunning silhouette, of the perfect hourglass figure.

I said, "You said that you posted a quote from my works."

"Got four hundred likes and about three hundred comments."

I went to her and said, "Open your legs."

She did. I used the towels to clean her. She closed her eyes and smiled.

I did too. I was cleaning my come away from Regina Baptiste.

This was a Hallmark moment. It could sell a million *Wish You Were Here* postcards.

I asked, "What do you want, most of all?"

"What do you mean, baby?"

"Most of all, besides fame, besides success, what do you want?"

"An unencumbered life."

A moment later she turned, faced me, looked in my eyes.

She whispered, "You are extraordinary."

"So are you."

"I'm hot, baby. You have me sweating like I'm back in Spanish Wells."

I adjusted the a/c, made the suite a little cooler to take away the heat.

She said, "You came a lot. Jesus, you came a lot."

I made more hot towels, cleaned her again. Done, I tossed the towels across the room, made them land near the bathroom, same as I had done with the first set of towels.

"James Thicke, don't throw stuff on the floor. I know you didn't grow up in a barn."

I picked up the towels and took them into the bathroom.

She said, "You have good hygiene. I love that about a man."

I said, "You said that you had a few

hundred likes and a few hundred comments."

"I love it when they LIKE me. I love to know that they are paying attention to me. It's crazy. I have a hundred thousand people following me on Twitter."

When I came back out she was on her side, covers pulled back from her naked body, watching mc like I was the statue of David.

She said, "Stand right there."

"Why?"

"I want to look at your fabulous body, James. You look good to me. So damn good."

"You look pretty good yourself, Baptiste."

She said, "Whoever you were waiting on tonight, booty call or you love her?"

I put on a smile. "Why do you ask?"

"I guess I ask you things so I can understand the man I've admired for so long."

"What are you trying to understand?"

"Me. You. This moment. We know each other now. Biblically. That can't be erased."

The conversation was getting too deep. I felt her pain now. And she felt mine.

She said, "So, you said that people want to drink what I drink and eat what I eat."

"That's why endorsements are so amazingly profitable. Brings in the lost sheep."

"Fame attracts nothing but fools. They go to a church because I go there."

"Yeah. The shallow follow the celebrities, not the preacher."

A moment passed with her regaining her composure. "Your lips are so sexy."

"Yours too. Both pair."

"Come here. Come here and touch me again."

When I joined her on the bed, she turned over on her side and faced me.

She whispered, "So they flock to church simply because a celebrity is there."

We kept the conversation thin, moved away from truths and emotions.

She put her hand on my head. I kissed her thighs. She guided my head and I licked her for a while. Her fingers touched my face, and she looked down, watched me savor her. Guttural hums. I tasted desire and all conversation ended.

I made her get on her knees, put her coveted ass in the air, and I slid inside. We moved around the bed. Positions changed, morphed from one into the next, and at some point she ended riding me sideways. I held her waist and let her move against my length. As she moved and rocked into me, I moaned and squeezed her butt, moved and rocked with her, my curt breathing and primal sounds like words of praise that let her know how good she made me feel.

Regina Baptiste moaned, "I'm coming baby I'm coming shit baby I can't stop coming."

The faces that she made, the intense and vulgar moans, that was what Regina Baptiste looked like in the throes of passion, how she behaved and made love and fucked and set her primal side free and freed her sexuality and expressed herself behind closed doors, this was her real face, not the pretend orgasmic faces she had made in many films. It was the same face that I'd see when Johnny Handsome fucked her and that tape made it out to the rest of the world.

I slapped her ass, and my orgasm held me captive a short while. As I came down from that high, I slapped her coveted backside again and again and again, each slap exhausted and without power, but she trembled when I smacked her ass. Trembled like she was coming again.

She did. And not long after, I did the same.

Six thirty was only an hour away. I wanted her to never forget this one-night stand.

She cuddled up next to me and said,

157

"You're a beast, James. You're a fucking beast."

"You're wide awake."

"I'm wired. Close your eyes if you want. I'll watch you sleep."

I sat up. "I didn't come here to sleep. Like I said, you're too attractive to sleep with."

But I did close my eyes. I did fall asleep. And as soon as I did the phone rang. I jumped up alert. Wake-up call. Six thirty. The party was over. She sat up, then went to the bathroom. When she came back she had on a robe. Paradise was closed and hidden from my eyes. Another fresh hint of happy powder was on the tip of her nose. I wiped the blow away.

I dressed and at the door she said, "I did it with the legendary James Thicke. Wow."

"I was with Regina Baptiste. Might have to rent a blimp and tell the world."

She whispered, "You were really good, James. I should bake you a cake."

"I had a good time, Miss Baptiste. Wish we could meet again. But I know we can't."

"It was both fun and worth it."

I stepped out into the hallway. She closed and locked the door behind me.

As I took my lethargic Walk of Shame, I yawned and checked my cellular. No text messages. When I made it to the lobby,

Driver was already waiting, crossword puzzle in hand.

CHAPTER 13

The next night, I sat at a red light in the turning lane at North Vermont Avenue and Los Feliz Boulevard, hands gripping my steering wheel, cars behind me blowing their horns. I closed my eyes like I was praying. Then I grunted. I put my hand down on top of her head, felt her swallowing. She finished and slowed down the passionate sucking and stroking action.

A moment later, Regina Baptiste raised her head from my lap.

She pulled her seatbelt back on, wiped the sides of her lips and smiled.

Regina Baptiste said, "The secret is to use the Listerine strips. Better than Altoids."

I drove away and blended with traffic that always moved at a madman's pace. We'd had dinner at the Vermont. I had on jeans, jacket, and another colorful T-shirt. THE CLITORIS IS THE MOST AMAZING PART OF A WOMAN'S BODY. She wore a little black dress. High heels.

Regina Baptiste's BMW 650i was parked back at my estate, the home that, once we had married and she had broken both faith and my spirits, I would leave behind.

That night. Calm breeze. Carmageddon at midnight. In a city surrounded by mountains.

She whispered, "You're good company. That road head was my saying thank you for another great evening. You could make me forget my sins and turn me into a saint."

"Do saints give road head?"

She laughed. "I could suck you all night."

I held her hand as I drove, my finger tracing her palm.

I asked, "How much time do you have?"

"I need to get back home." Her smile vanished. "Bobby's going to Skype me from Oslo."

"I wanted to show you around my property."

"Sorry. He's calling me in two hours. I have to be there."

"I can have you out of here in about an hour."

She looked stressed, suddenly anxious, had worry lines appear across her forehead as she bit her lip and looked at her watch. "I guess that I can squeeze in about thirty minutes."

Right then her cellular rang. She looked at the number and answered.

It was her publicity team. It was a short conversation that sounded like bad news.

She said, "I haven't seen it on the Internet as of yet. Google it. Text me. No, I won't get to talk to him for about two hours. There is a nine-hour time difference. He's on the frickin' set. What the hell do you want me to do, fly to Oslo and shut down his movie? Be real. Yeah. Bye."

As soon as the gates to my home opened, Regina Baptiste took it all in. I rolled into the two-thousand-square-foot garage; a garage that looked like it was part of the Louvre or Musée d'Orsay. Engine humming, I jockeyed past my fleet and her BMW. When I parked the Maybach, we sat there and held hands. The satellite radio was on a pop station, the music down low.

"Your screenplays have been very profitable, Mister Thicke."

"I have other investments, Miss Baptiste."

"You're killing Hollywood. I tracked the bottom line for your projects online."

"You've been following the money."

"Everyone follows the money. Cruise gets sixty and Sandler makes twenty million a film. We all follow the money. The people who forget the business part of show business die broke."

"You get six mil a picture."

"You're following my money."

"Googled you this afternoon."

"And half goes to the IRS. Twenty percent to management. Ten percent to agent. Accountant gets her cut. I have an assistant. I pay my parents' bills and mortgage. I have to feed my retirement accounts and maintain my investments as well, which have disappointed me."

"Still, six mil a picture is pretty good."

"Kidman gets sixteen a project. Witherspoon, Diaz, and Zellweger get fifteen. Theron gets ten. Compared to them I'm a cheap date. I make two million a picture less than Aniston and I work harder than all of them put together. Each dollar on me makes ten at the box office."

"Still, better than working at the drive-thru at McDonald's."

She smiled. "I have always loved your work."

"You're good at what you do too."

"And you never have any scandals or bullshit going on."

"Nobody cares about the private life of a writer, not even other writers."

"Screenwriters and television writers have

the advantage of being able to write and no one sees their cute little faces. You can write for Cruise or Roberts or Clooney, and no one has any idea who made them look good. My face is my calling card. My gender is my calling card. You can remain anonymous. You can write male or female characters. You're not in a box."

"We're all in boxes. Some bigger, some smaller, but we're all in boxes."

"Your box is an eight-thousand-square-foot estate behind gates and brick walls."

"Throw in a warden and it's a prison."

She was solemn. "I'm learning what really hard work is. I used to watch television and imagine the easy time the screen stars must be having in Hollywood, but the last few years have taught me quite another story. You can work hard, and then you have to work harder. Your main job in Hollywood is looking for a job and looking for a job is a full-time job that doesn't pay. I'm in a business where the average woman retires involuntarily by the age of twenty-nine."

"They have women older than that working at Burger King."

"And most of them used to be actresses."

We kissed again, kissed for a while, felt each other up, and then we got out of the car.

I said, "I'm surprised that you got in contact with me. You had your agent call my agent."

"That's how we do it in Hollywoodland."

"Sure is. Still, it surprised me. I thought you were done with me."

"I wanted to see you for dinner. This morning I arrived home to a surprise and it sort of threw me for a loop. I needed to get away. I figured you would be good company."

"Something happened?"

"Nothing that I want to talk about. Didn't mean to say that much."

Her phone rang again. Her publicist. She took the call and moved away from me, walked around my white, spotless garage. Talking, moving between anger and moments where she shook her head and laughed a laugh that expressed irony. She touched the cars. Rolls-Royce Ghost. Bentley Mulsanne. Maserati Quattroporte S. Porsche Panamera Turbo. She passed my favorite, the Maybach 62 S. Paused at the Audi A8. BMW Alpina B7. Lexus LS 600h.

She finished her call and came back to me. "All of your mouthwatering toys."

"And Regina Baptiste."

"I bet that you've gotten laid inside of all of these cars."

165

"Not by you. But we can if you want to. Would love to reciprocate for that road head."

"Can't. My publicist is panicking and just talked up all the time that I had left. Told you. I really need to be home in time for this Skype call. It's been scheduled all day long."

"You make the call sound more business than personal."

"It is. Trust me, it is. And I am not one to forsake business for pleasure."

"So my time is officially up."

She pouted. "I have to go. I told you that I could sneak out for dinner, but I have to go."

"Bobby Holland's not home for a few more days."

"He'll Skype me in a couple of hours. We have a few things . . . to discuss."

Again, when she mentioned Bobby Holland, her disposition changed, went south. Unhappiness had made her put on a meat dress and dazzle everyone at the event last night. That same unhappiness had sent her to a bar and put her on a barstool next to me.

I asked, "You like who you are when you're with him?"

She swallowed and shook her head. "Don't

ask me that."

"What about now? How do you feel while you're with me?"

"This is new, Thicke. This isn't even real. Besides, new always feels better until it becomes old. Holland felt new. But he never felt like this. This is a diffcrent kind of new. New becomes old then we go after what's new again. We chase that feeling like we chase our dreams. I'm new to you too. Are you with the movie star or the woman? Which are you with?"

"You're a movie star? No shit? I thought you were an accountant."

"What makes me any different from the rest of the women that you've taken to bed?"

"You're from Montana with Spanish Wells and UK roots. Your personality, you have something that makes you stand out. You're naturally beautiful too. Most women up here have implants, capped front teeth, and contacts to give their eyes a better shade. You're all real."

"I had my nose done."

"Just when I thought you were perfect. Thanks for bursting that bubble."

"I was lured here by the Hollywood lucre, just like everyone else, Thicke."

"Maybe. But we all are."

"There are a million women here who are

prettier than I am. I just got lucky."

"You have something that no one else has. It's indescribable. And marketable."

"Nothing like a beautiful woman peddling tampons and Midol."

"You should have your own clothing line. Your own perfume. You should be like Elizabeth Taylor. And you should be spending your nights with a better man than Holland."

"Interesting answer, Thicke. Interesting answer on a day like today."

"Stay."

"What?"

"I want you to stay the night. I stayed with you a night. You owe me a night."

She paused. "Is this about sex?"

"Stay and we can find out."

"How do you see me?"

"You're a hardworking and determined woman. I'm a hardworking and determined man. For me the diligent, strong-minded woman is in itself an aphrodisiac."

She almost smiled. "Describe me as a film. Tell me how you see me."

"You'd be a Spanish film with lots of music and dancing, a character with a dark side in a movie with good wine and decadent food, familial obligation, and lots of laughter."

We looked at each other again.

She said, "You'd be a French film, introspective, witty, realistic, and lusty with urban grit."

We kissed for a very long time. Kissed until we both had hungry looks in our eyes.

I whispered, "Stay."

"We've already done enough damage. I cheated on Bobby Holland. I'm sure a few women are trying to figure out why you're off radar and where you've been for the last few hours."

"We don't have to have sex."

"Don't do this, Thicke. This was just supposed to be a nice dinner date. An escape. Told you I had a very bad morning. I have to be home soon to take this important call."

"Stay."

"No. That's not possible. And don't be forceful with me. It's a turnoff."

"Please?"

She paused. "Did you just say please?"

"Yes."

Again she paused. "And if I stay?"

"Stay."

She moaned and kissed me again. "B I have to go home and do my laundry."

"How many excuses do you have?"

"I really have to do my laundry."

"Bring it here and do it."

"Serious? I can bring my basket of jeans and Agent Provocateur here and wash?"

"I have three washers and three dryers and a laundry room the size of a McDonald's."

"James, *we've done enough damage.* And I can't be here. *You know I can't be here.*"

I pulled her to me and kissed her shoulders, her neck, pulled her dress away from her shoulders and took her breasts out, sucked and licked each one until she almost exploded.

With her nipple between my teeth, as she panted, I whispered, "Stay."

She took a breath, moaned, and squirmed. I put my hand between her legs, massaged her with my fingers. She moaned. I eased a finger inside of her. She moaned louder.

Regina Baptiste stared at me, her chest rising and falling. "Wait a second."

She adjusted her dress, stepped away and took out her cell. I pretended that I didn't care who she had to call. But I did. Even then, after only being with her one night, after one dinner, I cared. Whoever she called, her body language never became intimate.

She came back to me and asked, "What's your address? My assistant needs it."

"She's coming tonight?"

"She's going to walk the dogs tonight and

bring my laundry in a few hours. She's wonderful. She's from Turkey. Well-spoken and so professional. Today was the worst day that I've had in a long, long time and she really helped me keep my head on straight. Some days it seems like all I have are enemies in this business. Love her to death and trust her with my life. She does everything, no matter what, and never complains. She'll be here with laundry by ten."

"Not Bobby Holland's laundry. Leave his skid marks at his house."

"I don't do his laundry. I've never done his laundry. Only do my own."

I told her my address so that it could be fed into her assistant's GPS.

She stepped away again and continued her phone call. It looked like her publicist had called again. Minutes passed before she nodded, hung up, and came back to me.

She licked her lips and smiled. "So tonight I'm Spanish and you're French."

Minutes later we were in the shower in my master suite, eight shower heads on, picking up from where we had left off in the car. Regina Baptiste had her back to the wall and I was down on my knees servicing her. Water from one showerhead cascaded down my face and neck. When I stood up, Regina reached for one of the showerheads and I watched her while she placed it between her long legs, watched her find heaven as the stream pulsated on her clit. Her mouth opened, eyes closed, and her left hand held the wall. I watched her come twice. It was like watching a dream. Then I took her from behind, worked her slowly, one hand wrapped around her waist, the other cupped over her breast, fingers twisting and pulling at her nipples.

Not long after, we put on white robes and stepped outside. Underneath she wore her Agent P thong and I had my jeans back on. We stopped by the pool. There was a bivouac, in case I ever wanted to sleep outside under the stars. She was impressed with the property.

She said, "The bottom of your pool is painted so beautifully."

"The pool's floor is blown glass sculptures inlaid, with heavy flat glass over top."

"How much does something like that cost?"

"Too much."

"Tell me. Over one hundred thousand?"

"Ten times that."

She stared at the art for a moment. "Pool

is heated?"

"Seventy-five degrees."

She dropped her robe and stepped down into the shallow end, created ripples.

She said, "I love your spread. So peaceful here. So tranquil. I need this environment."

"Thanks."

"I thought you'd retort by saying you like the way I spread my legs."

"I love that too. But the road-head could make me give up all other forms of sex."

"Sorry if I was too rough. I was pretty aggressive."

"Very. Tonight you look like you're filled with aggression."

She looked at my world within a world. "This is a wonderful place to hide."

"Thanks. There're bigger homes around. Especially going up toward the amphitheatre. Lots of old money. The people who the people who make decisions report to are up there."

"I love this area. Everyone here is rich and dresses so casually. I love it."

She went in to her neck, walked around for a couple of minutes, then went underwater, swam, and touched the bottom. She surfaced and looked up at the dark sky before she came back out. I sat down and she swam lap after lap. She swam aggressively. With anger.

When she had finished I met her with a big white towel.

I asked, "Feel better now?"

She dried her hair. "Not even close."

"Want to talk about it?"

"We can have sex again later. Sometimes a good fuck makes it all seem better."

"When you're stressed out, you like to have sex."

She nodded.

She was still upset, the tension palatable.

Barefoot, hair wet, no makeup on, in a long white cotton robe, Regina Baptiste followed me, her hand hanging onto two of my fingers, as we retraced our steps, moved from room to room, took in the trestled-ceiling living room with arched doorways. She loved the bathrooms and bedrooms. She smiled when she saw the eating area, the Bouquet Canyon Stone flooring, the formal dining room. She inspected the pots, pans, and Viking appliances.

She said, "I love to cook. Well, I used to."

"You don't cook at all?"

"As an act of rebellion. Let Bobby Holland feed his own whiney regrets."

"You okay?"

"I'm fine."

She looked at the time on the microwave,

lips pulled in, concerned and angry.

I stepped away to go to the bathroom and when I returned she had a credit card in her hand. She had poured blow and done a line from the top of my counter. She wiped away excess power with her fingertips, and then she massaged her gums. She stared at me a moment.

We stood in the window, staring out at the new pool with waterfalls in an oversized backyard that had trees and walls that gave total privacy.

She reached into her purse and handed me a DVD.

I asked, "What's this?"

"My work. I forgot that I had brought you a reel of my best work."

I popped it in the system and turned the projector on, the system playing footage first from her latest film, then all of her work for the last decade. The two-hundred-inch screen showed her wholesome image as a young mother in an action film. She was astonishing kicking butt on the big screen. In one film she was an action hero. Then in the next she was all dolled up and walking a modelesque sashay that would be imitated by many, a walk that she had worked on for weeks with a pageant coach, a man who helped her with her image and taught her how to sashay down the red carpet, how to stop, how to pose, how to have that movie-star appeal at all times.

She said, "Since you convinced me to stay, you should tell me about your next script."

"One day, maybe."

"No way your number-one fan can get a little sneak peek?"

I grinned then shook my head. "Nope."

"The sex scenes in your scripts are the best in the business."

"When they, anyone, only talk about the sex, that is a gross underestimation of what the material is about, and that takes away from the character and plot development."

"Oh, I agree. I agree totally. It's the same for me. If I do a film and at the junkets they only talk about the damn sex scene, which, on camera, is only a few seconds, it pisses me off."

"They don't understand what's going on in the script."

"Or what's going on in a movie. For example, no one understood *Monster's Ball*."

I nodded. "I can't argue that point. The sex made the plot a moot point."

"It was about pain. Pain so deep that they both thought they were going to drown from the anguish. Pain is a bitch. No one comprehended the pain, the grief; the need to feel connected, to feel something other than misery. No one took in the purpose of the sex."

"They could've made the same movie without the sex scene."

"It was needed. She tried to fuck her pain away. Besides, sex is never really about sex."

"Controversy made the movie sell."

"To the stupid and shallow, yeah. We don't exactly live in a literate or literary country."

"Made the movie sell like iced water in Hell."

"I'm not saying that for your ego, but you're good at making actors look good with your words. It starts with the screenplay. Starts with the idea. You're part of the foundation."

"You're racking up the brownie points over there."

"Enough to see what you're working on?"

"Not even close."

As her image and voice filled the room, she took a cushion off the sofa and dropped it to the floor. She opened her purse and removed a Listerine strip, put it inside her mouth, smiled at me, motioned for me to come closer. I did. She lowered her body until her knees sank into the soft leather of the Italian cushion. She winked up at me as she unzipped my pants.

She said, "You'll beg to show me."

"Won't."

She said that she was wet, very wet, and started to talk dirty, let dirty and vulgar words come out of her pretty little mouth, gave me head, and massaged the area behind my balls.

"Your dick is amazing. You're so clean-shaven down here. You taste so clean."

I thought that what she had done in the car was the best blowjob ever.

I was wrong.

I opened my eyes and she was staring up at me, once again smiling.

She said, "I love that expression. You look so weak, so stunned. You are so into it."

Again I swallowed and moaned. She kept on masturbating me as her other hand opened her purse. Moments later, she sprinkled white powder across the length of my erection.

I took a breath and managed to say, "You need to take it easy powdering your nose."

"I'm just trying to fit in."

"You'll end up fitting in a coffin."

"Stop it. Right now all I'm worried about is you fitting inside of my mouth."

After she had inhaled the white, she licked my flesh and took some of me inside her mouth. The coke had eased into my pores.

It fueled my erection. I held her hair, guided her, watched her face, how it had changed shape, watched her with her mouth full, then I heard her voice, heard her talking in the film and turned my head, watched her larger-than-life image on my screen. As she took me deeper, I watched her in a film where she played the part of a nun.

She whispered, "Are you going to tell me about your next goddamn script or what?"

"You'll have to . . . stop doing that . . . let the blood flow back to my brain for a moment."

"Poor baby can't talk while I do this."

"No. I can't. Just like you can't talk while I'm licking you."

"Try. Come on. Try multitasking. Impress me, Thicke. Impress me."

I moaned and told her about my screenplay.

She stopped sucking me and used her hands. "Anybody interested?"

"The usual suspects; Cruise, Jolie, Bergs, Pitt, Theron, and Damon."

"Wide range."

"On this one, I did two versions. One with a male as lead, one with a female."

"A female lead is possible? I'm dying to get on board a project like that."

I said, "I have a meeting with Hazel

Tamana Bijou soon. A power meeting. I can bring up your name, see if there is any way that she can push to get you attached."

"No. If you do that, then this affair becomes a backroom casting couch."

"No it doesn't."

"If there are auditions, I'll tell my agent. I'll earn my way in. Not through you. And definitely not through Hazel Tamana Bijou. I've heard her conversations. I don't want to be owned by her."

She stood up. "Told you that you'd tell me."

She kissed me, smiled, and led me to the living room, to the Italian sofa, and then she rested on her belly and raised her white robe up, pulled it until it bunched at her slender waist, and grinned back at me. I didn't pull her thong off, just tugged it to the side. She was already wet. I barely touched her, but she shuddered and moaned like she was dying. I tossed my robe away, let it fly to wherever gravity took it, and went inside her with eagerness and ease.

With a soft smile, with a broken voice, she whispered, "You have talent, you know that?"

"What does that mean, Regina Baptiste?"

"Do we have to talk about all of this now? While you feel so good inside me, is that really the conversation that you want to have? Or do you want this conversation. Like that move?"

"You've been holding out on me."

She took me on a ride that became wicked, and its own wretched fire burned with incredible noise and fury. I led her into the master bedroom and we both staggered across the suite and collapsed on the king-sized bed. We looked at each other and breathed in silence.

CHAPTER 14

Regina Baptiste said, "James, this script is fucking brilliant."

Three hours later her assistant had come and gone and we were inside my laundry room, a room painted golden and filled with framed posters from some of my favorite movies. *Casablanca. Fort Apache. Doctor Zhivago.* Akira Kurosawa's *Dreams. Unforgiven.*

Regina had grabbed my dirty clothes and put all of our laundry together, used one washing machine for dark colors; another for whites, and the third for bright clothing.

Her assistant had brought her more clothes. Now she had on wrinkled Levi's, her hair in a ponytail and was wearing my DON'T FUCKIN' JUDGE ME T-Shirt. Regina Baptiste was on top of the middle washing machine, my script in her lap, a grin of victory on her face.

I was seated at the folding table, Gunnar

Staalesen's *The Writing on the Wall* in my hand. Regina Baptiste had texted her assistant and told her to bring it with the laundry and extra clothing. Regina Baptiste read the one and only copy of my script as I enjoyed Gunnar's work, a story about a man named Varg Veum. That name would stick with me for a lifetime.

She said, "You actually use a typewriter?"

"The rumors that you have heard about me and my typewriter are true."

"Get out."

"I've used the same typewriter since I started writing. My mother bought it for me."

"You're amazing. I know I keep saying that, but damn I am impressed."

Before I knew it the dryer buzzed. That load of sheets and towels was done.

She commenced folding our dark clothes; boxers, T-shirts, jeans, panties, socks, thongs, and bras. I put the novel at my side and picked up my Nikon, took photos of a priceless moment.

No makeup. Hair pulled back. I let her become a domestic queen and I went back to reading. But a minute later, the second dryer buzzed. She went to the dryer and opened it up.

She said, "Sheets. Help me fold."

I put the book down, grabbed one end of the sheets while she grabbed the other. The sheets were hot, and like a warm lover, felt good in my hands. We worked well together. Then we got to the part where we had to meet halfway, the part where we had to touch.

We held that position. She took the warm sheets from my hand.

She whispered, "Jesus."

"What?"

She leaned in and we kissed again. Short kisses. Fun kisses.

Her cellular rang. She had an app on her cellular and she could access Skype.

It was Bobby Holland. She answered and told him that she was doing laundry. Her camera wasn't on, but his was. I saw his face. I saw Bobby Holland right in front me.

She said, "You were supposed to call me two hours ago."

"We ran over. Had problems with one of the cameras. Where are you?"

"I'm home waiting on you to call. My publicist called me, Bobby."

I saw his long blond hair and blue eyes as I heard her smooth lies. He asked her to turn on her video. She told him that her camera wasn't working. He asked her to check the settings.

"A process server came this morning, Bobby. They gave the papers to my assistant."

"I'll take care of it, Regina. It will all be taken care of."

"Who is the woman?"

"Calm down, Regina."

"Don't act like I'm a fucking moron."

"It's a lie. They are trying to slander my name. I'm filing a defamation of character suit. My lawyers are serving them. When the truth comes out, you'll see that it's all a lie."

"How long have you known about this kid? I swear, Bobby, if one reporter, if one fucking camera shows up on our front porch . . . just don't fuck me over, Bobby. They called my goddamn publicist and asked for a statement. They didn't comment because they were blindsided."

She left the laundry room and went to the other side of the pool. A half hour passed before she finished her call and came back to the laundry room.

I asked, "You okay?"

"You folded everything."

"You were occupied."

"Thanks. I really need to apologize for that. But I've been holding that in all day."

She put her hand up to the side of my face and smiled.

She said, "So, what does that terse expression mean?"

A million thoughts were in my head. Regina Baptiste's expression mirrored mine.

It looked like she wanted to say something, like she was ready to tell me good-bye.

She asked, "May I stay the night?"

"Sure that's possible?"

"It's possible."

Then she pulled my pants down, yanked her own pants down, and turned around, her face so intense, her lips pulled in. I took her just like that. I went inside her and held on as she backed into me over and over. She cursed and moaned. This was her *Monster's Ball.*

Three more days went by. Regina Baptiste was still sleeping in my bed.

Driver came for us, and we sat the behind tinted windows of one of my luxury cars as he drove us to Geisha House for sushi, and from there to Club Mapona. It was the nicest and hottest club between Hollywood and Dubai, six dance floors and twice as many bars, an evening there costing as much as a month's rent in San Francisco. It was designed to keep riffraff out, but unfortunately, from hip-hop to the Hiltons, L.A. had moneyed riffraff and rich Poor White Trash. I took her into the owner's suite overlooking the spectacular club, a thousand-square-foot room that made the people who bought two-thousand-dollar tables in VIP look like they were in the slums. We had the suite to ourselves, along with top-shelf service, and privacy.

House music played and she danced and sweated and danced and laughed and danced.

She beamed. "This joint is your club?"

"One of my investments. Part owner. Not my favorite investment either."

"This suite is larger than my first apartment in Livingston."

"Nobody uses it but me. It has a full bath and a Murphy bed in case I ever want to stay."

"Or get butt-naked and get your freak on while everyone out there gets their party on."

"That too."

"Come here often? Pun intended."

I smiled. "I rarely come here. Mostly just to check on things."

She laughed. "Jesus. I had no idea. I've been here more than a few times."

"I saw you from up here. You were with

Holland. Hilton and Dash were here that night."

"*Small* house in Los Feliz. A *half-dozen* cars and each cost as much as a starter-home. This club that has a *two-hundred-dollar* cover charge. You're too modest for your own good."

The private line in the room rang and I took the call. When I was done, I went to the camera that showed people coming inside the club and saw the celebrity of the hour.

I motioned at one of the monitors. "That ruffian Johnny Bergs just entered the building."

"Oh. *People*'s Most Handsome Man of the Year. Friend of yours?"

"He's Johnny Bergs. I invited him down. Good for business, if nothing else."

That night. The fight at the club. We'd been in my suite, looking out of the one-way glass for about thirty minutes, dancing and people watching and drinking while Driver stayed at the car and waited, and it was just before one A.M. when the commotion at the bar pulled our attention.

It was Johnny Bergs and his crew fighting with a bunch of guys who looked like Jay-Z and 50 Cent and T. I. and Lil Wayne clones. At least five hundred paying Patrón drinkers were at the bar, most of them the Hilton, Kardashian, and Lohan types. Two drinks and they would have sex in the booths and bi-curious activity in the bathrooms. One of the drunken Jay-Z types came at Johnny Bergs and Bergs threw a hard right punch into his face and took him down. It was one-sided. The guy was smaller and already three sheets to the wind. Before the guy could get up and come back after Johnny Bergs, a T. I.-type jumped in, but the mean-looking guys in Bergs's party beat him down. The rest of the hip-hop guy's friends jumped in and Bergs's boys attacked them all, threw barstools, punches, bottles, and glasses. Regina Baptiste was in shock. "That girl in the dreadlocks is fighting with them."

"Which girl?"

"She was knocked down. She's on the floor in the middle of the crowd."

It took a good five minutes — drinks flying, women ducking, cell phones recording — before the bouncers had everything back under control. Johnny Handsome stood with his entourage. Then came the applause. They always applauded him for his wrongs. The crowd applauded him as the bouncers pulled the other guys, the riffraff that had much money and little class, out of the club, fighting with them all the way to the front door. I shook my head. Johnny Bergs was just as much riffraff as the ones ejected.

Regina Baptiste said, "Jesus. I bet that will make *TMZ* and *Entertainment Tonight.*"

One of the managers came up to the booth and explained to me what had happened.

He said, "Johnny Bergs sends his apologies. He heard that you were up here."

"I'm not here, Flaco. I'm never here. I'm not here now and never will be here."

"Sorry. Didn't know."

"What does America's favorite action hero slash lover boy want?"

"He got excited when I said you were up here. Something about a script that you wrote."

"Flaco, look. Tell him to get in line. What just happened? Besides another lawsuit."

"No idea. Bergs said that the other party started it. The other guys said that Bergs and his party stepped on their shoes and didn't apologize. Bergs said that he's always being challenged because of his action-hero status. He wants to come up and tell you in person."

"Who is he with? Bodyguards?"

"Most of them are his brothers. They just

kicked seven shades of shit out of those guys."

"He's with his family of felons."

"Should I let Bergs come up and apologize? I mean, he's Johnny Bergs."

Regina Baptiste looked distressed and shook her head over and over.

She said, "He's not one of my favorite people. I don't want to be in the same room."

I told my manager no, then instructed him to move the Bergs's party away from everyone else, to the VIP section in the red sector, and to send a bottle of Patrón to Johnny. He was in a party the size of a classroom, and when they started drinking, it would never end, so they'd buy more overpriced bottles, the tab would be sky-high, and the club would make up to ten thousand dollars off him and his followers within the next hour. So far as the fight, I instructed my manager to take the names of witnesses as well. Everyone on the floor who didn't leave, until last call, would get drinks at Happy Hour prices. And I told him to give a voucher good for two free admissions, a pass that would get them by the velvet rope. People loved to feel special.

I said, "In ten minutes, they will be back to dancing and grabbing every ass in sight."

"I'll have the boys in the box keep cameras on them."

"And at the end of the night, we'll put them in taxis and send them all home. That generosity plays well during arbitration. It will be impossible to sue the club after that."

"Paparazzi followed Bergs and his entourage here."

"If they followed Bergs, then they are hired by Bergs's publicity team to follow him."

"No doubt."

After he left, I again apologized to Regina for the drama that had taken place.

I said, "So you're not a Johnny Bergs fan."

When I asked, Regina Baptiste looked different. Arms folded. Her lips pursed.

"James Thicke, you actually have talent. People respect both you and your work. The business respects you. Here they respect you. You're so lucky. You have it made."

"What happened?"

"Nothing. Forget it. Let's have a good time. Didn't mean to spoil the night."

"Something happen between you and Bergs? I can throw him out too."

Her eyes watered. "Last month, I was at an industry party and he came over to me."

"Johnny Bergs."

"I tried to talk to him about work. He was

drunk, so his lips were real loose. His brothers were with him. So was his dad. That's a lowbrow family. Johnny touched me on my ass and told me that I was nothing more than eye candy. Something to fuck and he wanted to know when he would get a shot. I told him he had to be joking. It caught me off guard. I gave him a chance to take it all back. He laughed again and repeated that I was just eye candy."

"He did that in front of his entourage."

"He's bold. He said that whenever I was cast, directors and actors and everyone on the set were taking bets on who would get to hit this. He said that I was cast for the same reason all of the other pretty women on any project were cast, for sex. That was the only reason. He was drunk and in my face, laughing and smiling. He said it like it was no big deal. I walked away."

"I'll have him put out."

"Don't. Just let it be. You'll have to work with him one day too. Keep your relationship distant, yet amicable. Most of the people in this business don't like each other anyway."

"It's my club."

"People say that his family is worse than a gang. Say they beat and kill people. Did you hear about his accountant? Some of Bergs's money was missing and that family went to his accountant's office and beat up him and his staff. Then the accountant vanished."

"That's supposed to scare me? As far as I'm concerned, it's just another urban legend."

"James, you're a writer. Johnny Handsome is trained at karate and all kinds of stuff."

"So that makes me less of a man?"

"That's not what I mean. I'm just saying, don't cross Johnny Handsome on my behalf. You seem smart. Very smart. Business-minded. No need to burn a bridge on my behalf."

I reached up and moved her hair from her cheeks. She had the pretty-girl blues.

She said, "I'm attracted to you. I wanted to get to know you because I respect your work, but I love your mind. I love the part of you that no one loves when it comes to me."

"Not many people buy posters of brains. Tits and ass? Yes. Brains? Not so much."

"The night at the industry party, before I came to the bar, I watched you. I had watched you all evening. I saw you move by everyone, so unaffected by his or her celebrity and position in the business. Everybody was flocking to Hazel Tamana Bijou, and you just waved at her and kept going. Hazel was so Hollywood that it was ridiculous, making sure everyone saw her, going from person to person, that invisible timer going on in her head, spending five minutes here, five minutes there, brownnosing to the point it made me want to puke. But you, the way people came over to you, the way they couldn't wait to touch you and pat you on the back, so much respect. I thought, that's how I want to be. Like him. It aroused me. I imagined you and me being together like this. I didn't think it would happen. Then I heard that you were at the bar. I had hoped you were alone. And if you weren't alone, I was going to run her away."

Her cellular rang and a call from her beau Bobby Holland ended our conversation.

He would be back in four days and this deciduous love affair would come to an end.

She ended the call, opened her purse, hand shaking, and put white powder on her finger, then rubbed it on her gums before she took a quick and dirty swallow of her whiskey and Coke.

I asked her, "Do you love you?"

"What do you mean?"

"Doing drugs means you hate yourself."

"You're serving Patrón by the gallon and calling me out? I can stop at any time. This is nothing compared to what goes on in this club, and you know that. Women meet in the ladies' room to powder their noses and they use a lot more Peruvian marching powder than I do. They are addicted to this shit. Not me. It's recreational. No different than taking a drink. When I'm stressed, when I'm upset, a little helps to smooth things over and give me the clarity I need."

"How long have you been doing blow?"

"Okay, I won't do it anymore while I'm with you. I apologize. Seeing Johnny Handsome here, remembering what he did, how he treated me like shit, that stressed me out."

"Johnny Handsome."

"Since that thing in *People,* that's what all the women call him. Johnny Handsome."

CHAPTER 15

Within a week, we were living up under each other like we were husband and wife.

We left my estate jogging, blended with the pre-dawn crowd, and tackled the hills of Griffith Park. We ran until we were sixteen hundred feet above sea level, the observatory down below us. There were numerous trails that gave a beautiful view of Downtown, West Hollywood, Glendale, Century City, Torrance, Pasadena, Silver Lake, and for many, the main attractions were the fresh air and the Hollywood sign. Down below at the observatory was chaos, so many busloads of tourists. We were on a dirt trail that was over four miles long.

I said, "Tell me something about you, Regina, anything, something trivial."

She was drenched in sweat, no makeup, hair underneath a bandana, wearing a pair of my too-large sweats and tee. The T-shirt had a picture of a rooster and over its head

I HAVE A BIG COCK in bright yellow letters. No one recognized her. Either that or no one up here cared.

She panted. "You first. Give me an example."

"I like the toilet paper torn along the perforated edges."

She laughed. "That's crazy, James. But cool. Let's pick up the pace."

I ran in front of her, and when she caught up, our run changed to a vigorous climb. We caught our breath and I continued talking, "I hate to see a toilet seat up. You flush with the seat up and germs fly six feet. Gets all over the counter and toothbrushes. Grosses me out."

She said, "I thought you were about to get deep and ask me the type of questions that I would cringe at and have to answer by either saying no comment or pleading the fifth."

"I said trivial. Now you."

"I detest hairy balls."

I laughed. "I don't like single-malt Scotch."

"I don't like Anthropologie."

"Hmmm. I stole a battery from a neighbor's car one night."

"A battery? I can top that, James. When I was a teenager in Montana I stole a car."

"Wow. Regina Baptiste. Car thief."

"I was Regina Baptist then. There was already a Regina Baptist registered, and since every actor gets his own name, and mine was taken, SAG made me change my name."

"You're willing to do whatever you have to do to be successful."

"I am. Failure is not an option. Success by any means necessary."

When we made it to the top again, we paused and stood in the crowd, looked out at the city. She held my hand. She held my hand and I felt something that I wanted to fight.

My cellular rang. It was the club calling. I answered.

"You hear the word, Thicke?"

"I've been occupied, Flaco. What has happened now?"

"The guys that got into the fight with the Bergs, they were all found dead. All were shot."

"The club involved?"

"Not at all. We have them on camera leaving the club after the melee."

"Johnny Bergs and his crew were okay? Anything else happen after we left?"

"Nothing. They ran up a thirty-thousand-dollar tab. He put it on his Centurion Card."

"Were the brothers there all night?"

"They were there, but their old man wasn't. He's the most evil of the bunch."

As far as I was concerned, whatever happened had occurred away from Mapona.

From the perspective of being liable, that was done.

Then Regina's cellular rang. It was her assistant. Her assistant was at Bobby Holland's home, walking and feeding the dogs, sending out e-mails, rescheduling appointments.

We finished our calls and stood in silence looking out over the cities below.

I asked, "How do you feel?"

Regina whispered, "No dogs. No kids. This has been the perfect week. Perfect. It's nice to be away for a while. Nice to feel safe. Nice not to be stressed the fuck out about everything."

The eighth night we once again moaned and sweated on my bed. Its covers had been disheveled by lust; her vibrator and slices of mangos and honey were on my nightstand. Regina's cellular rang as she was about to mount me, her breathing labored and her body over mine, ready to ease down and take control; she ran her hands across her hair, tisked and shook her head, hesitated, and fell away from me. She looked nervous, as if her secret had been revealed. She screamed a short scream and bounced her leg before she took the call.

"Hey, baby. I was on the StairMaster. How's Oslo? What happened now?"

A fire of jealousy erupted to life inside me. A fire I had to extinguish as soon as it started.

Everybody wanted to meet someone new. Everybody wanted to but couldn't. Starting over was hard, so they kept what they had and pretended. Those were my random thoughts.

"Miss you too. Love you too. I know. I overreacted. My publicist overreacted. If you say it's a lie, then it's a lie. I'll be at the airport. Okay, my love. Can't wait to see you either."

She finished the call and lay next to me, biting her lip, fingers rubbing her temples.

That call changed her mood, jarred her from this reality that we had created.

I asked, "You okay?"

"Bobby Holland will definitely be back from Oslo tomorrow."

I pulled her to me, but she pulled away, stood up and went inside the bathroom.

She closed the door. The shower came on.

I took that to mean that we were done being lovers and would go back to being strangers.

I picked up my cellular. I was about to send my first choice a text message.

If I wanted to I could fill my nights with women who were the modern day equivalents of Lana Turner, Dorothy Dandridge, Rita Moreno, Marilyn Monroe, Nichelle Nichols, Pam Grier, Ava Gardner, Rita Hayworth, Doris Duke, Zsa Zsa Gabor, Lena Horne, Barbara Hutton, Eartha Kitt, Jayne Mansfield, Princess Grace Kelly, Denise Nicholas, and Eva Perón.

I'd been with many. They'd left my home pleased and rushing to get on their cellular phones so they could have conversations with their girlfriends and talk about my Rubirosas.

I dropped the phone and stared at the intricate details of the ceiling.

A little after four in the morning I woke up in my master bedroom suite with Regina Baptiste sitting up next to me. Her cellular was in her hand, its light illuminating her face as she sent someone a text message. She closed it and put it down, sighed, then looked back at me. I was on my side, eyes barely opened. There was no light on in the room, only a full moon outside.

She whispered, "He boarded his flight. I have to go. I packed everything while you were sleeping. My suitcase is by the bedroom door. Nothing is left but the basket of clean clothes."

"You were leaving without saying good-bye."

"You have the alarm set. It's impossible for me to leave with it wailing."

I told her the code. She wasn't a prisoner and I wasn't forcing her to stay.

She said, "Even if I act odd with you when I see you in public, these days with you, I had a good time. Eight days went by so fast. Feels like I just got here. Every day was a great day. Just had to say. When I see you again, we can give no signs that we know each other."

"You did a line, didn't you?"

"I'm stressed. Yeah, I did a line. Had a little of your whiskey too."

"Well, let me call Driver. I can drive your car and drop you off and he can follow in my car. You don't need to drive, not on drugs. Get a DUI and your career will take a nosedive."

"The moment that Bobby's plane lands, everything is going to change. It's too late,

James. What's done is done. I think that my career has already taken a nosedive. I feel it."

She hand combed her hair, picked up her laundry basket. But she put her laundry down and wiped tears from her eyes. Regina Baptiste, with no makeup on her face, with no rented dress covering her body, without the high heels; she looked so young and innocent.

"You're addicted to the blow, Baptiste. I can get you help."

"I'm not a damsel in distress. And don't look at me and treat me like I am one."

"Go get coked up and end up like Belushi and Phoenix."

"Fuck you. I make six million a picture. You're lucky that I slept with you. Do you have any idea how many men wish they could have one night with me?"

"How many have had you for one night?"

"Fuck you."

"How much blow have you done? Within a year your mom and dad will be dressed in black and both will be in Livingston crying and standing over your brand new grave."

She was motionless for over a minute. "I hate you for saying that."

"Heath Ledger. Brittany Murphy. Chris Farley. Judy Garland. Anna Nicole Smith.

Elvis Presley. Dorothy Dandridge. Brad Renfro. Lani O'Grady. And soon, Regina Baptiste."

A long moment went by.

"Your mom. Your dad. Standing over your grave, surrounded by the paparazzi."

"Be quiet."

"Get help. Or let me get you help. Your choice."

She took her white powder out of her purse, stared at it a while, then went to the bathroom. I heard the toilet flush. She came back empty-handed.

Eight nights earlier, if a text had come in as I waited at that bar, it would've been different.

We would've gone on as Hollywood goes on, passing each other at events, pretending not to know each other, with me snubbing Bobby Holland and barely giving Regina a hello.

And no one would have died.

I told her, "Stay."

"I have to go face this."

"You okay?"

"I'm starting to feel overwhelmed again. My head wants to explode right now."

"Holland won't be back until afternoon. You have a few more hours. Stay."

We kissed. She calmed down. I undressed her.

Moments later, she guided me back inside her. She wanted me back inside.

I whispered, "We don't have to."

"I want to. I'm sore, but I want to feel you."

As her walls pulsated and held me, I asked, "Could you love me?"

"Don't put your dick inside me, don't get so deep inside my head and ask me that."

CHAPTER 16

The ninth afternoon, the paparazzi were buzzing around outside my gates, waiting on Regina Baptiste to vacate my bed. Regina didn't call me to warn me. She didn't call me because in Hollywood, when tragedy struck, when the walls of Jericho came down, you didn't dial 9-1-1, you called your publicist, you called the magician who charged you tens of thousands of dollars to shape your image, and he scrambled to earn his retainer and handle the damage. So I hadn't been warned. Maybe I had been seen as part of the problem. Or simply the entire problem. Regina Baptiste was all about her career, as most in Hollywood were, and everything else was expendable. Half of the paparazzi followed Regina Baptiste's BMW 650i the way they had dogged Princess Diana. The other half waited on me, took photo after photo as I left my property, were dogging me no more than thirty minutes after Regina Baptiste and I had shared lunch and parted ways. I was on the way to a meeting with the power mogul and movie executive Hazel Tamana Bijou. By the time I made it out of my zip code, Hollywood already knew. The paparazzi had recorded Regina leaving my home, and then they recorded me leaving my own home, and it was all on the Internet, with time stamps.

Seconds later, it was posted on YouTube; minutes later, it was all over the Internet. One of the anxious paparazzi had used an iPhone, the video magnificent and the picture unambiguous. Minutes later it was news in the industry. Even then it was all about Regina Baptiste. I was only a writer. My face wasn't in magazines, or on Sunset Boulevard billboards.

Two days later, there was a twenty-six-foot U-Haul truck parked in front of my home.

On the front seat was a box and inside that box was a bottle of 1978 Balvenie vintage cask single-malt Scotch whiskey and a handwritten note from Regina's boyfriend Bobby Holland.

THE COKE HEAD BITCH IS YOURS NOW. GOOD RIDDANCE AND GOOD LUCK YOU FUCKIN PRICK.

Actress Regina Baptiste and Director Bobby Holland Split

15,407 Comments.

Regina Baptiste and Bobby Holland are no longer cohabiting and planning a family, a source close to the pair told UsMagazine.com. The seemingly perfect couple decided to call it quits, initially citing the difference in their nonstop work schedules, agendas that kept them apart for weeks at a time, as the main reason for the split of the once amorous couple. The power couple's reps released the following statement: "Addressing the media speculation regarding Regina Baptiste and Bobby Holland's relationship, they mutually have decided to part ways. The two remain friends and continue to hold the highest level of love and respect for each other."

However, *Us Weekly* reported that Baptiste was having an affair with writer James Thicke. CLICK HERE FOR VIDEO OF BAPTISTE LEAVING JAMES THICKE'S HOME.

Baptiste, 26, and Holland, 32, began

dating after being introduced at the Golden Globes. It's rumored that powerhouse Hazel Tamana Bijou was the one who introduced them. Following the awards show, Baptiste and Holland were constantly photographed canoodling. They were seen holding hands and appeared to be inseparable at both Cannes and Sundance. They vacationed in Hawaii, Norway, and Venezuela, were living together at his newly built estate in the San Fernando Valley, but the pair didn't officially announce their relationship for six months.

Holland Tweeted praises about Baptiste as recently as last week. He has said that she was the sunshine of his life. Yesterday morning his Tweet said that the sun in his life has gone down but will rise once again, new and improved. Her response Tweet, which came an hour later, said that Bobby Holland was "Never Mr. Right, only Mr. Right now." His retort came at noon, "If only she had more talent." Baptiste responded two minutes later. "If only he had more blue pills."

CLICK HERE FOR OTHER CELEBRITY SPLITS.

CHAPTER 17

Downey, California

Four days went by with Driver sending updates to the throwaway or meeting me at the Starbucks near Imperial Highway and Leffingwell Road. That was ninety-six hours with me being absent from my world of shame, away from actors and actresses and producers and agents and managers and homes with gates and guards and the foul breath of the paparazzi, but connected to news feed like that poison was the IV that slow-dripped and infused aggravation into my blood.

Incompetent talking heads had taken over. The controversy wasn't dying. Thanks to Facebook and YouTube, idiots posted all day long, created rumors, rumors that became stronger than the truth, and the lies burned brighter with each passing moment.

Regina Baptiste Interviews with all of

the Sexy Men She's Dated in Hollywood.

Regina Baptiste Pregnant with Johnny Bergs's Alleged 3rd Lovechild.

Regina Baptiste: Her Ex Bobby Holland Claims to Have 2nd Revealing Sex Tape.

Most of the interviews were made up. The lies stung as much as the truth.

Bobby Holland Ordered to Pay $940K in Child Support.

A judge has ordered director Bobby Holland to pay close to a million dollars to French actress Brigette Deneve-Marceau, who won a ruling naming Holland as the father of her eleven-year-old son. But a rep for the director says, "The judgment was a default judgment made without Holland being present. He looks forward to resolving this paternity hoax, and is awaiting the results of a recent paternity test to clear up this con job. Unfortunately there is no penalty for women who create such claims that both damage a man's character and eat up valuable time in our court system. When that happens, when those who file false claims are penalized for doing so, there will be justice in the world." Bobby Holland has two children from another failed marriage to Norwegian actress Liv Foss, known for her natural beauty, intellect, and complex performances. She has not worked for the past decade. Bobby Holland has been in and out of court, battling paternity issues with Liv Foss for the last decade as well. Bobby Holland is the former live-in lover of American actress Regina Baptiste. No children were born of their three-year relationship. Regina Baptiste is now at the center of a sex-tape scandal involving superstar actor Johnny Bergs.

Baptiste's Real Sex with Bergs: Demeaning or Empowering to the Female Species?

Regina Baptiste and our problems were mentioned unnecessarily in the thread about Bobby Holland, as if the dead relationship with that asshole now had a second life, as if that potential million-dollar debt was her responsibility. It was like Denise Richards getting new press every time Charlie

Sheen took a shit. Regina Baptiste would be in the thread of anyone she was linked to at this point. There was even a link to a man who claimed to be the high school boyfriend that she had left behind. He was working in Great Falls as a high school teacher. Television wanted to interview him to hear his story about the all-American who had played high school football, the good old Montana boy who was jilted by the glamorous superstar, the Lyle Lovett who was dumped by Julia Roberts. The beast abandoned by the beauty. He would talk. They would pay and he would talk. For spite. For attention. To settle an old score. A loser's last stand. Plus post-varsity football, he was an actor who never made it past doing high school musicals. People threw others underneath the bus of fame to make a buck. I'd been fucked over by producers, actors, agents; pretty much everyone in the business had acted in their own self-interest and run me over in the process. Some would have my scripts tied up for years. Others would forget me after the contracts were signed. In the name of business, I had done the same thing. And I wasn't ashamed. You survive swimming with the sharks by becoming the meanest shark in the waters. We were trained that way. Bobby Holland had fucked me over on a deal. Maybe in retaliation I had thrown Bobby Holland under the Fuck You bus years ago. But he was throwing Regina Baptiste under the bus at the time. Everyone threw somebody under a bus; then ran it forward and backward. And a new double-decker bus ran every ten minutes.

Johnny Bergs's name popped up on hundreds of pages. At the top was the announcement that they were running JOHNNY BERGS: BAD BOY ON THE EDGE on the bio channel tonight. His name was also in a new thread that led to a blog site. It was the crass comedienne who had been riding the coattails of Bergs's beating to make herself famous. Now she called herself The Baddest Whyte Bitch Dat Done Ever Been Born. She claimed that she had been threatened because of her stand-up act about the Johnny Bergs fiasco.

About six or seven motherfuckers came to my apartment complex in Universal City, I mean all of those big, big, corn-fed Men in Black suit-wearing motherfuckers showed up looking like they were ready to stone me to death. I'm not sure who they were, but some people say that they were Johnny Bitch . . . I mean

Bergs's brothers. I guess those thugs were supposed to scare me. One was so ugly my kids thought it was Halloween and threw leftover trick-or-treat candy at the sonofabitch. Then Bergs's punk-ass attorney sends me a letter to cease and desist doing my routine about Johnny Bergs because of some defamation of character bullshit. I exercise my freedom of motherfucking speech the way Bergs exercised his freedom to fuck the shit out of Regina Baptiste followed by his freedom to get the shit beat out of his ass. Running through the streets crying in the rain? I'm sorry, that's so gay that gay people don't even do that shit. Yeah, I said it. What the fuck he gonna do? Kill me? They have pissed me the fuck off and I'm going to do all I can to make that bitch miserable. I'm posting all of my shit on Facebook and YouTube and Twitter so pass that shit on to other people. I will be at the J-Spot, Laugh Factory, Comedy Store, and Club Savoy.

I checked my messages and there was one from one of the managers at Club Mapona.

"Boss, Flaco. Moses Bergs and his sons came into the club last night looking for you. That fucking lunatic acted like he was going to set the club on fire. Call me."

There was a knock at my door. I looked at the clock. It was almost six A.M.

I opened the door and Sweet Isabel was standing in the badly lighted hallway.

Like Patrice had been during her surprise visit, Sweet Isabel was half naked.

And so was I. I'd been expecting her. Another Post-it was on my front door too.

CHAPTER 18

The first day back, running was difficult. From the first step it was physically draining and emotionally trying. Sleep had been bad. My energy was down, but I pushed it, because with each step, I imagined stomping Johnny Handsome's face until it turned into mush.

"How are you holding up today, Varg?"

"This is more than three miles out."

"We're four miles out and you're starting to slow me down."

"I told you that I was good for six miles."

"Oh, well. I seem to have forgotten that part of the conversation."

"Why did you say it was three miles out and back?"

"When you befriend liars, it's best to practice the art of deception at every turn."

"Blimey."

"Blimey is old and outdated and only sounds appropriate when I say the word."

"Blimey."

"Interesting T-shirt you're running in."

"Thanks."

"That was not a compliment."

"Blimey."

My T-shirt was blue and said THERE ARE 70 WAYS TO SATISFY A WOMAN. ONE IS SHOPPING. THE OTHER IS 69. TOO BAD I DON'T LIKE TO GO SHOPPING. Hers read THE ONLY WAY IS NOT ESSEX.

Sweet Isabel maintained a steady pace. But a quarter of a mile later, I let her buns of steel go on without me. The super-fit, mature woman in the light blue running shorts and golden T-shirt pulled away one stride at a time, each stride stronger than the one before. I slowed down and turned back around, kept it moving at a good pace, kept stomping Johnny Handsome's face, weighed by my thoughts for another grueling half hour.

About a half mile before the finish line at Imperial Highway, Isabel passed by me.

She moved like the wind to prove a point.

She finished and waved, crossed at the red light, then kept jogging back to the complex.

When I finished my run, aching and out of breath, I jogged until she was out of sight, then stopped and absorbed the pain from the run, the pain of my life, and returned to being James Thicke. Sweat poured from me as I walked parallel to insane traffic. Morning was here. People were leaving lives they hated to rush to jobs they loathed. The Apartments rose before me like the villas of Argentina, the favelas of Buenos Aires, the anti-Hollywood of California.

When I made it to the area near the pool, Mr. Holder was leaning against the rail. We spoke, shook hands, and then he said, "It's almost the big day."

"The reunion with your daughter."

"We're meeting at TGIF. Would be nice to ride down there in that car of yours."

"You want me to drive you down?"

"Could you? We meet next week. She might get a kick out of seeing that Maybach."

"Would be glad to. If you want, I'll take both of you for a ride."

I stretched for a moment and after I'd caught my breath, I ran up the stairs to get a bottle of water. The neighbor living over my head was fornicating nonstop and making enough noise for me to want to call management and complain. Either that or buy whoever lived up there a better bed. The sun was coming up. I picked up my Nikon, cellular, and sunglasses, and then stormed back downstairs and stood near

Mr. Holder. He looked anxious. Today I looked and felt calm.

I asked, "You okay?"

He nodded. "Just thinking back. About what I went through with my daughter's mom."

"Kerri-Anne."

He nodded again. "From Kerri-Anne to Vera-Anne. Twenty years later."

We watched the people leaving for work. Mr. Holder stayed quiet while I photographed the Arabic, Dutch, Hebrew, Tibetan, Ukrainian, Mexican, Farsi, Mandarin, French, and German tenants as they exited the buildings. I took candid shots every now and then. Captured the hardworking people. Mr. Holder shifted and looked at all of the women. More than a few people said hello to Mr. Holder. He'd been here sixteen years and knew everyone by name.

His jaw tightened and he looked angry; it came and went.

He asked, "How long did you rent your apartment for?"

"Did a year lease."

"A year? That's quite a bit of money."

"My monthly mortgage is a lot more than that."

"So that much money, I guess it's just a

drop of water in the ocean for you."

"I'll write it off as a business expense."

"People here are struggling to pay their rent and you're throwing money away."

He shook his head and exhaled, but added no words to his thoughts.

My cellular rang. It was Driver. He was driving another customer to the airport.

He said, "Gray four-door car was in front of your house the last two days."

"Who?"

"No idea. Might've been parked longer than that."

"Get the plates?"

"I'll drive back by after I finish this run. If it's still there, I'll get the license plates."

We hung up and I took a deep breath. Mr. Holder still looked angry.

I put my camera down at my side and asked, "You sure that you're okay?"

Mr. Holder moved to one of the worn pool chairs and sat down.

I did the same.

"Thinking about Vera-Anna. I was on the computer last night trying to sort some things out. A few things have me troubled. So I'm standing outside, getting fresh air and thinking."

I said, "You never said how you met Vera-Anne."

"Met her right here. She used to live across the hall from me. She was working at a State Farm insurance office. Lost that job, then was working at a comedy club. Lost that job, and was getting evicted. It's a bad season for trying to find a job, and that's from top to bottom. I let her crash at my place for a few days, gave her a week to contact her family and move in with them, but by the third night, she got up from the couch and stood in my bedroom door."

"And one thing led to another."

Right about then, Vera-Anne came out of the complex. Tight jean shorts. Dark sports bra. House shoes. She was alone and had two Styrofoam bowls with her.

Mr. Holder said, "Where are the kids?"

"Brought you some chicken souse and Johnny Cake. Brought you some too, Varg."

"Thanks, Vera-Anne."

"You said chicken souse was one of your favorite meals, right?"

"Yeah. It is."

Mr. Holder snapped, "What did I tell you about leaving those children unattended?"

"They're watching television. Relax."

Vera-Anne handed him a bowl and a plastic spoon, then did the same to me.

Mr. Holder had a hard expression, a twitch in his lip, a rigid moment that I interpreted as him not being happy with Vera-Anne being generous with the food that he was buying.

I had accepted the gift and didn't know how to give it back.

Mr. Holder said, "I was about to come back inside anyway. Come on, Vera-Anne. You're a mother now. You don't need to be walking around with your ass hanging out like that. People will think you're advertising. And house shoes are made for wearing inside of the house."

She ran her fingers though her pink mane. "Poppa, take me to the Getty today."

He regarded her without expression. Then he turned to me, smiled as his eyes frowned, and we shook hands again, his handshake so firm, his eye contact so direct that it felt as if I were being challenged. He suddenly let my hand go and headed back toward his apartment. Vera-Anne followed. His steps were heavy, his head down, and hands inside of his pockets. Vera-Anne looked back, waved and smiled before she ran right into a heavy blond man as he exited the building. He was rushing, head down, and he almost knocked Vera-Anne over. They apologized to each other, then Vera-Anne glanced back, waved good-bye again.

The blond man hurried toward the parking lot. New face. He was large enough to be unforgettable. Hadn't seen him here before. The heavy man left in a hurry, refused to make eye contact with anyone. His shame told me who he was. He was a customer and had been here on *business*. If I went back to my apartment, no screams of passion would rain down from overhead.

I wasn't in a rush to go back upstairs. I ate the chicken souse and Johnny Cake.

Thirty minutes later, my enemy from the laundry room came downstairs.

She'd styled her long dreadlocks, made them look wavy. Part of her strong hair was pulled back while a lot of her powerful mane hung to her shoulders. She wore Roman sandals, jean shorts, and a T-Shirt that read YES I'M A BITCH, JUST NOT YOURS. Without warning, she reversed her course and came my way. I stood up. A man should face his enemy on foot. My enemy cleared antagonism from her throat and looked in my eyes, studied my face.

"You do look very familiar."

"From the laundry room."

"Yeah, I remember that."

"So do I."

She motioned at my camera. "You're a photographer."

"I've been called worse."

"I'm an entertainer and an inspiring writer."

"*Aspiring* writer. And an entertainer."

"That's what I said."

"What type of entertainment?"

"Personal entertainment. It depends on the needs of the client."

She nodded and gave me eye contact that tested my ability to read between the lines.

I asked, "Your book. What's it about?"

"The cruelty of men toward women."

"What's it called?"

"The Cruelty of Men Toward Women."

"You have a name?"

"Misty. I'm in E-313."

"I'm in E-213. Call me Varg."

"How long have you been living up under me?"

"Long enough to know you're a very busy woman."

"You look very familiar. I just don't know from where."

What broke the conversation was when one of the other tenants left the building.

It was a husband and a wife. They were holding hands and laughing like they didn't have a care in the world. Misty waved at them. The husband waved back. The wife looked, but didn't wave. He had on worn jeans and a green shirt. She wore Nike

226

workout gear, all black.

I asked, "Who is that big guy?"

"Ted Evans. He sells crappy used cars at a crappy Mexican car lot in Norwalk."

Mrs. Patrice Evans was walking with Ted. She glanced, and then looked away.

Misty tilted her head and asked, "What's your name again?"

"Varg Veum."

"Wait a minute. Have you ever been to a club in Hollywood called Mapona?"

Caught off guard, I paused and shook my head. "Can't afford it. You've been there?"

"Once. Clients that I went with got into a fight with that asshole Johnny Bergs and we were thrown out and Johnny Bergs and his party were treated like kings and shit. We didn't even get our money back and I heard that Johnny Bergs was given free champagne and free food."

"I'll make a point never to go up there. I'm more of a Bible study kinda guy anyway."

"Regina Baptiste's perfume is named after that place. That slut's all over the news. Heard she's pregnant by Johnny Bergs. Heard that she had AIDS. Heard she's doing porn now."

I stared at her. In my mind I was beating her the way I had beaten Johnny Handsome, holding her dreadlocks in my left hand and striking her in the mouth over and over, grimacing and spitting in her face and making her regret calling my wife a slut.

She asked, "What was your name again?"

I cleared my throat and said, "Veum. Varg Veum."

"Ugly name."

"Ugly world."

She studied my features for a while. The edge of her lips curled upward.

"Okay, Veum. Varg. Man with the ugly name. See you later."

She left in a hurry and I sweated like a man on the run from the unknown.

And just like that, I was no longer calm. I was beyond anxious.

Once again I could hear the thunderous applause.

I logged on and reactivated my Facebook account. Did the same for Twitter. As soon as I did, friend requests and strangers begging to follow me on Twitter poured in. Within an hour, I had more hits than three times the population of the British overseas territory Montserrat. I could only imagine the attention Regina Baptiste loathed right now.

Could only imagine the attention Johnny

Bergs was enjoying.

Worst of all, I heard that bastard Bobby Holland laughing at it all.

The tabloid fire was still burning throughout Hollywoodland and beyond.

There was nothing that I could do. Stress sweat drained from my face.

I had left my computer on; my Skype was up and running. I clicked on the icon.

Someone had tried to call me on the account that I shared with only a few.

It was the account that I used mostly to communicate with Regina when she was away at work. The screen name was STEVE-MARTIN. OBJECTOFBEAUTY. A comedian and his novel.

I looked up the profile and it was pretty blank. No information told me who this was.

My guess was the Bergs. Either Johnny Handsome or someone in his family.

Or maybe it was the comedienne who was capitalizing on the situation, *The Baddest Whyte Bitch Dat Done Ever Been Born*. I looked her up. Her name was Frances Johnson; another nobody who was trying to be somebody; another comic trying to get to the top of the barrel.

CHAPTER 19

Procol Harum sang "A Whiter Shade of Pale." Isabel played the vintage record when I entered her apartment. Her place smelled of fresh chocolate chip cookies. A hint of lavender came from her deodorizer, and her apartment was spotless, everything in its proper place. Her furniture was modest and very nice, a light brown sofa made for sitting and watching television, or sleeping, a dark green love seat and a wooden coffee table that held an arrangement of colorful fresh cut flowers. Her carpet was beige and freshly cleaned, the paint on her walls crisp. When I came inside, she changed records, put on Ann Peebles's "I'm Gonna Tear Your Playhouse Down." Like she had done at my apartment, I gravitated toward her literary novels. She had hundreds of books. There were books by British authors; those were separated from the rest, the majority of them decades old, many of them in hardback.

She said, "Be a gentleman and carry my bowling ball for me."

"Sure. I'll be more than happy to carry your ball. One day you might return the favor."

"Frisky wanker. I like you better as a cheeky bastard."

We headed out to her sports car, a red Nissan 350Z Roadster, and with the top down, she zoomed us up Imperial Highway into the city of Norwalk to Keystone Lanes.

We bowled six games. Isabel was all strikes and spares, her bowling form perfect, her hook on the ball remarkable, the spin on her ball amazing. She had three speeds, different hand positions. Her hips were squared like a professional, and she moved like a ballerina. When she broke a sweat and took off her jacket revealing a dark tank top, everyone looked at her physique. Her remarkable bowling had everyone taking notes. Her delivery was good, her explosion point perfect. She knew the terminology, Brooklyn, The Pocket, The Pick-Up, and bowled like a league bowler, never scored less than two hundred sixty, her top score two seventy-seven. Even though I never had a gutter ball, I only had six strikes and my score stayed under one-ninety.

When we were done I asked, "Want to go back over to Cerritos to Skate Depot?"

"Another day, you cheeky bastard."

I was out of The Apartments, out of my self-imposed claustrophobia, still a man on the run from a crime that he had committed, a man humiliated, and I just didn't want to go back.

My cellular rang. It was Driver. I didn't answer.

I didn't want to go back to being James Thicke right now.

I wanted to take on this part I'd created, become a method actor and make it mine.

Once at Isabel's apartment, we sat at her dining room table, Gladys Knight singing "Help Me Make It Through the Night" on the record player, and we sipped Earl Grey tea.

Isabel looked at me and asked, "Varg, who are you really?"

And just like that, as Gladys Knight sang, Varg Veum no longer existed.

Without remorse or hesitation, I told her who I really was.

She said, "Your real name is James Thicke."

"Mind if I turn your television on?"

I changed the channels and two movies that Regina Baptiste had been in were on.

Images of her as an actress five and seven years ago were on HBO and Showtime. By then, ironically, in the background, as my wife gave her stellar performance, Teddy Pendergrass sang from the record player, begged from the record player, and pleaded "I Miss You."

I said, "That's the woman I married, Sweet Isabel."

"Oh, my. She's definitely not a minger. She's posh and as lovely as Bettie Page, as stunning as Linda Christian. A woman who looks this good can wangle anything."

"It's all smoke and mirrors. I've seen her without her makeup."

"Oh, if she is your wife, you've seen her without more than just makeup."

"I've seen her doubled over and cramping and begging for stronger Midol too."

"And she went full monty on film and everything has gone pear shaped for her."

"She went past full monty. She took an R-rated script and knocked it down six letters."

"When I was growing up, they kissed and carried a woman to the bedroom door, then faded to black. You had to use your own imagination. And that we did. Now the camera follows them into the bedroom and stays there until the woman gets pregnant and has a baby."

"Pretty much."

She said, "Before becoming a school-teacher, I used to work in the film industry. That's where I met my husband. He did set designs. There were so many scandals back then. The alcohol. The drugs. So many men were marrying beards to keep their sexuality hidden from the public. So many lesbian or bisexual women were marrying men for the same reason. All the key and drug parties. It was the in thing. We were at a more than a few. And the murders. What they did to Marilyn Monroe was a shame. That business has always been scandalous."

"It has and always will be."

"Today, tomorrow, forever."

I turned the television off.

Isabel knew who I wasn't. And who I was. She had met James Thicke.

She said, "Well, when a woman shows you who she is, believe her."

Isabel moved by me and changed records. Dean Martin sang "Besame Mucho."

She said, "I love Dean Martin, but the Andrea Bocelli version of this song is much better."

Then we went to the kitchen sink. I shampooed Isabel's hair with a rosemary juniper scented shampoo, washed it twice as she asked me, massaged her scalp, slowly, and gently.

Dean Martin finished and I went to her record collection, an assortment that was as amazing as my rare books, and I gingerly took out a different record, Johnny Bristol's "Hang on In There Baby." Followed by The New Birth singing "Dream Merchant," George McCrae's "Rock Your Baby," and Al Green first singing "Sha La La" followed by him crooning "Simply Beautiful."

She said, "You're really good at washing me hair."

"Used to wash my wife's hair from time to time."

"Here's my two cents. You do what you want to. Women blame much on men, but in the end, they are challenging each other, and men benefit from that sparring. You can take the filthy job, or leave with your dignity. No matter how many women are going fully monty in movies, you don't have to do it. Who should follow the path walked by most idiots? Only other idiots do that."

"In film, to be the star, it's pretty much a prerequisite for a woman to do a love scene."

"There is a difference between a love scene and hard-core porn."

"What do you know about porn?"

"I'm not a bloody prude, you wanker. And not ashamed to say I've seen my share."

"Have you?"

"Enough to know there is a difference between a true lady and two girls and a cup."

I massaged her scalp for a while and she fell silent. While I ran my fingers across her scalp, I gazed at her wonderful, amazing build. A few times she moaned. I swallowed.

She said, "Well, I hope that she doesn't end up like Linda Darnell."

"Linda Darnell. *A Letter to Three Wives. Unfaithfully Yours. Angels of Darkness.*"

"Darnell was a wonderful American actress."

"American actress."

"British actresses are much better. But for America, Darnell was wonderful."

I nodded. "She was. For her time, she was."

"But notorious for her volatile personal life."

"Hollywood did her in."

"So they say. People never really know what burdens another might bear."

"Darnell became an alcoholic. Read about bad marriage after bad marriage."

Isabel said, "In the end, I guess that's what most remember. The scandal."

"Nothing is new. Even when it's new, it's not new. Scandals are like stories; all have been done before. All that changes are technology and faces. Sex. Affairs. Mixed-race babies. Actresses becoming criminals. It's all been done before. And will be done again."

When I finished with her hair, Isabel thanked me and pulled out her portable hair dryer.

She asked, "Would you like to stay and watch *Sonny Boy* while I dry me hair?"

"I'm going to go back upstairs for a while. I have to check on a few things."

"That got to you, didn't it? Seeing the missus on the telly just now got to you."

"I'll be okay after I die."

"Hopefully I didn't instigate too much."

"Not at all. I want you to feel comfortable around your cheeky and lying neighbor."

"Hopefully I didn't offend you."

"Of course you did. You outran me then beat me at bowling."

"Girl power."

She winked, then came to walk me to her front door, a yellow towel over hair colored the hue of the sun. With her hair covered, with it pulled up like that, she looked so much younger.

Without thinking, on impulse, I asked her

if I could touch her defined arms.

She told me that I could. I just wanted to touch her magnificent frame.

She asked, "So should I call you James?"

I said, "No. Call me Varg. I'm Varg for now. James has too many problems."

"I understand. I'm sorry that I pried the way I did. It's the way I am."

"You're a Brit. All of you cheeky bastards are nosey buggers across the pond."

As I put my fingers on her skin, Peabo Bryson finished his turn at the microphone, "Reaching for the Sky," and New Birth took to the invisible stage and sang the sexy song of praise, "Wildflower." I traced my fingers over her forearms, to her shoulders, then back down to her palms.

She closed her eyes and rocked like we were back in the seventies, slow dancing.

She had just as much appeal as a movie starlet, could easily define sexiness and a generation's taste in fashion. I wondered how her marriage had been, if she had been loyal.

She held my hand and I held hers as Smokey Robinson sang "Baby Come Close."

"Look at the dreadful and selfish way I'm behaving. Young enough to be my son."

"You don't look old enough to be my

mother."

Isabel whispered, "You best go before I'm tempted to carry you to the bedroom door."

"What would happen on the other side of that bedroom door?"

"A bit of how's your father."

"A round of how's your father would be interesting."

"I'd embarrass you."

"Blimey."

I leaned toward her, touched her lips with mine. I put my mouth on hers for seconds, and she opened her mouth to receive my tongue. I kissed her and focused on the sensation of kissing, tasted her, felt her, inhaled her. I kissed her for a long time, for the thrill of kissing.

When the kiss ended, she touched the side of my face and first licked her lips, then chewed at the corner of her bottom lip. She headed toward her bedroom and I followed her.

She said, "You're not a lazy lover are you?"

"I'm better in bed than I am bowling."

"So am I."

I stood in the doorframe, observing her, and she let her wet hair down, let it fall free, the first step to becoming this other person. She eased her firm bottom down on the edge of the bed, her hands at her side. I stood in the doorframe staring at her as if I were a mannish child staring through a peephole at a grown woman. Our eyes remained locked for a long moment.

She whispered, "Bring me your pain."

I took a step toward her and she moved, held the bed and slid down in a slow and sexy way, moved in slow motion until her bottom touched the carpet at the foot of the bed, her eyes still on mine. I went down on my knees in front of her and inhaled her. I sucked her earlobes, kissed her neck, touched her breasts, rubbed between her legs. She reached to me, pulled my tee over my head, laid it to the side, and then stared at my chest. Sweet Isabel rubbed my chest and her breath caught in her throat. She smiled. So feminine and so mature and still a lovely girl all at once. Her naughtiness had risen to the surface. I kissed her and her body moved, led me to the carpet and I followed, her legs opening for me, opening wide, the invitation clear.

I pulled her pants and panties away from her, then unzipped my pants and rubbed my erection against her, felt her slickness, and I moved up and down until I found her opening, until she sighed and held on as I penetrated, as I eased inside her. A long sigh escaped her. She swallowed. For a moment,

I didn't move. Finally I was in a safe place. I inhaled and shuddered from the sensation of being connected to her, the sweetness of being inside her, one of the most deeply emotionally charged moments of my existence. We'd become a beast with two backs, but I didn't move for a long moment. Even though she moved against me, even though my moans rose to my throat, I didn't move. I held myself there and stared into her eyes until she sighed and then I eased them shut. She held me and became a masterpiece of unbridled passion.

I danced with her rhythm, moved in a deliberate motion, moved in and out of her, measured her, watched her react, watched her until what I felt grabbed me and pulled me toward its heat. I stopped and shuddered again, and then she opened her eyes and gazed at me, a small smile on her face, a smile of unexpected pleasure, a sweet smile, her mouth barely opened and exposing the whiteness of her teeth and the pinkness of her tongue, her eyes dreamy. She blinked a hundred times and one at a time her hands fell away from me, rested at her side. She moaned in surrender. Maybe it wasn't submission, but that she knew I was married, she knew that the other me was married, that even if now I was Varg, the

James part of me was married, and if she didn't touch me now, if she didn't encourage me deeper inside her, she wouldn't be complicit in this crime, only a spectator. I eased out of her body, made one become two, and backed away, the sound of desire living in each inhale and exhale, and written across my face.

In a heated whisper she asked, "Done so soon?"

"Take the rest of your clothes off."

She removed her clothing. I removed all of mine. Her body was as beautiful as if it had been photoshopped. The weightlifting, the running, the yoga, the Pilates, the bowling, the dancing, her diet, her energy, it had kept her body powerful, lean, and youthful.

As I sat and held my erection, I hoped that I looked as good to her naked.

She moved her wet hair from her face and whispered, "You have a gorgeous cock."

"You're gorgeous. You're a work of art, Sweet Isabel, physically and mentally."

"I imagine that this is how Chet felt when he first saw Vera-Anne's youth unadorned."

"I imagine that she was tired of little boys and wanted someone mature for a change."

"You at that age and me at this age. Now I have become quite the hypocrite."

"We're all hypocrites."

"That we are."

"But seeing you in your natural state, it's a shame we have to wear clothes."

I kissed her body, sucked her toes, rubbed her bottom, then tasted her, licked her provocatively, licked her like she was melting ice cream. Sweet Isabel was truly sweet.

Sweet Isabel sat up on my lap. It showed in her face, the pressure that was building up, the need for an extraordinary release. She abandoned her ladylike ways, her politeness, became sexual and primal, moved faster, and without saying a word that I could comprehend, she demanded more. I turned her over, entered her, and met her every demand.

Sweet Isabel whispered, "Tea?"

"Sure."

She pulled her wet hair back into a ponytail, wrapped a towel around her mane, then pulled on a housecoat that matched her hair. When she was done, she smiled at me.

"You're a very skilled lover."

"Why, thank you, Isabel."

"My, my, my. You are much better at this than you are at bowling."

Isabel headed for the kitchen.

She called back, "So, do you really know seventy ways to satisfy a woman?"

I laughed, then took a deep breath, felt the stress from James Thicke's life overtaking Varg Veum's peaceful world. Finally gave in and took out my cellular. I called Flaco to find out what had been happening at Club Mapona.

He said, "Since this thing between you and Bergs has happened, one of the Bergs has been at the club every night. Not the same one, but one of them. Last night they acted out."

"Anyone get hurt?"

"Not yet. Police keep coming by asking for you too, but not often."

"Heard that too."

"Some hooker that he used to deal with was on CNN talking about him. These bitches. Man. She was telling about Bergs and drugs and said that he was on antidepressant pills, heroin, coke, and alcohol. She didn't paint a pretty picture."

"What's the atmosphere at the club?"

"People show up to see the place now, since they said you were part-owner in the press. The comedienne who's skewing Bergs, Frances, she came one night. She's loud and bad news."

"If she left her info, call her. If she didn't, look her up online. Let her and ten people in for free. Red sector. Three drinks each for free, but don't tell them until the tab comes."

"Just found her on Facebook. Sending her a message as we talk."

"Keep me posted, Flaco. Anything Bergs, keep me posted."

"You okay, boss?"

"I'm as good as I'm going to be until it gets worse."

"She told me not to tell you, but I feel as if I have to. I mean, I like her as a person and all that, but you're the boss. I work for you. So she's put me in a bad spot by having me involved."

"What, Flaco?"

"Regina Baptiste came here. She stayed in your suite two days. She was here right after that incident at the airport. She came in the private entrance, came after hours. Locked the door, broke down, never went out. No one knew that she was in there but me and her assistant."

"Where is she now?"

"Then she left. When the Bergs came by and caused a little noise, she panicked and left. She barely got out ahead of the paparazzi. She left and never came back."

I hung up, then lowered my head. It felt as if I was dreaming. As if I had gone crazy. As if I was outside of my body watching me. I had met wrong with wrong and beaten a man to settle a score that couldn't be settled. When I saw Bergs again I'd beat the little handsome that was left in his ass into the asphalt. I had been cuckold then committed adultery and shed no tears and felt no shame. My soul didn't understand this convoluted world, but my heart understood revenge. The world understood revenge. Revenge was the water that doused the fires of pain.

From what I had heard and seen, I was sure that the Bergs understood revenge as well.

The world laughed. Part of me wanted to scream. Every action created a reaction. Each reaction created another reaction. Violence begets violence. It was an endless loop.

Isabel called out, "Tea is ready."

I pulled on my pants and headed toward Isabel's kitchen. Anger pulled at me and I was thinking about leaving right then, was ready to leave this world behind and go on the hunt, go face my problems head-on, but I looked at Sweet Isabel, took in her school-girl smile.

I said, "You're blushing."

"I am. Like I'm twenty-one."

I watched her a while, my anger diminishing, Varg Veum taking control with every breath.

She said, "And how are you feeling? Thought that you might have nodded off."

"Mind if I put some music on?"

"Blimey. That's how we got started the first time."

"Are we done?"

"Are you waving the white flag of surrender?"

"I'm a Brit. We never surrender."

Moments later Gladys Knight sang and the scent of Earl Grey tea filled the air. We sat at the table, words few, music low, our fingers intertwined as we sipped our tea from plain white teacups. Mine was sweetened with honey. She took hers with milk. A Brit to the bone. When I was living in the UK, my mum and father both took their tea the same way. That made me smile.

Isabel put her foot in my chair, between my legs, slid her toes up and down my penis.

"I could be your mother."

"But you're not. Not with the things that we've done."

"Should I feel horrible for allowing such a thing?"

"You should feel wonderful. You should feel very naughty and wonderful."

"How cruel the gods can be. You at that

age, and me this age."

"Very cruel. Or simply very smart. Smarter than the both of us."

This was how it had been with Regina and me at the start. She had come to me, had found peace inside of my home, had escaped all that had troubled her and found tranquility and freedom.

Regina Baptiste had run away from Bobby Holland, had come to me in pain, had wanted to escape for just one night, cocaine and sex the drugs she used to make it though the night.

And now I had run away from the world.

Sweet Isabel came to me, pulled my pants away, and then took me inside her mouth again. I sat back, sipped Earl Grey tea and released inarticulate sounds while she tortured me. She did things that I couldn't imagine Sweet Isabel would ever do, her skills surprising, made me moan and slide out of the chair until I was on the floor. I squirmed and she followed me, controlled me as if she had invented fellatio and forgotten to patent her creation. Then she held my butt and encouraged me to thrust. Her oral sex was intelligent. She handled me perfectly. She squeezed my ass, wanted me to feed her, wanted me to thrust. In slow motion I moved in and out of that warmth.

A while later, as I stood firm, as I tingled, we headed back toward the bedroom. Along the way, when we were in her hallway, I took her against the wall, took her from behind with water from her wet hair draining down her back, with her soft cries rising, then with her facing me, her strong legs wrapped around my waist. Just like that, with us connected, I held her buttocks and carried her, took her, eased her down on the bed and reciprocated the oral torture that she had given me in the kitchen. The skin across her lower back shivered and soon she pulled me up to her face.

We kissed and kissed and moved as if time was on our side.

It was as if every nerve ending was awake. My moan was so joyous. She reacted as if she felt the same. She held my back and I felt ten fingernails drag across my skin, ready to dig in deep and brand me like I was her property and this was her plantation. I grabbed her wrists and held her hands at her side. Then I let her hands go. Stroked her until she grabbed me again. I didn't care if she took fire and iron and branded her name across my back and chest.

While I was here, there wasn't an endless tape playing inside of my head — no Johnny

Bergs, no more Regina Baptiste, no threats from Bobby Holland, no Mapona, no Hollywood.

Finally, I could no longer hear the applause. Finally, there was a moment of peace.

Sweet Isabel moaned and moved with me and showed a young man who was the boss.

I kissed Sweet Isabel and moved deeper inside. I was safe inside these walls.

Right or wrong, I felt safe and at home inside the walls of Sweet Isabel.

News for Regina Baptiste

msnbc.com

Regina Baptiste no longer in the running for *Bodyguard* Remake

8 hours ago

Once considered to be the perfect fit for the project, Regina Baptiste has been removed. Just weeks ago she was in negotiations to reprise the role that Whitney Houston brought to life in the 1992 classic. Speculation is that since her real sex film with actor Johnny Bergs leaked, along with the negative publicity that has followed, she was no longer considered a fit for the project. Regina Baptiste has lost several contracts as the result of the untitled film, including endorsements with L'Oreal, Tampax, and St. John. She has, however, been offered two parts in porn movies, one starring Ron Jeremy and the other Mr. Marcus. Both were turned down. Ironically, Johnny Bergs has been offered a contract to reprise the role of the bodyguard that had been played by Kevin Costner.

Los Angeles Times (blog) — (6000) related articles.

News for Regina Baptiste

gossip.com

Regina Baptiste and Johnny Bergs the hot new Hollywood couple?

1 hour ago

Regina Baptiste and James Thicke have both been MIA since Regina's on-film sex-capade. Rumors are Miss Baptiste has filed for divorce from her husband, award-winning screenwriter and entrepreneur James Thicke. Also there are pictures of her with a baby bump. Could she be preggers with Johnny Bergs's child? That would be one beautiful baby.

Hollywood Gossip (blog) — (700) related articles.

CHAPTER 20

The next morning I ran with Isabel again. I stopped by her apartment and we had a quickie. She had an appointment and I had things to do as well. Back inside my apartment I installed my magicJack and called producer Hazel Tamana Bijou's cellular.

"James, you saw the news on the movie. Not only that, but a Disney project that Regina was up for has been pulled. And word is that The Powerful Agency is letting Regina Baptiste go."

A pain ran through my chest. "She's losing her top-shelf management team."

I took a breath and shook my head. "Par for the course. Rats leaving a sinking ship."

"Everyone is melting down. Regina Baptiste is a brand, a business in and of herself."

"A multimillion-dollar-a-picture business. She makes money and all who work for her in Hollywood can send their kids to private schools and buy winter homes in the Caribbean."

"First. Bobby Holland. He's called a dozen times. He wants to meet with you."

"Forget Bobby Holland. I'm concerned with Johnny Handsome."

She told me that word on the street was that Johnny Handsome was with his Malibu lawyers and Rodeo Drive plastic surgeons. Johnny Handsome's injuries had been severe and the humiliation forced him into hiding. And his publicity team was trying to do damage control, put a spin on the street fight so that their action hero didn't go from being the next Schwarzenegger to being seen as the next Screech. He didn't want shots with him looking beaten up surfacing, but the one that did had spoken a million words. Those Web sites had been shut down, but people were forwarding those shots in e-mails, and the tape of them having sex was still out there. It wouldn't die. It would live on, would move from laptop to laptop the same way the world had passed around the photos of Rihanna after her battle with Chris Brown, same way they had passed around the fourteen-minute sex tape that Colin Farrell had made with Narain in 2003.

Hazel said, "They're paying people off. They are buying the rights from anyone who videoed anything so that the moment it is posted they can order it removed from the Internet."

I told Hazel that the paparazzi were in Los Feliz. All of my employees had confidentiality agreements and none could say one word to the press without risking a major lawsuit for breech of confidentiality. Like everyone else in the biz, I was covered on that end.

She said, "But that has never stopped information from being leaked. Workers are people who might be quiet on the job, but each one has friends and intimate relationships. Everyone who holds your secret, pillow talks with someone at the end of the day. There are no secrets. Only truths that have not been revealed and spread across *Page Six*."

"And you, Hazel? Do you pillow talk?"

"Let's not go down that road, James. Let's not."

At my regular haunts in Los Feliz, the paparazzi had made contact with more than a few waiters, at least one from each shift, and promised cash and their photos posted online as well as a video of them sent to *Entertainment Tonight* if any of them sighted me and called it in.

I asked, "Is Regina Baptiste shacking up with Johnny Bergs now? If she is, get me his primary home address so I can pack up a U-Haul and throw her belongings on his doorstep."

"Geesh, James. I have no idea. No photos have been posted. But they have posted photos of you and Regina Baptiste. People are curious about you. You two were in Nassau at Arawak Cay eating at Twin Brothers. They have you at the Starbucks in Cable Beach."

"They loved her in the Bahamas. The islands claimed her as their own."

"That they did. They have others of you driving and Regina as your passenger as you left City Market at Lyford Cay. Again they focused on her, so you're not clear. If I'm not mistaken, they have you in pictures with Whitney Houston, Celine Dion, and Anna Nicole Smith."

"Anna Nicole Smith? They dug up some very old pictures. Geesh. One site has posted an old article from two years ago. 'Regina Baptiste has left Bobby Holland and has been spotted holding hands with a man identified as James Thicke. Click here for photos of them having tea and muffins at Abbott's Habit in Venice, photos of them on the back lot at Universal Studios, having Jamaican dinners at Will's in Inglewood, and at Borders bookstore at Howard Hughes

Center. Regina Baptiste tweeted that she was in love again and she is engaged.' "

"Sounds like an RSS feed. Are you back online?"

"You should read some of the comments that people are leaving. They hide behind their fucking computers and write page after page of mean shit about me. They said mean shit about her. The world is an ugly place."

"I'm here for you, James. Others, all of your friends, we are on your side, but our roar is not as loud as the roar that comes when a superstar actor and beautiful actress enter the arena. You're in this, you're a big part of this triangle, but to many, you're only an extra on the set."

"The crew applauded."

"James, on another note, and I know that you're stressed, but business is business."

"The earth will go around the sun no matter what tragedy befalls us."

"The project that you're working on for The Powerful Clients is still due. They want me to remind you. I know that I'm not your agent, but they know that we have a working relationship."

"Business is business and we're in the business of show."

"They want that *Boy Meets Girl* script, no

257

matter what is going on in your personal life."

"Yeah. I'll need the money for the down payment on the payoff of the fuck-my-wife-on-camera-in-front-of-the-world lawsuit. Nothing like having a man fuck your wife then suing you."

"James."

"Come on, Hazel. Laugh. That was funny. Me paying a man for fucking my wife."

"As a friend, I could have a third party broker a meeting between you and Johnny Bergs."

"You're talking mediation and a settlement with a confidentiality clause."

"Meeting with an arbitrator might be the best route for everyone involved."

I said, "Nation shall rise against nation, and kingdom against kingdom."

"Costs money for a nation to fight a nation. Let's not wage a war."

"Wars are fun. Men get to kill each other and no one goes to jail."

"Johnny Handsome is a rich, vindictive man, James. He takes after his old man. Everyone knows that. Johnny Bergs can be evil."

"So am I. Well, he's better looking. Well, he was better looking."

"But in this industry, in this business,

you're not Johnny Bergs, James."

"He earns the industry more money, so I'm the disposable one."

"You know how it is. And you know most line up on the side of the moneymakers."

"Sounds like you know something and you're not telling me."

Hazel Tamana Bijou hesitated. "We'll talk soon."

"Hazel."

"Yes, James."

"You're so formal with me."

"We're professional. We keep it professional, James."

"Is it awkward talking to me about this crap that's going on with Regina Baptiste?"

"I've worked with Regina in some capacity for the past decade."

"You know what I mean. Because of you and me."

"On the record, there is not now, nor has there ever been, a you and me, James."

"Of course. Off the record, Hazel."

"At times. Not as hard as it was when I first found out about you two."

"I'm sorry. That was something that we never addressed."

"For what, James? As you said, the earth continues to circle the sun, no matter what."

"Things didn't work out between us. And

the way you found out about Regina Baptiste."

"I guess that if I had come inside the bar that night, things would have been different."

"What bar and which night are you referring to?"

"The night you were with her. The night she came looking for you. I was still there when she had come back. Regina Baptiste was on a mission to meet with you. The script. Everyone was talking about your script. You were everyone's next big paycheck. She had asked me where you had gone and I had told her. She didn't know that you and I were . . . she didn't know."

"No one knew. That's how you wanted it."

"I stood and watched you and her drinking and flirting. She was living with Bobby Holland. I didn't think that she would betray Bobby Holland like that. But a woman is a woman."

"You watched us at the bar."

"And a man is a man. You and Bobby Holland weren't friends, but you knew each other."

"Okay, Hazel."

"I watched for a while. I thought that I had sent you a text. You didn't reply. Not long after, I left. Then the next day, I saw that I had sent the text to James Cameron, not to you."

We laughed laughs that weren't really laughs. They were chortles of discomfort.

I said, "Hope the message that you sent wasn't too salacious."

"I said that I was still in the lobby, that I was outside the bar, said that I saw you chatting with Bobby Holland's wife. I jokingly called her his wife back then, and then I asked if you could meet me back at my office to go over an urgent contract that needed your signature. I always talk in code. I never text or e-mail anything that could come back to bite me in the end."

"You never said."

"Well, by the time I heard from you again, over a week had gone by and you and Regina Baptiste and Bobby Holland were breaking news. You were on the way to my office to meet with me, and the news was breaking. I called you and told you and you never made it to my office, not that day. That was a fire. Maybe if I'd just come inside the bar that night, all would be different."

"You didn't call me for at least a week."

"You didn't call me either, James. And Miss Baptiste suddenly wasn't available."

"I'm sorry, Hazel."

"No need to be, James. We're great friends now. We had fun for months. We watched foreign films in your screening room. We quaffed the best of wine and made love. Each experience was nice."

"Nice?"

"I adored you. You were fond of me."

"Adored and fond. Okay."

"My nerves were shot back then. I confided in you back then."

"You were pretty stressed. You left and went to Atlanta to go hiking for a few days."

"And you were an attentive lover. Part of me had hoped for more. Watching you flirt with Regina Baptiste that night, well that was like watching you flirt with my daughter, and I guess in many ways it put things in perspective for me. I'm not an actress so I don't need to compete for the part of leading lady in another short-lived film. Whatever we had, it was good while it lasted."

"I'm sorry, Hazel. I don't know how it happened, to be honest. It just happened."

"No big deal. Hollywood is worse than high school. Everyone switches partners and it seems like a big game of musical beds. The circles are so small that it seems almost incestuous. We live in a world where there has to be a press release when people date and a press conference when they break up. Everyone out there thinks that they are entitled to the details of your personal life. The best thing that anyone can do is never open that door to the public. People out there are ignorant, small-minded and as vicious as the sixties. And now this. This is an outrage. Despite so many levels of wrongdoing, they praise Johnny as if he is the new Brad Elvis Jesus Presley Pitt."

"Wait, skip the Johnny Not-Handsome talk for a minute. Rewind this a bit."

"No need to rewind. No point going back. Flow forward like a river. James, I understand how complicated we were as human beings. I don't process relationships the same way dime-store novels and trendy magazines with pretty pictures of new clothing and perfumes and articles about celebrities encourage people to process their complicated existences. We work in an industry where everyone writes fairytales, but no one lives a true fairytale."

"I know."

"We have extravagant weddings followed by record-setting divorce payoffs."

"God bless prenuptials and all the assets that they protect. Amen."

"We sell the snake oil called love to the public and we make a lot of money making them believe a well-written lie. You know people the same way I know people, James."

"Look, we can meet at some point, Hazel. We can talk face-to-face. I think that I never really felt like more than a boy toy to you, to be honest. Let's meet and clear the air."

"Let's not open that door, James. It's closed for a reason and forever."

"Two years and you never said a word."

"Don't do this, James."

"Do what, Hazel?"

"You picked Regina Baptiste. It didn't turn out right. Now you're reaching back. It's too late to play what-if with us. You have to play what-is. This is your bed, James. This is your bed."

"This is my bed."

"I used to be like Regina, the young girl that all men gravitated toward. I work in a business where mature women, beautiful women over forty, if that old, don't want to be seen in a love scene. In film, they view a woman of forty, fifty, sixty, seventy, eighty, as being sexless. Maybe not sexless, simply not sex worthy. And being sexless is definitely not the case. An older woman in love is beautiful. But for some reason, they find the beauty of it disgusting and pathetic on film. At most, if shown, it's the look of consent, no real kissing, no undressing, him with his shirt off, if he's young, and the woman fully dressed. They are afraid of mature women."

"Love the way you changed the course of the conversation."

"On another note . . ."

"Back to being professional."

"I had hoped that you would be around to meet my daughter. Nia Simone is almost as brilliant a writer as you are. Almost. Would have been great to employ your services as a script doctor. But the timing is bad. Studios are interested in an apocalyptic sci-fi screenplay that she has written and I will be in meetings on that matter. She is going to be here for a few days."

"Take care of your daughter. And tell Nia Simone congratulations. Blood is thicker."

"I have to take care of you too. You're *my* star. I brought you into this business."

"I'll figure out how to fix this shitstorm I started."

"You didn't start it, James. But you definitely didn't help it with what you did."

"He put his dick inside my wife. I was supposed to kick his ass."

"Of course."

"And I have to pay."

"But the question you need to ask is if it was worth it."

Hazel Tamana Bijou hung up and went back to the church where Hollywood was their Father, box office sales were their Son, and the Holy Spirits were made by Patrón.

Socks on my feet and still in my dirty workout clothes, I went and stood in the shower, water as hot as I could take it, screaming. My cry of frustration echoed, hit me in my face like rapid punches from an invisible enemy. I screamed and slammed my fist into the wall two dozen times. This might end up being my real life, luxury lost, using a stained shower-tub combo behind a clear, plastic shower curtain. Clothed and soaking wet, I went to Underwood and put in a sheet of paper, my fingers moving at the speed of light, the keys clicking and clacking, that sound calming my nerves, bringing my blood pressure down, opening my head and the room.

Calmer, I walked away from the words I had typed over and over: RELAX BREATHE.

Between the dawn and the light, and the occasional afternoon delight, Hazel used to ride me like a wave, showed me the side of her she never showed in business, drove me insane with more than physical desire for her, desire that would never have been reciprocated beyond an occasional statement of *adoration*. And frustrated, I'd moved away from her Trinidadian shores to Livingston. Then I could taste her salt, her secret kisses like wine, and it compounded everything. I repeated what she had said, "I adored you. You were fond of me."

Hazel Tamana Bijou had thrown away the nights we'd shared, had forgotten how she used to touch me in the night, masturbate me back to consciousness and make love to me, but vanish before day broke. Intimately, I'd never see her at first light of any day. Only in the evenings, the late evenings of our affair. I'd never been invited to her home, not when it wasn't a group gathering, and never for an overnight stay. The text would always read something like: WOULD LIKE TO DISCUSS AN URGENT CONTRACT THAT NEEDS SIGNING TO-NIGHT. H. BIJOU. Or maybe: I HAVE A SCRIPT AND WOULD LIKE TO GET IT DE-LIVERED TO YOUR HOME FOR IMMEDIATE DOCTORING. Or simply: LOS FELIZ. 9:30 PM. She had bowdlerized what we'd done from her mind and now I wished that I could expurgate Regina Baptiste from mine. Hazel was a smart woman, and in this town, the talented made the money for the educated. Regina Baptiste wasn't a slouch. She was a very smart woman as well. My type.

I'd never been attracted to magazine reading girls with low vocabulary who thought that learning was a waste of time, or that ambition was for other people.

I saw Hazel Tamana Bijou in my mind. Her image was here, across the room, on my bed, making love to an image of me. She had doffed all of her fine clothing; every fashionable item gently folded or hung up. Each piece of her jewelry and her watch sitting on the dresser, the right side, near the edge. When she made love, she wanted to be totally nude, no adornments, not even earrings. The room was darkening, became obscure as the memory became clear, as the memory forced itself to the surface of my mind. My memory matched the time of day. Late evening. We were kissing. Deep, passionate kisses. Then slow deliberate kisses, trying to prolong the apex of our passion. She kissed beautifully. My tongue penetrated her, her mouth open and accepting. Then she did the same, sucked my tongue as if it were her vagina tightened around my penis, sucked and pulled me. And while she did, I entered her. Her moans intensified and she tried to move away from me, her primal side unleashed, all of our social graces put on pause. This would have been our second time that evening. The first time,

I had her on her back, my hands underneath her ass, squeezing her as I licked circles and figure eights and teased the edges before pushing my tongue deeper inside of her sweetness. Sometimes she sat me on the armless red leather chair and straddled me, took me with the control that she had over Hollywood. I saw all of those possibilities; saw all of those versions of us, until it settled into one. She reached underneath the covers, stroked me until I woke up, then kissed me as she stroked me. She was a hard woman in the office, but a gentle lover in bed. After she had woken me again, I smiled at the way I made love to her. I loved her and that image of me and I smiled. There was no escaping memory. My hands touched her short hair. Her hairstyles were always short, chic, mature, and professional, very cosmopolitan. She ran Hollywood, had A-list actors on speed dial, and she looked the part during the day. But now, in that vivid image, she was a sexy woman. She started to fall off the bed, but I didn't let her go. As that image of me pulled her back to the bed, as he kissed her and repositioned himself between her legs, I stood in the doorframe. I watched us make love from the bed then back down to the floor. It became intense. I hadn't realized how we had looked, until now. It was a wonderful madness. She made glorious faces. A moment later she had me on my back and she mounted me reverse-cowgirl. She was good in that position, a position where she had all the control and could move back and forth over my length as she touched herself. I watched her, looked in her face for some sign of love, thinking that was why she turned her back on me when we had sex, because she was feeling her love for me, and with tears in her eyes, with her back to me in a dimly lit room, I could feel her body, but I couldn't feel her heart, couldn't see her lips moving as she told me that she loved me, her soft words drowned by my escalating moans, my eyes closed so I missed seeing the tears in her eyes when she turned to look in my face. I remembered that she always paused. I had thought that she paused to keep her orgasm at bay, to elongate the moment of ecstasy, but she paused because she felt more than adoration. I watched her. She looked at me, looked at me with tears in her eyes as she sat on top of the oblivious version of me, the me who held her ass and pulled at her until she moved again, until she once again moved back and forth and tingles ran across that vision of my aroused body in powerful waves, waves that pounded the shores of Trinidad. I watched her. She looked at me. She saw me. She saw me watching her, watching them. She tilted her head to the side and pulled her lips in. Exposed. Tears rolled down her face. I saw my own face. I saw the stunning ugliness in my face. Orgasm was arriving. The itch was too strong. She had left me with an itch so intense, so powerful that in that moment, I would kill her to get it salved. I watched that younger version of me as he grabbed her ass, tried to sink his nails into her ass to get her to move again. But she was looking at me now, the *me* that was reaching back. It was almost as if she could see me, as if she were looking into the future, and she realized that she wouldn't be there. We broke our stare and she went back to him. She did move for him; she moved and she felt as much as he did, on fire, her itch becoming intense as his continued. I knew how my orgasm arrived. I knew how my body worked. I knew what that version of me felt. As it built up in the backside, the frenular delta, and traveled down his penis, as it felt like the fire and itch moved all the way to his perineum and sat there, became more intense, gripped his testicles and made him clench his buttocks. He was out of control. So was she. Lips pulled in, rocking, hoping for a different end, I watched them come together. They shared transcendence. They were above the universe. They were divine. They were with God. I watched him exhaust himself inside her. I watched her in rapture, fighting to get that fire out of her body. Her orgasm faded in increments. I watch her reluctantly return to this world. Then she sat on him in those moments after, breathing heavily. Not moving away. He held her hips, ran his fingers up and down her spine. She licked her lips and sighed as they disconnected, no longer two, no longer transcending, no longer divine, no longer with God, back as they were before. No words were shared. Moments later, she pushed up her elbow and ran a hand over her short hair; then she moved her legs, swung them around and put her feet on the floor. Both hands on the mattress, she pushed down and stood up slowly. She looked at the exhausted man in the bed. A man younger than she. She went to the bathroom and I watched him fall asleep in her two-minute absence. I watched her ease back into bed with him, touching but not cuddling. She was wide awake. Wired. Restless. Afraid to cuddle. Afraid to disturb him. Afraid of attachment. Or afraid of rejection.

I had no idea. But she took a finger and traced the edges of his face, his lips, his nose, studied him in silence. She reluctantly pulled herself away from him, her touch ending with a sad expression, and I watched her dress to leave, yawning, pausing in the doorway to blow a good-bye kiss. The words *I love you, James* leaving her lips, unheard. The room was filled with pain and poignancy, muted frustrations, longing and misunderstanding.

And outside those windows, dark skies were becoming lighter.

With daylight came clarity. Lucidity was rarely the best friend of intense emotions.

Then, as she vanished, leaving with her jewelry still off so as not to make a sound, with her shoes in one hand and car keys in the other, he jerked awake, jerked as if his life support had been taken away, its power abruptly cut off. He reached for her and woke up to an empty bed.

The disappointment on his face made me shake my head.

Hazel was right. Revisionist history would not give me a better reality.

I was in search of tea and sympathy, looking at dead days past.

We get what we deserve.

At this point in my life, I wished that my

choice, if I had a choice, had been the opposite way, Hazel, not Regina. I would have been with a woman whom the world hadn't seen naked, a woman whom magazines hadn't dissected and chopped up into sensual body parts, a woman whom only a few men had seen in special, intimate ways. It would have been nice to be with a woman whom I could take to dinner without someone interrupting us, could accompany to Jamba Juice without someone rudely barging into our conversation and asking for autographs, running up to us and snapping photos without so much as a hello, seeing us talking and intruding as if I were the invisible man, or even worse, the insignificant man.

It would be nice to be with a woman who, when it went wrong, if we went into a death spiral, it wasn't on radio, television, billboards, and every news and gossip page and blog online.

I growled. "Johnny Handsome."

Pulling my wet clothing from my aching body, I knew that I would have to pay.

The problem with having means was that even when you were being done wrong and retaliated, people who did you wrong had the right to sue for getting their just due. It was a life's savings for an eye, never an eye for an eye. Johnny Bergs had been a burglar and burglars had more rights than home-owners in this country. A man could break into your home and he had to be facing you and armed for you to shoot him and get away with blowing his brains into the wall.

"Thicke?"

"Driver. What's going on?"

"I went by. The gray car is gone. I went by there off and on. It never came back."

"Think they changed cars?"

"I took photos of all cars parked near your gates. Got shots of license plates."

"Wait. Any word on Baptiste?"

"She's vanished off the face of the earth. She never came back to the estate."

I paused. "You think the guys in the gray car did something to her?"

"I'd say they were waiting on you. But people are crazy, so I have no idea."

"I should take my gun, drive up there and have a conversation."

"Bad idea. Sit tight until I can take you. The owner at Wolfe Classic Limousine sent me on a job. Heading to San Diego. I'll come check on you when I'm done and make it back up this way."

"I'll handle it, Driver."

"Thicke, sit your butt down. Don't do like

you did the night you beat Johnny Bergs in the streets. That night, if you had waited on me, I could've been your buffer. Stay where you are."

I looked across the room at my .38. "I'll do my best to wait on you."

CHAPTER 21

"Varg? Varg? Hey, Varg."

Hours later, I was in the musty hallway on the first floor, right outside of the laundry room, back against the wall, head down, hands in fists as I washed my water-soaked workout clothes.

"Varg, what are you up to?"

I didn't look up. Hearing *Varg* didn't click. My conversation with Hazel Tamana Bijou had left me numb. And my wife remained heavy on my mind. That video of her and Johnny Handsome had been reactivated, was playing inside my head. And Bobby Holland's phone calls and threats were there too. Plus there were the other noises that were outside of my head. On one side, I heard a vacuum cleaner, on the other I heard an argument, and from yet another direction, I heard televisions and laughter as half the floor watched *Jerry Springer.*

"Varg, don't act like you can't hear me.

Something must be heavy on your mind."

When I caught on, I turned around. Vera-Anne and her two kids came down the hallway, passed by a Mexican family, an Asian woman, and seven preteen children who were roaming about unsupervised. Vera-Anne had on a tight white skirt and black fitted top, low heels, and nice silver jewelry. She smiled and came into the laundry room.

She said, "You're doing laundry again? I'll bet that you'd make a good husband."

"Have to beat the crowd. Half of the machines don't work."

She chuckled. "Poppa was looking for you this morning."

"Was he? What was it about?"

"His daughter, of course. Are you going with him to meet her later?"

"I had forgotten about that. That's this evening. Are you going?"

"I'd have to take the kids. Too much trouble. And then the bill for dinner would be a lot higher too. His daughter is older than me, you know. Might be too creepy."

Vera-Anne made small talk for a moment, small talk and intense eye contact.

She said, "You have a girlfriend? Somebody up there enjoying your nice art with you?"

"Are you trying to hook me up with one of your friends?"

"Oh, hell no. I wouldn't do that. Then I might get jealous. Know what I mean? I've been cooking and feeding you and I would hate to fatten frog for snake. That wouldn't be right."

I smiled a cautious smile in return, one that was meant to correct her course.

She said, "I'm making pea soup and dough for lunch."

"Never had that before."

"Then you really should come by and let me feed you. I make mine with turkey meat."

"Will Mr. Holder be there?"

"He'll be gone all day. He's in L.A. getting a haircut and shopping for a new suit."

"The kids?"

"It's their nap time. Come by. I haven't had a chance to have you to myself. We can get better acquainted and talk without Poppa or Isabel being in the room. Wouldn't you like that?"

She was standing a few feet away, but her scent was all over me. She watched me, her stare electric and sordid as she waited for my response to her indecent proposal.

I said, "Your cooking is great, but I'll have to pass on lunch."

"I am interested in knowing you. If you ever want to hang out, sneak away to a museum or an art show, that would be cool. Would be nice to go with somebody who understands me."

"All I need to understand is that Mr. Holder would not appreciate that."

"He doesn't appreciate art. I need to connect with a man who appreciates art."

"He appreciates you. You really need to be grateful for a man who appreciates you."

She grinned a disenchanted grin, her perfume and sexy dress all gone to waste. She nodded, and they headed down the hallway, her ass wagging, as her kids kept chattering away.

Then she left her kids down the hallway, paused, shook her head, tapped her foot a dozen times, took off her eyeglasses, put her hand on her hip, and gradually walked back to me. She let her pink hair fall down, hand combed it free, then undid two buttons on her blouse.

In a much stronger voice she said, "Is it because of Poppa?"

"Your kids are standing right behind you, Vera-Anne."

"Is it because of my kids? Do you have something against single mothers?"

I said, "Mr. Holder is taking care of you

and your kids."

"*He's not my husband.* He's *never* going to ask me to marry him."

I said, "Real talk. Not many men would do that, take in a woman and two kids."

"I'm not asking you to take care of me and my kids. You're probably as broke as everybody else around here. If you live here, you must not be doing so good yourself."

"You're a smart woman, at least you seem to be."

"I am smart. I'm very smart. And I'm very ambitious."

"I'm just an angry man who has no love for overly *ambitious* women right now. And in this case, the word *ambitious* is a very kind euphemism for a much stronger, unfriendly word."

"Okay, I'm having a blond moment. What's a euphemism?"

"What you're doing, not cool. Be as good to Mr. Holder as he is to you. Only dogs move from dog to dog and only a female dog will stand still while male dogs line up to take their turn. You have two kids. Shut down the ride. If that's what you're doing, shut down the ride."

Her smile lessened. This impromptu audition for the part of leading lady wasn't going the way she wanted. And just like that, tears streamed out of her eyes and her chest heaved.

Her children played behind her, oblivious to their mother's situation. I thought she wanted to run away from me, but she didn't want her kids to see her face. She leaned into me and I put my arms around, held her until she calmed down. When I pulled away, she didn't let me go. Her body was too warm, her breasts were too soft, her breathing too hot, and she held me too close. I eased her away from me. She wiped her tears away and then apologized.

I asked, "Are you okay?"

She looked up at me, pulled me to her as she tiptoed and kissed me, and then she rushed her tongue deep inside of my mouth. I pushed her away from me and shook my head.

"Vera-Anne, that was wrong on so many levels."

"It didn't feel wrong."

"Most wrongs don't feel wrong. Especially when they taste like grape bubblegum."

"You look like you have a lot of potential. I mean, I know you're not rich, but you seem to be smart, almost as smart as I am, a metrosexual with good taste, so I know you're not going to stay in a dump like this for sixteen years. All of that art that you have, I don't care how you got it. I don't care where you stole it from. We could help each other in so many ways. Poppa has been here for *sixteen* years. Since I was in the first grade. He's a nice man, but he's a loser."

"Damn. That's how you see me? That's what you think of Mr. Holder?"

"It's more than that. Poppa is twice my age. His daughter is older than I am."

"You knew that before the first kiss, right? You knew it before you had sex with him."

"I knew it. But damn. He lectures me all the time. It gets on my nerves after a while. He lectures me when we go to bed together. That's not right. It's like he's my daddy one minute and then the next he's ready to dick me half the night. I can't stand living with him most of the time."

I took a deep breath and said, "Have a good rest of the day, Vera-Anne."

"And by the way, if you ever change your mind before I change mine, I'm fixed."

"Never said you were broken."

"You know what I mean. You wouldn't have anything to worry about, if you're worried."

"That's not letting the ride shut down."

"Not shutting down the ride. This is a damn good ride. More fun than all the rides down at Disneyland and Magic Mountain combined. I just have to pick better passengers."

She put her glasses back on, buttoned her blouse, and went back to her kids.

On the second floor of building E, Mrs. Patrice Evans lingered impatiently near my apartment door. Her arms were folded underneath her breasts, back against the wall.

No high gates. No guards. No Dobermans. Too much access to my front door.

She met me at my door and snapped, "Who's the bitch you were with by the pool yesterday?"

"Misty. She lives upstairs."

"Has that bitch been over here?"

"You better leave, Mrs. Evans. Get off my floor. Time to go back to Mr. Ted Evans."

"I'm sorry. I'm sorry."

"Don't be sorry. Just take that attitude and leave."

"Can I come inside for a few minutes?"

I took a breath and said, "Just to talk."

"Just to talk. Nothing else. I only have twenty minutes anyway."

She followed me inside my apartment and before I could put the basket of clothes down in the living room, she was naked on my comfy bed, beckoning for me to come to her.

"Varg, Varg, oh my God, Varg. Shit."

Patrice's leg trembled. Then her entire body did the same.

"Oh my God you're angry oh my God I pissed you the fuck off oh my God I love this."

Then I heard rapid applause. Someone was clapping for us to continue.

I looked up and frowned. The noise that I heard wasn't a standing ovation.

Someone banged at my door like the Gestapo was coming to take us away.

I held her mouth, muffled her screams, and held her like she was my hostage.

I cursed; then in a frantic whisper I asked, "Ted follow you here?"

She couldn't answer. Drowning people couldn't hear anything, not even their own cries. Again I looked toward the door. Then I looked at the dresser, where I kept my gun.

She swallowed, continued struggling to breathe, and panted, "Who . . . who was that?"

Chest rising and falling, I panted, "What have you gotten me into, Patrice?"

Patrice jumped up from the bed and hurried to the front door, still naked. She held her breasts, opened the door and looked out, then slammed the door, made sure it was locked.

"Are you fucking insane?"

"I've had enough. And if Ted was out there, he would've known that I've had enough."

I looked toward the door, listened for a lunatic, but she pulled my face back to hers.

She said, "It's too late now. What's done is done."

She pulled at me and I gave in, mounted her and she took me inside her.

Patrice whispered, "Don't stop. This is my time. This is my twenty-minute vacation."

I looked toward the door, listened for her husband, but she pulled my face back to hers.

"This is my time. Give me some more Norway loving."

I moved with her, resumed that fast pace and felt that sensation pick up from where it had left off, felt it coming at me too fast. She whispered and begged me, sounded like a woman desperate to please a man so she could feel like a woman.

My muscles strained and my toes curled. Orgasm pulled me into its current, into its momentum, and I fought against its power, but it turned me primal, pulled me into its gravity.

When I was empty, I collapsed next to Ted Evans's wife the same way that Johnny Handsome had collapsed next to mine. Anger rose. Then the timer on Patrice's watch went off.

She said, "If that was Misty banging on your door, I hope she got an earful."

Within seconds, Patrice was dressed. I went and flushed the condom, then came back and pulled my clothing on, my eyes on my front door, listening for an intruder.

Her cellular rang and she looked at the caller ID. She rejected the call.

Her cellular rang again and again. Two more times she rejected his call.

Her husband kept calling. I didn't know if he was calling from the other side of the complex or right outside my door. I told her to wait a moment and I went back to my bedroom and grabbed a jacket. Then I followed her fast pace to the front door and undid my locks.

I slowly pulled my door open, hoped that it didn't sing on its hinges.

A couple of neighbors were in the hallway. Patrice stayed sequestered inside my apartment until I told her that the hallway was empty from end to end.

I wiped sweat away from my eyes and said, "No one is out there."

"Wonder who that was. Doors don't knock themselves."

"My guess would be that it was Ted."

"Ted would still be there. With one of his guns, maybe two, one in each of his hands."

"This has been fun. But it might be time to stop."

"We can't stop."

"Why not?"

"Because I have hundreds of Post-its."

"Patrice."

"Check your car, if you have one. If I were a woman at your door I would've left to go fuck up your car. That's what I would do. You'd come out and I would've taken keys to your paint job. Or I'd be out there busting out your car windows. Then I'd throw bags of shit inside."

"Guess it's a good thing that you don't know if I have a car."

Her cellular rang again and Patrice took off running back toward her apartment.

I said, "Run, Forrest. Run."

That was when I let the jacket fall from my arm. Underneath was my loaded .38.

Gun hidden, I rushed my anxiety by tenants and jogged downstairs to the parking lot.

The Apartments was a U-shaped monstrosity, my parking spot far away, at the bottom of its ugliness, my apartment located on the left side of that U toward the middle facing the 605. My car was there, covered. I used a generic car cover much too large for the vehicle. My Maybach hadn't been battered. I knew that, but I checked anyway. If it had been assaulted, the remote would've sent me a warning. The remote would tell me when anyone came near.

Then arrived a moment that I hadn't adumbrated.

A luxury vehicle crept down the side of the series of worn, three-story stucco buildings. Bentley Continental Supersport. It stopped and its V12 engine purred like an animal primed to attack. Scowling, I stood facing a coupé that cost close to three hundred thousand dollars. This was the dramatic entrance of a celestial being. It was the return of Regina Baptiste.

CHAPTER 22

The Bentley purred. Regina Baptiste shifted inside the car, but the Bentley didn't creep any closer. She sat, parked, and waited. Like she was waiting for time to reverse itself.

I saw her and I saw that film of her and Johnny Handsome inside of my mind.

Again I heard the applause.

While images resurrected anger, she raised her cellular and motioned at me.

Jaw tight, heart galloping, sweat growing on my neck and brow, I nodded.

Seconds later, my cellular rang.

Regina Baptiste faced me and called me from her hands free as she pulled at her hair. She had dialed my fucking number and that felt like burglary inside my peace of mind.

Her music was on. Janis Ian's song "At Seventeen." It was the song that she played when she was at her lowest, a song that took her back to when she was Regina *Baptist,* a brown-eyed girl in hand-me-downs who had dreams of coming to Hollywood and becoming a star.

She rubbed the bridge of her nose and, in a broken voice, whispered, "I love you."

"Regina Baptiste. If you did, it would be in your actions."

"Baby, James. I disappointed you. I know that I did. I let you down."

"You did."

"I don't know what to say. I miss you. I need you. I can't handle this crucifixion, this perpetual character assassination. This shit is driving me crazy. I want to slit my wrists."

"Thought you had fled to parts of Europe with your publicist."

"The paparazzi was either following me or waiting on me everywhere I went."

"I'll bet they were."

"Like I was the Duchess of Cambridge. Only they were shouting horrible things at me."

"You love cameras and press. And all press is good press, right?"

"Everyone has turned so mean. I can't handle this. This is too much for me."

I paused. "You're okay?"

"You know I'm not okay. Do you care? Do you even care how I am, James?"

"Put the pity party on pause and put on your big girl panties."

"I've fucked everything up that I have worked for."

"Including this marriage."

"Are we over, James? I need to know if we're over."

"How did you find me?"

"Your Maybach has Lo Jack. I called them and they told me where all the cars are parked. Everything else is home, and you're not home, so I followed the missing car."

"Smart woman. But Montana women are the best of the best."

"What is this place? Why has your car been here for over two weeks?"

"Right now this foreign country is my safe haven."

"Are you staying with someone here?"

"Does it matter? You vanished on me, Regina Baptiste. Just like you did the first time. Just like you did when you left my home and were going back to Bobby Holland. That night the press came after you and you left me hanging. I should've known how things would be then."

"I'm going to get out. Is that okay?"

"No."

"Why not?"

"Because I said so. The moment you get

out, do you see all of those nosey fucks over your head? They're looking at your shiny Bentley, wondering who is inside. Wondering who is dumb enough to drive a Bentley that cost more than they make in five years into a dump like this."

"I'm getting out. Talking like this is stupid."

"Regina, please, think about your press, as usual. The moment you get out of that Bentley, everyone will start taking photos and video and before you can get to me so I can curse you out and choke you to death, they will be posting you on every site, and everyone from here to small villages in Nairobi will know where you are within the next ten seconds."

"I'm trapped inside this car."

"It's not like you're in a room at a Motel 6. Not as large, but it has fewer roaches."

"I'm this close to you and I can't hold you in my arms."

"Have you talked to the rest of your family?"

"They hate me. My parents are ashamed. They told me not to come to Montana. The newspapers and reporters are in front of their home. They can't leave either. They're trapped."

"Welcome to infamy. Fame is just the interregnum between being unknown by many and unloved by most. What where you thinking, Regina?"

"Please, James. Help me. I can't think. I can barely breathe. Tell me what to do."

"First, you contact H. G. Wells and get his Time Machine."

"I'm serious, dammit. Damn you, James. Tell me what I should do."

Her faltering voice weakened me and my savage heart struggled to pound with the civilized beat of love. I looked up at the windows. So much profanity and clamor was overhead. Noise pollution, air pollution, and ground pollution set the backdrop for our emotional moment.

Regina asked, "What are you doing parked in this disgusting place?"

"I'm here degrading myself by having meaningless sex with strangers to fill a void."

"You have a mistress?"

"Of course."

"Don't joke like that."

"Do you hear a laugh track? No, you're used to applause at the end of your sex scenes."

"Please. Don't do this to me. After that message you left me, the way you talked to me, the threats you made, the things that you said, trust me, it took everything to reach out to you."

"Where did you go first? Let me guess. You ran to your publicist."

"I'm sorry. I wanted it fixed. I wanted it shut down before you found out."

"You wanted to cover up what you had done."

"You dislike me. You really dislike me."

"What happened on set?"

In the softest, frailest voice, she whispered, "Come get in the car with me."

"No. Talk to me first."

"Why can't you get inside the car? We can leave here, drive around, and talk. We can go down to Long Beach and park by the Aquarium, or park on a side street in Bixby Knolls."

"I don't want to be responsible for what I might do. So what happened?"

"I was having problems with the scene. Working with Johnny was horrible. I hate him. You know that. I fucking hate him. I had complained about working with him for weeks. That's why they wanted to do that love scene last. They had hoped that our chemistry would be better. The new scene was important. After everything else was done, they wanted me relaxed."

"That scene was not in the script I delivered. It wasn't fucking important."

"What was I to do? Alan Smithee wanted that scene. You know he gets what he wants."

"From what I saw, there was no problem. Unless you consider the fact that only half of Hollywood and all of the goddamn world saw Johnny Handsome riding you bareback a problem."

"I've been freaking out. I'm losing my mind. I don't know how it got so out of control."

"You fucked up my script."

"What's more important? Me or that script? Nobody cares about the script anymore."

"Were drugs involved?"

"No. You know I'm clean. You know that."

"Speak up. Be a woman and answer."

She sighed and her voice weakened, "I'm clean, James."

"Were drugs involved?"

"No. None were involved."

"Last time asking."

She took a deep breath. "Some."

"You just went from none to some."

"I was stressed."

"Everyone alive is stressed. And right now, as you're parked in the Village of Stressed-out, you're looking at their king. Well, maybe not king. More like court jester."

"So much pressure was on me to finish

that picture."

"Some. Define some."

"Things became . . . for me . . . tense . . . so much stress . . . I broke and did a line."

"You did a line."

"I was encouraged. To do what I had to do to save the show. To make it happen."

"Keep the blame where it belongs."

"It . . . it came unexpectedly . . . I freaked out . . . and I broke down."

"Where did you get it?"

"It's not important."

"Where did the cocaine come from? Who supplied you with the drugs on set?"

"I was in Johnny Bergs's trailer. And somebody brought the drugs."

"Johnny fucking Bergs."

"Yeah."

I said, "His fucking name is going to be in my obituary and on my damn tombstone."

"It will probably be on mine too. Over mine in larger letters and brighter lights."

"Let me get this right. You were lounging inside Johnny Bergs's bed on wheels."

"Not alone. Never alone. A few of us were in there."

"What others?"

"Just others."

"You've been clean for two years."

She whispered, "The moment before,

James. No matter what happens, there is always a moment before. Nothing happens suddenly. Nothing. Even the unexpected has a moment before. You're a writer. You know that. I'm an actress. I know that. We create based on the moment before. What happens next is always driven by the moment before. A building blows up. But there was gas left on and fire left on. We see car accidents being set up. The moment before. Every scene that I step into, I must know my moment before. When an actress doesn't know her moment before, she's not prepared, she's vulnerable, and everything that comes after is fucked and won't make sense to the audience. It's out of context. This entire scandal, this shit that's pulling me down, it's all out of context. Every scene that you write, you have to know the moment before. Even in life, when we don't know that there is a moment before, there is a moment before. Even for the ignorant, there is a moment before. They just don't know it."

"What's all this rambling about the moment before?"

"The moment before I did the coke . . . there was a moment before, James."

"The moments after you did the coke are what matters. When they put the coke out in front of you like it was a buffet at an anti-Betty Ford clinic, you had choices. To watch, coach, join in, or walk the fuck away. What did you do, Regina? Which choice did you make?"

"I did that one line. Regretfully. I haven't touched the shit but once in two years."

"I worked with you. I chartered a private plane and took you to rehab under the radar. I spent twenty thousand a month to sneak you into the Crossroads Center. And when you didn't like it there, I put you on another private jet and sent you to The Sanctuary in Australia. I did it away from the press. I fucking protected you. I've protected you since I met you. I got you clean before anyone knew that you were on coke. Bobby Holland got you on coke. I got you off."

"Fuck Bobby Holland. I don't ever want to hear his name again."

"I married you."

"I asked you to marry me, James. I asked you because I loved you. I came to you with the prenuptial. I wanted nothing from you. Just your love. That's all I wanted. That's what I need from you right now. I need your love. If I have that, then I can get through this."

"I did more for you than Bobby Holland

299

ever did and I have asked you for nothing in return. First you fuck Johnny, then you hang me out to dry, leave me with no warning, just book a flight then vanish into thin air; no calls, not one text."

"That wasn't me, James. That wasn't me in that film."

"What do you mean that it wasn't you?"

"That was Sasha."

"Who the fuck is Sasha?"

"I was so deep in character that Sasha took over. I was so overwhelmed, so deep in character that I *was* the character."

"You're blaming Stanislavski? Is that who we're going to sue at the end of the day?"

"Regina didn't exist anymore. I was there, but I was way in the back of my mind; just a whisper of me remained. The Regina part of me that remained was so small, like a drop of water in a glass of tea. I was lost in make-believe, so lost that fantasy and reality changed places. I was lost. Baby, I don't know what happened. It was as if I had blacked out. I woke up from a dream surrounded by people, naked, next to Johnny Bergs."

"With his come all over your body. It was dripping off your hands."

"I freaked out. And he didn't have the sock thing on his penis. His penis was supposed to be covered; you know that. But it wasn't. I swear, baby, that was not me. That was Sasha."

"Am I supposed to believe you or my lying eyes?"

"It was Sasha."

"Blaming Sasha is an easy out."

She cried for a while before she asked, "Will we be able to fix this?"

"Can you do a worldwide memory wipe?"

"You want a divorce?"

"What do you think?"

"Okay. Fine. I'll call my attorney and we can start the goddamn divorce, you insensitive sonofabitch. I need you right now and this is how you're going to fucking treat me."

"Don't turn this around. I saw the goddamn tape. Most men hear about their wives cheating on them, and a few might walk in, but not many get a high quality film directed by one of the best in the goddamn business to show them the details and the money shot."

"Alan Smithee forced me to work that scene. I told you that; you know that."

"Did he put Johnny Handsome's dick inside you too? How did that happen?"

"No need dragging this out. No matter what I say to the press, no matter what I say to you, you're all the same. You're just like them. I'll have you served as soon as I can."

"Fuck you the way you fucked that loser Johnny, you slut."

"No, fucking fuck you. I'm embarrassed. I'm scared. I've been with my therapist for days. I'm really messed up and I need you right now. Look, I fucking need you, James."

"Maybe you should go cry on Johnny Handsome's nut sacs."

"Yeah, maybe I'll do that. Maybe I'll drive to his Bel Air estate right now and suck his dick. The world wants me with him anyway. That would be my best move right now."

"Always thinking about career first."

"Just like you."

"You're probably already sucking his dick. Surprised you didn't swallow on camera."

She snapped, "Yeah, I'm sucking his fat dick and his hot come tastes good. His come is thick and rich and like boysenberry and tastes better than yours. I went to his trailer and sucked his dick every day we were on the set. I sucked his dick to wake him up in the morning and I sucked his dick to put him to sleep at night. I sucked his dick this morning and I'm imagining sucking his dick right now. Is that what you want to hear? You want to know that his dick feels better than yours? You want to know that you never made me go into Sasha mode and he did?"

I closed my phone with a snap, tried of going at it like we were Alec Baldwin and Kim Basinger, and I moved my coat and pulled my gun out. My wife saw the gun. And I saw her anger. I saw her tears. I saw her madness. I saw that she was broken. She was insane now.

Regina Baptiste revved up the car, made it lurch like she was preparing to run me over.

And I was a man gone mad.

She made the RPMs kick into the red.

I walked toward the Bentley, each step deliberate, and my rage was clear.

My cellular rang again. Regina's smiling face popped up on my caller ID.

I answered again.

She yelled, "I do love you, you know. If I didn't, I would run you over for abandoning me when I need you the most. Alan Smithee, Johnny Bergs, everyone has done me wrong."

"You are deranged. I haven't heard from you in how many days? Not one message in two weeks. Who abandoned whom, Regina? Who fucking abandoned whom?"

She revved the engine again. She revved it

as if to officially announce that she was inside of a very expensive weapon. I made sure she could see the loaded .38 at my side.

She said, "I love you. Remember that. I love you."

Then the call ended as abruptly as our relationship had started.

Boy meets girl. Boy kills girl. Girl is immortalized like she's the new Marilyn Monroe.

She put the Bentley in reverse and backed away in a hurry. She had been trained to drive in a movie where she played a cop, then trained again in a movie where she played the wife of criminal whom she helped escape, so she handled the car extremely well, better than a professional.

Visions of Johnny Handsome flashed behind my eyes.

It was time to go after Regina Baptiste too.

But I looked up and saw dozens of faces looking out of their dirty windows.

I left what was almost a bloody disaster and stepped across refuse and broken glass, moved across the filth that defined my new world. I pushed the red button and the Maybach went back to sleep. Sweat rained from my face and down my neck and my hands remained in fists as I walked away.

That Bentley had come into my world and now I had not a fucking word to say.

She had come on her hands. And I had had blood on mine. Johnny Handsome's warm come had stained her flesh. Johnny Handsome's warm blood had stained mine.

But in that moment, no one existed in my mind. I was a lone planet in a unique solar system, a planet that circled one shining star. Everyone had been removed. Everyone except Regina Baptiste. That was the power that love, that Regina Baptiste had over me now.

I could buy anything I needed but I couldn't pay to make that moment vanish from my reality. I had been bombarded by a million thoughts, each moving at the speed of light, all colliding in my brain, and now it felt as if I was walking through an endless, shrieking blackness.

That was why I didn't feel the heat and see the problem that was stalking me.

CHAPTER 23

The elevator was out and there were over a dozen people crowding the stairs. It looked like rush hour at Ellis Island and the borders at Tijuana. That was why no one's anger stood out. Not the frowning man in the sagging pants. Not the six women yakking violently at each other in Vietnamese. Not the irritated man in a pinstriped suit and presidential-looking tie. Not the arguing East Indian couple. As usual, I would rush by them all and make no eye contact, keep to my side of the crummy hallway as if it were my carpool lane on the 405.

But the man in pinstriped the suit did a double take and shouted, "James Thicke?"

Hearing my name crippled my livid pace. I slowed down and directed my scowl at him. He had a black Tumi messenger bag hanging over his shoulder. He had an equine face with a bulbous, hawklike nose. The kind of guy who had to put on a thousand-dollar suit to get a dime-store hooker to notice him.

The suited man repeated my name. Then he snarled, doubled his fists, and exploded. He ran at me with violence, the same fast and furious way that I had gone after Johnny Handsome.

He swung fast, threw an impatient round-house punch that was meant to separate my head from my neck. My world was set on fire, red with pain. The gun and jacket that I held, both fell and tumbled to the dull brown carpet in the hallway. Another blow came my way. The blow hit my forearm and the impact sent pain up my arm, from my hand to my shoulder. He threw a third blow before the second one had finished doing its damage. I bobbed and felt his knuckles swish past my nose. He had thrown all of his weight into that blow. It was a hellified haymaker that took him off balance. Unrelenting, I did my best to knock him galley-west. My blow missed the side of his head. He came at me like he'd been waiting for this moment all of his life. He swung another roundhouse punch. This time I countered. My blow exploded into his chest. Pain registered in his eyes. He staggered. I charged at him, aimed for his throat, but my next blow caught the side of his face.

That knocked him away from me.

My world on fire, pain rising like a flood, I snapped, "Who the fuck are you?"

He barked, "You sonofabitch. You didn't think that you could ambush a Bergs brother and just walk away without getting your clock cleaned, did you? You sneak attack one of us and you attack all of us. I'm here to set the record straight, motherfucker. I'm here to beat your motherfucking ass then put your head on a stick and take it back to my brother."

Apartment doors opened on the fight. Neighbors spied or stepped out into the hallway.

Now we were both blocked in and the slender hallway had become our narrow ring.

It was a violent, noisy fight that moved from wall to wall and up and down the hallway, the curses flying back and forth like we were the background rappers in a Lil Wayne cut. The bastard caught me with a couple of quick lefts that put bee stings across my face. He grinned like he was going to torture me until he decided to beat my ass into the dilapidated carpet. But I went full throttle, snapped off a left-right-left-right-double-left-double right to his head, most missing, but at least four finding parts of his face and at least two catching the bridge of his nose.

Tasting his own blood enraged him.

He screamed and came at me swinging, caught me with a stiff left.

Then I was stunned, frightened, enraged, and once again humiliated.

He said, "I'm going to fuck you up even better than Johnny fucked your pretty little wife."

I exploded and went after him with a Sugar Ray flurry and Mike Tyson blows.

He ducked and stumbled, but I hit that bastard until a blow landed dead square on his jaw. His lights didn't go out, but the rheostat inside his head eased the bright lights down to dim.

He was down for at least an eight count. I needed him down for ten.

Barely able to breathe, ribs aching, I staggered, rubbed my throbbing hands, and picked up my jacket. I didn't have brass knuckles. What I was going after was my loaded gun. He looked up, surprised to see my .38, the same way a kid would be surprised to see a magician pull a pissed-off rattlesnake out of a hat. He'd never seen the gun on the floor as we fought. My coat had fallen with the gun, had left the .38

covered except for the edge of the short barrel.

I said, "Say it again. What you said about
your brother and my wife, say it again."

His shirt was ripped, damn near pulled
off his body. His face was red, eyes swollen.

My jeans were ripped. My face ached. But
nothing ached more than my hands.

"Johnny fucked that slut and he fucked
her good."

I raised the gun and hit him a half dozen
times, would've kept beating his ass but I
was too spent. His face was a brand new
ugly, his jaw broken, and blood ran from his
head like a river in search of an ocean. Then
somebody came up behind me and pulled
me off that ugly sonofabitch. He pulled me
and I took a wild swing and missed him by
the width of the face of a watch, then was
ready to aim the gun at him and pull the
trigger.

It was another man in a dark suit. Six-
foot-two. Driver.

Hands extended in front of his body, he
said, "Thicke. Calm down, man. Don't do
it."

Driver looked at me, his eyes wide, his
concern deep, but after what he saw, he
stepped out of the way. Sweat ran from my
skin like water. I pulled back the hammer

on the gun.

Driver said, "You don't want to do that, Thicke. Trust me. You don't want to kill a man. You do, and you'll have to live with that shit the rest of your motherfucking life."

Driver and I held eye contact. His professional words had changed from being as smooth as butter to as rugged as the streets. And I saw part of him that I knew nothing about.

Bizarro Bergs extended his arms, shook his head vehemently, palms out, and begged.

I said, "I'll count to ten. But I'm going to start shooting at three. One . . ."

He saw madness, saw the look of a raging bull, the insanity of *Taxi Driver,* and crawled away from me as fast as he could, scampered like a crab, grabbed a door knob and pulled himself to his feet, then took off running and limping and stumbling, never looking back.

Chest heaving for air, I turned around and scowled beyond Driver at my multiethnic neighbors. One of them looked Scandinavian, a man with long blond hair with hints of gray, a face with a thin, scruffy beard that actually reminded me of Trond Espen Seim, the actor who played Varg Veum in the movies. He had his iPhone up high, was recording the melee with a wide grin on his face.

He looked tough. Hard-boiled. As if he was a better fighter.

Driver saw that smart-ass smug sonofa-bitch and was on him in less than a second. The man had some size, looked rough around the edges, a man who lived for a barroom fight. But Driver was a man who protected his clients. He grabbed the man by his throat and ripped the cellular phone from the man's hand. Driver tossed me the phone, then drew back like he was about to knock that man's head through the wall. But he didn't. When Driver let the man go, he staggered like he had been shot and col-lapsed to the carpet. Driver and I stared at each other, both surprised at how fast that second fight on the card had ended.

I told Driver, "Give the man his phone back."

"I don't think so. You just bought this phone."

"Did I?"

"Yeah. This kind man sold it to you."

"I didn't hear him sell it to me."

"It was a silent auction and you won."

"Yeah. You're right. He did sell it to me. Begrudgingly, but a deal is a deal."

I took out my wallet and threw four hundred-dollar bills at the man's feet.

Driver said, "It's an iPhone. Give him one

more for good measure."

"That's all my cash."

Driver took five twenties out of his wallet and threw those into the pile.

He said, "I'll expense you."

Then I looked at the terrified man. I looked into his eyes, a gun in my hand, sweat on my brow, blood on my clothing. "Don't make me come visit you, neighbor. Don't make me. Just so you'll know, this isn't a toy in my hand. I practice at the range twice a week. Center mass nine times out of ten. I've never shot a man, but I've been itching to find out what that is like. I'd do it just to say that I did it. Don't make today that day, neighbor. Don't make today that day."

Driver smiled a courteous smile and extended a hand to the man, then pulled him back to his feet. The man stood up, two inches taller than Driver, but the fear in his eyes made him look like a munchkin facing a pit bull. The man took the money and retreated back inside his apartment, slammed his door hard as if that was the blow he wished he'd had the nerve to deliver to Driver's jaw. Driver knocked on the man's door until the man opened the door.

The man looked at Driver. He wanted to

look tough, but fear had him by its claws.

Driver said, "You want to redo that rude exit? I feel offended."

The man nodded, closed his door slowly, softly, gently, and the click was barely audible. Then I regarded the crowd of spectators. Driver did the same.

With authority, Driver announced, "Fight's over."

Half of them applauded the way people in the business did when the credits rolled at the end of an art house film. Curtain was down. Show was over. Then they all went back inside. As soon as their doors closed, the music began blasting in a half dozen incongruous languages.

I looked down at the suit coat that Bizarro Johnny Handsome had left behind.

I told Driver, "He ran off and left his coat."

Driver said, "He abandoned his expensive messenger bag too."

He picked up the bag and looked inside. Then he looked up at me, his expression serious. Resting inside the bag were receipts from McDonald's on Firestone and a loaded .380.

He said, "The McDonald's he went to was in Norwalk. That's one city over. My guess was that he'd met someone there to buy the gun. Then he came over here looking for you."

"How did you come to that conclusion?"

"That's what I would've done."

"That's what I would've written. Including the suit. It kept him from looking like a thug."

"You messed that man up pretty bad."

"He was ugly when I met him. Just uglier when he left."

My mind flashed back to when I was in bed with Patrice. He had been the one knocking on my door. But Patrice had run out into the hallway naked and that had thrown him off.

Her drop-in that was inspired by jealousy might've, on this day, saved my life.

I said, "He came looking for me with a gun inside his man-bag."

Driver walked to the end of the hallway. He walked at an easy, confident yet cautious pace. He spied to see if anyone else was coming. I went the opposite way and did the same thing. He didn't see anyone. Neither did I. There was no sign of Bizarro Bergs, just a trail of blood that led to the stairs, then blood spots on the wall where he had used his hands to keep from falling on his face as he fled. I was hurting, but I wasn't going to let it show. Pain screamed as my adrenaline level came down. We rushed inside my apartment. There, along with Driver, I had two new best friends. One was named Green Alcohol. The other was named Ice.

I said, "I could call the police."

"Not a wise move."

"I could call the police and tell them that Johnny Bergs had sent a hitman after me. I could dial 1-800-PAPARAZZI and have my face and story all over the web in an hour."

"Thicke. You pistol-whipped the man."

"I pistol-whipped a sonofabitch who was coming to shoot me in the back of the head."

"Gangster."

"My fists were hurting too bad to hit him again."

"Brick. Pipe. Coffee pot. Always hit a man with something. Hands are delicate."

"Thanks for the advice."

"I'll bill you for that too. And I need to use your computer."

Driver took the iPhone that I had just bought from my neighbor across the hallway and scrolled through its files. He used my USB, connected to my Mac and downloaded all the man had recorded while I was doing battle in the hallway. Then Driver reset the iPhone, cleared all that the man had recorded, deleted all of his pictures and contacts, and put it back to factory settings. After that, Driver stepped outside my door and banged on the door across the hall. Twenty seconds later, he came back with the money he had just paid the man for the phone.

Driver said, "The hallway fight is on your computer now. The tough guy across the hallway doesn't have a copy. No one does but you. We paid him for the phone before we took it, so he can't say he was robbed; then we sold it back to him for seven hundred dollars."

"We paid him five."

"Restocking fee. Plus a nominal charge for resetting his phone."

"So I made two hundred bucks on that transaction."

"Fifty. I had to walk across the hall and agent the negotiating."

"You should've asked for eight hundred."

"I did. He pissed his pants and swore on his mother's grave that was all he had."

"You went soft."

"I'm a gentleman. So I lowered my price for the man."

"Kind of you."

Driver gave me my part of the money. As I put it inside my pocket, I told him that

Regina had been here. I didn't tell him about the argument, what I said, or what she had said.

Driver rubbed his chin. "She sped away right before you came upstairs."

"And five minutes later an ugly Bergs attacked me."

"She brought him? Is that what you're thinking? That she's in bed with the Bergs?"

"No. She had just found me. He was here first."

"Or he followed her. A Bentley is easy to follow."

"No idea."

"And he came with a gun."

"If he had brought flowers and candy, I would've been offended."

I took a desperate breath, a breath that didn't slow my galloping heart. New reality. It felt like I had been lucky to get out of that one alive. I put both guns on the coffee table.

I said, "The Bergs have arrived."

"Moses Bergs has sent his sons, at least one of them, to your front door."

I said, "Driver. Call my wife. Make sure she is okay. If she's not, vanish and go handle it. If she is, then she is and let her be. Either way, don't tell me. Just call her and see."

He took out his cellular, stepped into the kitchen, and made a call.

I stared at those guns. It looked like my .38 had had a baby and named it .380.

Driver was only on the phone for about two minutes. He ended the call and came back.

He didn't say and I didn't ask.

Cars blew their horns outside my window. Freeway traffic was piling up.

I said, "Driver, what you said in the hallway . . . you killed somebody."

"If I told you, then I'd have to kill you."

I nodded and left it at that. Every man was entitled to own his secrets.

He said, "But it changes you. Hypothetically speaking. It changes you."

"What does?"

"Killing changes you. And you will not welcome the change. You will become as dark and moody and as black and ruthless as Hollywood. Murder is a thorny and complex subject."

"Murder?"

"Self-defense. And even when it's self-defense, it still feels like murder."

A sudden knock at my door made us both jump and face the door.

I called out, "Who is it?"

"Holder."

I relaxed. Driver didn't.

I opened the door and Mr. Holder came inside. His expression was off and I read that to mean that the neighbors had been talking about the melee. He closed the door behind himself; saw me, looked at Driver, then back at my injuries. My ragged clothes and bruised and bloodied face was a novel of pain. The two guns on the table were another short story waiting to be told.

I said, "Driver, this is Mr. Holder."

"Driver. Is that your name or your occupation?"

"It's what you can feel free to call me."

That drew the line between them. With that, Driver backed away and checked his watch.

He was putting Mr. Holder on a timer.

Mr. Holder asked what had happened. I told him that Johnny Handsome's brother had found me. That meant that Johnny Handsome knew where I was. He wanted payback for that beating in the rain. I had been located. I wasn't running away. So it was only a matter of time.

Mr. Holder said, "So Regina Baptiste left her throne and came to our part of the world."

"She might have been thrown out of her kingdom."

"And right after that movie star left, you were attacked."

I touched my face, spots that ached and felt swollen. "I was attacked."

"Just like you attacked that boy in Hollywood."

"Yeah, I know. It's a vicious cycle."

He shifted on his heels and look at the carpet. "Got a minute?"

"I'm in the middle of a crisis right now."

His jaw tightened, then released. "I just need a minute."

"What's going on? What did you need, Mr. Holder?"

He looked at me again, his smile rugged. "It's personal."

I looked at Driver and nodded. My guess was that Holder wanted to borrow money.

Driver said, "I'm going to walk the hallway and come back."

Then he left Mr. Holder and me, left the way a bodyguard would step away from the President if he were about to have a conversation with a Prime Minister.

Mr. Holder said, "The fight you had up here, it's the talk of the building right now."

"Figured that. A better fight will come along before the week is over."

"So Johnny Bergs's brother was banging on your door with a gun in his bag?"

"Banged a couple of times, for a good minute nonstop. But I didn't go to the door then."

"In the bathroom?"

"In the bedroom. I was occupied. That probably saved me from being . . . hurt real bad."

For a moment, the strong-backed man with dimples and cleft chin looked uneasy.

He took a shallow breath and asked, "Who were you up here sleeping with?"

I knew what he was asking. So I felt obliged to answer. "Mrs. Patrice Evans."

Mr. Holder looked relieved; then he shook his head. "You and Mrs. Patrice Evans?"

"Yeah. She came by. She was out there the night I moved in."

"You barely said two words to her. How did that come about?"

"Abruptly and without foreshadowing. At least from my point of view."

"I *know* Ted. We're not best friends, but we're friends. He used to come by and play dominoes with me and Vera-Anne and Isabel. Just letting you know that I know him too."

I opened and closed my hand. Mr. Holder looked me over, still shaking his head.

He asked, "Did Ted's wife see your Maybach?"

"No one has seen my car but you."

"They go after athletes and lawyers. They all want to have sex with a man who is somebody. Men like you get put at the top of the list. They know you're rich. It shows."

"People in this complex have brand new Benzes, BMWs, and Range Rovers."

"People here fake being rich. For them being rich is a fantasy. They have nothing."

"As far as they know, I'm no different."

He snapped, "Did you kiss Vera-Anne today when you were in the laundry room?"

He caught me off guard.

"Were you holding her and kissing her in the hallway in front of her kids?"

I took a breath and shook my head. "I didn't kiss her. I'd never disrespect you."

He took a breath and his bottom lip trembled. "James, look. Her little boy talks to me."

"You really need to calm down, Mr. Holder."

"He said that you had your arms around his momma. So, did you?"

"She chatted, offered me pea soup. I declined; then she went home."

"The boy seems to think differently. And let's get this in the open, James. She likes you."

"Vera-Anne likes the art in my apartment.

Pictures and glass sculptures. Not me."

"Say nothing, James. Say nothing right now. Fuck. She hasn't bought a roll of toilet paper to wipe her ass or a tampon to stop her blood, and the moment you show up, after all I have done, after all that I have spent, the moment I leave, she's out in the hallway in front of her kids kissing you? This is the worst moment of my life, so do me a favor and say nothing."

"Mr. Holder, that's not what happened."

"I went through this shit with my daughter's mom. I told you that. Never again."

My face was aching, the pain from fighting Bizarro Bergs still fresh, and I was already in another unexpected fight. This was harder than the battle in the hallway. Bergs had come to kill me in cold blood and now Holder was in my space assassinating my character.

He said, "Don't take it out on us."

I snapped, "She came on to me."

He took a breath, and exhaled fire and hurt. "The moment I left, she came on to you."

"But I've never touched her. Not like that. She gave me a hug."

"I see. You hugged her but you didn't touch her. She touched you. Front to front."

"She was crying. So I hugged her to calm

324

her down."

"Crying. Oh. She was crying. That's how she ended up in my bed. By crying."

"Well, she didn't end up in mine."

"How do I know that? How do I know what happened when those kids took a nap?"

"Are you serious? Look at her, and then look at Regina Baptiste. Look at her, and then look at my wife. Grab a magazine and hold my wife's face up next to Vera-Anne's face. There is no comparison. And my wife is a hard worker. My wife makes . . . she makes a lot of money . . . and Vera-Anne makes zero. You said that you can't get Vera-Anne to get up and go to work and I can't get mine to stop working. Vera-Anne is nice; she's a good cook; but she's not Regina Baptiste, even with Regina's problems. Sweet Isabel pointed out that she's under-educated and doesn't care. So, yeah. She came on to me. And nothing happened. Absofuckinglutely nothing. Why in the hell would I go after her? You're my friend. At least you were my friend."

His headed lowered and he opened and closed his hands.

I said, "I'm sorry. But when you come at me like that, you get what you get."

"No, no. You said the truth."

"Hate that I had to say that. Don't mean to be disrespectful. But you left me no choice."

"You could buy my life, but Johnny Bergs is more famous than Jesus. I don't mean this in a *disrespectful* way, but that is the truth. He slept with your wife and there is very little outcry from a Christian nation. Immediate gratification. They're hooked on immediate gratification. They're tired of waiting on Jesus so they've made man their Jesus. What women have done to Johnny Bergs out there, the idolizing, that's what women are doing to you here."

"Look, I know you're in pain, pissed off, but that's where I draw the line, Mr. Holder."

"You've been in The Apartments for a few days. Men have been trying to get some of Ted's wife for years. She won't go near another man. But she comes to your door just like that."

"Don't fucking blame me because I've made better choices than you and you're fifty years old living in a dump like this. Don't fucking come into my space and try and attack me. I'm nice, but I'm not that fucking nice, *Chet.* You'd better adjust your attitude. This is not the day."

Then he stopped talking, but his body

language remained hostile.

Two guns were behind him and my bloodied face and anger were in front of him.

Mr. Holder said, "My car is not worth mentioning. I'm living the life of a poor man. I live with a woman who has two kids. You drive a Maybach. You're rich. You're married to a movie star. You wedded one of the prettiest women God ever made. I'm stuck here. You have options. You've accomplished a lot at a young age. You've done more with your life than I have with mine. You have nice things. I have nothing to show for being on this planet for fifty years."

"My wife has a porn tape. I'm on the run. And I'm sitting here with you."

"*You're here by choice.* You're here because you're not man enough to face your problems. You're hiding. Your wife did you wrong and you're afraid to stand up and tell the media how you feel. You tucked your tail between your legs and ran to the ghetto to hide."

We stared each other down. We were moments from a bloody shooting.

There was a tap on the door. And we both jumped.

I swallowed my new anger and called, out, "Yeah. Who the hell is it this time?"

"Driver."

I let Driver back in. He had a baseball bat in his hand. A Louisville Slugger. He'd been to his car, then double-checked, had looked for the rest of the Bergs Brothers.

Driver said, "Everything okay in here?"

"Nothing that I can't handle. What about out there?"

"Not a Berg in sight. I'd bet they think you're calling the cops."

"That or they're taking the one I beat to the emergency room."

"This is just the quiet before the storm."

"People think that I'm a joke until we have to go one-on-one."

"Obviously. They don't know how you get when you're pissed off."

"No they don't. Johnny Bergs knows. And so does one of his fucking brothers."

"You look pissed off."

"I'm moving from storm to storm. And only a hurricane can beat a tropical storm."

"Sure about everything being okay in here? Do I need to intervene?"

"All is good. Like I said, my friend, I can handle my own problems."

Baseball bat in hand, Driver sat on the leather sofa, the leather sighing under his weight. He laid the baseball bat across his lap, patted it three or four times for good measure.

Mr. Holder regarded Driver for a short second. Driver returned the favor, unblinking.

I said, "Are we done here, Mr. Holder? Or do you have other accusations and insecurities and lifelong failures and bad choices in relationships that need to be addressed?"

Mr. Holder said, "What matters now is getting ready to go see my daughter."

"Look, Mr. Holder."

"What is that, Mr. Thicke? What does the young, rich man want to say now?"

"Look. Did you still want me to drive you down there in the Maybach?"

"No, I'll drive. I'd hate to show up and have her think that I'm somebody that I'm not. Or I'd hate for her to see you and get distracted. If she sees you, your car, she might not see me."

"I can arrange for a car service to take you down and bring you back."

"I need nothing from you, Mr. Thicke. Like you, I'm my own man. Always have been."

"I was just offering. I owe you from helping me move in. A promise is a promise. No matter what was said, no matter what you think, I'm a man of my word and I've been your friend."

"A man has to make money, or he's not seen as a man worthy of being in this world."

"It's not about the money."

"When a man doesn't have money, *it's always about the money.*"

Mr. Holder took a breath, looked anxious, and then he opened the door, ready to exit without saying good-bye. But he opened the door on Vera-Anne's crying face. She was on the other side of my door, face red, pink hair pulled back, jean shorts and a black T, no sandals, as if she had run up here right after Mr. Holder had come to confront me. I didn't know how much she had heard. But her face, the way her body trembled, her guilt was suffocating. Her chest rose and fell with her anxiety, and her neck was damp with stress sweat, her palms the same.

She saw my face, my bruises and looked like she was about to scream.

Mr. Holder snapped at her, "What are you doing up here?"

"I'm sorry, Poppa."

"What are you sorry for?"

"I didn't mean to do anything wrong. It was just flirting. It wasn't serious. I mean, I did hug him. But nothing happened. If he told you something did happen, he's lying.

He's been looking at me and I was just being polite. He kept saying that we're almost the same age. Then he kept asking me to put the kids to sleep and come up here by myself, but I turned him down."

"He told me that you were crying. That's the same thing you did with me. I told you that I was just trying to help you and your children, that I was trying to be nice, and you got off my sofa and came into my bedroom crying. You cried your way into my bed. You tried that with him."

"He's lying."

"You undressed and stood in my doorway naked, breaking down with tears in your eyes."

"Don't believe him."

"And I held you, and you whispered in my ear, and like a fool, I took you into my bed."

"He just wants to break us up so he can have me."

"I told you that I was too old for you. I knew that you were too immature."

"I love you, Poppa. You know I love you."

"You said age meant nothing and you'd be better to me than any woman I'd ever met."

"My kids love you too, Poppa. You know how much my kids love you."

"And you made me feel things no woman had made me feel in over two decades."

"Varg is a liar."

"You have no idea who this man is. That adds insult to injury."

"He's nobody. I bet that everything in his apartment is stolen. He's a bum."

Mr. Holder spoke in a voice so calm it was terrifying. "You started packing yet?"

"Packing? You're really putting me out over this?"

"We had issues before he showed up. But I guess I just chose to ignore those issues. I can see the future. You'll cheat on me. You didn't do it today, but you will at some point."

"You're putting me out over Varg? I don't like him. He's not my type; you know that."

"Eventually. If you haven't already. Loving you has made me a fool."

"What are me and my kids going to do? Where are we going to live? How will we eat?"

"You have two kids. That's two men who need to be feeding you and them, and maybe it's time for them to grow up, for you to grow up, for them to feed their seeds, not me."

"Please, Poppa. Please. I haven't slept with anybody since I've been with you."

"Vera-Anne, I'm not stupid. I hacked your e-mails. Been reading your e-mails since you moved in with me. I've read everything that you've written about every cute boy or man that you've met on Facebook, and I know how you like good-looking men. Those are your words. If you see a good-looking man, you have to go introduce yourself. You have to get his phone number. You have to friend him on Facebook. Those are your words. And so far as our new neighbor, since you first came up here uninvited and met him, you have wanted to be with *Varg Veum.* Every word you've sent, I read. I want you packed and gone by this time tomorrow."

"You're a hacker?"

"I can't go through this again. I just can't. You know how my first wife did me."

"You've been reading my personal e-mails?"

"That was two decades ago and I still think about it, still feel resentment to this very day."

Vera-Anne screamed, *"You're a hacker."*

"It's better than what you are, Vera-Anne. Much better."

"I fucking hate hackers. I sleep with your old ass and you hack me? *How dare you."*

His expression was hard, judgmental, a mix of rabid disappointment, cups of sadness, tons of disbelief. He looked at her like he wanted to stab her over and over and over.

Mr. Holder pulled the door closed behind them and her cries followed, her begging and pleading and promising to be a good woman echoed, followed him up the hallway.

Driver said, "When I stepped out, she was in the hallway by your door eavesdropping."

"First Regina Baptiste, then Bergs and now this shit with Holder and Vera-Anne."

"So far as Holder, welcome to the ghetto. Young girls like that are dangerous. He's a sucker, being played like that. Crap like that usually ends with bloodshed and body bags."

I nodded and punctuated the moment with a deep sigh of regret. Then I shifted my mind, moved back to my real problems. My problems were the problems that mattered most.

One of the Bergs had found me. That meant that they had been looking for me since I had beat Johnny Bergs in the streets of Hollywood. And Johnny Bergs was probably orchestrating this revenge. I remembered the fight at Mapona. The rumors about the missing accountant. The boys who had been found dead after they had fought the Bergs.

Anxiety and fear tried to rise up. I refused to fall apart.

Driver moved the bat from his lap. "All of your cars have tracking devices."

"I know. That's how Regina found where the car was parked."

"I could've taken it back to the house the day you came here."

"I know that you could've."

"You didn't go too far. Less than an hour. You wanted Regina to find you."

I nodded. "Next time I'm hiring a stupid driver. You're too good. Like a damn detective."

"Crossword puzzles keep the brain sharp."

I made myself a cup of Kona coffee, gave the same to Driver, and we waited for Godot. Driver was hanging around, probably to make sure I didn't take the guns and go retaliate.

I had plenty of time to be afraid of what was yet to come.

He asked, "When Mrs. Thicke showed up, how did it go?"

"Emotional and immature. We both digressed to being primates. Became hurt children."

"Like Holder and that young girl did."

"Compared to us, they were pretty mature."

I sipped my coffee to calm my out-of-control nerves.

Driver said, "I missed the start of the fight, but you handled yourself."

"You can look at it on the computer."

He hesitated, and then he loaded the file and watched.

He analyzed and said, "Mean jabs. Your form's not too bad, considering that you were in a street fight. I could help you with that hook. And never drop your opposite hand."

"Well, just look at the part where I beat his ass. It's not the damn Olympics."

"You have a great fighting instinct. Relentless. Like you grew up brawling. Brothers?"

"Two older, two younger, all bigger, all stronger, all faster, none smarter."

Driver said, "Then you woke up fighting and you went to bed fighting."

"Sure did. We lived on top of each other. Laughter. Depression. My mother and father in one bedroom. Six boys in either the living room or the other bedroom. And no books."

"You overcompensated. Bought everything you never had as a child."

"We all overcompensate. Material things.

We buy too much. In the quest for love. We don't know how to love and we try and we end up loving too many of the people who are not worthy of our love. What we don't have drives us to obsession and we overcompensate."

"You've never mentioned anything about your family. Never in an interview."

"I don't do tragic interviews. I don't want strangers hearing me talk, and thinking that we have somehow bonded, then coming up to me as if they know me and telling me how shitty their lives have been. I grew up in areas that would make this place look like the W hotel. People hear that I grew up in London and think that I had the keys to Buckingham Place and an audience with the queen. London was horrible for my family and me. It was horrible for me. I went three, sometimes four days without food. I had a can of beans once. You know what I did? I hid it from my family and saved it. I was afraid to eat it because it was all that I had and I didn't know when I'd get another can of beans. I made a can of beans last six days. But London was harsh. And for a while it wasn't much better here. That was how things were when we were growing up, before we came back to the States. I saw people eating and I used to pretend that I wasn't hungry. I'd go to school so hungry that I thought that I was going to pass out. We all have shitty lives. It's not supposed to be that bad in a Christian nation. Mr. Holder was just talking about a Christian nation. The hypocritical values of a Christian nation. This nation was built on the blood of a carpenter who was nailed to a cross and tortured until he died. We're programmed to accept suffering and are addicted to tales of woe and sorrow and stories about suffering."

"And we're also addicted to crucifying and throwing stones and spears at the suffering."

Mr. Chetwyn Holder's diatribe had derailed me from my real mission and gotten to me.

I took a breath. "Anyway. Yeah. I just told you things that I've never told my wife."

"And they won't leave this room unless you take them with you."

"God bless confidentiality agreements."

"I'm a man who did two years in jail for not telling. I did someone else's time."

I nodded. "Well, whoever you did time for, I hope they appreciated it."

He said, "You had a pretty big family. Had no idea."

"Big family, small flat. My parents were

not happily married, and I grew up as an introverted and reserved boy in a house of domestic turmoil. That introversion is what made me a writer. The brothers are what made me a fighter. That's why it was no problem going after Johnny Handsome. I have a reputation to maintain, even if that rep is only inside my head."

Driver remained without judgment. He said, "Fighting. It gets in your blood."

"It stays there. Dormant at best, but it stays there. Mine has been activated."

"Bloodlust."

"I'm up to two guns, but I'm still outnumbered."

"I can't fight your physical battles for you. But I can keep the odds even. Not in your favor. Just even. If it's between you and one man, I'll do what I have to do to keep it that way."

"So you're up for a fight, need be."

"Just let me know if I need to change clothes."

Maybe some part of me needed a reason to beat someone's ass and feel good about it. The high from that victory was a drug too. Now two boys from the Bergs family were far from being handsome. I had done more damage to Johnny's brother than Pac-Man had done to Oscar in his final eight rounds. I had beaten his ass in front of a hallway filled with people.

I said, "My family. When we were living abroad in Hackney and Tottenham, those were the days. Those were the soup days. They used to get up at five thirty in the morning. I'd get up earlier. Around five. It was the only calm time in the house. Thirty minutes of silence. I'd speed-read a few chapters of a book; didn't matter if it was bad or good. My mother would get up before my father. She woke up praying. Noisy and praying. Never prayed with her lips shut. The noise would start. Brothers would start to get up. The race for the bathroom would commence. When we came here to the States, it eventually became better. My father worked all over. Laborer. Handyman. Mechanic who loved cars. My mother worked in a factory, processing paperwork, dealing with new or rehires, separation notices, doing whatever they did in HR. My typewriter, she bought it from a shop and gave it to me. It's my most prized possession. Not the cars. Not the house. Underwood matters the most."

"You talked to your family since this started?"

"No. They'd only depress me more than I am already depressed."

"Pick one person. Call them. Make one phone call and check in."

Driver wasn't just having a conversation. He was getting me to talk, calming me down.

I left Driver seated with his coffee and stepped into the bedroom with my iPhone.

That was when I called my family. I talked to one of my brothers, the youngest, the one that I was the closest to, the one in film school back at NYU, and told him that I was fine. He wasn't being bombarded with e-mails and hounded by the local press. He still had our family name, the ugly British name that I had been born with and changed when I started working in this business. He was concerned. I hadn't returned calls. Or e-mails. Or texts. I had vanished. I was good at vanishing when stressed. Everyone had been worried. They loved Regina. But everyone did. She was beautiful. She was rich. She was talented. Trifecta. My brother told me that they were all in shock, trying to understand what couldn't be understood.

I gave him twenty minutes of talking, then told him to spread the word that I was fine.

What would happen next was outside my field of vision.

Then I let him go and went back in the

front room with Driver long enough to tell him that I needed to get cleaned up. He told me that, if I didn't mind, he'd stick around for a moment. I told him that my iPad was next to Underwood and he could surf the Internet while he waited.

He reached into his pocket and took out a crossword puzzle and a pen.

He waved the puzzle in the air and said, "I'm covered."

I didn't have high gates. Or Dobermans. But I had a guard at the front door.

I yanked off my mutilated and soiled clothing and showered, then dressed in a different pair of D&G jeans, pulled out a tee with a picture of a veiled Middle Eastern woman. Only her eyes could be seen; across the top the phrase read GENTLEMEN PRE-FER BURKAS.

I sat on the bed and took a deep, deep breath and still smelled Patrice.

From the front room Driver called out, "Thicke."

"Yeah."

"A lady came by. She looked like Audrey Hepburn, Helen Mirren, and Julia Roberts."

"British accent. Very classy. Elegant."

"Told her that you were in the shower. She didn't leave a message, but she left a book for you. Said she was at Barnes and

Noble, bought it for you and wanted to leave it."

"A book by Gunnar Staalesen. The character Varg Veum."

"As soon as she left, another tall and slim woman with dreadlocks stopped by."

"Misty Mouse."

"Didn't tell me her name. Just said to say she stopped by. She left a manuscript."

"The Cruelty of Men Toward Women."

"I left both packages sitting next to Underwood."

I looked at my cellular. I had left it on. It was vibrating nonstop.

Regina Baptiste, or Sasha, or whoever in the hell she was now was calling nonstop.

And I had text messages from STEVE MARTIN.

The message read: REGINA B ASS.

Driver called back to me. "I just got another message from Steve Martin."

"Me too. Just got one from Steve Martin too."

Driver hesitated. "Could be an anagram."

"Now you're making it into a puzzle."

"Actually, I'm an Occam's razor kind of guy."

"I think it's a joke. Regina Baptiste's ass. Or Regina's big ass."

"Like I said, could be an anagram. Or just

343

Regina Baptiste's assistant."

I paused. "That's not her assistant's name. Her assistant is a young, Turkish girl."

Driver said, "They could be looking for her assistant, trying to get info on your wife."

"I think it's a joke. Regina Baptiste's ass. She has shown her assets to the world."

Driver said, "Well, on that note, Thicke, I have no idea who it is or what it means."

And there were quite a few calls from an unknown number.

I asked, "Are you getting a lot of calls from unknown or blocked numbers?"

"Ever since this started. They started coming in that night you beat Bergs."

"Answer any?"

"We were in red alert that night. Only talked to you. I let them go to voice mail."

"If they call again, answer. I'll do the same on this end. Might be the Bergs."

My phone vibrated again. Then came the text from Bobby Holland.

He told me what he had.

And to make good, he played thirty seconds of an audio of Regina Baptiste.

For the first time in over two years, Bobby Holland had my attention.

CHAPTER 24

Driver followed me toward the parking lot. I carried the Louisville Slugger. We took the long way, not the expected route, cut through other letter-coded buildings. When we made it to the parking lot, Driver motioned. The Bentley was parked at the L of the buildings.

He said, "She's back."

"She never left. If she did, she didn't go far."

"She's scared."

"Yeah. She's scared."

"And alone, James. No matter how many fans she has, she feels alone. Everybody in the world has forsaken her. I'm talking about the people that she really cares about, not the ones that get a paycheck because they're riding on her fame. She has been forsaken."

"Did you have to say it like that, Driver?"

"Yeah. I had to."

"Forsaken."

"Forsaken is a powerful word. Very biblical."

"I could fire you."

"Then I'd walk down there and start working for her."

"At a raise."

"I'd lower my fee for her. She's nicer than you. You can be a pain at times."

"I figured you'd say that."

In the land of the blue-collar workers and paupers, Regina sat in a chariot made for a queen. My cellular rang. My wife was calling me the way Patrice's husband called her.

I answered.

"Regina."

"James."

I held the phone for a long moment. "Bobby Holland called."

"That narcissistic, psycho, bootlicking, Nazi creep."

"Yeah, that Bobby Holland."

"Don't talk to him. Please. Don't talk to him."

"Too late."

"What did he say, James?"

"He has something that he's trying to sell."

"Blackmail is so cliché."

"Cliché, but effective."

She went quiet with her words, her breathing coarse and riled.

She whispered, "Come here. Please."

I hung up the phone. It was time to try and be more mature than emotional.

I handed Driver the baseball bat and he waited where he was. I looked up at the dirty windows, saw a few residents staring down; then I headed toward the Bentley. A moment later, I opened the passenger door and climbed inside a space cooled to seventy-three degrees. The car felt more comfortable than anyplace I'd been since I had landed here. I evaluated Regina Baptiste. This broken-down version. Her body was wracked with guilt, tension, grief, anxiety, fear, and worry. She'd lost weight over the last two weeks. My guess was that she was down at least ten pounds. She didn't look like the woman on the billboards anymore. Eyes swollen and red, tissue in her left hand, she looked disordered and molested. She was barefoot and wore ripped jeans and a black T with white letters that read: DEAR GOD, WHY IS IT SO HARD TO WIN THE LOTTERY?

I said, "Bobby Holland has another tape."

Her swollen eyes widened with concern. "What happened to your face?"

"Ran into a Bergs."

347

She wiped away her tears. "Johnny Bergs?"

"One of his brothers. Well, I ran into his fist is a better description of what happened. His brother came looking for revenge right after I saw you down here."

"Are you serious? Are they following me?"

"Don't touch my face. Don't touch me at all, Regina."

"I'm sorry."

"Did you set me up?"

"Of course not. Are you crazy?"

"Was jumped in the hallway right after you drove away angry."

"He beat you up?"

"He looks worse. A lot worse. Half of it because he was born that way."

"You need to go to your doctor."

"Maybe tomorrow. If I'm not in jail. But jails have the best doctors for free."

"James, don't play like that.'

"We'll get to chatting about Johnny Bergs. We need to talk about Bobby Holland."

"He's scum."

"It's true then."

"Yes. It's true."

I closed my eyes, my headache strong. "Was this so-called tape before me?"

"Does it matter?"

"Was whatever's on the tape, whatever he has, was that before we married?"

"It was before you. But the public won't care. Marilyn Monroe has been dead for decades and they're still buying nude photos and film, trading it like it's on the stock market."

"I know. The difference is Marilyn Monroe is dead. Most associated with her are dead."

"I don't need any more bad press. My parents, they don't need me to have any more bad press. My family doesn't need any more shame. I've humiliated everyone. I'm more worried about my family than I am the rest of the world. My family is my world. I haven't dealt with this yet, this Johnny Handsome thing. I want it to go away, but the less I say, the more they lie. They are printing that we had had an affair for years, that I have Johnny's love child, all sorts of crap. They're saying that every love scene that I've done in a movie is *authentic*."

"You're worried about your family?"

"That means you too, James. We're family now. Like it or not, we're family."

"Bobby Holland. Let's focus on him for the moment. What does he have?"

"Whatever Bobby has is different. And over four years old. We were together back then. We were a couple. I was crazy about him at first. He recorded us all the time, innocent stuff, recorded every little thing I did, most of the time without me knowing it. I trusted him back then, so it didn't matter. But he recorded me saying and doing things that could end my career. We were loaded, getting loaded, and just being fools. No one needs to see me that way. No one needs to hear the things that I said. We're all mean-spirited in private. It was a private moment."

"Regina. Anything else I need to know?"

"The has-been line in Hollywood stretches for miles, across fifty states and into every country. Always a short line of stars. But the line of has-been gets longer every fucking day."

"Still quoting my works."

"One false move and the sky will light up with the brilliance that can only come from a falling star. When they fall, they all go to the same place. They all fall into the pit of nothingness."

"Two years after we met at a bar, you're still quoting me."

"Feels like I'm living one of your dark screenplays right now, and that's not cool."

"I'm living it too. More fun writing it than living it. Much more fun to write."

A moment passed.

She said, "I had an incident on the plane."

"I heard."

"They disrespected me and put me off the fucking plane like I was a criminal."

"You attacked a flight attendant."

"After the verbal assault. She insulted me and I threw champagne in her face."

"That's not nice. Makes first class look like no class."

"The bitch deserved it."

"Well, throw Coke next time. Clear liquids are no good. They come out too easily."

"You should've heard what she said to me. How she treated me was horrible."

"A Johnny Handsome fan."

"The head of his fan club. Bitch is lucky that I didn't yank off her tacky front lace weave."

"Assault charges?"

"I have to wait to hear from the FAA. My attorney will handle it."

"Sounds like at least a fine. But that's cheaper than a full-blown lawsuit."

She held up her cellular. "Look at the responses to this so-called news. People behave pretty much the same way most newspapers write, on a sixth grade level, for the unlearned and the immature. They never see the big picture, judge everything in shades of black and white."

We let another moment pass.

She said, "The morality clause."

351

"There is a morality clause in marriage too."

She nodded.

A morals clause was a provision in her contracts that prohibited certain behavior that would garner bad publicity for the product. Sexual acts. Drugs. Common in the business. The film studios wanted to protect their brand. If the polls were low, if Regina Baptiste had forfeited the respect of the public, she would be of no use to the moneymaking machines and everyone could fire her now. Without a memo. What Bobby Holland had could make a difference. She had fallen, but she wasn't on her back. Bobby Holland could destroy her with ten seconds of a tape that had been made years ago. I hated what she had done, but I had to protect her. That was part of the contract that I had made with her, morality clause or not.

I said, "You need a bath."

"And you need a medic."

She put her hand on mine and I interdigitated our fingers, clasped our hands together. She leaned toward me and I leaned toward her. She put her forehead against mine, closed her eyes, and gently pushed her head into mine, did that as she tried to find some physical way of reconnecting with me, any small way, and she emphasized each word.

"I'm so sorry, James. I am so sorry. The pressure was too much for me. I broke."

We stayed that way a while.

She said, "Seems like nobody cares what happens to me. I'm bad luck overnight."

"I care."

"I'm talking about everybody else in the world."

"In this world, your problems and my problems, they are nothing. Your world is falling apart. Mine is falling apart. We think the world is falling apart. That's not the truth. Since this happened, we haven't passed by anyone who cares about what troubles us because they are too caught up in what is troubling them. I'm in a village of people with bigger problems."

"Everyone is abandoning me."

"They don't want to be bothered with you because every relationship is reciprocal. When you touch something, it touches you. Nobody wants bad luck or career-ending publicity."

A moment passed. Her phone rang over and over and over. Calls from friends and management and UNKNOWN were all rejected before the first ring had completed.

She said, "You're not wearing your wedding ring."

"Johnny Handsome fucked you and it fell off my hand. When a butterfly flaps its wings."

She rubbed her temples and asked, "With whom are you staying here?"

"Your eloquence is returning."

"With whom?

A twinge of anger returned. "It doesn't matter."

Her voice fractured, "A woman? You're here laid up with some woman?"

"If I do have a mistress, it started after this happened, after I saw that tape, after I saw Johnny Handsome's cock inside you like he was your husband and it was your wedding night."

She moved her head from mine and sat back, eyes closed, tears falling.

She took her hand away from mine. We had disconnected.

The car smelled of her body and my cleanliness, but it also smelled of severe depression and anger as well. Her depression had a stench more powerful than my anger.

She said, "Thanks for being honest."

"Wish that I could say the same to you. You should've called me first."

"Would you have understood?"

"No. But at least I could have been prepared."

"Do you understand now?"

"No. But once I see your old flame Bobby Holland, he thinks that I will."

"Don't go."

"I'm trapped between a guy you fucked and one who wants to fuck you over."

"You don't have to go. I'll let my lawyers do what they can do."

"Which, in this case, is nothing. They can do nothing. You know that there is no choice."

She wiped her eyes.

I asked, "Have you been sleeping with Bobby Holland since you left him?"

"No."

"Kiss? Any type of intimacy? Digital? Oral? Anything?"

"Nothing."

"How did he get all of my phone numbers?"

"No idea."

"He has numbers that only a few people have."

"Like me, your agent, your manager, and Hazel Tamana Bijou."

"And none of them would give him my numbers."

She nodded and I left it at that.

I asked, "Johnny Handsome?"

"I don't know what to call what happened."

"What does Johnny Boy call it?"

"An accidental fuck."

"An accidental fuck."

"When I went off on Johnny Handsome, after the shoot was done, I was in his trailer. I was livid. He was on cocaine and E. He didn't know where he was or whom he was with. He claims that he doesn't remember. He had no guilt because he claims that he couldn't remember."

"An accidental fuck."

"He called it an accidental fuck. Not me. When it as over, I felt as if I were raped. I felt like I was a whore on stage in Amsterdam, drugged and raped while everyone applauded. It was rape, James. I didn't want that. That's the way I feel, to be honest. I feel as if I were raped."

"Looked like buyer's remorse on film."

"No, rape."

"Cocaine fucked you first. Johnny Handsome was second on that train."

"Fuck you, James. Fuck you. Get out of my car. Get out of my goddamn car."

I didn't say anything. Part of me wanted to apologize, but that part lost the battle.

She quieted and wiped her eyes again.

"One helluva drug. Cocaine is nobody's friend."

"I wouldn't know. But I guess it is a helluva drug. And for you, an old friend."

"It was seconds. Less than a minute."

"To me it was a lifetime."

"Why is sex so powerful? Even when it means nothing, it's powerful when it shouldn't have happened, when it was fucking accidental fucking, that felt like rape."

She reached for my hand. I moved my hand away and shook my head.

She said, "I disgust you now."

I didn't answer.

My cellular rang. I looked at the caller ID. It was Driver. His broad back was to us, giving us privacy, watching out for us from that direction. Sweet Isabel passed by in her car, but she never looked our way. She passed by Driver just as I answered, then turned and vanished.

I said, "Driver."

"Thicke, sorry to interrupt, but it's urgent."

"No problem."

"I just talked to somebody who said that they were Steve Martin."

"And during my darkest hour, what does Steve Martin want?"

When I said that, I looked at Regina,

looked for some sign that said she knew about Steve Martin, some recognition. Nothing was there. She rubbed her forehead and let me talk.

"This cat sounds shaky, but that's just nerves. It sounds legit. Not like some cloud-cuckoo-land crap. Steve Martin wants to meet. And I think that you should."

I told Driver, "He can wait. I have a more important meeting scheduled."

"You need to talk to Steve Martin first. I'll text you the number so you can come to your own conclusion, although I think that you need to stop everything, return that call right now."

"Why right now?"

"Steve Martin said you have one hour to return the call and meet, so call now."

Driver didn't say why, but I trusted his judgment. Right now I was too numb to make a decision on my own. I had no instinct. All of the choices I'd made so far had been bad or wrong.

I dialed the number that Driver had sent and asked, "Who is this?"

"Hello, Mister Thicke."

"Steve Martin. What can I do for you?"

"I'm trying to do something for you."

"Okay. What can you do for me?"

"The night that the thing happened to

Miss Baptiste, I was the fly on the wall."

"There were a lot of flies on the wall that night."

"Not like me. You're talking about on the set. I'm talking about before."

That paused me. Confused me. "What good does that do me?"

"I can show you what happened and you can see for yourself."

"It's of no value."

"You're with Miss Baptiste right now, aren't you?"

"I am."

"Is she doing okay?"

I ignored the question. "The other thing; it was already sent to my cell phone."

"Not this. The recording that I have was taken before that happened."

"What am I missing?"

"I'm in Venice. Abbot Kinney and California Avenue."

"Just e-mail the information to this phone and I'll get back to you."

"No. This stays on my phone and my phone only. This will never be mailed out. Look, I'm tired. If you come now, if you get here within forty minutes, I'll wait and can show it to you."

"How much will it cost me?"

"Forty minutes."

Steve Martin hung up.

I ended the call and told Regina Baptiste, "You smell."

"I need a hot shower. I've been sleeping in the car the last two days."

"Go upstairs to my luxurious apartment and get cleaned up."

"There are so many people here. Someone will see me."

"There are no paparazzi here. And right now, with your hair unkempt, with your face swollen, and those bloodshot eyes, you're not recognizable. You could stand next to one of your movie posters or billboards and no one would think that you were Regina Baptiste."

"Geesh, thanks. I look that bad, huh?"

"Put your scarf over your head. Put your shades on. You look famous or interesting because you're in a Bentley. Once you get ten yards away, no one will notice you, but they will still notice the car. No one will expect to see you here. Even if they recognize you, they'll say it can't be you, not here. You can't go anywhere else, not in this area, not in this car, and not be noticed. This isn't Sunset or Rodeo or Malibu. I'll have Driver get you inside my apartment."

"You have an apartment here?"

"Yes."

"Since when?"

"Since you fucked Johnny Bergs."

"When I go up to this . . . your apartment, then what?"

"I'm going to take my checkbook and meet with Bobby Holland."

"Let Driver take you. I don't want you to go alone. Don't trust Bobby Holland."

"This isn't Driver's concern. Sometimes a man has to handle his own business."

She repeated, "Sometimes a man has to handle his own business."

"Or the business of his family."

She pulled her lips in, then smiled a little. "Okay. But do you have to do it alone?"

"Yup. Ask Johnny Handsome. I'll have to meet with him again too."

"This isn't the wild, wild West."

"I beg to differ."

"You're not a cowboy."

"But I'm feeling like John Wayne."

"John Wayne is dead."

"Then I'm feeling like Bruce Willis."

A moment passed. She asked, "Can I touch your hand again?"

"No. I don't want to feel your touch right now."

She shivered and asked, "Are you filing for a divorce?"

"Yes."

Her tears came back, fast and swift. She nodded and asked, "When?"

"As soon as I find a synonym for Thesaurus."

I gave her my hand. She pulled it to her face and kissed it a half dozen times.

I told Regina to drive toward Driver, and stay close to the building, close enough so no one could look down without taking the dirty screens off of their windows.

Driver came to the car. We traded. He gave me the baseball bat and I moved into the captain's seat and put Regina Baptiste in his care.

Driver said, "I'll call somebody to come help her with whatever she needs."

"Are they trustworthy?"

"I trust them with my life, and that umbrella covers you and Miss Baptiste. No additional confidentiality clause needed."

"Okay."

"And I wouldn't be comfortable taking care of her in the way that she needs to be taken care of at this juncture in her life. A woman should look after a woman."

"Agreed and understood."

I eased back out of the car and went to Regina. I hugged my wife.

She said, "What everybody is doing is wrong, especially Bobby Holland."

"The business isn't about right or wrong. It's about what sells and what doesn't sell. We're in sales. Not the business of morals. Unless morals sell, then we sell morals."

I released her to Driver and climbed back inside her second favorite car.

Her first favorite car was still the Ford EXP that she had driven from Montana.

It was time to attempt to unravel mistakes that were impossible to unravel.

That car was long gone, in her past. Like I hoped that all of this would be one day.

I thought about Mr. Holder and Vera-Anne. He wanted redemption.

I imagined that he was reunited with his daughter, laughing and smiling, while Vera-Anne was crying and packing, her children crying as well. Varg Veum had a simpler life.

It had become a painful existence, but it was pain of the normal, bearable kind.

But I let those thoughts go away. Bobby Holland owned my mind right now.

When I drove away, it seemed like every eye in the complex was on me. Music stopped bumping, televisions turned off, conversations ended, and people stood in their windows. I passed by Mrs. Patrice Evans and her husband. They were outside arguing. They saw me and stopped. Both stared at me like I was the grand marshal in the Thanksgiving Day parade.

Her husband's eyes were on the car. Patrice's eyes were on me, her mouth wide open.

I didn't know Mrs. Patrice Evans. My name was James Thicke and we'd never met.

By the time I took to the 605, I was being followed. It was an older gray car. I didn't know if it had anything to do with Steve Martin. If felt like a setup. I maintained the speed limit and let drivers zoom around me. The gray car stayed ten car lengths behind me. At least two people were inside. They followed me down the 105 to the 405 and into the streets of Marina del Rey.

CHAPTER 25

A naked man ran down Abbot Kinney,
streaked down the center of the two-lane
strip that was filled with high-end shops and
overpriced condos. He wore headphones
and New Balance shoes, his pace an enviable six-minute mile. Nobody cared. As long
as he didn't slow traffic, no one would give
a damn. It was Venice, the land of the
grunge, home of the strange, where the well-
to-do rubbed shoulders with vagrants, their
wardrobes pretty much the same, a good
place to start a sociological study, a better
place to end it.

I found street parking and slowly got out
of my car, but not unnoticed because the
Bentley stood out like a black tuxedo at a
ragged jeans party. People would look, but
not many would look twice. This was the
Maserati, Porsche, Lamborghini zone.
There were Honda Civics, various Nissans,
Ford, Chryslers, and Jeeps and cars that

should be at Pick-A-Part too.

I was being followed. Just as they had followed Regina Baptiste to find me, they were still following me. Plain car, gray, four door, ten years old. I had bigger issues to deal with.

I fed the meter then stood next to my car with the baseball bat at my side.

There were no paparazzi. Not yet. But I had a half-block walk to get to my destination.

Down here what was strange was a man with a post-fight face dressed in jeans and loafers and a baseball bat at his side, but the crude T-shirt that I wore helped me fit in with the rumpled men in Way Fair glasses, flannel shirts, flip-flops, unshaven faces, and disheveled dos.

Carrying a bat was too obvious. And if whoever was in the gray car was equipped the way Bizarro Bergs had been equipped, it made no sense to carry a Louisville Slugger into a gunfight. I left the bat on the passenger seat and picked up the messenger bag Bizarro Bergs had left behind. That bag would send them a message. At least I hoped that it would, as I hoofed through a section where men and women alike took pride in looking homeless, maybe to keep the destitute from petitioning them for tax-free handouts. Within three minutes, I was at the corner of California Avenue and Abbot Kinney Boulevard. Abbot's Habit was a local dive, a coffee shop that boasted of having the best sandwiches in town. I loved their muffins. The scent from coffees, teas, bagels, and subs on rosemary bread lit up the small space, a space of concrete floors, exposed fixtures and white ceiling fans that didn't cost a lot. Wooden tables. Minimalist. I came down here often. It was strange that Steve Martin wanted to meet here. Steve Martin knew me. And more than as being Regina Baptiste's husband.

Whoever was following me didn't leave their car. They knew I'd be back. The Bentley was insurance that I'd return at some point. The hour limit on the parking meters gave them an approximate waiting time. They'd been after me for days. Another hour wouldn't matter.

I took a breath, opened and closed my dank hands. Dozens were seated outside, many with their mutts and pedigreed dogs on a leash, a few with kids that needed the same restraints.

No paparazzi.

I adjusted the Tumi messenger bag on my shoulder.

This haunt was one of my favorite places.

It was one of my wife's favorites too.

I stepped inside, waited for someone to approach me. No one did. There was a long line at the deli, a line that went out the door. There were about twenty four-seat tables throughout the bare-bones space, all taken. Soulful music was on, but not a soulful person was in sight. I looked at my watch. Five minutes left. Most of the people in the room worked in the business in some way, the number of scripts and sides that were on the sturdy tables a dead giveaway.

A woman was seated at the last wooden table before the bathrooms. There was a book on the table. Steve Martin's *An Object of Beauty.* The dark makeup, dark lipstick, dark tattoos, a half dozen body piercings that I could see, the overall, rebellious, gothic appearance made her look like she had been transported from a post-apocalyptic world, one beset by cannibals and hunger, a place where the sun no longer shined and darkness and freezing cold were a man's blanket. She wore dark jeans and a suit coat over a trendy tank top that said DON'T EVER TAKE SERIOUSLY ANYTHING A WOMAN TELLS YOU RIGHT BEFORE OR DURING HER PERIOD.

I stopped in front of her. First she looked up, then she closed her book.

She said, "Nice to see you again, Mister Thicke."

I nodded, but my mind was processing the word *again*.

She said, "Your face . . ."

"It will heal. At least I think it will. If not, I'll have to get a new passport photo."

"Looks like you got hit by a truck."

"And the other guy looks like he was run over by a six-engine train."

"Johnny Bergs?"

"One of his representatives."

I looked around, didn't see any more of the Bergs brothers, saw that gray car still parked down Abbot Kinney, and I groaned out some pain that I didn't realize I owned as I took to the straight back wooden seat. Two tables over was a woman writing notes on yellow Post-its. Standing in line at the deli was an older man with a much younger woman. Beautiful older women were here too. As soon as I sat down, I set my phone down on the table close to me.

She said, "No cameras."

"None here."

"I mean, no cell phones."

"In case my wife or my associate need to reach me."

"Could you power it down and put it inside your pocket?"

"Why?"

"Trust issues."

"I trust people better when I have my phone at my side."

"They make me nervous. Turn it off. Or I'll walk."

I did what she said. Outside, a woman in jean shorts and a purple L.A. Lakers hoodie over her pink bikini top went speeding by on Rollerblades, followed by a messenger speeding by on a bicycle, followed by a jogger who actually wore clothing. The line at the deli remained long.

I asked, "What's your name?"

She smiled. Her look told me that I should know. Mine told her that I didn't.

I said, "I know you. You look familiar."

"This is how I dress, express myself, after work. You've only seen me at work."

I nodded. There were a million jobs in the city. I had no idea which job was hers.

She smiled like she was disappointed. "You came alone, Mister Thicke."

For a moment, in that instant, I was still Varg. Or wanted to be. Varg's reality wasn't pleasant, not at the moment, but it wasn't as traumatic and taxing as this. I blinked it away.

I said, "I did."

"You passed by in the Bentley. You usually

drive one of the other cars."

I nodded and tried not to look uncomfortable. "I do. Usually."

"The Mercedes."

"Yeah. The Maybach."

"The guy who usually drives you around?"

"He's not here. That's who I was leaving my phone on for."

She took a breath and said, "Best served cold, is what he said. Best served cold."

"He who?"

"On set. The director said that that night it all happened."

"Alan Smithee."

"Not Alan Smithee."

"Who?"

"Bobby Holland."

"He was there."

"He was there. He was always dropping by the set."

"Was he taking directing lessons from Alan Smithee?"

"To see Miss Baptiste."

"They were seeing each other?"

"More like he was always after her."

"How did she respond?"

"I could tell she wanted to call security. But she wasn't going to let him intimidate her."

"How did he get on the set that day?"

"Friends with Alan Smithee. Friends with Bergs. Could've bribed somebody."

"You said you saw everything that happened."

"I saw what happened. I can show it to you. When I'm comfortable with you. I've been tossing and turning since this happened, not really knowing what to do with what I have."

"You were a fly on the wall somehow."

"I was."

"And you're telling me that no one saw you."

"I was as invisible as a black man in a film about World War Two."

"Black man during World War Two."

"Heard this black guy on set say that one day."

"Where were you?"

"I was sitting next to all of them."

I looked at her severe gothness. "Why didn't they notice you?"

"Because I'm nobody important."

"And you were sitting next to everyone who was important?"

"Important people only notice more important people."

"Welcome to Los Angeles."

"And I taped their entire evening. Well, most of it."

372

"How did you manage that?"

"I use my cellular. I pretend that I'm on the phone, hold it up to my ear, only the video is going. They see the side of my head and think that I am chatting, but I'm videotaping everything."

"Pretty slick."

"Not really. But people do that all the time, then post on YouTube. Half of the guys walking down Venice Beach with their phone up to their heads are getting T&A shots and videos on their phones. Everyone who has a phone has a video camera and that makes me nervous."

"That's why you wanted my phone off."

"And if you had had a pen in your pocket, I would've had you remove that too. They sell pens that record now. Pen camera, button cameras, and keychain cameras. Everyone has a video on his or her phones. People are recording people in their most personal moments."

"Bad experience?"

She nodded. "I've already had a bad experience with a guy, which I will not get into."

I let that topic drop and said, "Steve Martin. *Object of Beauty.*"

"That's my favorite book at the moment. Years ago it was *Shopgirl.* I connected with that character. The one taken for granted, struggling, overworked, overlooked. And I was dating an older guy at the time. When I finished reading the book, I left him. It was inevitable."

"I'll have to pick up a copy of each before I beat Johnny Bergs's ass again and go to jail."

"She doesn't deserve what has happened to her. She's Regina Baptiste and they're treating her as if she's nothing more than a hooker who just got off the Greyhound bus at Union."

"They treat hookers at Union better."

"She was better with you. I've watched her. She was good, but when she connected with you, she became great. I saw the exponential change. When she was with Bobby Holland, she couldn't take a photo without him trying to get in the shot. And he wanted his name first. Bobby Holland and Regina Baptiste. You never stole her limelight. You never tried to steal her press. You stood in the back and smiled. That was awesome. When a woman has the right man, the right influences in her life, she goes from good to great. When she did *SNL,* her show was as popular as when Steve Martin hosted. She was funny and she killed in every skit."

"Steve Martin."

"I'm his number one fan."

"Who are you?"

"You don't remember me, do you?"

"No. I don't."

"I'm the nobody who hears everything because when you're a nobody people talk in front of you as if you've never been born. They send me for drugs and if I get busted, not only will no one come to help me, but I will lose my job. I'm the flunky. I lose my job if I don't score coke and I lose my job if I refuse to go. Whatever one refuses to do, someone else will do with a smile."

"Trapped."

"Like she was. He was her pimp, if you ask me."

"Who?"

"Bobby Holland. When she was with him, he was more like her pimp. He kept that birdie in a cage. You set her free. The world owes you a debt of gratitude for that. She was only an actress before you. After you, she was international. And she deserved it. She's talented."

"I bought enough publicity. Helped her make better choices. Pulled a few strings. But she did all the heavy lifting. She was the one giving her body and soul to the business."

"What did you get in return?"

"I had the privilege of seeing her happy."

"Well, that's corny."

"Matches my attire."

"What did you ask her for in return?"

"She made me breakfast every now and then."

"You're demanding."

"Try to be."

"You're a regular Hitler."

"I made her boil eggs and make toast. Three eggs and two pieces of toast."

"A real monster. Making her boil three eggs. Shame on you."

"And toast. Don't forget the toast."

"In the oven or in a toaster?"

"I let her use the toaster from time to time. I like my toast from the oven."

She said, "You didn't really ask her for anything."

"Well, it was Regina Baptiste singing, dancing, and making me breakfast."

"Priceless."

"I did the same for her, but in your eyes, it wouldn't have the same weight."

"You did it all for her."

"I did."

"Why?"

"Not because she's Regina Baptiste. We're . . . we were a team."

She smiled as if that was what she wanted to hear.

She said, "I love your wife. And I care about her deeply."

"Is this the part where you tell me that you're lesbian lovers."

"Not even. I'm straight, but she could make me embrace the rainbow."

"You sound like you're her number-one fan."

"More important than that. I'm her number-one employee."

I nodded. "You're Regina Baptiste's assistant."

"Ninety percent of the interviews that she does, she never sees. But I have watched them all. I sit in her office and watch them all. Most of them she no longer remembers doing; most things she no longer remembers saying. It's amazing to me. Whenever she interviews, she's different, super fun, super funny, very entertaining, very serious when need be, and her word choice, if she's on BBC or CBS or PBS, fits the comedic nature or seriousness of the broadcast or interviews, always on point. That Montana girl is smart."

I nodded in agreement. My mind was on the gray car waiting up the block.

"When she works, it's amazing to see the

actress inside her take over. When she interviews, not when she first started, but later, a few years later, after having done so many press junkets and chat shows and print interviews, autopilot kicks in."

"So you've been on her team for a long time."

"I know her and I can tell when she is on autopilot. I'd be bored too. Same stupid questions. Same answers. You already know everything and there is nothing new to talk about. But she collected and filed as many of those interview moments as she could on DVD. She said she wanted everything for her records. For her memoirs. For her unborn children."

She was to Regina what Driver was to me. She knew things about my wife that I would never know; she knew things that my wife would never share because no one shared all.

She said, "She can't know that we met. She can't ever know that . . . that . . ."

"That you record her private moments with your phone."

"I record and it's for me. It's just for me. I mean she's Regina Baptiste."

Again I thought about Driver and whispered, "Occam's razor."

"What was that?"

"You sent messages to Driver. You got his number from Regina's contact sheet."

"I was trying to find you. But I was scared to say who I was. I didn't want to lose my job. I break the confidentiality clause, I can get sued for everything that I own plus rights to *my* unborn children. Actually, I was worried about you for a minute. After that . . . film was online, after it was online, I was hoping you didn't go out and kill Bergs. That would have devastated Miss Baptiste."

I looked at her. "You dress plain when you're at work, not this . . . dynamic."

"I dress dull and girly. There is a dress code. Miss Baptiste has a dress code for her employees. Skirts or slacks and low heels. If we wear jeans they can't be ripped or faded and heels are a must with jeans. I wear long sleeves all the time so my tats don't show. Wear an acceptable shade of mascara and lipstick. I have to look a certain way at work. Basically, I have to look professional. Which to me is just plain boring. But she's nice and pays well."

"So I've met you before. But you didn't look like this. Am I correct?"

She nodded. "You met me the night she spent the night at your home. When she was still living with Bobby Holland. I brought her things to wear. I brought her her laundry. And other things. A woman needs things when she's away from home. While she was with you, while she was so happy with you, I covered for her by texting Bobby Holland and pretending that I was her. My job is to assist, and that was what I did. While she swam in your pool, I went by Bobby Holland's and walked his dogs. I called and rescheduled all of her meetings. She put the world on hold. I picked up what needed to be picked up. That week I was in and out of your home. Still am. But mostly I work out of her production company. I'm at your estate a lot. The guards, the gardeners, the maids, the mailman, the pool boy, the FedEx man, the ants, the bougainvillea, the fir, the palm trees, they all know me. They all see me. Especially the bougainvillea. You're always out in that remote part of the property where you write. I could hear you out there. That typewriter that you use clicks and clacks like you're back in the sixties. You're a serious typist."

The woman facing me probably knew Regina's social security number and the password to all of her accounts. She might've known mine as well. Not much surprised me, not even the gray car that had followed me here from The Apartments in Downey, but this did. I let a moment pass, a moment of guilt, a moment of preoccupied and busy rich-man's guilt, before I faced the woman who knew all about me and my life, the woman who had been a fly on my wall as well, and then I took a slow, anxious breath and asked, "So, Steve, what do you have for me?"

She took out her iPhone and slid it across the table to me.

She said, "My name is Alice Ayres."

"Alice Ayres."

"Alice Ayres from Toledo. Before that Detroit. But mainly from Toledo."

"You're lying. You're Turkish."

She smiled. "I was born in Gaziantep. My name is Asiye Fahrunissa Karaca, but after 9/11, I started using the name Alice Ayres. I'm a screenwriter too, but not nearly on your level. Screenwriter, playwright, and poet. I plan to write a novel one day soon too. I'm going to write about the horrors of Hollywood. Or maybe it will be a play. Not sure at this point."

I said, "Alice Ayres. I don't mean to rush, but I have another urgent meeting."

She nodded. "What I have on this phone is worth millions to keep the world from seeing."

When she said that, I swallowed. I looked

381

at her and said, "Millions."

"I'm not a good judge of these things. But you can decide."

She slid me earphones and started up the video. As soon as she did, what I saw was Regina Baptiste. She had on ripped jeans and a wrinkled T-shirt, red with black lettering. DON'T JUDGE ME. She was with Bobby Holland. She was with her old lover. The man she had lived with for three years. He had on jeans and a collared shirt, black sports coat, sunglasses, his hair long and blond, his eyes startling blue. And they were alone inside a trailer. The trailer was from Luxury Fifth Wheel, one that was famous for comfort and size, and was like a two-bedroom apartment of soft leather and shining wood. Wooden cabinets. Dinettes. Side-by-side refrigerator. Satellite television. Living room with two sofas. Bedrooms with king-size beds.

There was a familiarity between them. An uncomfortable familiarity. I saw the familiarity that had been between old lovers, people who knew each other beyond the intimacy of sex. They knew each other's likes and dislikes, foods, favorite songs. She remembered how he felt inside of her and he remembered what it was like to be inside her. The longing in his eyes was unmatched by the longing of any man for any woman on this planet. It had power. It wasn't blatant, but I was a man who walked among men and I recognized the truths that men tried to conceal. I knew our ways, our techniques for masking sadness, madness, outrage, and pain.

"Relax, Regina. You're stiff."

"Won't argue that point."

"Regina, you need to do what you used to do."

"Which is what exactly, Bobby?"

Watching them, I was living on tenterhooks, bent nails inside my skin, stretching.

Behind me, as I was pulled into the video, as I stayed beyond my hour on the meter and received a forty dollar ticket from an ambitious meter maid, a man in jeans and a black jacket, black baseball cap, and Ray-Bans came inside Abbot's Habit, entered through the door at California Avenue, moved by the deli, looked around, turned left at the end of the deli, saw me seated with Alice Ayres, my back to him as I watched the video, then he took steps backward and left the place that made the best sandwiches in town, unseen by my distracted and angered eyes.

CHAPTER 26

"Johnny Bergs is fine, but who wants to sleep with a man that can't beat Greg Brady's ass? Could you see that in a prison scene?"

The audience roared with laughter.

"And once again, if Johnny bitch . . . I mean Johnny Bergs . . . has an issue with the shit I'm saying, he can bring his bitch ass to the comedy club. Every show I do I am leaving a ticket for his bitch ass at will-call. Now let's move on to other shit . . . like these pilots at Southwest . . . did you hear that rant? I thought that I said some foul shit. Talk about some hard-core gay bashing. I guess if this comedy thing doesn't work out for Tracy Morgan, he can change careers and apply to be a pilot there. Does Johnny Bergs fly Southwest? Has anybody even seen that motherfucker since he got his ass kicked? That motherfucker James Thicke needs his own fan page for doing that shit. That mother-fucker went cowboy on Bergs. Shit, I bet Re-

gina Baptiste got fucked that night. Bergs got fucked up and Baptiste got fucked by a damn caveman."

She acted out a caveman sexing a beauty queen. When she imitated the troglodyte having a barbaric orgasm, once again the audience applauded and roared with laughter.

"Then that Neanderthal James Thicke looked at Bergs. You're next, bitch. Put that Vaseline down and take it like a man. Oh, stop crying. Take it from me the way Regina Baptiste took it from you. Fair is fair, bitch; fair is fair."

Outrageous laughter.

CHAPTER 27

For the second time I played the video on the iPhone that I'd procured from Alice Ayres. The trailer from Luxury Fifth Wheel came on the screen. Regina Baptiste. Johnny Bergs. Satellite television on in the background. Regina on one plush sofa. Holland on the other, legs crossed, hands on knees. Johnny Handsome's trailer. Regina's trailer would be the same. Equal billing, equal trailers, names in alphabetical order over the credits, Baptiste before Bergs.

Alice Ayres was in a cushy chair that was facing the wall, her phone facing the room, facing dead-on two sofas that were at angles, almost in the shape of a V, her position perfect.

Regina and Bobby still looked like a couple. That familiarity burned my eyes.

"Relax, Regina. You're stiff."

"Won't argue that point."

He looked concerned. Truly concerned.

He wanted to fix what was wrong. But he also looked like an owner who had found his favorite rebellious bitch that had run away.

"Regina, you need to do what you used to do."

"Which is what exactly, Bobby?"

There was a pause. A knowing look washed across her face.

"What you used to do, Regina."

"Which is what, Bobby Holland? What is that?"

"Improvisational tricks. Trust exercises."

With that answer, she took a deep breath. "I'm doing fine."

"You're horrible. And you know you're horrible. Talking to you as a director."

Regina Baptiste smiled. He had hit her Achilles' heel and she smiled.

I smiled too. Like I was a cheerleader, I smiled at that small victory. The girl from Montana was a Los Angeles girl now, a transplant that had been hardened by the business. We all were in some way. We were in a racist, bigoted, sexist business where racism, bigotry, and sexism seldom created a lawsuit. Every time someone offended you, each time a director or an actor or newspaper tried to cut you down, you couldn't tuck your tail and run away. You met all of the bullies head-on. You took the challenge, each meeting, each audition your personal *High Noon.* She was in a showdown with Bobby Holland.

She looked across the trailer at him then asked, "Suggestions? As a director?"

"Stop being married in your mind. Johnny touches you and you become frigid. You're not connecting to the character. Tickle his prostate and suck him until he comes."

"Cute."

Bobby Holland moved to her sofa. "Sense memory always helps."

She smiled. "I have sense memory of wearing a strap-on to please a Norwegian man."

Bobby Holland shifted. Her blow had stung. Her jab had been quick and swift.

He said, "I'm just saying to loosen up and let go and touch him like he's your lover."

"Well, this scene is not in the script. That's the problem."

"Use sense memory. Remember how we used to be. Imagine us."

"Imagining you and being with Johnny, I'd laugh until I puked."

She did laugh. In his face, amused by her own insult, she laughed.

Bobby Holland smiled the smile of deep hate. He put his hand inside his pocket for a moment, just a moment, as if checking to make sure something valuable was still there.

It was. He nodded to himself, then once again looked toward Regina.

"Improvise, Regina. Go off book and let the camera capture honesty."

"Alan Smithee and his script changes. What James wrote was perfect."

"If it was perfect, there would be no need for changes."

"It's perfect, Bobby. End of story."

"He's too arrogant to see his own faults. And you're equally as blind."

"Why must every director have to put in his two cents and rewrite what is written?"

"The same reason every actor or actress shows up and wants to change what is written to fit his ego. You've never once changed a character's lines? You've never gone against a director and thought that you had a better vision? You've never once modified a character written by someone else and said that your character wouldn't say or do something that was written? You never once felt superior to the creators? You've never wanted to change one single action, an action that you thought, even though great for the character, was not good for you, personally, as an actress? You've never run across a single word that your ego refused to say?"

"You know the answer to that."

"I know I know the answer. For years, I entertained all of your complaints."

"Your point?"

"Actors want to show up and tell the writer what the character he created would do, as if the writer now is incompetent and they can see inside the mind of a character that someone else created. That's as ludicrous as explaining man to the god that created him. That's the director's job. To step in and raise the mediocre scripts up and make them worth watching on film."

"Why are you here, Bobby?"

The look in his eyes, it was a mixture of anger and sadness, longing and need. For a moment he opened and closed his mouth, no words coming out, but what he wanted very obvious. He wanted Regina Baptiste. He wanted to ask her to make love to him again. He wanted her to open her legs for him and give him bragging rights, if not closure.

Bobby Holland looked confident, confidence a mask that we all wore. Winners wore confidence. So did the ones who waited tables. Here the homeless were confident.

He swallowed and said, "Relax, Regina.

You're amongst friends."

"No."

"Really."

Regina smirked, her eyes taunting. "I heard they went with someone else on the Bruce Willis film. You were attached, but they have cut you lose for some reason. You were in the running for directing *Last Stand* and *The Tomb,* and I guess something didn't work out there either."

"I was going to direct Schwarzenegger in his comeback film."

"What happened?"

"There was a conflict."

"You were fired."

"There was a conflict."

"Why are you here on the set? Applying for a position as best boy?"

"So now, as I try to help you, after all I have been to you and done for you, you insult me."

"Why are you on set? You have absolutely nothing to do with this project."

"Business with Alan Smithee. And I needed to talk to Johnny Bergs. I need to talk him into coming on board a project. I'm not here stalking you, if that's what you're implying."

"You want Johnny Bergs to work with you again. Good luck with that one."

"Maybe you can put in a good word for me. For old times."

"Look, that's between you and Johnny. I have my own issues and I'm trying to remain focused. Right now I am frustrated. Shit. I don't know what to do to make this scene work."

Then her cellular rang. She answered with a smile. She was talking to me. She had lowered her voice and smiled and told me that everything was fine. Blew me a kiss. Hung up.

She said nothing for a moment. She looked troubled. She had lied.

She was afraid. Her mask of confidence shifted on her face; then it fell.

Bobby Holland was angered.

She exploded, "What will it take to knock out this fucking scene?"

When her scream died he said, "Guts."

She looked at him as if he had just appeared. "What about guts."

"Where are your guts, Regina?"

"I have guts."

"Not any more. Not any more. You used to have guts. Now you're resting on the laurels of work gone by. You haven't done anything brilliant in a very long time. No guts, Regina."

"I have guts. Don't ever challenge my

work ethic. You know that I'm dedicated."

"You don't have the guts to give Hollywood want it wants. You're a hack. You're not committed to your craft. You married James Thicke, moved into a life of luxury, and went soft. Where is your daring? Now in every role you're the same character, only with a different hairstyle. You're walking through the parts in different clothing. You're not acting."

"I am acting."

"You're no longer becoming the character. You're just being you and reading what's on the page like you're a newscaster. Everyone arrives in L.A. hungry. Willing to do what they have to do to make it in Hollywood. But the women. What happens to most of the women?"

"Stop, Bobby."

"They fall in love, get married, or worse, have babies, and when babies come, professional laziness sets in. They lose that edge, soften up, and put their hair in ponytails so they can go play soccer mom. Cinderella fantasies do them in every time."

"That's what happened to your first wife."

"And I'm watching it happen to you."

"I've had enough, Bobby."

"Someone has to say it to you. A woman gets married and then there are certain roles she is willing to do, only certain parts she will play because now a man is in the way of her success, and now she will only go so far. The single, the young, they come in like wolves and soon actresses like you are losing your edge and playing their moms on the Disney Channel. And when she joins the mommy club, I mean in real life, it's off to the daytime chatty women's issues gossip talk shows to chat about breast-feeding and losing ten pounds and makeovers."

"Nothing wrong with any of that."

"Please. All of that hard work to end up sitting on a couch with people who haven't worked in two decades. Is that what you came here from Livingston to do? Sit on a sofa and talk about breasts, weight, and babies? I watched my ex-wife do that. As if that clichéd accomplishment was her manifest destiny. Any girl that's bleeding can have a baby."

"Any man with good sperm can make one. Your point?"

"There is nothing special about having a baby. They're all over. Hell, they have extra babies all over the world that nobody wants. That's why it's so easy to swoop into a third-world country, get a bucket of KFC and a darkie on the side, and come right back to the U.S. The world needs to be neutered because there are regrets crawling everywhere."

He stopped and let his words seep into her pores.

Regina wiped her eyes with the back of her hands.

He saw that victory and said, "When you were with me, you still had that edge. I made sure you kept that edge. You look good. You look better than ever, but the truth is that James Thicke has made you soft. Love has become an anchor and you can no longer rise."

The first tear broke free, ran down her face, rolled around her chin, went down her neck.

He said, "You flop this and you're done."

She licked her lips, wiped her eyes, and searched for a tissue.

He said, "Your last movie came in at number three and slid out of the box office and went to DVD and iTunes in record time. You're doing an imitation of an ambitious actress who used to be Regina Baptiste. You're becoming a caricature of Regina Baptiste. A lookalike."

Her face reddened and she swallowed.

Bobby Holland said, "I still love you."

"What was that?"

"I still love you. I need you to know that.

I need you back in my life."

"If you had loved me from the start, Bobby, then maybe things would have worked for us. You loved me after I was gone. It was too late. All you can do now is keep loving me from behind closed doors. Keep staring at photos and imagining what could have been. Keep fantasizing and masturbating. Whatever you do, that's beyond my control. I'll never do the same. I'm married, Bobby. I'm married to the best man in the world. Even if I never reach number one at the box office again, even if I never reach number three or five or seven, I'm number one is his heart and he is number one in mine. I know, that sounds corny. But being in love is corny. I'm from Montana. I was raised on corny. And hopefully I'll be corny until the day I die."

"If you no longer care about being number one, if you're willing to dump the movie for the guy and are no longer willing to sacrifice the guy in the name of the film, you're done."

She rocked and sucked her bottom lip as she clapped her hands nervously.

He said, "You might as well get back in your car and drive back to Montana. You're on the downside. Go ahead and step down and let a better lioness take over the watering hole."

Then, as Regina Baptiste sat next to him and cried, he took out a package and an American Express card, made a line of white powder on the table, took a hit, then motioned to her.

He said, "Get your edge back."

He put down four white lines.

He whispered, "Let go and be Sasha. Every woman has a Sasha inside of her. It's like in the movie. There is a battle going on inside of you. A battle between the black and white swans inside of you. The black swan is what got you here. Let the black swan win and you win."

Regina Baptiste stared at the cocaine for an endless moment.

He said, "The picture is over budget. This day is already into the twelfth hour. Everyone out there is depending on you. Everyone is angry and tired. You're letting them all down."

She closed her eyes and hummed and rocked and shook her head, all in a gentle way.

He said, "This will get you over your hump."

Tears fell. She looked exhausted, exhausted from dieting, from lack of sleep for the last six weeks that she had been working. Lines formed across her forehead. She cringed, and I knew that her headache was strong. More tears came. She massaged her temples. She rocked. Had it under control. Then more tears came in a torrent. She wiped her eyes.

She stared at the white lines.

Shivering.

And as she cried, she leaned forward, closed her eyes, and inhaled her old friend.

Bobby Holland smiled. "Best served cold, Regina. Best served cold."

She didn't hear him. The high was taking over. The cocaine was in her blood.

That was when Johnny Handsome walked in, as if on cue, as if he had been complicit in this moment, as if he had left his trailer in order for Bobby Holland to work his magic.

All-American Johnny Bergs had a stunning woman on his arms. Brunette eyebrows and blond hair parted down the center, black leather pants, high heels, and a form-fitting golden top. The thermostats on her chest told that it was a chilly night. She looked like a model. Johnny Handsome and his lady paused, mouths opened in shock. Regina was busted with the cocaine. She looked up at Holland, coke on her nose, too late to turn back now.

Bobby Holland smiled. "Bergs. This will help you loosen up on set. And I bought you some ecstasy too. We know how you like that. How are things going with you, Bergs?"

Johnny Bergs set free a big smile. "Alan Smithee just chewed me a new asshole. I was coming back to figure out how to work off some stress before we went back on set."

"Then you need this. You need this as much, if not more, than Regina does."

Johnny Bergs joined in. A sucker for peer pressure, the kind that made a man live fast and die young. Bobby Holland handed him the extra goodies. Johnny Handsome took his drink and dropped in a pill. I assume that it was E. His female friend followed suit. She was excited, bubbly, smiling the widest smile in history, high on being around celebrities. She had crossed the velvet rope into the land of excess.

The new girl said, "You're Regina Baptiste."

Regina ignored her, then stood up and went to the bathroom.

The girl said, "We are the same size. Me and Regina Baptiste. I read that in a magazine. From the neck down, we could be sisters. I am much prettier."

Bobby Holland asked, "Who is your lovely

female friend, Bergs?"

"Her name is Piroska Anastazia Dorika Vass Torma."

She said, "You said that almost perfectly, Johnny."

Bobby Holland heard her accent and smiled. "You're Hungarian."

She smiled. "Ya."

"What brings you to Hollywood?"

"I come here to America to study my English, become a successful movie actress."

"How long have you been here?"

"Two days. I rent a one-bedroom apartment with five others in Hollywood."

"Well, welcome aboard."

"You're not from here."

"I'm Norwegian."

"What is your name?"

"Yngvar Vimar Bakken. But Bobby Holland is the name I use over here."

"Are you too an actor?"

"Director."

"Directors are very good. They are very, very important."

"Every movie has one."

"That is why they are important."

"How old are you?"

"Eighteen."

Bobby Holland smiled. "Where did you meet her, Bergs?"

"She's an extra. Met her an hour ago. Plucked her from the food line at Craft Services."

She corrected him, "It was ten minutes ago."

Johnny Bergs pulled her face to his and shoved his tongue down her throat. He was a man who made twenty million a picture French kissing a woman who made between fifty and a hundred bucks a day. That day was overtime, so she was making a killing, by her standards.

Piroska smiled and asked Johnny Bergs, "Would you like head now?"

"Not right now."

"When do I have to be back to be an extra again?"

"You don't have to be back until I say you have to be back."

They went back to kissing, his hand first freeing a breast, then fondling her.

Regina came back. She sat down, ran her hand over her hair.

Bobby Holland smiled at Regina. He leaned close. She shook her head. Feet away Johnny Bergs was experiencing adoration and acceptance as Bobby Holland treaded in rejection.

He leaned closer to Regina and said, "Since this is where we are. Best served cold, as they say. I have something else to talk to you about. It's a tape of you. Of us. But mostly of you. You're doing lines. We're in Norway. You say some harsh things. Things that could be taken as being racist. You might remember that day. The police had stopped us."

Regina looked at him. I saw fear. She knew what he was talking about.

"You're joking, Bobby."

"I have it."

"You deleted that."

"I kept it. I have more than that."

As Johnny Bergs took his hands and massaged Hungarian breasts, Regina Baptiste stared at Bobby Holland. She swallowed. High. Nervous. Not sure if he was serious or joking.

He did a line, then smiled. "Do another line for good measure."

And the party that led to destruction began.

Bobby Holland. He was the instigator. The brokenhearted puppet master.

He didn't make Johnny Bergs and Regina Baptiste cross that line. He didn't strip down Johnny Bergs and call in a fluffer, then violate my wife. But he tapped into their insecurities, their pride, and gave them both gentle nudges. The man behind the curtain.

The Wizard of Tinseltown. Or just simply the harbinger of the moment before my life went to Hell.

Johnny Handsome looked across the room and did a double take, looked into the camera, at the phone, the fly on the wall as she pretended not to notice what was going on.

He pointed and asked, "Who is that girl?"

Regina Baptiste looked that way, paused, then said, "That's my assistant."

Bobby Holland said, "Where in the world did you come from?"

Alice Ayres said, "Toledo. I came from Toledo, Ohio."

Johnny Handsome looked at her, sat back in shock, blinked over and over, then pointed at her as if she had magically appeared. "When did you get into my trailer?"

"Just walked in."

"I have two gorillas being paid good money to be my security standing outside my door."

"I tossed them a banana and they let me in."

Regina said, "I thought . . . hold on. I thought that you walked in with me and left."

"I did. I left. I went to your trailer. Just came back to check on you."

Regina looked at the door, then at the assistant. "You walked by me and sat over there?"

"Just now. I came in behind Johnny Bergs. All of you were pretty busy."

Regina said, "God. I'm so exhausted right now. I'm sorry. Didn't see you come back."

Johnny Bergs said, "Hold up. You said that you walked in here just now behind me?"

"That's why your security guard didn't stop me. And you were busy getting acquainted with the Hungarian girl. She's very pretty, by the way. Built sort of like Miss Baptiste."

Johnny Bergs laughed. "You're a fucking ninja. I love this chick. She's a fat ninja."

She grumbled, "I'm not fat. I'm a size six. Fucking overrated, arrogant bastard."

Bobby Holland said, "What are you over there doing?"

She heard him; the way her breathing changed told me that.

Bobby Holland repeated, "You, chick with the Steve Martin book in her lap. What are you over there doing? What are you doing here in Johnny Bergs's private trailer?"

She said, "Waiting on Miss Baptiste. My name isn't Steve Mar—"

"What are you doing?"

"Mister Holland, we've met before on

numerous occasions."

"Well, you may have met me, but I've never met you. What are you doing?"

"I'm doing my job, Mister Holland."

"Which is what exactly?"

"My job is to assist Miss Baptiste. I work for Miss Baptiste."

"What are you doing over there on the phone? That doesn't look like work."

"I'm talking to my boyfriend. I need my dog walked. He's my assistant tonight."

"Do that outside. You don't need to be in here. And forget everything you see."

Regina said, "She's blind in her ears and can't hear with her eyes."

Bobby Holland said, "That made no sense."

Regina told her assistant, "Meet me at my trailer in twenty."

"Okay, Miss Baptiste. Will you need anything else before I step out?"

"Here, take my cellular. Send my husband a message in about five minutes."

"What should it say?"

"He's very busy working on his next screenplay."

Bobby Holland said, "*Boy Meets Girl.* Has a director been attached?"

She ignored Bobby and looked at her assistant. "Tell my husband that I was just checking in and I'm stressed, but okay. I have my second wind. His name is James Thicke."

"I know his name, Miss Baptiste. I've met him quite a few times. Nice guy."

"I know you know. I was just saying that in case someone else had forgotten."

Alice stood and walked by them all, the camera phone panning the impromptu party as she made her slow and easy exit, phone still on and recording until she stepped outside of the trailer into a section that looked like bungalows on wheels. She was good with the phone. Damn good. A reason we all had to beware. Still recording, she left that cocaine session, stepped into the light outside of Johnny's trailer. She panted, frantic, speaking to herself in what sounded like Arabic. She didn't stop talking to herself. Her breathing was harsh. She was excited and kept going. She hurried by actors waiting for makeup, by a crew complaining about being on the set this long, people bitching about the attitudes of stars, about Regina, about Johnny, about Alan Smithee, about the pimples on their lucky-to-be-working asses. She passed the other actors' trailers, none as big as the one they had given Johnny Handsome and Regina Baptiste. Wardrobe trailers. Honey wagons.

She walked a short distance, kept her phone up to her ear, like an actress waiting for a director to call cut, recording all she passed, as if she'd give herself away if she put the phone down too fast. Then she jerked when she heard somebody shout.

"Steve Martin. Slow your fat ass down."

"Shit. Bobby Holland is chasing me. I am so busted. Oh shit; oh shit."

She lowered the phone and Bobby Holland's expensive loafers came into frame.

He demanded, "Miss Baptiste said for me to tell you to give me her phone so I can get that asshole James Thicke's phone number. Give me all of his phone numbers right now."

"She didn't tell me —"

"Give me the fucking phone, bitch."

He took Regina's phone from her. While Alice Ayres protested, he stole my numbers.

He said, "One word to her, one word, and I'll make sure you never work in this city again."

Then, with that clichéd threat, he dropped Regina's phone to the pavement and walked away. With her phone, Alice extended her arm and recorded Bobby Holland storming away.

Alice Ayres looked into the phone, tears in her eyes, lips quivering, shaken.

Cursing in Arabic. Then the video recording on the phone abruptly went black.

CHAPTER 28

Bobby Holland's luxurious spread was still
in the valley. The same home he had shared
with Regina Baptiste. He leased at the end
of a cul-de-sac, the street very quiet, at least
three miles in from the closest freeway. The
evil puppet master waited on me outside his
three-thousand-square-foot home, curbside,
with his hands behind his back and a Cuban
cigar on the tip of his lips. I parked four
houses down. Intentionally. When I looked
back, there was no gray car. Bobby Holland
extended his right hand and I did the same.
We shook hands.

He said, "You're in the wife's car."

I nodded.

He asked, "She knows that we're meeting?"

"Only if you told her."

He asked, "What's in the man bag?"

I took the Tumi bag from my shoulder and
allowed him to look inside.

He said, "It's empty."

I let his observations stand and offered no explanation. I carried it so whoever was following me in the gray car would think otherwise. At least I hoped that they would.

Bobby Holland was dressed like he'd just returned from an event. He had on jeans by Simon Spurr. He also wore a very nice watch, the Montblanc Nicolas Rieussec Chronograph Automatic, the version that came in 18k red gold. On his feet were velvet slippers that looked like they were by Wellington Black and a Ralph Lauren wool turtleneck. Head to toe he was impressive, dressed in the casual attire of a formerly rich man who aspired to return to that status.

He tossed the last of his Cuban cigar and we headed toward his ranch-style home.

I glanced back again. The gray car was parking two houses beyond where I had parked. Bobby Holland looked back too. He saw the gray car. He didn't question it.

Holland's furniture was Spanish-style and elephant heavy. His living room had more celebrity photos than the walls at The Dresden. If you walked in and read the press that he had framed as well, you'd think that he was in the same category as DeMille, Stone, Lumet, Kubrick, Eastwood, Cameron, and Spielberg. There were *vestiges* of his native Norway, The Geirangerfjord, The Royal Guard in Oslo, Bryggen Wharf, Lillehammer, Vigeland Park, and the Holmenkollen ski jump, but they paled in comparison to his collection of celebrities at his side. It looked like he owned show business. I took in Hollywood and Norway as I followed. Beige carpet. Pure white walls, expensive paint, very European from what I could see. All the doors off the hallway were closed. There was no music on. No television. The house was quiet and held the sweet stench of lust, gluttony, greed, sloth, wrath, envy, and pride. Outside of those aromas, the only thing that I could smell was the scent of chlorine coming from the pool in the back.

At the end of the hallway facing the pool and a well-landscaped area was his administrative center, a room that had at one time been a master bedroom. It had a wooden ceiling and a modern ceiling fan. There were a lot of things I pretended not to see, including the stack of yellow Post-its; Post-its took me back to being Varg Veum. This wasn't his world. So I focused on the Golden Raspberry Award, a Razzie, the award for cinematic sins. It rested in front of his twenty-seven-inch desktop, a Mac, and was positioned at the corner of his mahogany desk. Other awards were present too, some on his bookshelves and inside glass cases, but the Razzie was by itself. It belonged in the same category as The Golden Turkey and Stella Awards and Bad Sex in Film. I pointed at the Razzie, an award segregated from his other positive achievements, a bastard child at an orphanage waiting on an adoption that would never come.

Bobby Holland said, "Sandra Bullock has one. Halle Berry. Michael Bay. M. Night Shyamalan. Eddie Murphy. Many have accepted their shame. So I accepted mine as well."

"I've never been nominated."

"We all have bad periods."

"Women have bad periods. You made bad films."

Then I gave in and looked at the massive collection that would disturb me.

His office was filled with movie posters and covers from magazines, all the posters in expensive frames, all the magazines laminated. *Elle. Harper's Bazaar. Good Housekeeping. Famous. Vogue. People. Women's Fitness. Marie Claire. Sel. InStyle. Bis. Croissant. Filament. Hennes. Lucire. Shape Magazine. VeckoRevyn. Bitch. Rolling Stone. Sports Illustrated* Swimsuit Edition.

The cover spoof by *Mad Magazine.* All were of Regina Baptiste. Between the movie posters and the laminated magazine covers, there had to be at least one hundred photos, one hundred different outfits, and one hundred versions of the same woman staring at me, enough to give me vertigo. Regina Baptiste in formal gowns, ripped jeans, a karategi, form-fitting workout gear, with her hair down, pulled back or done up like it was in the forties, in futuristic styles, on the beaches in Florida, in Paris, in Russia, in London. And in Norway. A stack of magazines was in the corner. All covers with Regina Baptiste. No matter which way a man turned in this room, Regina Baptiste smiled at him. This was an altar for religious worship. His private conventicle, a place to fantasize and masturbate. There were only photos of Regina Baptiste. No one else existed in this room. He probably had a gallon of Vaseline and tissues inside of his desk drawer. His bedroom ceiling was probably wallpapered with the same images.

Witnessing my discomfort, Bobby Holland smiled, his eyes dark clouds turning gray.

He said, "Have a seat."

There was a black conference chair facing his desk. I made myself uncomfortable on its hard black leather. Bobby Holland took the king's chair behind his mahogany throne. There wasn't a lot to be said, not at this stage in the game, so I cut to the chase.

Right away I said, "If you can't have her, you'll help destroy her."

"I won't destroy what I can profit from. Not at this point in my life."

"You would exploit her like that? With something from years ago?"

"Regina Baptiste has become a religion."

"And all religions are exploited."

"Of course. Religion is about power and money. Which brings me to my agenda. I need financing. I need a big project. This is my moment to come back. That will take money."

I took a breath. "How big of a loan are we talking about?"

"I'd never borrow from you."

"I'm offering a low-interest rate this month. You'd get a free keychain too."

"You'll *give* it to me and you'll do it with a smile."

"Why would I do that, Holland?"

"Because you love her. Like a fool you love her. You love her like a fool."

"I could walk away."

"You won't."

"You're right. I won't. And I won't walk

away from Regina."

"But one day you might go away to write a screenplay and come back and she's in somebody else's bed. She's done that once. Maybe more than once. She left that model she was dating and came to me. That tells you who she is, Thicke. She is loyal only to herself."

"Anything is possible."

"Or she could go away to work six weeks on a film and never come back to you."

"Like I said, anything is possible."

"You're in too deep, Thicke. She has you. Like she had me."

"Sounds like she still has you. From your redundant office décor, looks that way too."

"And that's the only thing that we have in common, Thicke."

"Yeah. The only thing."

"Actually, may I ask for permission to withdraw my last statement?"

"Permission granted."

"She doesn't have me, Thicke. No, this time I have her."

"Seems that way."

He smiled. "I hate you, Thicke."

"Never been too fond of you either, Holland."

"Her publicist liked you better than me."

"Well, all of your headlines began to be

about a child support battle. Women hate men in child support battles. Women hate women who support men in child support battles."

"Women take what is none of their business and pretend as if it's happening to them."

"That's why Rom-Coms sell so many tickets."

"But in my case, women do project and protest trivial things too much."

I said, "I won't call it trivial, but I won't argue with you on that one."

"We're almost friends now."

"We're as close to being friends as the sun is to Uranus."

"Uranus."

"Funny word."

"So funny that I forgot to laugh."

I said, "No way we can kiss and make up?"

"We crossed the Rubicon a long, long time ago, Thicke."

"When was that? When did this war between you and me begin?"

"The morning the paparazzi took her photo leaving your home."

"I thought that our Rubicon was long before that."

"It was."

I said, "You should've sent me a memo."

"I tried. You sued me, then never returned my calls."

"I guess I hurt your feelings. I'll send flowers and a photo of my wife on your birthday."

"Most, if not all of this could have been avoided."

"What's the bill?"

"I should've drowned her in my pool. I should've left her coked up and let her drown."

"A bit dramatic, don't you think?"

"The things I let her to do me. She loved to tickle my prostate and suck me dry. Has she ever done that for you, James? That hurts."

"Bet it does."

"No, I mean the way women take all of your secrets and sashay away smiling, take all of their tricks to other men and pretend those tricks are their own invention."

"What's the bill?"

"When I met her, she was beautiful, but she was a lousy Montanan fuck."

"What's the bill, Holland?"

"From what I saw on the video, she has definitely improved."

"Where are you going with this, Holland?"

"I'm trying to befriend you."

I said, "Enemies closer."

"Enemies closer, bill higher, if you prefer."

"I'd never ask an enemy for a favor. And you'd have to get a promotion to become an enemy. So when you bill me, bill me with that in mind. I'm not here to beg or ask for favors."

He said, "I'm showing you that you're not special. You're just the fool who is next."

"The bill is what's next."

He smiled. "The bill should be enough to make you feel like a fool."

I nodded. "Depends on what you're selling."

He turned his Mac desktop until the screen faced me. It was already set up. He tapped ENTER and QuickTime played. Twenty-seven-inch screen. Video camera set up in a bedroom. My wife. Younger. Cocaine on the table. Laughing. Naked. Talking about the industry. About the people in the industry. Evil things about Hazel Tamana Bijou. About gays. About the Jews who ran the business. The stuff that all of the two-faced people in the business said behind closed doors or when they were in a place where they didn't have to be politically correct. The things no one wanted to hear or see in print. All Regina. Before the level of fame and success that she had now. A frustrated Regina, angry at a bitch named

Hollywood. Holland was there. Invisible. All directors were invisible. Never seen. Always there. Lots of cuts. Cuts that made it sound as if Regina was answering questions. Interviewer unseen. Whatever Bobby Holland had said had been bowdlerized. But the world wouldn't care, not even if she had been reading from a script. I pushed the screen away from me, gently, until it face Holland.

"No wisecracks, James?"

"No wisecracks."

"I'm disappointed."

"The bill?"

"To start off, I want two cars. Two of your delicious cars. I want the next script. I want five million transferred to an account to be specified next week. Regina will sign on to the project. Someone else could rise to the top on your words, but they will not on this script. Not the one that has everyone talking. And I want you to coax Regina into coming on board. If she passes on this one, I will show the public all that I have and make it so she won't be able to get a reality show. She will work through my production company. Only her contract will be different."

"You want enough money to buy an

island, total control and top-shelf talent for free."

"She will be paid."

"You know what her asking price is, right?"

"She'll work scale. Like the nothing she was when she came here."

"You can't leave her alone, can you?"

"I can leave her alone. I just can't escape her. The same way Aniston can't escape Pitt and Jolie. Debbie Reynolds couldn't escape Elizabeth Taylor, not even when Taylor was on her deathbed. If we can't fucking escape them, if we have to endure this ridicule and torture until our deathbeds, if that one relationship defines us, then we must use it to our advantage. No, I can't escape Baptiste. She left me and went to you, but she's never left me."

"You threw her out, packed her up, sent her to me in a U-Haul."

"But no paparazzi. If there had been no paparazzi, it would've been a private matter."

"That was kind of you."

"That whore made me seem like I am less of a man. Wonderful spin on my misery, don't you think? Every direction I turn, I see her face. If I'm on a plane and read a magazine, I see her face. On the side of the road, a bus passes with her face. Every interview that I have done since then, her name has come up. Every interview, the same questions. Not about my work or my children, not about my skills as a gifted and underappreciated director. How did you lose the most beautiful woman on the planet? Anyway. Regina Baptiste and you, James Thicke, even if no one knows who you are, you and your wife are a gold mine right now. *Boy Meets Girl.*"

"My most recent labor of love."

"You took my labor of love. I want yours."

"I could pen you another one."

"No. I want *Boy Meets Girl.* Regina Baptiste, you'll get her to sign on."

"I'm married to her, but I don't own her."

"She loves you. Love is the invisible slavery. Love is a debt. She betrayed you and she owes you and because of that emotional debt, she will do whatever you ask. After what she did with Bergs, after what she did in front of the crew, the guilt she feels, the love and trust she has for a prick like you, and she'll do it just to please you. And she'll be in it with Johnny Bergs."

"That in and of itself will be interesting."

"Oh, it will be. Regina Baptiste. With the director she dumped in a screenplay written by the husband she cheated on starring with the man she cheated with. Can you see it now? Maybe I'll hire her other lovers as extras. That poor slob she left back in Livingston would love to have a five-and-under. Regina surrounded by all the men that she's either fucked or fucked over. But in this case, she's fucked us all. Can you imagine the torrid interviews?"

I nodded.

He said, "Regina Baptiste. I lived for her, James. You destroyed that."

"You fed her cocaine like it was pixie dust."

"The problem was I just didn't feed her enough."

"You're out of control, Holland."

"Quite the opposite. I'm in control. I'm driving and I own the car."

He turned his Mac desktop until it faced me again; the video was in a loop.

I said, "I don't need to see the video again."

He left the monitor facing me, that video playing over and over.

"So, my asking price is pretty low, thinking long-term here. How much money she would stand to make versus how she would lose or never make. She would be blacklisted overnight."

"And you want my money and my cars to

make it go away."

"Ah, your toys look great in photo shoots. Your home and your toys, but you're upside down on your mortgage, so your home has no real value at this point. Oh, they love your estate. They love it because she lives there. And she looked as if she owned the world when she took a photo in front of each of your cars, in different outfits."

"The article was a nice puff piece. Pulled in the shallow and materialistic."

"Loved the way she said that you were the first man she had ever loved. She told me she loved me a million times and all of a sudden you became the first man she loved. Never mind the boyfriend she left back in Livingston. There were other men. She discounted and devalued every man who'd ever come into her life until the moment she betrayed me for you."

"Never knew you felt that way."

"On national television she said that no man had ever been as good to her. She made every other man who had loved her nothing. My kids saw that. Kids that she lived with for three years; kids that she sat at the table with at Thanksgiving and Christmas, she didn't mention. Not one word. I ceased to exist. They ceased to exist. Once my career wasn't as good as hers, I ceased to be of value. She did to me what the studios have done to many. I was dedicated, but no longer profitable, so I was expendable and forgettable and regrettable and laughable. The wedding pictures were magnificent. You looked good standing next to her."

"Okay. Looking around your office, you looked good next to her too."

"But any man looks good standing next to Regina Baptiste. Quasimodo would look like Prince Charming. You, her first love. Her first husband. She made it sound like she was a born-again virgin on her wedding night. The happy wedding pictures were everywhere. Regina Baptiste. The Girl From Livingston. Montana to Hollywood. It's impossible to escape her."

"You can't escape her. She casts a long shadow. A very long shadow."

Bobby Holland asked, "Enjoying the video?"

"Like a 9/11 terrorist enjoyed Gitmo."

"James, I could fuck you in your ass right now. Or have someone else fuck you in your ass while I did a line of coke and sipped champagne and broadcast it live online."

"You do have a noose around my neck at this point."

"You're mine. Like she was mine, now

you're mine too. Success buys access. With her name, once again I will have access to everything."

"What's the cost?"

"I told you."

"Sorry. I was numb. I can hear better now. Repeat it for clarification."

"It will cost you three cars."

"You said two."

"Well, now it's three. I want five million of your money. Better yet, make that five point two five. Penalty for stealing what was mine. I want the rights to *Boy Meets Girl*. I want to own it. I want my name on it as primary writer. You can stay on as co-writer. No. As original story by."

"Déjà vu."

"You sued me. You rounded up the best lawyers in Hollywood and sued me."

"And won."

"You sued for conversion, for copyright infringement, for false designation, for violation of statutory rights, misappropriation, violation of privacy, everything but sodomy."

"I don't think sodomy is illegal in Hollywood. Not sure, but I can double-check for you."

"Yes, I am still crossed about that. We'll reduce you, even though you did the hard work, to being an idea man. I will take credit as the screenwriter. I want Regina Baptiste to sign on as the female lead. And I want Bergs to show up and do whatever it takes to make this a hit."

"I can't control Johnny."

"Oh, but I can."

"How?"

"Thanks to you, I have him."

"What do you have on Bergs?"

"I have a noose around his neck and a vice grip on his balls."

"If you say so."

"Regina Baptiste and Johnny Bergs. I want them seen together at Jamba Juice. And I want Regina laughing like she's a goddess sitting with a goddamn god. I want them seen on vacation together. On a beach with white sand, half naked and frolicking. Better yet, I want them photographed on the nude beach, Hawksbill Bay, in Antigua. I want her topless on Pointe Tarare and Seven Mile Beach. If I want them to fly off to Africa and adopt a baby, they will do that too. And I want them seen with the swingers going into Trapeze down in Fort Lauderdale. But for now, days of photo ops. Lots of talk about this wonderful moment they've shared. That will keep the rumor mill going. They're a gold mine now. Their next movie will open with numbers that rival James

Cameron."

I said, "I'll have my lawyer draw it up."

"No, we'll use mine. And my confidentiality agreement as well."

"Sure. We'll use yours. But my lawyer will have to review it."

"You will sign it as is. But you can use your own pen."

I paused. "Sure."

"Right off the bat, as a sign of good faith, that will cost you three cars."

"You are obsessed with my cars as much as you are obsessed with Regina."

"I want them detailed and delivered within the next forty-eight hours."

"Sure."

"Losing those cars will hurt your pride, won't it?"

"Sure will. But I can only ride in one at a time anyway."

"I want the Maybach. I want the Bentley. I want your favorite and hers. I'll text you the third. I haven't decided. More than likely it will be the brand new Maserati."

"I don't have a brand new Maserati. Mine is two years old."

"Then you'll have to order me a brand new one."

"And the cash?"

"The money will be transferred to an account in Norway within fourteen days."

"Was hoping you'd accept a personal check."

"No paper trail."

Defeated in battle, bested by Bobby Holland, I prepared to stand up.

He commanded, "Sit. I'm not done with you. Not yet."

I nodded at my new master and sat back down, a thin smile across my face.

He said, "I need the truth."

"Sure."

"Thicke, the paparazzi being outside your gates when she left your home after your nine-day fuckfest, the way they dogged her everywhere she went, she blamed that on me."

"I know she did. I blamed that on you too."

"*But I didn't call the paparazzi.* I'm not that low."

I said, "She was your most prized possession. You were a man scorned."

"She was mine. And I loved her too much to shame her."

"In other words, it would've been a bad career move."

Bobby Holland stared at me. "The paparazzi."

"What about them?"

"When she was at your home betraying me, how did they know where she was?"

"Did you have her followed?"

"I should've had her followed, but I didn't. It could've been that guy who drives you around. He looks like he would sell you out. Or it could've been anyone who works on your staff. A cook. A maid. A gardener. The pool boy."

"None of those people called."

"Why are you so sure?"

"All of those people adored her from the start."

"That leaves only one possible answer."

"Which is what, Holland?"

He bared his teeth. "You called the paparazzi."

My breathing smooth, I possessed a face devoid of any readable emotion.

He said, "It wasn't me. It wasn't anyone else, so you say. It had to be you."

With much effort, I smiled. "I made that call. Holland, I called in the paparazzi."

Bobby Holland raised his right hand and showed me his hidden gun.

It was a .45.

The eye of the gun looked directly at me, center mass.

The gun looked angry. But not as enraged as Bobby Holland.

CHAPTER 29

Holland had pulled his hand from underneath his mahogany desk and there was his HK .45. My confession had stung Bobby Holland. In that heated place, where there had been strong hate for me before, now there was extreme hate. Rage and murder danced around in his eyes. He held the gun on me. Pointed it at the center of my face.

I said, "Just remember. Hard to get five million and three cars from a dead man."

He held the gun until his arm started to tremble from either its weight or his frustration, then slapped the gun down on his desk. He picked it back up, walked over to me, and slapped me twice, once for each cheek. He took a breath and shook his head, outraged.

He went back to his king's chair and sat down before he snapped, "Why, Thicke? Why?"

I touched my face. Bottom lip busted,

swollen. Tasted my own blood.

Again he snapped, "Why?"

"I wanted her."

"You called the paparazzi. You did this to me."

"This is life, Bobby Holland. This is the big league. We take what we want."

"You did this to me and my children, Thicke."

I said, "I called the paparazzi, Holland."

He shook his head at me and scowled. *"Why why why why why?"*

I snapped, *"Because I wanted her, you moron."*

"Be careful what you say, Thicke. I could still shoot you."

"You could've shot me when I first came in here."

"You fucked her a few times and lost your mind. You could have had her and sent her back to me and I would have been none the wiser. That's what we do in this town. You broke the rules, Thicke. You could've had your thrill and moved on to a hundred women who look better than Regina Baptiste. You had your notch in your bedpost and you could've moved on."

"I wanted her for more than sex. I wanted her for more than photo ops at poolside with exotic kids and cute dogs. I wanted her to live with me behind my gates."

"Were you lonely?"

"Yes, I was lonely. I was lonely and I wanted her to keep me from being lonely. But most of all, I wanted her to be happy. I wanted her off drugs. I wanted to force her hand. You didn't see her there. You didn't see her with me at my estate those nine days."

"Everyone is happy at Disneyland, Thicke. The crippled, the terminally ill, everyone."

"You didn't see how happy she was when she was away from you. Letting her go back to a scum like you, no matter if she still loved you, would've been wrong. If I had let her go back to you, she'd be dead by now, career dead at best, physically dead at worst."

The shouting ended and once again a hostile silence settled between us.

Holland looked at his gun. Hands trembling, he picked it up and moved it to the side.

He asked, "She knows that you betrayed her confidence with one phone call?"

I shook my head. "She still blames you. And I fucking like it that way."

He said, "You were the bad guy in all of this, Thicke."

"In your story, maybe. Not in mine."

"You made the first domino fall, Thicke."

"I'll never be the bad guy in my own life."

"That's why they have the word *denial* in the dictionary. Look it up. Your picture is right there, you self-centered, backstabbing, narcissistic, piece of shit prick."

"You won't shoot me, Holland."

"Why so sure?"

"Beige carpet. No plastic put down. Besides, you have no idea who knows I'm here."

"You said that no one knew."

"I said that I didn't tell my wife."

"Who knows you're here?"

"I have friends with me. They're parked in a gray car, two houses behind mine."

"The car that pulled up behind you."

"They're with me."

"Who are they?"

"Take your gun. Go see. They just might have guns too."

I sat in silence, longing for the life that I had created in Downey.

I said, "May I leave your wonderful museum now?"

"No. School is still in. Still much to learn."

"Whatever you say, Holland. Whatever you say."

"I'm surprised that you haven't thrown a fit and made threats, Thicke."

"If I jumped and screamed, kicked walls and ripped off my shirt, threw chairs through windows, with the cards that you're holding, you'd only demand more scripts, money, and cars."

"You know me so well."

I rubbed my eyes and dragged my hands down my cheeks. My face was still numb from his blows. The taste of my own blood remained strong inside my mouth.

"I outmaneuvered you."

"Knowing what I know now, I never would've gone after Johnny Bergs. I would've come after you, Holland. I would've driven up here to pay you a visit on that rainy night."

"You're feeling stupid, aren't you, Thicke?"

"Being stupid hurts a man like me. I'm disappointed in the way I acted."

"Johnny Bergs got the bad end of the deal."

"He sure did. Outside of getting to fuck my wife, he sure did."

Bobby Holland lit a Cuban cigar, puffed, leaned back in his chair.

I let a second pass before I said, "Question?"

"Go ahead, Thicke?"

"Why now? You've had that tape of her

since before she left you."

"I kicked her out."

"I stand corrected."

"I packed her belongings and kicked her out."

"Why now?"

He hesitated, then shifted, uncomfortable. He pulled his lips in then said, "Maybe I just wanted her to fall from a great height. Thanks for getting her up there, James."

"What changed? Something's changed. Why are you coming after us now?"

"She's high enough to fall and make the earth shake, tsunamis rise, and the gravitational spin of the world to become permanently altered. It's up to you if she actually falls that far."

"This is more personal than business."

"Oh, when the paparazzi showed her leaving your property like she was Princess Diana leaving Kensington, to have it be the conversation in every meeting or interview that I went into, to have it as the primary conversation on my own set, to have to contact my publicist and issue press releases, to have it overshadow me and my accomplishments, especially when she made her snarky sexual comments on Twitter, when I dealt with her betrayal and your ego, that was personal. This, the cars, the script, the payout, James, all of that is simply good business."

I nodded.

He said, "You called the paparazzi. I should make you give me four cars."

Weighed down by emotions, I looked out of his window. Stared at his swimming pool.

He said, "And since you're involved, I'll show you one more thing."

He turned the screen toward me again. It was a video of me attacking Johnny Bergs. It was crisp and clear, as if it were a shoot on a set. I saw me storming past the camera with a tire iron in my hand, rushing up to the Porsche and smashing Bergs's car window. Then, enraged, I pulled him out and beat him. As rain fell, I pounded the man into the pavement.

Bobby Holland said, "Money can buy you access to anything. Now I have Bergs. This is what he would hate for the world to see. He'll work for me again. With a smile and a pay cut."

On the video, Johnny Handsome fled as I jumped back inside my car and sped away.

I looked at Bobby Holland, once again surprised.

He said, "Don't sit there like this is a silent movie with no subtitles. Speak up."

"Was thinking."

"Share your thoughts."

I said, "*Chinatown.* This feels like *Chinatown.*"

He nodded. "Hollywood is *Chinatown.* The bad guys do win. The rich always win."

Another moment went by with me in a trance, staring out at his pool.

"You still with me, Thicke? No jokes. Your voice is gone now. No arrogance."

I said, "You win. I love her. I want to protect her. Always have."

"Was she worth it?"

"Doesn't matter the cost. She's priceless."

"I'm enjoying the outcome. I get to tear your playhouse down."

He puffed on his Cuban cigar, the scent of his victory.

I smiled an affable smile and said, "Mind if I have one to go?"

"Sure. As a matter of fact, I'll give you two."

"So kind of you. You are truly, truly a thoughtful and generous man."

"One for Regina. Bill gave a cigar to Monica. It will remind Regina of old times."

"I'm sure."

"I look forward to working with her again."

"No doubt."

"Despite this, despite the past, she was

always a joy to work with."

"The cigar and I'll be on my way."

"The cars will be here in forty-eight."

I nodded. "If not sooner."

He stood and we shook hands.

Then he sat back down and spun around in his luxurious red chair to open his humidor and remove cigars from his private stash. He was smiling the smile of a well-earned payday.

I growled, *"Yngvar Vimar Bakken."*

Those three words halted him. When he snapped back around I was no longer on the opposite side of his desk, but I was on his side, standing over him, a deadly grimace on my face, his Razzie raised high in my hand. He moved, jerked to grab for his gun. I brought the statuette down hard, struck the side of his head, parted his beautiful blond hair, hair that sang of virility, and it changed to a beautiful shade of red, the hue of the lipstick on a two-dollar whore. Shock and pain contorted his once overconfident face. He tumbled out of his chair, collapsed onto the carpet without so much as a sigh. Bobby Holland was down for the count.

Driver was right. It was more effective to use a solid object than a fist.

I stepped over Bobby Holland and moved his gun. I picked it up and tossed it across the room. It thudded when it hit the carpet. Then I thought twice, imagined him some- how crawling to that gun and shooting me. I stepped over Holland again and retrieved the gun. I dropped it inside the Tumi bag. A second later I stepped over him again and opened his desk drawer. Found a stash of cocaine. With the stash were specialized spoons and other tooters, mirrors and CD cases, things he used to make bumps or lines. And there were hundreds of straws. He had more straws than Mrs. Patrice Evans had Post-its. Sharing straws was like sharing needles. There was something else there. Oral syringes. He was a plugger, at least part time. A pegger and a plugger. He used the syringes to inject cocaine into his anus. Some men injected it anally and some women did the same and vaginally as well. Women always had more stores at the mall and more options. Not many people talked about it. Social taboos. But show business was a country of its own. This was Bobby Holland's private life. This was his office stash. This was what he kept handy.

A man like Bobby Holland would always have a supply close at hand.

Inside another drawer were bills and lawsuits, some filed by him against various companies, most from companies that were suing him. The one on top was from his ex-wife. The one under that was the bill for the other kid. The DNA test had come back and not in his favor. He was in debt on a kid from over a decade ago. Just like the news online had said, close to a million owed. The next from the IRS was demanding just as much within the next thirty days. He owed everyone from his attorneys to his gardeners.

Inside another drawer was a roll of duct tape on top of a stack of photos, all of Regina Baptiste. Duct tape and photos of my wife. Made no sense. Regina was locked away in a drawer and held down by a half-used roll of gray duct tape. But there it was. It looked like a threat. A promise to keep her enslaved. As Bobby lay on the floor, bleeding and moaning, I kicked his gut twice. He had slapped me twice. I issued equal punishment. I was a fair man at heart. He groaned and wheezed and murmured obscenities that offended my sensibilities. I had on good shoes. My shoes were of greater value than his. He didn't appreciate their soles.

I said, "Just wanted to make sure you were still alive."

I used his duct tape to bind him. Hands behind his back. I taped his ankles together.

Did the same for his knees. Enraged, I picked up one of his magazines and ripped out an elegant photo of Regina Baptiste. I balled it up and shoved it inside his bloody mouth, then used more duct tape to keep it there. He made disgusted faces like he didn't appreciate the taste of my wife anymore.

I kicked him again, that time out of spite. My shoes wanted to, so I let them.

Bobby Holland at my feet, I looked up at the stunning images of Regina Baptiste.

Then I gazed out at the beautiful moonlight reflecting in his swimming pool.

CHAPTER 30

Holland slithered across the concrete. Face bloodied, he did his best to do the impersonation of a two-hundred-pound snake and struggled to escape. He was trapped. I was trapped too.

"Slapping me was no good. You should've shot me in the face, Bobby Holland."

He squirmed and scraped his flesh on the concrete, went nowhere fast.

"But there was no profit in shooting me, right? No cars. No cash. Slapping just added to the humiliation. I bet that made you feel superior. Bet that made you feel real superior."

Cool breeze on my skin, air whistling through palm trees, the scent of the desert and chlorine filling my heated lungs, lungs that burned after dragging Holland from his office to the backyard, I stood at the edge of his swimming pool, head aching, and fists firm on my hips; head back, looking up at the moon. It felt like I was in the deep dark hell of a life that belonged to somebody else. There was only one direction that we could go from here. I frowned down at him, angry at my life. Regina Baptiste was inside his mouth and he still wasn't satisfied. I put my loafer on the side of his neck, adjusted my weight, and made him stop snaking around in vain.

I asked, "How's that last laugh working out for you, Holland?"

He fought for a moment; then his panicked expression looked up into my angered eyes. His eyes were so wide they looked like two moons reflecting the moon above. His fear was magnificent. No actor had ever portrayed the level of fear that Bobby Holland owned. Now he realized how lucky Johnny Handsome had been. I gathered a mouth of spit and was tempted to shower his face, but I didn't. I didn't want to be gross. Or cliché. I spat it away into his pool.

I took an iPhone out of my pocket. It was the one that I had obtained from Steve Martin, aka Alice Ayres. She had had a film that was worth millions, a film that could shake Hollywood, and all she asked me to do was take care of the parking ticket on her car. I paid her for her iPhone and she was cool with that. There were decent

people out there. Decent people were ignored while the scoundrels were praised. I
held the iPhone in front of Bobby Holland's
eyes and played the video. At first he was
confused. Me, James Thicke, holding a
video of him. When he realized what it was,
surprise took root. Extreme surprise. Bobby
Holland, on set, verbally abusing Baptiste,
giving cocaine to Baptiste and Bergs. Bobby
Holland. Functional cocaine addict. Baptiste might have been screwed in more ways
than one, but Holland knew that his time
had come. I set the iPhone on record and
pointed it at his face. I became the director.

I said, "We're beyond the Rubicon. Rubicon is the river that, once crossed, guaran-
tees war. Not all wars are loud. Some are as
quiet as this one. It's time for us to move
onto the battlefield."

Face bloodied, Holland kicked his legs in
vain. The duct tape that had his hands
bound behind his back was better than
shackles. Duct tape was around his ankles
and knees too.

"Exploit me. I'm a writer and no one will
care. It's about the story. No one remembers
the writer. We're simply the unnamed and
unnoticed angels who work for the gods.
You can put Donald Duck across the front
as the screenwriter; no one will care but the

lawyers at Disney."

His eyes widened with an emotion that was miles beyond the exit to fear. Stripped down, I was an animal. And so was Holland. Right now, he was a zebra watching a lion close in. His muscles flexed and strained against his binds. He did that until he exhausted himself. His heartbeat was accelerated. And underneath his turtleneck, the hairs on his body were on end.

"No one applauds screenwriters. Well, no one but other screenwriters. Everybody else thinks that they can just slap us around. You picked the wrong screenwriter to slap around."

I pulled over a chair and set the iPhone up for a wider shot.

"This is for your family, Holland. After it's been edited. I'll show them who you were."

I emptied my pockets, put my car keys and wallet and other phones inside the Tumi bag, tossed the messenger bag to the side. I took off my shoes. Bobby Holland continued freaking out. His body was in fight or flight, but he wasn't able to satisfy either primal urge. He exerted intense muscular effort. I stuck my toes into the water. The water was cold.

I said, "Zugzwang. Eight-letter word.

That's where you have me, Bobby Holland. In this game of chess, you have left me in that position. No matter what I do, I can't win. Bravo."

I squatted down next to Holland, grabbed him, and dragged him down into the frigid waters of the pool. He struggled until the water covered his face. I would've undressed him first, but I wasn't the type of man who found joy in undressing other men.

"My pool is heated, Holland. I'm going to catch pneumonia murdering you. This is haphazard. Like throwing furniture into a truck and moving to Downey. Unsystematic and haphazard. If I had known that this was how this would end, I would've at least worn duck hunting boots. And I would've driven to your home in a car that wasn't mine."

He tried to fight the frigid waters, again his battle in vain. I stood over him like I was his conscience. Watched him struggle to breathe as spit gathered in his mouth and he was forced to swallow that spit to keep from choking to death on his own saliva.

"You have to have Regina. You need her fame. There is no substituting her type of talent. She's bigger than the script. She will never be as large as her own brand. She's Regina *Baptist* and she's fighting every day to live up to the standards of being Regina *Baptiste.* Behind my gates, she didn't have to be Regina Baptiste. She was the girl from Montana walking around in flip-flops and wrinkled jeans from the Salvation Army. Yeah, she still shopped there. She wore ten-thousand-dollar dresses on the red carpet, but at home she wore five-dollar jeans and tees."

He kicked and splashed water in my face, but I pushed his head underwater, submerged his face for around thirty seconds, the water numbing my hands. When I pulled him up, he was shivering and twice as terrified, a man who could see his own cold, cold death on the horizon.

"Take my cars. Take my money. Slap me. I can deal with that, Holland. I can make more money. I can buy more cars. My wounds will heal and the scars will add character to my face. Be corrupt, I don't care. But you went too far. You fed my wife coke. You fed her coke. She's not your girlfriend anymore, Bobby. She's not the girl from Montana you used as your eye candy. Regina is my wife. You shoved coke up her nose. I can't forgive you for that."

I put him under again, then brought him up and watched him struggle to breathe.

I waited until he could because I wanted

447

him to hear every word that I said.

"You know that this deal wouldn't be the end. You'd keep coming back. You'd bankrupt me. Or you would break Regina. You'd have her in Beverly Hills seeing a psychotic-and-Botox-faced shrink twice a week. You'd watch her drug up and waste away like so many other actresses have. You'd make her spindly, stick skinny, and dejected just to make a buck."

I put him under again, that time for only fifteen seconds.

"The tape. Bergs and my wife. The tape of me beating Bergs. The tape you showed me. The video that I showed you. And the one where I beat Bizarro Bergs. Almost had forgotten about that one. We have enough tape to edit and make a feature film at this point. It's getting to be too much. Too fucking much. I'm numb. But I applaud you. This session of sex, lies, and videotapes is Oscar worthy. Your best work to date. Bravo, Holland. You have directed this well. You might have figured out when to start this bullshit, but you just didn't know when to stop."

He made muffled sounds, did his best not to choke as he begged for his life.

"Bobby Holland. There's no begging in blackmail."

He shivered and closed his eyes and the begging, the supplicating continued.

"I didn't beg you, did I? Probably would've done you a lot of good to stop at five mil and two cars. I would've complied. But five mil *two hundred and fifty* thou and *three* cars? You've over-bid on *The Price Is Right* on that one. Payment requested became ludicrous."

He prayed. When scum like Bobby Holland prayed, religion became a punch line.

"Take a deep breath, Holland. Take a deep, deep breath."

He did and I took him under again. He had a new stench. The rancid aroma from terror dancing with horror overpowered the reek from the Seven Deadly Sins. The disgusting odor of helplessness came in third. I held him under for close to a minute. I held him under and each moment I looked down at him, as carbon monoxide bubbles escaped his lungs, I held down someone different. I held down Holland. I held down my wife for being so weak that she let Bobby Holland's drugs seduce her into a so-called accidental fuck that was broadcast worldwide. I held down Mr. Holder. I held down Vera-Anne. I held down Hazel Tamana Bijou because she had sent a text to James Cameron and not me. I held down Johnny Handsome. I held down Bizarro Bergs. Then, once again, I held down Bobby Holland, the evil puppet master. The bubbles escaping him became fewer. I felt him struggling. His neck muscles tensed. His back. His legs. My hands were again numb. He ran out of energy, didn't fight as hard. Then he had a burst of energy and struggled once more. He fought to live. Again I brought him up and watched him suffer to remain amongst the living. It took another minute before he stopped suffocating. Right now he loved life more than he did my money. He wanted a lungful of desert air more than he did my wife. Now he appreciated the simple things in life. I dragged him to a corner and placed his head in the concrete wedge. I needed to open and close my cold hands, get my circulation going, find warmth. My legs and feet were doing better. But my hands were in and out of the water and the night air did me no more favors than it did Bobby Holland. He had to use his leg and neck muscles to keep from slipping back into the water. He shivered and couldn't kick. All he could do was open his eyes, concentrate, breathe, and listen to me.

"I want you to feel what you put my wife through. I could have killed you right away.

But you made my wife suffer for years. Now you have ruptured our marriage. We suffer. You suffer. Even if I did this all night, that would be too kind, you piece of shit. Be glad I'm nice."

He was weak, but determined to stay alive. He got his feet underneath himself. I stood where I was and watched, wondered what good that would do. Hands taped behind his back, bound at his knees and ankles, he tried to hop away in fear. On the second hop, he fell and went underwater. I waded through the water, pulled him back up, and turned him face up. He struggled to breathe again, his chest expanding and contracting, begging for decent respiration.

He was in excruciating pain. And still his pain wasn't enough to satisfy me.

The moonlight glowed in his terrified eyes.

I pushed him under the water again. This was tomorrow's news. This would be the RSS feed that would be on fire for forty-eight hours. This would be what would cause the media to orgasm. There was something else I knew, but couldn't prove. But I felt it in the heart of my gut.

Someone had sent that explicit video of Johnny Handsome and my wife to my phone. They had sent the video to a phone number that only a few people had access to. The crew wouldn't do that. Alan Smithee wouldn't want that leaked. But it was leaked before the night was over. Bobby Holland was on the set. He had stolen my numbers from Alice Ayres. Maybe Alan Smithee had rejected Holland as well, and part of that was global retaliation. Same for Johnny Bergs. Holland had sent that video to my phone, had sent it to Hazel Tamana Bijou's phone, and posted it online for the world to see. It had done damage to everyone that he had loathed. Bergs. Baptiste. Smithee. And me. As I gritted my teeth and held him under, it was all clear to me. My wife had rejected him. He'd had two years of pining over a love that had first cheated on him then celebrated that affair with a spectacular wedding made for a queen. She had broken the rules. When a woman left a man she was supposed to do worse, not better. When he had come on to her in Johnny Bergs's trailer, that last rejection was too much to bear. She had laughed in his face and he had attacked her where she was the most sensitive.

Bobby Holland was the butterfly that had flapped its wings and caused a hurricane.

I remembered what Driver had said about murdering or killing a man.

He said a man was never the same once

he took the life of another man.

But sometimes a man would never be the same if he let that man live.

He had fed my wife cocaine. He'd attacked her self-esteem and fed her cocaine.

He had fed her cocaine.

Cocaine.

I left him terrified, floating on his back, and eased out of the water. I hurried back to his office, pool water dripping everywhere. I stepped over the shattered Razzie and bloodstained carpet and took the cocaine from the top drawer of his desk. I took his packet and grabbed scissors to cut the plastic that housed the South American imported powder open.

When I got back to the pool, Bobby Holland had flipped over in my absence. He was wiggling like a fish, about to expire. I turned him over and he was happy to breathe again.

Happiness became strife when he saw me waving the Bolivian marching powder.

I said, "Benzoylmethylecgonine. From the leaves of the coca plant. Nervous system stimulant. Cocaine. For Eric Clapton, it was a wonderful song. Tonight, for Bobby Holland, the man who insufflated the drug, for what you did to my wife, this will be poetic justice."

I cut open the end of the package, then used the scissors to bring out a small amount. I sprinkled the cocaine inside his nostrils, used the scissors as a makeshift spoon and administered it a little at a time. He knew his options. Sniff, sniff, sniff or get flipped over.

"I sat and listened to you talk. I let you ramble out your verbal manifesto. I gave you a chance to extricate yourself from this atrocious predicament. I didn't hear one word of apology. Not one fucking apology. You took me for granted. I don't fancy myself as being a tough guy, Holland, but I am. I might dress like I belong on the yard at Princeton, but that's just my costume. Now. This is what I could do for you at this point. I could ask Regina to do a small part. A part that requires one day of shooting. And on that day of shooting, you're to be barred from your own set. I could do that. But I'd never insult my wife by asking her to work for you."

With each breath, eyes wide, he tried to not suffocate, and the drug absorbed into his mucus membranes lining his sinuses. He had to inhale the coke because all things living had to breathe. He had to be terrified of getting a nosebleed, because that would do him in; he'd drown in his own blood. I told him that this was what he had done to my wife. This was what the video on his Mac had showed her doing with rolled-up banknotes and hollowed-out pens. He didn't enjoy the blow now. Not when he was in water. Not when it would increase his heart rate. Blood pressure. Might make him vomit. Could make his muscles contract. Or he could pass out.

"You can take your last deep breath. Or you can go under and start drinking water. Bet you hate that you have a home with a pool. And before you start drinking, I just took a piss."

Bobby Holland shuddered and took a deep breath, as deep a breath as he could with cold water and brisk air contracting his lungs. He gathered air and closed his eyes. Over five million dollars and luxury cars were no longer on his mind. All he had left was regret. Regret for fucking with me, the Londoner born in San Francisco. I wondered what that felt like, knowing this was his final moon, mine the last face, the last person he'd fucked over reminding him that Hollywood was built on secrets kept as quiet as a silent film.

"For now, here are words of comfort. I might go to jail for this. I know I will. And when I do, Baptiste will be free of both of us scoundrels. We lose. She wins. Say good night, Gracie."

Then I flipped him over and pushed his head under water.

I was seconds into sending Holland into his watery grave when the lights came on in one of his bedrooms. The bedroom was on the opposite side of the home. He wasn't home alone. Bobby Holland struggled, legs bound together, turned harshly, kicked like a mermaid, made water splash in my face and out to the concrete at the edge of the pool. Lights turned on in a hallway, seconds later in the kitchen. Somebody moved around then came to the back door. I lowered my body into the water, hid my face, and held Holland under. But the Tumi bag was on the ground. So were my shoes. The windows were closed. The night air was too cold. So I guessed that we hadn't been heard all evening, not inside of his office, and not out by the pool. Bobby Holland fought and I held him down. But I wanted to escape. For me there was no escape. I felt my heart beat, felt panic trying to kick in and take control, wondered if I would have to kill someone else just so I could finish my business with Bobby Holland. The sliding glass door opened and a Coca-Cola shaped silhouette appeared. As I fought to drown Bobby Holland, she stepped out onto the patio, but not into the moonlight. I held Bobby Holland's head down and he fought to turn over and get air. I held him and punched him in the lungs. Right now I needed him quieter than a new tenant inside of an old graveyard.

Bubbles escaped his nostrils. He inhaled. He jerked. Then he stopped moving.

The silhouette stepped out into the backyard. A bare-naked woman in stiletto heels.

It was the silhouette of Regina Baptiste.

She called out for the dead man in the pool.

CHAPTER 31

"Yngvar?"

It was the silhouette of Regina Baptiste, but relief came when I realized that it wasn't my wife wearing that beautiful shape tonight. She had loaned it to a woman from another nation.

"You can not hide from me. I hear you splash the water. You try and scare me."

The accent was both as soft and strong as it was glamorous and exotic.

It was a woman whom I had seen before, and for a moment I didn't know from where. The fear of being recognized ran high and now I was breathing like I was gasping for air. Then it came to me in a rush that I had seen her attractive face earlier, but we had never met.

"Yngvar, it is so beautiful in America tonight."

I pulled Bobby Holland close to the wall and replied. "Ya. Beautiful. Like you."

458

The scissors were near the edge of the pool. I eased my right hand out and pulled those to me. This was the problem with killing a man, once you started, only God knew how many people you would have to kill in order to get away. What had been done couldn't be undone.

Even in death, Bobby Holland had me with a noose around my neck.

I did my best Bobby Holland imitation and said, "Come get in the pool."

"I tell you that I no like to swim and you tell me to get in pool again."

"Ya."

"I sleep a long, long time today. The Benadryl make me so sleepy."

"Ya. Antihistamines will do that."

"My allergies feel much better. But I am still so very tired. And very lonely in bed."

Her blond hair was no longer parted down the center. It had personality now, styled with pins and curls, locks in soft waves with the ends curled under, just like glamour women of the past. Looked like she had just stepped out of the 1950s. The wind picked up and whipped her locks into her face. I'd only seen her in the video I'd received from Alice Ayres, and then the former model and aspiring movie actress was wearing black leather pants, high heels, and a formfitting

459

top that smothered her breasts. It was the teenager from Hungary. The fifth person who had been in Johnny Handsome's trailer. Like a Valkyrie sent to escort Bobby Holland into Valhalla, Piroska Anastazia Dorika Vass Torma came toward the pool. Her silhouette never stopped reminding me of my wife. And in the darkness, which was probably where he kept her, the lights being off inside of his home being a tell, she probably felt the same, until she spoke, up to the point of entry. She was the perfect body double. Like John Derek had done when he had gone from Linda Evans to Bo Derek, Bobby Holland had found him a duplicate, body-wise, of the same woman. The winds blew in my direction. She was wearing Mapona, the scent of Regina Baptiste. The Hungarian's walk was inebriated. Her steps slowed as her heels clicked along the tiled walkway. She ran her hand over her hair and gazed at the moon, then she smiled like the eighteen-year-old woman-child who had more child inside of her heart than woman. Innocent, naïve, and hungry. Out of the millions of people in Los Angeles, I would've never expected her to be here.

But I understood Bobby Holland better now. He'd found a new love and now he could destroy Regina. The new girl had taken the place of the old love. Now he could blackmail.

She called out, "Yngvar?"

I squatted down, the frigid water at my chin, scissors in my cold hand, and moved down the side of the pool, one step at time, dragging Bobby Holland's corpse as if it was my security blanket. I worked the scissors and freed the duct tape around Bobby Holland's mouth.

"Ya. Piroska."

"Oh, you're down there."

"What is it?"

"I have my Choo shoes. The ones with the brown leather and snakeskin and many straps and six-inch wooden heel. Don't splash the water on me. I will not think that funny."

"I left you a present, Piroska."

"Did you? Where?"

I peeled the duct tape away. "Down at that end of the pool where you are."

"Yngvar. Bobby, I will not get in the pool. My hair is too lovely."

"Relax, Piroska. It's not in the pool. Look down."

Her heels clicked and she brought her nakedness to the edge of the pool. By then I had Bobby Holland's face away from her. I splashed water to make it sound like he was moving. I splashed water and hoped that would keep her from coming too close.

She stayed where she was and said, "I'm horny."

"Get in the pool."

"I will wait for you to get out."

"Get in with me."

"No. My hair. And don't splash water on my Choo shoes."

She saw the package of cocaine that I had left down at that end of the pool.

She squatted and picked it up. "For me?"

"For you, Piroska. For you."

She paused. "You sound strange."

"This is my swimming voice."

She picked up her present and walked back inside the house, her walk a little faster now, and her inebriation high. She disappeared and I worked with Bobby Holland. My hands were numb and I worked in desperation to cut the duct tape away from his wrists. I turned him over but he kept flipping, kept floating away from me. Living men were stubborn and dead men never cooperated. I grabbed his sweater and pulled him until I could get to his pants. Turned him over and cut the duct tape away from between his knees and ankles. I used the scissors to cut away his turtleneck, then unbuckled his pants. I had to pull those off.

Just as I finished, the door opened again and Piroska returned, credit card and mirror in one hand, cocaine in the other. Now she had on a big housecoat. She was out here to stay.

She was coming in my direction as the cellular rang. It was the cellular that I had gotten from Alice Ayres. That stopped Piroska. She was six feet away. I hid behind the body of a naked dead man. She looked into the pool for a moment, saw Bobby Holland naked, moving his limp arms in a casual motion, then she hurried toward the phone, heels clicking fast.

I said, "Let it ring."

"You have a new phone now?"

"Ya."

"You promised me an iPhone."

"We will get you one tomorrow."

"The new iPad?"

"That too."

She applauded and smiled and looked out toward the pool.

She sounded more than happy. "How long will you swim in that cold water?"

"Not much longer."

"Don't drown."

"Will try not to."

She laughed. "The cold water makes your balls so small. Looks funny to me."

A moment went by. She came back in my direction. Saw Bobby Holland's face, eyes open, but not blinking.

I moved his arms and asked, "You okay?"

"I want to give head before I go to sleep again."

"Ya."

"And get head at same time."

"Ya, ya."

"Stop imitating me. Always imitating me."

"Ya, ya, ya."

She laughed.

She started back toward the house, but halfway she turned and came back.

She said, "I wait for you."

"Go wait for me in the bed."

"Your home is so large and I am lonely. I wait for you here."

She went to the lounger and took out the blow, made lines on the mirror, used a straw, and sniffed. She held her head back and waited on the narcotic to kick in. I let Bobby Holland go. I gathered all of his wet clothing, then remembered he had on a watch that cost as much as one of my cars. I waded back and removed his watch. I almost forgot the most important thing. The one thing that would make his death read like murder. I opened Bobby Holland's mouth and fished out the page from the magazine. The last thing that he had tasted was the image of my wife. The last face that he had seen was mine. Then I gathered his clothing and crept back to the end of the pool near the house, where I had entered. I had to move across the waters and ease by her as she sat in the lounger moon bathing. The scissors were tucked inside my belt. Behind me Bobby Holland's body floated out into the moonlight as Piroska Anastazia Dorika Vass Torma took a package of cigarettes out of her pocket, lit up, and stared at the sky. She took two puffs then laid her cigarette inside an ashtray that rested on a small glass table.

I quietly got out of the pool, body weighted down by fear and the water that had taken up residence inside my clothes. Piroska turned on her side for a moment, faced the opposite direction. I put the damp clothing on the concrete and pulled the scissors from my jeans.

Water dripped from every part of me and I gathered up Holland's wardrobe. I crept across the grass and found his garbage cans on the side of the house. I deposited his clothing there. The gate was in front of me. I could slip out and leave this crime scene. But I had to go back. My shoes were poolside. Plus there was more. Bizarro Bergs's

465

bag was a Tumi. That meant that it was registered. Most Tumi products were registered at the point of purchase. If that bag were to be found at the scene of a poolside murder, the police might connect me to the bag because Bizarro Bergs would rub his ugly face and wounded pride and tell them that I had stolen it from him, and do that with a smile that only a mother could love. The same for the iPhone. If the police showed up at Alice Ayres's door, it wouldn't matter if she was Regina Baptiste's number one fan, that bird would sing whatever song kept her walking the streets with the free.

Corrupt acts had gotten me here. And more corrupt acts would have to buy my freedom.

I took slow steps, scissors gripped in my hand, raised high and prepared to strike. I'd stab her like Norman Bates. Like many said O. J. Simpson had done Goldman in Brentwood.

When I made it to the woman who had a physique that mirrored my wife's, she was motionless. She was wrapped up in her housecoat, a hand between her legs, snoring lightly. She'd fallen asleep touching herself. I stared at the teenager, her hair made up like a starlet. She was just another woman-child, another nymph, another barterer who had just gotten off the bus, enamored by the titles of men and the things that they owned, This was the life that Regina Baptiste had lived before she met me. I lowered the scissors, then held my breath as I gathered the iPhone and Tumi bag that held Holland's gun. Body numb, shoulders hunched, I shivered, swallowed, and looked out at the pool. Bobby Holland floated in the moonlight.

I whispered, "Not *Chinatown. Sunset Boulevard.*"

With minimal breathing and no musical accompaniment, I crept away from the scene of my crime, took steps backward, awkward steps, each step feeling arthritic and rooted in pain, until I made it to his rented house. I coughed and spat into the shrubbery and looked back. The picture painted by Greed hadn't changed. The man who had drugged my wife and slapped me twice hadn't been resurrected. I put my shoes on, opened his door, and eased it shut.

At any moment I expected to hear a woman-child wail louder than a banshee.

Back inside the office, water dripping down my face, my jeans and T-shirt clinging to my body like a second skin, I dropped a beige throw rug over the bloodstain in the carpet. I disconnected his Mac, rearranged his desk, put other awards in the place of the one missing, scripts and books where the computer had been, so that it wouldn't look like it was missing. Straightened up his office, wiped anything that I had touched, picked up the broken Razzie and the Mac and the Tumi bag, wiped the doorknob and the handle on the back door, then made a trail of water to his front door. The computer would have to get reformatted, then trashed. If there were other copies of his madness out there, if that evidence was stored in other places, only time would reveal. The Razzie and my shoes would have to get thrown away. Same for my clothing. Shivering, I made it to the Bentley, climbed inside and turned the heater on high.

Driver had called me on the throwaway phone.

My wife had called my iPhone a half dozen times.

Hazel Tamana Bijou had called thrice.

There was more bad news. I knew that. I felt that. But now wasn't the time.

And as I sat there, my nose running, hands wrinkled from being in the pool, both phones rang again. This wasn't the time to take calls. Especially on the iPhone. The moment that I answered, the GPS would triangulate my position and put me at the scene of Holland's murder.

As I pulled away, as I felt an awful, awkward sense of rightful vengeance mixed up with fear and caution, the gray car that had escaped my mind like a bad conscience, it followed me.

Like it or not, from the womb, Death followed us all.

CHAPTER 32

Fresh bullet holes decorated the Bentley by the time I made it back to the shadows in Downey. A short detour had been made, one that took me on Skirball Center Drive, an access road of Los Angeles's 405 Freeway in the area between the valley and UCLA.

The left headlight was dead, murdered by a bullet of unknown caliber. A second bullet had left its mark on the windshield. My left ear bled from being grazed by a third bullet that had been meant for my head. Nobody was taught to aim for an ear. The same thoughts remained with me; corrupt acts had gotten me here. And corrupter acts had either bought my freedom or sealed my doom. Bloodlust had taken hold of me. Bloodlust had taken hold of them.

How many more bullet were holes in the Bentley, I'd need daylight to be able to tell. There was no other place to take it, not right now. If I'd gone to Los Feliz and the paparazzi were still stalking, one photo of bullet holes in my windshield would have done me in better than any video Bobby Holland had on his Mac.

I pulled to the side, coughed off and on, dehydrated, hungry, head still aching, and battled with my nerves, remained as calm as I could as I spied around the land of graffiti and rubbish. Sweet Isabel's car was parked a few cars away. So was Mr. Holder's.

My cellular rang and I jumped. Hazel Tamana Bijou called yet again.

Seconds later, Driver called again. About five minutes later, my wife called once more.

My voice mail on the iPhone was full, had been full since I left Los Feliz, so I couldn't receive more unwanted messages. I had no idea how to retrieve messages on the throwaway.

A caravan of cars sped by, from Range Rovers to Pintos. A few threw trash out of their windows as they rolled by. Tonight The Apartments was as calm as the Las Vegas Strip. It was a barrio of restless people. The troubled rarely slept the sleep of the gods.

Water saturated my clothes and tugged at my body as if Holland was still trying to pull me down, trying get his fingers and death grip into me. My nose was stuffy for a moment, but I blew it and was able to inhale a dry, cool breeze that carried a hint of smog. If that arid breeze were a painting, it would be colored by death and tinted by the undertone of danger.

I pulled up next to my Maybach, took in the shadows of this hard-boiled part of my world, the world of the other me, the man whom I had created when stress and anger had won the battle with logic and common sense. For a moment, inside my mind, I heard the echo of gunshots. Felt the weight of the .45, felt its rapid kicks inside my hand. It wasn't like being at the range. On the range, targets didn't move. On the range, targets never screamed and fired back. On the range, I wore earplugs to keep the explosions from deafening me. The ringing was still in my ears and even though my hand was empty, I felt the gun kick over and over. I felt it the way an amputee still felt his missing limb. I felt that weight of that gun inside of my hand. I had to shake off what had happened on Skirball Center Drive. And that reminded me. I dug inside my pocket and took out the spent .45 shells that I had collected from the pavement, and threw them all over the concrete wall into a barren lot. I closed my eyes and listened to the gritty sounds coming from the freeway, then to the wisps of music from scurrilous songs that had lyrics as pleasing as inhaling smoke. In the distance was an irritating hum. Someone was cleaning his or her carpet in the night.

Police sirens screamed in the distance. Their wail rushed in my direction.

Holland had wanted three of my cars and five million two hundred and fifty thousand.

The police wouldn't care about the motivation, only the end result. I was a murderer. My crime first-degree.

Despite all that had happened, those sirens took me back to what had brought me to this moment. Sirens screamed and the only thing that played in my head was seeing Regina Baptiste with Johnny Handsome. If I closed my eyes, that movie would play in my dreams like a chcap movic at a dollar theater that had a bad projector and one screen. The preview would be short and look like the opening moment of *Sunset Boulevard,* not the final moments of *Chinatown.* Bobby Holland face down in a pool while a coked-up, Benadryl-taking, Norwegian beauty entertained herself and fantasized about getting her star on the Walk of Fame.

The parade of police came toward The Apartments. Then the howl continued down

Imperial Highway. Shaking, I rubbed my hands for warmth, then removed the car cover from the Maybach. I moved the Bentley to the far side of the complex, parked in visitors, covered the car and all of its injuries, and headed toward the buildings. Not until then did nausea grip me.

Soaking wet, I gagged and regurgitated, threw up with a hostility I'd never experienced, a suffocating brutality, like my body was trying to purge itself of compunction and bad memories.

When I finished, I realized that I wasn't alone. Near me was a man as dark as an open road. Driver was watching me. He saw me, soaking wet and at my worst, then waited for me to finish embarrassing myself and wipe my mouth with a corner of my damp shirt. I didn't want him to see me. I didn't want him involved. But now he'd witnessed this moment and it was too late.

I looked at him and I knew that he knew what I had done. This was easier than any crossword puzzle. Occam's razor gave the most logical answer and that answer was the best fit.

For whatever reason, I knew that he had been in my position. It felt as if I had been on my feet one thousand and one nights. But all I wanted to do was take off my clothes, drink Jack Daniels from the bottle, and go to bed. Any bed that had a mattress made of rocks and glass would feel kinder than my life felt right now. Exhaustion pulled but anxiety and fear were on the other team in that vicious tug-of-war.

Driver disappeared and came back within five minutes. He brought me a dark towel, jeans, shoes, and a T-shirt. *Si vis pacem, para bellum.* When he saw that I was bleeding from my ear, he went back upstairs and came back with peroxide and bandages. By the time he'd returned, I had stripped, dried off and changed. As cars passed by and televisions played above, I emptied my pockets before I wrapped my wet clothing and shoes tight inside the wet towel, then coughed and carried it all to the Dumpster. I came back, saturated my ear with peroxide, and dressed my wound.

I asked Driver, "Anybody come by my penthouse suite while I was gone?"

"Mr. Holder came by again. He looked troubled, but not as mad as before. Said that he'd just left meeting his daughter and would like to talk to you again, if that was okay. Just passing on the message. The pretty British lady came by again. She looked worried this time. The lady who left the manuscript came back a while later, the one who has the dreadlocks. Said to tell you Misty Mouse stopped by and she'd catch you later. She asked me if you had been to Club Mapona. The girl with the pink hair, Holder's PYT, I was walking the area looking for Bergs brothers and saw her coming back from the store with a ton of empty boxes. Still upset and coming apart at the seams. And somebody left a blank yellow Post-it on your door."

"Sounds like it's been pretty busy."

"Needless to say, the traffic at your door hasn't impressed Miss Baptiste."

"I don't see any paparazzi here, so I take that to be a good thing."

"No one has seen her. She's in bed. Since the news came, she's been in shock."

I used the stucco wall to keep my balance. "What news?"

Driver paused. "Jesus, Thicke. I guess that you don't know about the shooting."

Again I felt the kick of Bobby Holland's .45 in my hand.

Just as we rushed to the second floor, my cellular rang again.

It was Hazel Tamana Bijou.

This time I answered. Hazel was crying. She was frantic.

CHAPTER 33

Johnny Handsome was born in Granite, Oregon, and worked his way from obscurity to international fame. His prized face was, some said, insured by Lloyd's of London, the same business that had underwritten the shipping of human cargo when Britain was a chief slave trading power centuries ago. In the business of show, insuring a face, a hand, a nose, legs, buttocks, any type of bodily insurance wasn't unusual. Lloyd's of London insured all things narcissistic and unusual, from taste buds of a food critic, to Betty Grable's legs, Merv Hughes's moustache, the legs of dancer Michael Flatley, Ken Dodd's buckteeth, and Abbott and Costello's *Who's on First?* routine. Decades ago, Bruce Springsteen had insured his voice for six million. The ten-million-dollar policy that insured Johnny Bergs's face couldn't insure his reputation. As far as the public was concerned, it was worse than if

Woody Allen beat Sylvester Stallone. Johnny Handsome would never recover from being beaten into the ground by a screenwriter. Johnny Handsome's team had rushed in and bought all evidence of their A-list moneymaking box-office sensation getting his ass kicked by a screenwriter who was well known inside the business, but unknown beyond the reaches of Hollywood. A beating and an avalanche of publicity had garnered Rihanna sympathy and boosted record sales. An action-hero-romantic-leading-man getting his ass beaten had the opposite effect. For Johnny Handsome, it was castration. There were no groups that protested straight men getting their ass kicked, even when blindsided. He had gone into his pockets, dug deep and done his best to cover up what had been done. But one of the videos that showed Johnny Handsome getting beaten on Sunset and La Brea had escaped his deep pockets. Bobby Holland had purchased only one video. Only one was needed when blackmail had become your business. It was easy to hear Johnny Handsome beg not to be hit in his face. The audio was modified, the sound of the rain and the traffic and the blaring of horns stripped away, and with clarity you could hear him begging.

"You're not so fucking tough when you don't have a gang of Bergs with you."

"Not my face, James. C'mon, man, don't hit me in my face again."

"You fucked my wife and e-mailed it to me?"

"You broke my fucking nose. Thicke. I'm going to fucking sue you for this shit."

"You can't sue me if you're dead, Johnny Handsome. You're not that fucking good."

"Please, man. Please, stop fucking hitting me. James . . . please . . . please . . . please . . ."

My rage was immeasurable, as was Johnny Handsome's fear.

The videographer had added English, Spanish, French, and slang subtitles, the latter as a joke that turned the horrific night into sheer comedy. Johnny Handsome. Begging for his life. The owner of the video was a Hispanic woman, a camerawoman who kept her hi-res video camera at her side as she drove the streets of Los Angeles County. She never knew when she would run across a Rodney King scenario. And this had been her lottery. She had taped the best parts; said that she was already taping the car in front of her, some asshole who had cut her off and she wanted to get the license plate on the car as they sat at the intersection of Sunset and La Brea. So her camera was already rolling on that rainy night as she saw me leave my car and storm toward Johnny Bergs's prized Porsche, and caught the bulk of the confrontation. She had captured my rage. She taped me breaking the car window and pulling Johnny Handsome into the streets, Johnny Handsome screaming for help, me pounding his face, then Johnny Handsome running like he was trying to escape a raptor in Jurassic Park.

Bobby Holland had bought that video before that night had ended. Holland knew that was his guarantee that Johnny Handsome would work with him again. And again. And again. Maybe a gag order could've been placed on that video, but not before it had gone viral.

Bobby Holland had begged, borrowed, and stolen, and come up with enough cash to satisfy an opportunistic citizen and outbid Johnny Handsome on his own video the way Michael Joseph Jackson had outbid Sir Paul McCartney on the rights to the Beatles' catalogue. That's what friends were for. Bobby Holland owned that video. He owned the best video from that night. He owned part of Johnny Handsome's legacy. He owned part of my legacy as well.

That shame that had come after my humiliation had put me on the run and put

Johnny Handsome into a death spiral that crashed him into the pits of his own personal Hell. I'd been too busy dealing with my own pain to have any fucking empathy. I'd been running. And Johnny Handsome had been hiding. Waiting for wounds to heal so he could get his handsome face fixed. What I had done had been devastating, but it took more than my rage to get to his ego.

What had pushed Johnny Handsome over the edge were the jokes from one unknown blue comedienne. A high school dropout who'd had a kid at sixteen then went to comedy open mic on a dare, seemingly overnight had been catapulted to fame for her routine on cable and her "Who wants to sleep with a man who can't beat Greg Brady's ass?" That routine had been a sensation on YouTube the next day. Within one day, the comedienne had garnered over one million hits; in four she had sixteen million. More than enough people were following her now to make her an instant star. She had redefined the public perception of Johnny Bergs the same way comics had changed the perception of Richard Nixon post Watergate, her jokes wicked enough to make Johnny Handsome a strong punch line, powerful enough to make the comedienne almost as popular as Justin Bieber was when he started out — thousands of friend requests on Facebook, tens of thousands following her on Twitter, comedy clubs racing to book her while she was hot and popular enough to draw a crowd to buy the honestly overpriced drinks, and that was enough to get the comedienne invited on both daytime and nighttime talk shows, as well as CNN and BBC.

Johnny Bergs is fine, but who wants to sleep with a man that can't beat Greg Brady's ass? Could you see that in a prison scene? Johnny Berg confronting Greg Brady in the prison yard, next scene, Greg Brady butt fucking Johnny Bergs like he's on the bitch end of Brokeback Mountain?

No matter how many times she said that, the audience roared with laughter.

That stand-up routine was enough to earn that comedienne a coveted spot on Sunset Boulevard at the Comedy Factory. And she had posted a four-minute comical reenactment on *Funny or Die,* that reenactment featuring a look-alike for the one and only Greg Brady beating the shit out of a look-alike for Johnny Handsome. It said a lot about culture. We lived in a culture of crassness, from the reality shows to the routines at the comedy clubs. We lived where people felt as if they had to disrespect others to earn respect. Being mean in a world of intellectual barbarians was more profitable than being polite, especially if people laughed in the end.

Hours ago, after that rising star had finished her thirty-minute set, twenty-five of those minutes spent ridiculing and lambasting Johnny Handsome, she left the stage to a standing ovation bestowed on her by a room filled with breast implants, liquid face-lifts, facial contouring, wrinkled correction, and tummy tucks. The faithful clients of Botox, JUVÉDERM, Restylane, Perlane, Artefill, and Dysport, poster children for penile implants and vaginal rejuvenation, they all cheered and applauded the rising star, a nobody that Hollywood would now embrace.

Casting directors and reps from most of the studios all wanted to meet the comedienne to talk about rushing to develop a sitcom, about her being featured in a film with top-name A-list clients, about doing a comedy special for cable and branding herself.

Johnny Handsome was waiting for her outside, alone, in the cool breeze and clamor and never-ending line of headlights and brake lights that defined the glamour-filled and pothole-ridden section of Sunset Boulevard. There were a lot of mentally strong people in Hollywood, but there were also a bunch of overly inflated, weak mind-fucks who couldn't handle the dark side of fame. Most of the egos in Hollywood were so fragile that they made a porcelain teacup seem as thick as The Great Wall of China. We were all scarred; the deepest scars invisible to the naked eye. One crass woman had made the world laugh at Johnny Handsome. One comedienne had made the world laugh at his name like it was funnier than the word *Uranus.* Humiliated, he had stood outside the venue and heard her use his shame as a punch line, heard the audience laugh at him for an eternity.

He had heard them applaud her insults. Applause was acceptance.

The applause did him in. Her acceptance had echoed like his rejection. His humiliation.

In a crowd of hundreds, as people gradually recognized him and whispered his name, Johnny Handsome stormed up and touched her shoulder. When she turned around prepared to shake a hand or greet a new fan or give another autograph, she saw a sweaty man, a superstar in pain, a god who had insomnia and nervousness. She saw a version of Johnny Handsome that the world wasn't supposed to see. The comedienne saw Johnny Handsome with his face black and blue, bruised from the emergency plastic surgery that had been done to mend his broken jaw, nose, and other injures, weeks of anger and disdain seated in his deep blue eyes, and for a moment, she couldn't have known who he was.

He was no longer Johnny Handsome. He was Johnny Grotesque.

He was on pain medications. A little Patrón was in his blood. Blow lined his nostrils. Zoloft was in his bloodstream. And most importantly, a gun was in his hand. She had to have experienced recognition. And a flash of fear. Her mouth probably dropped open and the smile she had turned into pure horror. He shot the comedienne just as she was into the second minute of her fifteen minutes of celebrity and he was living in the last minute of his, stood at point-blank range, pulled the trigger three times and killed her verbal abuse and punch lines and career on the sidewalks of the Sunset Strip, billboards illuminating the dark road to excess and fame. She had killed on stage and Johnny Handsome murdered on the pavement.

An eye for an eye. A career for a career.

Her fans ran from her as his had abandoned him. Nothing was funny. No one laughed. No one applauded. Maybe Johnny Handsome knew that you could kill the comic, but you couldn't kill the joke. Or he knew that Bobby Holland had a video and it was just a matter of time before it surfaced. But he had no idea that at that moment he was free of Bobby Holland. He had no idea that Bobby Holland was taking his last swim and I was on Skirball Center Drive. No one wanted to be a has-been in Hollywood. No one wanted to be a falling star. No one wanted to be a nation's punch line. The brave drew their videophones as if they were all working for C. B. DeMille, getting that perfect close-up. Police cars pulled up and officers drew their weapons. The Strip was always filled with police officers and bouncers who kept nobodies out of the VIP sections of life. This had happened on the streets. This wasn't an issue for the bouncers.

Traffic came to a halt and the police shouted for Johnny Bergs to drop his weapon.

He hadn't been able to sleep. His anger was high.

The anxiety had been unbearable.

Two weeks of insomnia had been excruciating.

He'd killed the comedienne and the agitation and restlessness remained.

He had let his father down. He'd never be able to face Moses Bergstein again.

I'd beat his ass and the Bergs family had become America's new punch line.

Johnny Handsome gazed at the brilliance and decadence on the snaking Sunset Strip, stared at a sliver of an amoral world that rivaled the debauchery in both Times Square and along the Las Vegas Strip. No one grew up in Tinseltown. This was where many understood life as a child, thought as a child, and would never put away childish things. Girls just wanted to have fun and boys just wanted to get laid in the land of exotic cars and high-end pussy and endless drugs. He stared at his larger-than-life illuminated billboard, smiled a final narcissistic smile that said he had made it from a small town that no one had ever heard of and crawled to the top of the barrel of well-manicured crabs. He had been a priest of the city. Another god who was praised at the box office. Jaws wired shut, face black and blue, Johnny Handsome put the gun to his temple.

Johnny Handsome drove a 1954 Porsche 550 Spyder, just like James Dean.

Maybe, like his idol, Johnny Handsome had always wanted to die young.

The old were forgotten and died long after their careers had ended, but only the young were immortalized. Die young, live forever. Like Dean, he'd never age. He'd never grow old.

As police shouted, horns blew, and his disloyal fans screamed, Johnny pulled the trigger. His suicide was captured from countless camera angles.

Everything was posted on Wikipedia the moment the bodies hit the pavement.

The crazed fans remained loyal. They didn't stop videoing and photographing the brain matter or the spilled blood. The rest was on YouTube before the paparazzi had arrived. And of course, once again, as dozens of camera phones recorded it all, Facebook, MySpace, Bebo, Friendster, hi5, Orkut, PerfSpot, Zorpia, Netlog, Habbo, LinkedIn, Ning, Tagged, Flixster, Xanga, Badoo, MiGente, StudiVZ, and Twitter were all ablaze.

CHAPTER 34

Driver's friend was very nice-looking. She was dressed in a black suit tailored to accentuate her shape. From first glance, she came across as a serious woman with sensuous eyes and full lips, everything accented because her hair was pulled back into a professional bun. When I came in with Driver, she was seated on the sofa, crossword puzzle in her lap. She stood up, her hands behind her back. I reached to shake her hand and introduced myself. She introduced herself as Panther.

Then our conversation ended as unexpectedly as it had begun.

Regina Baptiste came out of the bedroom. She had on one of my T-shirts — SHHH . . . I'M HIDING FROM THE STUPID PEOPLE — a pair of my running shorts and a pair of white socks, all of my clothing swallowing her. Guilt was a helluva drug and it looked like she was overdosing.

She said, "Johnny Bergs killed himself."

I nodded. "I heard. Driver just told me."

I went to her and put my arms around her for a moment. She trembled and cried. There were layers upon layers of angst inside her body and it all rolled through me.

She had turned on my laptop. Not the one that I had just bought, but the one from home. She had connected to Slingbox and was looking at the news via the television at our home in Los Feliz. People were dropping flowers and leaving candles on Bergs's star on the Walk of Fame.

Then I turned to Driver and his employee. It was an awkward moment. I went to Driver and shook his hand. I told him to go get some rest. Said I'd call him in about twelve hours. He nodded. Then his coworker said good night to my wife and me, and they left us in this apartment.

Less than a minute after they left, Regina's cellular rang. And so did mine.

For the first time ever, Bobby Holland's ex-wife was calling on Regina's phone.

War and death had the power to make enemies become friends.

Hazel Tamana Bijou's assistant was calling on mine.

I didn't have to answer to know that

Bobby Holland had been found dead at his home.

The man who would play video and cast aspersions on everyone was dead.

As my ear bled, as my hearing returned to normal, the gray car remained on my mind.

After I had left Bobby Holland's home with a Tumi bag over my shoulder and a computer in my left hand, the gray car followed me. I *needed* them to follow me because whoever was inside that car could place me at Bobby Holland's home. That would be worth another five million. But I didn't think they were interested in money or scripts or convincing actresses to be in their films. Fear was in my heart. Fear of the unknown added to the chill that had me coughing. It had to be Johnny Handsome coming to do his own dirty work. They had found me. I didn't want to be in an area that had cameras. Not while driving the Bentley. A Bentley was the opposite of the gray car. A Bentley was a comet on a starless night.

After I sped down the 101 and merged onto the 405, traffic became as busy as it would be at noon. The gray car remained less than four car lengths behind me. I put my signal on when I came up on Skirball

491

Center Drive, a strip of road that made a loop with Sepulveda Boulevard and Mulholland Drive. They changed lanes two seconds after I did. Bobby Holland's gun was restless in my lap. I'd made sure that it was loaded before I exited the 405 at Skirball Center Drive. When I made it to a strip that was far away from the 405, I made a U-turn and faced them. They drove closer before they stopped. Baseball bat in hand, I stepped out of my car and stood next to my door. Three doors opened on the gray car and three men stepped out. One had a goatee, and half of Johnny Handsome's looks. His father. The other two were his sons. The largest had the same equine face with a bulbous hawk-like nose as the one that I'd met before when I'd been attacked at The Apartments. The one next to him was like the Bergs that I had met earlier in the day, another knuckle-dragger; only he looked like a chupacabra with a goatee, his hair slicked back on his head. Then a fourth man got out. From what I could tell, he looked as good as Johnny Handsome. My guess was that two of them had different mothers.

One more was inside the car. In the backseat. He had been riding the middle spot.

The man who looked like the father of the

pissed-off Bergs said, "James Thicke."

"You're burning a lot of high-priced gas following me all over town."

He nodded. "You're soaking wet."

"Who are you again?"

"You know who we are. We are the fucking Bergs."

"What can I do for you, fucking Bergs? Need directions somewhere?"

We stared for a moment, the traffic behind them, the coldness of the night on my skin.

"Thicke, you should've taken that hostility out on your wife, not my boy. My boy just did what a man is supposed to do when he's between a whore's legs. That's all my boy did. And my boy did it well. If you had a problem with that, if anyone should've been beaten, it was her as a lesson of how a lady behaves. That should've been your slut of a wife. You beat her ass and mess up her money, not my son's money. You beat your goddamn wife. You've damaged my son's reputation. You cost him two movies. He's not happy about that."

"Why didn't Johnny show up to deliver this little message?"

"Oh, he can't be involved. I've waited two weeks to give it some air."

"Are you Bergs coming at me one at a time, or is this like a gang initiation?"

"Oh, we didn't come to fight."

"You said that like I should be scared."

"You're facing Moses Bergstein. You should be fucking terrified."

"Four of you. One of me. We could just be nice and start a basketball team."

Without looking at his boys he said, "Abraham."

His second equine-faced son opened the trunk of his car. Then Poppa Bergs motioned.

He said, "We can do this quietly or we can do this the hard way."

"You're not going to shoot me, Moses Bergstein."

"Mr. Bergstein to you, you haughty sonofabitch."

"You're not going to shoot me."

He looked at his sons; his boys looked at each other. Then the patriarch of the Bergs fired four times. The headlight to the Bentley was hit. The windshield was hit three times. My heart rate increased, but I didn't jump. The Bergs came together and stood side by side. The shortest of the clan was around six feet. The tallest was about six-foot-five. All had broad shoulders. They wore snarls and deadly faces while the patriarch held the gun.

Moses Bergstein said, "The next shot

494

won't miss you. Drop the bat or . . ."

I dropped the bat and shivered. I was wet and cold and the chill that had settled into my bones refused to set me free. When I kicked the bat away, Moses lowered his gun and looked at his boys. He did that as if to say that this was how a man did things. The easy way. He looked at his boys like they were all fuckups who hadn't lived up to his standards. He'd made them come after me. While they had that moment, I took a deep breath, and pulled the .45 from behind my back. I started shooting. It wasn't the time to think. I pulled the trigger over and over.

Moses went down first. He had to. He had the gun.

Then it was too late to turn back. On the range, I was nine out of ten.

Once a man had killed a man, killing more men was nothing. It was all the same punishment. The state couldn't kill a man twice. And a man couldn't go to Hell more than once.

I kept pulling the trigger. Once it started, it was impossible to stop.

When I was done, my ears rang, deafness took control, and for a moment, the world was a place of sight, not sound. That scared me more than the shooting. My adrenaline was high and my fear and paranoia and fight or flight had become a monster. I took deep, deep breaths and now made myself think. Being deaf terrified me. Now I couldn't hear and couldn't breathe and it felt like I was the one underwater. I cursed and panted and cursed and tried to relax my clenched jawbone. Bobby Holland was somewhere out there floating in the frigid waters of a swimming pool and now four Bergs were on the ground decorated in blood and lead. I jerked and expected a dozen more Bergs to appear out of nowhere. No more Bergs were in sight. Only the one left seated in the car. The one that had been put on punishment like he was a bad child. He didn't get out and start shooting. Gun aimed, like I had been trained by LAPD when I took shooting lessons with Regina Baptiste, again for her part in a film where she had to handle firearms, breathing hard, body aching, teeth clenched, I went to the car, clothes sloshing, moved fast through the sole headlight from my Bentley. He was in the backseat, panicked and doing his best to crawl over the seat to get into the front so he could drive away. He'd seen his father go down, then saw his three brothers being gunned down as they tried to run away from speeding bullets. He saw me, saw my gun, then opened his door, stepped out, faced me trembling. He nodded then came toward me, jaw broken, lips tight, anger and tears in his eyes. His old man had tended to his injuries, but hadn't taken him to the hospital, probably as punishment. He looked down at his dead relatives, his chest rising and falling as tears rolled.

Bizarro Bergs stood straight and looked at me, dared me, his breathing hard and macho.

I snapped, "Why didn't you leave this between me and Johnny?"

The ringing in my ears had died down enough for me to hear the edges of my own words. Still, they sounded like they had come from far away. I repeated what I had asked and heard better. He tried to say something. But it was gibberish, made no sense. Not at the moment.

I tossed him his Tumi bag and told him to look inside. His gun was there. The .380 that he'd brought to shoot me with was back in the bag. It was clearer to me now. He was to stick the gun in my back and lead me away from The Apartments. He'd seen me, lost control of his emotions and ended up in a fight. He didn't stick to his father's much simpler plan to be patient and take me. I'd put his gun back in his bag as I drove from Bobby Holland's home.

The last Bergs brother exploded in grief and anger and reached in to take his gun out.

He aimed it at me and pulled the trigger to blow my brains out. Nothing happened. It was empty. If he had used guns before, if he was the type of man that his father seemed to be, he probably could have told by the weight of the gun. He was praying for a bullet to be in the clip. I wasn't that stupid. He looked at me, incensed and defeated. He dropped the gun and looked back at the dead men. Then he turned back and looked at me. I looked him in his eyes. He dared me. Traffic whizzing by on the 405, moon watching us, I shot him in the head.

I picked up the baseball bat and tossed it back inside the Bentley. Next I wiped down Bobby Holland's gun and dropped it near my car. Death in the air, I rushed back inside my Bentley and left the dead men where they were. I returned to the 405 and drove north, connected with the 101 and headed toward downtown L.A., imagining ways to get to Johnny Handsome.

Halfway back to Downey, as I stared through bullet-cracked glass, the nausea kicked in.

Not until then did I feel the stinging in

my ear. I touched my pain and my hand came back red.

I'd almost died. I'd almost been shot in the head.

By the time I made it to the 605 Freeway, I figured out what the last Bergs had said.

He'd said, "Because we're family, you sonofabitch. Nobody fucks with the Bergs."

The news report on KTLA said that the police arrived at the scene on Skirball and the registration on the .45 led them back to Bobby Holland's home. The front door was closed, but it wasn't locked. I had left it unlocked when I had left. They called out and moved from room to room, saw no one, then paused at his office, stood on top of the rug that covered Bobby Holland's blood. What was all around the room grabbed their attention, made them look up and not down. For a moment, as radios squawked, they took in the outstanding shrine and the magnificence of Regina Baptiste. A moment later, they snapped out of their own fantasies and headed outside. His stunning eighteen-year-old Hungarian lover was still drugged out and unconscious by the pool of death, a package of cocaine at her side, powder on her nose, and her slender hands between her shapely legs. She looked tempting when the police showed up with their guns drawn. When they touched her shoulder, she jerked awake. First she smiled at the boys in blue, despite their guns being drawn, smiled until she saw Bobby Holland's naked body facedown in the pool. She stared for a long moment, called Bobby Holland's name over and over, allowed what was going on to register, and then she shook her head and screamed. She screamed that she had told him not to go swimming a few minutes ago, said that they were just talking, that she was lonely and he was going to swim then come to have sex with her, that they were going to do the six nine and she was going put on the strap-on and make love to him the way he liked so much, that she was waiting on him to finish his swim and feel asleep. She said that it must have been the Benadryl, and even though she had done some blow, she couldn't stay awake, and that after Bobby Holland had handed her the blow, she had been excited and hadn't paid attention, cried that maybe she could've saved him but she hadn't wanted to get her Choo shoes and beautiful hair wet. Then tears became anger and she snapped that Bobby Holland had fucking drowned himself and fucked up her life and she would have to go back to being a waitress at Roscoe's Chicken and Waffles on Gower and Sunset and move back into a crowded and smelly one-bedroom apartment with five other people on Hollywood and Franklin. Piroska Anastazia Dorika Vass Torma wished that she had never left Johnny Bergs for Bobby Holland. They asked her if she was familiar with Johnny Bergs. She did her best to calm down, repeated what she had screamed, that Johnny was her ex-boyfriend. They had been boyfriend and girlfriend for almost two weeks and it had been very nice while it lasted.

"Did Johnny Bergs want you back? Was there a fight over you between them?"

"Johnny call and call and call. Look at me. I am beautiful. All men want me back."

"Was Bergs fighting with Holland?"

"Every one fights with Bobby. Every one is jealous of him."

"So Bergs and Holland were at odds over you."

"Bobby tells me not to cry and tells me how beautiful I am. That I am more beautiful than Regina Baptiste. And he tells me he can put me in movies and make me a star, a better star than her. I go home with him. I leave Johnny Bergs and say nothing and go with Bobby Holland. Bobby brings me here and eat my poosy and make love and treats me like I am the better special woman in the world. We do some drugs and he laugh and have fun while I wear strap-on for him and make love to him like a dog. He laugh and tell me that he e-mail the video of Johnny Bergs and Regina Baptiste having sex to the world. He hated her. I didn't like her. She is rude. Very rude. He make her famous and she leave him for a writer. I would not leave Bobby, ever. He Tweet that the sun in his life had gone down two years ago, but now it had risen again, new and improved. He was talking about me. But now that fucker is dead. He is fucking dead. He die right in front of me. Why would he do that to me? Fucking idiot die in front of me."

"Try and focus. You saw Bobby Holland swimming tonight?"

"He talk to me while he swim. He ask me to swim with him. I tell him no."

"You went back inside?"

"No. I watch him. We talk while he swim. He tell me that he buy me new iPhone and iPad tomorrow. Now he dead. How will I get my new iPhone and iPad now?"

"I need you to focus. You and Mister Holland were here alone?"

"Yes. He tell me to wait out here while he swim."

"So, confirming, it was just you and Mr. Holland here this evening?"

She nodded. "Mister Police Officer, I have a very serious question to ask you."

"Yes?"

"Will I be in the big newspaper and on all the television talk shows now?"

When she stood up, she dropped her package of blow. She bent at the waist and accidentally-on-purpose gave law enforcement a view of her derriere, a view that made them all pause, and she quickly picked up her blow, her final gift from Bobby Holland, stuck her fingernail inside, then sniffed and felt the rush before she dropped the package back in her pocket.

"I'm sorry, ma'am."

"I am so sad right now. So very sad."

"Did you just snort cocaine in front of us?"

"Would you like some, handsome police officer?"

Tears in her eyes, she extended the package to the officers. The officers looked at each other. This was Los Angeles. This was planet Hollywood. They had seen stranger. When she was handcuffed and led through the house, as they all stepped where I had stepped, touched things that I had touched, when the front door opened on a sea of news reporters, on bloggers who were outside streaming live on the Internet, she kicked and yelled that she wished that she had never left Hungary for Hollywood. She yelled that everyone did cocaine and they were picking on her for no reason. All she wanted to do was be in the movies like Julia Roberts. That was all she wanted to do, come to Hollywood and be the next *Pretty Woman* of the world.

Around the time Driver was pulling out of The Apartments, miles away in the valley, Bobby Holland's ex-wife's BMW X6 turned and sped down his cul-de-sac, angered because Bobby Holland hadn't returned her phone calls. He'd been busy. But I doubt if she cared. The ex-wife was frantic, her luggage crammed inside with her children and the three dogs. She had managed to get custody of the dogs as well. She had to make it to LAX in time to catch her flight to Norway. After a decade of being absent from the cinema, she was finally working again, back to being an actress. She had been cast in a film in Europe. She still had a chance to work. She had also been cast in London for a twelve-week run of Shakespeare's *Much Ado About Nothing.* Bobby Holland had refused to grant permission for their kids to leave the country for three months, and he managed to obtain temporary custody of his kids. That custody would lower his child-support payments and give him leverage in a custody battle. Those notes were in the files that were inside Bobby Holland's desk, files that would vanish and find their way to the media. His angered ex-wife slowed down when she saw all the police and the news vans out front. At first she thought that Bobby Holland was filming at his home. At first. Then she looked up in the sky and saw the news chopper overhead. There was an ambulance out front too. She cursed and shook her head as tears ran down her face. What mattered to her the most was her film and that it was Bobby Holland's court-ordered days to watch the kids and somehow Bobby Holland had, once again and for the last time, managed to fuck up her life.

As she and her children opened their car doors, before she could yell for them to stay inside the car, she heard a woman screaming, then saw her fighting with the police. They stood back and watched a half-naked woman being forced inside the backseat of a police car.

News for Johnny Bergs
msnbc.com
The death of Johnny "Handsome" Bergs
5 hours ago

After killing comedienne Frances Johnson on the streets of Sunset Boulevard, Johnny Bergs took his own life as hundreds looked on. The same night, his father and four brothers were found gunned down on Skirball Center Drive.

CLICK HERE FOR OTHER CELEBRITY SUICIDES

Los Angeles Times (blog) — (8100) related articles.

News for Bobby Holland
msnbc.com
The death of Bobby Holland
3 hours ago

Director Bobby Holland, a suspect in the murders of both the brothers and father of Superstar Johnny Bergs, was found dead at his home. Sources say that after a drug-filled evening, he had fallen, or possibly hit his head diving, and drowned in his swimming pool.

Sources claim that only a few hours ago, the gun used to kill the late Johnny Bergs's father and four brothers was traced to film director Bobby Holland. It appears that Johnny Bergs and Bobby Holland were at odds over a very beautiful woman, Piroska Anastazia Dorika Vass Torma. Torma is an aspiring actress and an extra on Bergs's last movie.

CLICK HERE FOR SEX TAPE SCANDAL WITH REGINA BAPTISTE

Rumors are that Torma is in the U.S. on false documentation claiming to be eighteen, but is a sixteen-year-old runaway. She has been dubbed the "Hungarian Lolita." Torma informed the media that she is selling her life story to a New York publishing company. The untitled book has been optioned.

Los Angeles Times (blog) — (8100) related articles.

CHAPTER 35

As six members of the Bergs family and Bobby Holland were being put in drawers inside the morgue, as they were being placed in deep freeze, I stepped out of a nice hot shower. After I had washed away the scent of fear and anger and stench of murder, I looked at my trembling hand, the hand that had pulled the trigger and saved my life, and waited for it to calm down, waited for the tremors to subside. I closed the lid, sat down on the toilet, and practiced breathing in a steam-filled room. I left the water running in the sink, used that to create sound, and massaged my temples for a while before I picked up the iPhone that I had been given by Alice Ayres. I didn't play the video that she had shown me, but I played the one where I had drowned Bobby Holland. The sound was on mute, but I remembered all that was said. I grimaced and watched it like I was watching *Faces of*

Death. I wasn't happy about what I had done, but I told myself that what I had done was necessary. I convinced myself that there was no other solution. Protecting Regina Baptiste was my job. I was about to delete the video. Keeping it was too dangerous. But I heard Regina let out a painful groan and stopped.

I called out, "Are you okay?"

"Come here when you get done."

Then I turned the water off and brushed my teeth before I went to the bedroom, the bedroom that belonged to Varg Veum, the bedroom that now had Regina Baptiste sitting on the edge of the Italian bed. It was a bed that she had sat on many times, a bed that we had made love on a thousand times, but here, in this apartment, sitting on that bed, in this dreary lighting, she looked out of place. This rundown apartment complex, this wasn't her world. But the way she looked, the way this place had fit what I felt inside, it seemed to fit her now as well. Her cellular was at her side, still ringing, now ringing nonstop, as she wallowed in endless tears, her head lowered, as if invisible strings were pulling her down. With effort, she raised her face.

I asked, "What else happened?"

Her lips trembled as she smiled at me.

But it wasn't really a smile. Her look was unsettling. Her muddled expression was new to me. But so was everything that had happened today. She shifted and held that expression, our emotions disjointed, but she looked as if I should know. Something else had happened since I had showered. Something serious.

She sighed and shook her head. "You always drop your clothes where you are."

"And you never tear the toilet paper along the perforated edges."

"Clothes on the floor. I hate that. My mother raised me that way. In that way, I'm like her. I need things orderly. I'm anal like that. And you know that I am anal like that, James."

I nodded. She was about to tell me something else. It was in her eyes.

She said, "I was going to empty your pockets before I hung your pants back up."

Again I nodded.

She whispered, "I always empty your pockets. Your shirt pockets. Jacket pockets. And pants pockets. My mother does that for my dad. And I do the same thing. Like my mom."

"You have a habit of doing that."

"You have a habit of leaving things in your pockets. You always leave money in your pockets. I have found so much money in your pockets. And valuable things that you should put away."

A moment passed before I managed to ask, "What did I leave in my pockets?"

She opened her right hand. Bobby Holland's watch rested in her palm, the Montblanc Nicolas Rieussec Chronograph Automatic, the version that came in 18k red gold.

She said, "I bought a watch like this for Bobby Holland. Three years ago."

I took a deep breath, but didn't say anything.

She said, "I spent one hundred and thirty thousand dollars on a watch for him. He wanted this watch so badly. And I bought it for him. One hundred and thirty thousand dollars."

I swallowed and rubbed the back of my neck before I released another sigh.

Her voice splintered, "It's engraved. From me to him. This is his watch. This is the watch I bought. The leather band is wet. It's soaking wet. And now it smells like chlorine."

We held eye contact. Her tears came faster. Occam's razor once again.

She whispered, "Jesus. This watch could be a needle in your arm, James."

I clenched my teeth.

She whispered, "James, how did this watch end up in your pockets?"

I didn't answer.

She went on, "You smelled of chlorine. Your skin was very cold. Like you'd been wet. And your eyes are bloodshot. Chlorine turns your eyes red. You know that and I know that."

Ill at ease, I pulled my lips in and set free a hum of angst.

"Driver came up here and grabbed fresh clothing. I knew something was wrong. You didn't answer my calls. I called you for hours. And when you came back, your hair was wet."

I said, "Let it go, Regina."

Then we were quiet again.

Her words almost incoherent, she said, "Bobby drowned. He drowned in his pool."

She trembled and ran her hands through her hair, more unsettled, more uncomfortable.

She swallowed, then asked, "Did anyone see you?"

I didn't reply.

She snapped, "Did anyone see you?"

"Not that I know of."

"You murdered him and kept a souvenir."

"That is not what happened."

"Jesus, Jesus, Jesus."

She remained on edge. I didn't know if she was my wife or my enemy.

But every other time, when a crisis appeared, she had vanished.

"Regina. Maybe you should leave. Put some distance between us."

"I'm not leaving."

I snapped, "I want you to leave."

"I'm not leaving."

"Leave. You can leave, walk away, and decide how you want to handle this."

She yelled back, "I'm not leaving."

"You run from everything else."

"I'm not running anymore, James. I'm never running again."

I leaned into the wall. She bounced her legs and let her tears fall on that damned watch. As a dozen emotions moved between us, the apartment shrank, became smaller than a jail cell.

She lowered her voice, "Did you leave any evidence?"

I paused and felt the tension rising. Clips from each video played in my brain. Beating Johnny. Regina and Johnny. Bobby giving her blow. Drowning Bobby. Shooting the Bergs.

She repeated, "Was any evidence left behind, James?"

"Not that I know of."

"Not that you know of? What the hell does that mean, James?"

"Something is always left behind. A footprint. A handprint on the wall."

"What did you leave, if you left anything?"

"Nothing that would connect it to you."

She lowered her head and rocked. "Jesus, is that what you think I'm crying about? Me?"

"Or over Bobby Holland. The way you're holding that watch, over Bobby Holland."

She threw the watch at me, threw it hard. It hit the wall and landed near my feet.

I picked it up and tossed it back. It landed on the bed next to her.

"James, I'm worried about you."

"And I'm fucking terrified."

"What if they find the videos he had?"

I said, "What Bobby Holland had on you, I took. I took his computer. If he had backups, no idea. He had things on you. I saw a tape. And he had Johnny Bergs by the balls too."

Saliva made her lips stick together when she managed to ask, "What did he want?"

The money, the cars, her talents, my script, Johnny Bergs, I told her what he had wanted. She listened without moving for a while; suddenly she shook her head in outrage and disbelief.

"Then what, James?"

I picked the watch up and stared at its face. "I baptized him and left."

"Then what? Did you stop anywhere?"

"Yes."

"Where?"

"I was being followed."

"Who saw you, James? Who followed you?"

"Johnny Bergs's father and brothers."

"The Bergs?"

"I pulled over and killed them."

Her head jerked up and her face twisted in a brand-new shock, her mouth wide open.

"Repeat that."

I said, "They had come to kill me. It was self-defense. Bobby Holland was murder. The rest was self-defense. If you want to turn me in and save yourself, I'm not going to stop you."

"Jesus, Jesus, Jesus."

"Actually, it was Moses."

"What was that?"

Again I took out the phone I'd been given by Alice Ayres. I'd left it sitting on the dash when I had faced the Bergs. It had recorded Moses shooting at me. Threatening me.

Then with me off screen, Moses was shot. His boys froze. One by one they all died.

"I shot them all. I killed them all."

"They had come to kill you because of me."

"Because I beat Johnny Handsome's ass."

"You attacked him because of me."

"He humiliated me and I humiliated him."

"Jesus, Jesus, Jesus."

"Stop saying that. Will you please stop saying that?"

"I feel sick. I feel ashamed."

I pulled on my pants and went and sat in the living room.

She came in after me and stood over me.

Her voice trembled as she said, "I don't care how many people you killed, I don't care if you ran over babies in your car. I don't care. I'm your alibi. Understand that. We've been together all evening. We've been together for as long as you say. I'm your fucking alibi, James."

"No, you're not."

"Yes, I am. And if you go against me, I'll kill you with my own hands. I swear I will."

Regina Baptiste stood over me, shaking her head, palming a dead man's watch. Then she went into the kitchen. Pots banged. The refrigerator opened. A chicken was taken out. So was a chopping board. Chicken was cut up. A big pot of water was put on the stove. Potatoes were cut up. Carrots. Yellow onions. Allspice, garlic, salt, dried red pepper, and lime juice were added. When the pot started to boil, Regina walked by me, that watch in her hand, and went back into the bedroom. She went into the bedroom and slammed the door.

There was a knock at the front door and my heart sped up.

I wondered how many Bergs there were. And how many knew where I lived.

I stood and opened the door without asking who it was. If they had come for me, I'd go. I'd go and leave my wife where she was, safe and in the bedroom. I'd go quietly.

But it was Mrs. Patrice Evans, dressed in her workout gear with a big smile on her face. She winked and brushed right by me taking her clothes off as she hurried toward my bedroom.

"I have thirty minutes. Come fuck me, Varg."

The bedroom door opened and Patrice screamed and ran back into the living room gathering her clothing. Jaw tight, Regina entered and stood where the hallway touched the living room. She looked at Mrs. Patrice Evans as if they were the only ones in the room.

Patrice stared at my wife for a moment, stared at her as if she looked familiar, as if she was trying to place her face, then she backed away from Regina. When she made it to the hallway, she took off jogging. I watched her as she ran by oblivious neighbors. After I closed the door, I looked at Regina. She shook her head and bit her bottom lip. What had just happened mattered to her. It looked like it mattered to her more than the death of Bobby Holland. Or the death of Johnny Handsome. A new devastation had been added.

I sat down on the sofa. James Thicke took a seat in Varg Veum's complex world.

Regina said, "We have bigger issues."

Regina went to the kitchen to check on the food, she saw that it was done, and she turned the stove off.

She came back and stood over me. She sat down at first, then she lay down on her side, put her head in my lap and closed her eyes. I listened to the sirens in the distance.

She cried soft tears again. "It wasn't a revenge fuck, James. It was accidental. It was an accidental fuck. It wasn't a luck fuck. It wasn't intentional. It wasn't adultery. It was accidental."

While she shook her foot, I rubbed her hair and massaged her temples.

She said, "Mine wasn't an affair. It wasn't. I swear that it wasn't."

"It was still broken trust. Broken trust makes it easy to embrace temptation."

"It wasn't me. I was lost. It was Sasha."

"You didn't tell me that Bobby Holland was there."

She stopped shaking her foot.

Johnny Handsome was dead. I didn't want him dead, but his death gave me no sorrow just as killing Bobby Holland would never give me any grief. That said a lot about me. About the man I was. I didn't like my wife crying over men who had been inside of her, accidentally or not. I'd killed a handful of people in the last few hours, and that was what troubled me the most.

I had killed all of those people and not one of those deaths bothered me.

She set the table and we pulled up the barstools and sat down.

No matter who died, no matter the loss, the living had to continue feeding.

She said, "We have to throw away the watch. No souvenirs. We break it and toss it. It's registered. We can't chance anyone finding it and trying to pawn it. Best to have it vanish."

I nodded and ate a piece of chicken.

A thousand moments went by before I said, "Dinner tastes good."

"Thanks."

Din rose up around us, the din that came with this world. I had grown used to the noise. I could tell that it grated on Regina's nerves.

I put the dishes in the sink and heard a loud noise coming from outside the bedroom window. I went and looked, saw a U-haul had pulled up outside and stopped near the entry to this building. The police didn't travel in U-Hauls. On edge, I went back to the sofa. Regina came over and lay down, put her head in my lap again, her breathing as disturbed as mine.

She whispered, "I wish I had been there to help drown him too."

While sirens wailed and the neighbor over me finished a round of sex, we stayed just like that. Then we watched the news on my laptop, read RSS feeds, read comments on Facebook and Twitter, moved from there to at least fifteen other social networking sites, took in comments that were a combination of sorrow and meanness, jokes and laughter at the expense of the dead. The bloggers were roaring like the many-headed beasts they had become. People were killed every day, but when it involved the famous, it was actually treated as if it were a crime. There was video of neighbors being interviewed outside of Bobby Holland's home, neighbors that cried and said how he was a wonderful man, a great father to his kids, and a leader of their community.

There was also a video of a police tow truck taking the Bergs' car away from the scene of the crime up at Skirball Center Drive. Banners read: WHY DID JOHNNY BERGS KILL HIMSELF? WAS THE MAFIA INVOLVED? DID ZOLOFT CAUSE JOHNNY BERGS TO BECOME SUICIDAL? TWO OF RE-GINA BAPTISTE'S LOVERS FOUND DEAD. REGINA BAPTISTE: IS SEX WITH THAT DIVA A DEATH-JINX? Computers were being seized from Johnny Bergs's home. There were prayer vigils, pointless interviews with his publicist, and candid words from his grief-stricken fans. We endured that bullshit as long as we could, watched until we couldn't stand the news. Then we forced ourselves to disconnect, went into the bedroom and undressed. Regina Baptiste. Here. Undressing. Stripping until she was naked. It struck me as odd for a few moments. Very surreal and distant. I was afraid to go to sleep. She looked overtired, too exhausted to rest.

The furniture was familiar to her, but the environment was a foreign country.

She rubbed my chest. "James."

"Yeah."

"I need to feel good, James."

"Now's not the right time."

"I need to feel good."

I was angry with her. But I looked at her, saw how desperate she was to reconnect with me. Saw how she needed my acceptance right now. Then I looked at her as she rolled over on her belly and reached for me. I stared at the woman whom many had died over in the last few hours. She was a queen who could start a war that could ruin a nation. A man had killed himself because of her powers and I had killed another man to save her. She had set Hollywood on fire and the fire would burn the way Chicago did back in 1871. I touched her much-desired figure and the rise of her round backside. I touched all things that men and women desired, all the things that were marketable. She looked at me, and with her expressive face and eyes that held her emotions, she seduced me as Hollywood had seduced her. I lay on her back and moved against her. I entered my wife again.

"I've missed you, James."

Tears rolled from her eyes. But not enough to wash this day clean.

Despite the drowning, despite the killings, my mind couldn't process the concept of an accidental fuck. Maybe one day it would.

Today, as numbness and anxiety danced, I was liberal, but my mind just wasn't that open. Intentional, yes. Rape, yes. Accidental, no.

She stopped me. "Not so rough, James."

She hadn't told Johnny Handsome to slow down. She had moaned for him the same way. Now I was the one drowning. Drowning in a memory that I'd never escape.

"James, James, not so rough."

I slowed down, slowed time down, and listened to her breathing. I had to not see Regina Baptiste. I had to pretend that she was someone else. Hazel had rejected me. Patrice would never be good enough. I needed a better woman. I pretended that she was Isabel. I pretended that she was the mature woman with the beautiful body. The mature woman who loved books. The beautiful woman with the British accent and wicked sense of humor. Isabel with the long beautiful hair.

My orgasm was immense and her body went into spasms. My orgasm was voluminous, as if I had never orgasmed once in my life and had saved it all up for this moment. It was embarrassing the way I took her, the desperate way I pounded her, the way I held onto her to get resentment out of my body, the way I showed her how fucking angry I'd been with her for days on end. And it was equally embarrassing the way she came, the way her orgasm came in waves.

When it ended, I rolled away from her as if I had been with a whore, my chest heaving.

I was a new man now. Not Varg. Not James. Someone in between. I looked at Regina Baptiste. She looked as strange to me now as she had the first night we'd been together.

She asked, "Why are you looking at me like that, James?"

I turned my head away, took control of myself, purged evil thoughts.

A moment went by.

As I sweated, I said, "I need to tell you something. Something that I did."

"Is this something to do with a woman?"

"No. Well. Yeah."

"Okay. What?"

My mind was on the revelation that had Bobby Holland ready to shoot me. If he had shot me over that lie, then he would be alive. I confessed. I told her that I had called the paparazzi. I told her that I had set this thing in motion. I'd made the first domino fall.

She said, "Impossible."

"What do you mean?"

"It's impossible because . . . I called the paparazzi."

I said, "I called them early that morning. Before you showered."

"No. I had called them. I'd called them the night before. They were waiting for me to leave the night before. Leaving your house in the middle of the night, being caught, that would have been more dramatic. When I had awakened and watched you sleeping, I had already called them. I had called them while we were doing laundry. That's why I was going to leave you and not say good-bye. I had to call them again and let them know to be at your gates in the morning."

I paused. "Why did you?"

"Nine days with you changed me. I wanted James Thicke. I wanted you."

"Did you?"

"I wanted that thing with Bobby Holland to end. I embarrassed him and forced it to be over. I knew his ego. He had to feel as if my leaving was his doing. It had to be his idea. But it was my planning. If I had just left him, who knows what he would've done to my career?"

"He was controlling you."

"Two million over the last two years."

"You paid him two million?"

"Yes."

"He didn't tell me that."

"I gave him a mil up front. Transferred it to his Norwegian business account. But he kept coming back for more. He needed money to keep his kids in private school. His rent. The note on his car."

"You never told me."

"I know. I just knew that I wanted to get away from him."

I let a moment go by. "Your paparazzi were out there with mine."

She said, "It was more than me. I called for other reasons too."

"What other reasons?"

"Since we're putting everything on the table."

"Okay. What other reasons, Regina?"

"I wanted that other thing you were in to be over too."

"What other thing?"

"Hazel Tamana Bijou."

I paused. "Hazel. Did she say something to you?"

"I saw Hazel Tamana Bijou. When we were in the bar, that first night, I saw her reflection in the mirror. I saw her and thought that she was looking for me, and then I realized that she had come looking for you. The way she left, I know she had. She saw us and there were tears in her eyes. Women like Hazel don't cry. And she cried for you, James. That's how special you are."

"You were jealous."

"She inspired me. I told you that I was obsessed with you. You would've been my first one-night stand. You know that I'm not that kind of girl. Not even when I was on coke."

"You knew that I was waiting on her to call me."

"I knew. But I wanted you for me. I loved you. I had studied you. I knew your work better than you did. I was obsessed with you. I loved your mind. I loved you inside out. I told you that and I meant it. And I still mean it. What I am to others, that's what you are to me."

"You love me."

"Yes."

"Like when you told other men."

"When I told other men that I loved them, I was only acting."

"You engraved it on their watches."

"One watch."

"You had it engraved."

"That was fiction. That was a well-written lie."

"How do I know you're not lying now?"

"You have to trust me."

I was exhausted.

Two weeks of dealing with Bergs, two weeks of being a man who called himself Varg Veum, two weeks of little sleep, two weeks of being in this self-imposed hell using stress and anxiety as my mattress and pillows. But I made love to her. Because this could be my last chance to love my wife before I was dragged away and got only approved conjugal visits.

We stood up. When I moved by the dresser, I looked out the window. So did Regina. First I looked at the U-Haul. Mr. Holder was loading up the truck. Vera-Anne was down there too. Her children were with her. Vera-Anne was crying. Mr. Holder didn't look happy either, but he was a man of resolve and he was moving forward. He was sending her away. I had killed men and didn't feel as guilty as I felt for what was going on between Vera-Anne and Mr. Holder. It wasn't my business. It wasn't the business of James Thicke. That May-September affair wasn't my concern. Their needs and insecurities had been here before I arrived. Even though at that moment it reminded me of Bobby Holland packing up Regina Baptiste's life and sending her to me, even though I wanted to know where Vera-Anne and her kids were going, my concern, James Thicke's concern, came from the right of where Mr. Holder and his sobbing ex-lover and her two primary concerns were standing.

Regina was looking that way, unconcerned with the distraught strangers down below.

We saw them at just about the same time. We saw the men and women walking and jogging and running this way with cameras. Professional cameras. We saw the residents of the building congregating. Cars were slowing down trying to figure out what was going on.

Regina said, "No, no, no. It can't be."

I closed the blinds and we peeled back one section and peeped outside.

Two stories down were at least three-dozen people with cameras.

The paparazzi had arrived and they had managed to sneak onto the property.

Misty Mouse was out there. The girl that I had had a confrontation with in the laundry room, the neighbor who lived above me, she was out there with them. Dark jeans and a pink and green T-shirt. I LOVE BUK-KAKE. She had recognized me. The day by the dry pool, when she asked me what I did, she didn't know then, but be it online or on the news as they talked about Regina Baptiste and Johnny Bergs, she had recognized

529

my face and finally called in the paparazzi. *Cruelty of Men Toward Women.* She'd brought the book by here because she wanted to see my face again. She'd wanted verification because seeing me here made no sense.

She wanted to see how much Varg Veum looked like James Thicke.

But maybe when she had come inside my apartment, she had seen all the magazines that were on the coffee table, and each magazine had Regina Baptiste's face on the cover.

Or maybe she had Googled Club Mapona and saw my face with the other owners.

With her dreadlocks framing her face, Misty pointed toward my window and cameras flashed in rapid succession, like a gun being discharged at the enemy on Skirball Center Drive.

I wondered how much they had paid her. Probably less than her hourly clients.

This was her revenge for our tense and almost combative moment in the laundry room.

Her revenge for being tossed out of Club Mapona with her now-deceased clients.

Touché, bitch. Touché.

My enemy glared up at my window and kissed her teeth.

Regina Baptiste asked, "Did you fuck her too?"

"Nope. But I folded her lingerie. That pissed her off."

As the commotion grew, Mr. Holder paused loading the U-Haul. He wiped sweat from his brow and looked toward Vera-Anne. He saw that she was still crying. Her babies were crying as well, but she was looking up toward my window, maybe because everyone else down there was gawking at my window. The attention of the paparazzi had her. Mr. Holder raised his head and looked at the window of the man who had brought his problems here and made Hell that much hotter for all of its occupants. And with the paparazzi, I was making it that much worse.

Regina Baptiste said, "They found me. They're still dogging me."

"I'll get you out of here."

"Are you scared?"

"I'm terrified."

My wife lay down on the carpet, and pulled me down next to her.

She swallowed. "No one saw you."

"No."

"No neighbors."

"No."

"No barking dogs and no kids."

"And I didn't use my cellular. And when I had the shoot-out on Skirball Center Drive, I used Bobby Holland's gun. I wiped it down and left it at the crime scene with the Bergs."

"And you stole Bobby's computer?"

"I did."

"You threw away all of the clothes that you were wearing."

"And rearranged his office so it wouldn't look like it was missing."

We lay there for a while, each inhale and exhale redefining who we were. Screenwriter and actress. Murderer and co-conspirator.

A cuckold and a woman betrayed as a result of her own action.

She wiped tears from her eyes again, wiped away tears like she was trying to wipe away both pain and death. She failed to stop the tears. Regina Baptiste was on her stomach. Her head turned to the side, facing me.

She said, "About this marriage."

"If you say it was accidental, it was accidental. If you say it was Sasha, it was Sasha. It wasn't you. It wasn't the woman that I'm with now. It was someone else who looked like you."

I ran my fingers over her body again.

Outside my window, outside of the world that once belonged to Varg Veum, the rumble grew. There were the standard Vietnamese curses and Caribbean insults flying out of the windows, the blowing of horns as the paparazzi was being rained on by profanity from men, women, and children, the outcries from a many-headed beast.

I moved closer and kissed her lips.

She whispered, "The cameras are waiting on us."

"Let me call Driver."

"I'm calling a mover. I'm going back home. You're coming back home too."

"You need better clothing. When you step outside, you need to look sizzling."

"Vera Wang would be nice."

"Regina. We're in the middle of a recession. No need to go Vera Wang."

"You're right. This is the real world. Not the-red-carpet-and-velvet-rope world."

"Nice jeans, a nice sexy top with a little cleavage, and you can go all out on the shoes."

"Let me call my assistant."

As the racket outside became more irritating than a raucous shivaree, Alice Ayres arrived wearing a nervous smile. She was dressed in beige slacks and heels, simple jewelry and looked nothing like the woman

I had met at Abbott's Habit. Her dress, her demeanor, everything was different. She was here, but never in the way, highly unnoticeable. We exchanged greetings but she didn't look me in my eyes for more than a second. She never had. Hours after she had given me her cellular, hours after she had shown me a video of Bobby Holland feeding my wife cocaine, Bobby Holland had been found dead. She kept herself busy helping Regina put on her makeup, doing Regina Baptiste's hair, doing all the things that Regina Baptiste asked. Not long after, Driver returned. Panther was with him. She remained stationed by the Bentley. She made sure that it remained covered. When all had died down, she would drive it from here and take it to a shop in East L. A. Driver knew a Mexican named Pedro, and Pedro had connections.

I stood in the bedroom and looked down on the crowd, a crowd that yelled out how much they loved the woman named Regina Baptiste. A teenage girl stood on top of a car and started singing "Who's That Girl," the song that Regina had sung on *The Graham Norton Show*. As the East Indian girl sang, little by little, the crowd joined in. When that ended, another girl started singing "At Seventeen," and every woman in the crowd, no matter what nationality, joined in like it was a preplanned flash mob. It was a cultural festival. Brazilian. Asian. African. Mexican. East Indian. Native American. Russian. American. European. Pakistani. While the multitude chanted Regina Baptiste's favorite songs and yelled out how much they loved her and begged her to come out and say hello, a moving crew showed up to start packing up my apartment. They came in and began dismantling the life of Varg Veum. Regina Baptiste's name had more pull than my American Express Black credit card. The commotion had become too loud, like a rock concert. Neighbors had called friends and friends had driven and walked and taken the bus and Metro over from all parts of Los Angeles County, and a cavalry of policemen had to be dispatched to stop a riot from breaking out. Outside was a madhouse, but the second floor of building E had been cleared. It would be that way until we made it down to the first level. Today the elevator actually worked. The elevator opened and the shouting came like an explosion. They were all waiting. These were her supporters. Celebrity worship had taken root.

She smiled, but I knew that she was afraid. Afraid that one fool would be in a window the same way Oswald had waited in a library window for a motorcade to pass by. Or that someone would get as close to her as Jack Ruby had been to Oswald.

She was their religion of the moment. But not everyone believed.

However no blogger, no newscast, no post on Facebook, no Tweet, no one in this universe would be able to crucify what this crowd believed in. Controversy had made her brand larger.

Sleeping with Johnny Handsome had somehow made her more admirable and enviable. I couldn't change that. Johnny Handsome had become the new James Dean.

Johnny Handsome had just died. No one would ask her what it was like to sleep with a dead man. People only fantasized about sleeping with the living. Sane people, anyway.

Regina being called one of the last women that he had had sex with would sell magazines. I wouldn't like that, but I couldn't change that either.

James Thicke was just her husband. Just a writer. Her name was above the title of this moment and I was just another guy with his name rolling by in the credits. I was fine with that.

Patrice's face was a speck in the crowd. We made eye contact for a moment. Her expression was bewildered. She tried to figure out who I was. She wanted to know who the man that she had bedded for the last two weeks really was. Mr. Holder and Vera-Anne were at the back of the U-Haul; the U-Haul was now packed with the life of Vera-Anne and her children. The rental was blocked in by traffic and a swarm of people. Vera-Anne's mouth opened in surprise and awe. Above us, everyone who had resided on this side of the building had their windows open and had ringside seats.

All of this had happened because of Misty fucking Mouse.

Because of a fight that the Bergs clan had had inside of Club Mapona.

Driver led us through the crowd. Six-foot-two and able to move them all out of his way. With her assistant at her left side, Regina Baptiste kept her head held up high. If they had hated her in her absence, in her self-imposed hiatus, they sure as hell loved her now.

She asked, "What should I do?"

"Just don't be remorseful. No matter what has happened, don't be apologetic. The world hates weak people. Even weak people despised weaker people. Be gentle, but remain unapologetic. Be Donald Trump. Be George Bush. Even when you're wrong, you're right."

She had no publicist, so I assumed the job for the day. I protected her, but I also did what was best for her. There was a young man in the crowd wearing headgear that had a small camera attached. He was a blogger and he was streaming this moment live on the Internet. We were being broadcast in real time. I motioned at him, then told the police to let him through. The guy was surprised and amazed. He was side by side with Regina Baptiste, capturing the moment and broadcasting it live for the entire world to see. This was his fifteen minutes of fame.

In Hollywood, fans were putting flowers on Johnny Handsome's star.

In the valley, two kids were crying because their father had drowned.

A young Hungarian woman sat in a holding cell, crying, with no one to bail her out.

As the enthusiastic crowd pushed and squeezed her, Patrice watched me.

And so did her husband. He was a tall man, pale skin, red hair, and freckles.

Mr. Holder watched Regina Baptiste. He stared at my wife with an unhidden envy.

And so did Vera-Anne as she held one of

her children on her hip, the other by the hand.

I'd bet that Hazel Tamana saw this too, was watching this on the news or on the web.

I had watched Regina Baptiste, from actress, effloresce into a shining star.

I'd seen her fall. And now she was rising again.

Regina Baptiste shook hands. She hugged people. She touched dozens. People cried. A few fainted. She smiled for photos. She laughed and kissed people on their cheeks. And when asked about Johnny Bergs, she expressed the proper amount of admiration blended with sorrow. They wanted her to sing. They begged her to sing that song by Janis Ian.

Driver helped put her on top of a car and the way everyone cheered, you would think that she could walk on water and raise the dead.

But the girl from Montana acted, sang, and danced. In this world, in this country that was a trifecta. For many, for thousands, for millions, that was all that it took to become a god.

And wearing a very short black dress that had long sleeves and cleavage, add to that a belt that made her figure stand out, and a pair of insanely incredible turquoise Louboutin heels helped. She was right. They wanted to see her dressed up like a movie star, not as one of them.

Her singing and greeting her fans lasted twenty minutes. The blogger captured it all. A large section of the world had seen the cultural festival, had front-row seats. They had seen how everyone was on the same page, how everyone was ecstatic, how everyone was getting along. I hadn't seen that spirit in this complex since I had arrived.

Police surrounded me, but not one said a word to me. Not one arrested me for murder.

Hours ago I was the star of the show, drowning one man, then killing the Bergs in a roadside shootout, and now I was an extra in this movie, a movie that starred Regina Baptiste; at most my part was an Under-Five. When I was with her, it was always about her. Once again, I was the bit player, atmosphere. Hundreds of cell phones were pointed our way, taking photos and recording. Something touched me deep inside. Part of me wanted to cry. But I smiled.

I'd remember this day to the other side of my death.

Regina said a few words, and when she spoke, whatever she said became the gospel according to Baptiste. She said that a lot of lies had been told about her, said that the small-minded and greedy had attacked her over the last few weeks, and that each lie had hurt her family and for that, because she was all about honesty and the truth, every magazine that had printed a lie would be sued. They applauded her. They lauded her attack on yellow journalism.

When my wife was done, Driver and the police helped Regina down from the top of a vehicle and she came to me. She hugged me, her body once again shaking from being nervous, wiped away tears, then held on to my hand, showed them that I was her leading man.

Within a day, she would have 7,586,777 views, 23,374 likes and 477 dislikes on this moment. Not bad. Not bad at all for the daughter of a Conky Joe from Spanish Wells.

She raised her voice and said, "I thought everyone hated me."

"Everyone loves you. And anyone who doesn't adore you, anyone who screams out anything differently, will hear an echo in that place where their brains should be."

We walked hand in hand, swaggering on the promise of life, cameras flashing, the eyes of the curious reflecting in our sunglasses, approval, envy, and disdain brightening and heating our faces, the hottest scandal in Hollywood at the moment, a scandal that had to be embraced and confronted head on or the flames of judgment would kill us, and the fire was our fire, the fire was ours to claim, and we'd ride the waves of fame and infamy until the next scandal arrived.

That was when I thought about the video of Bobby Holland being drowned.

When Regina had found Bobby Holland's watch in my pocket, she had pulled me off task. The video hadn't been deleted. I'd been distracted by confessing what I had done, her cooking, Patrice showing up in search of a good time, and trying to close this emotional and dangerous chasm that had grown between Regina Baptiste and me. Then the paparazzi had appeared and caused an avalanche of her fans to end up outside my window. I'd left the phone behind. The crew was packing and I had left the damn phone behind. I had slipped and left the one thing that could damn me to prison for the rest of my days. The expression on my face didn't hide that panic. I had failed to delete the video of Bobby Holland dying by my hand. The shootout with the Bergs was on that phone. And so was the coke session with Bergs,

Holland, and Baptiste.

Once I had put Regina inside the car, her assistant joined her on the rear passenger side. I was at the rear driver's side. Regina was on her cellular. Everyone was calling her. Her old agent. Her old publicist. The director for *The Bodyguard.* The director of *A Star is Born.*

Alice Ayres had been in the apartment. Something told me that she hadn't gone into the bathroom and stolen her iPhone. I hadn't seen her go inside the bathroom. I had to be sure. As we sat, I sent her a text message and asked her if she had retrieved her cellular.

Without looking at me, she sent a text and told me she hadn't.

I asked Regina if she had seen an iPhone in the bathroom.

She told me that she hadn't noticed. She had been distracted as well.

I told Driver to wait. But he couldn't. The police directed us forward.

Enough was enough and the citizens of Downey wanted their city back.

Not everyone appreciated or was thrilled by the madness.

We had to escape while the police had the roadway open from the apartment to the entrance of the 605 South. The phone was left behind. I called the number of the movers, and they put me in contact with the workers. The packing crew said that they hadn't seen a cellular in the bathroom. They looked all over. No phone. Phones didn't vanish. Someone had it.

CHAPTER 36

There were moments when a man saw his life very clearly. Clarity wasn't always a good thing. Back at The Apartments I'd walked to the third floor to return Misty Mouse's odious and poorly written manuscript, *Cruelty of Men Toward Women*. When I made it to that level, six young men were entering her apartment. Looked like it was bukkake time. Since the venal woman was occupied, I left her novel propped against her front door and headed down one level.

Over one hundred Post-it notes had been stuck on the apartment door at E-213, enough to fill the wooden door from top to bottom, enough to imply desperation. I peeled them all off. When I opened the door, part of me had wanted the space to be as it was, but the apartment was barren, empty, devoid of life. There were indentations in the carpet where the furniture had been. Across the hallway, the neighbors were playing Steely Dan. "Do It Again." That song remained thunderous after I closed the door and searched from room to room. In the kitchen, I looked inside the cabinets. In the bedroom, I searched the closets. I searched the cabinet under the sink in the bathroom. Nothing had been left behind. The videophone wasn't here.

I'd already unpacked everything in Los Feliz. It wasn't there either.

Above me, the sounds from Misty Mouse's working on her cheap bed never waned.

Inside the bathroom, jaw clenched, I stood and looked at the covering for the toilet's cistern. First I stared at the bathroom sink, then at the counter. I noticed it then. I ran two fingers across the top of the counter and looked at my fingers. Anger rose. There was an abrupt knock at the door. I wiped my hand on my pants and went to the door. It was Mr. Chetwyn Holder.

I invited him inside. He had on jeans and a polo shirt. He glanced at the red writing on my black T-Shirt. SUPPORT FINE ARTS. SHOOT A RAPPER. He looked around and saw that the place was empty, hollow, nothing to absorb sound, except for the carpet.

His voice had a slight echo when he said, "The other day . . ."

"Don't worry about it."

He nodded. "That was something else. What your wife did, all the people, that was something else. She made a lot of people happy. She's a talented woman. No matter what she did, the world loves her. I guess that's how it is when you can sing and dance."

I nodded then asked, "How did the reunion with your daughter go?"

"I thought she wanted to talk to me about the wedding. She did. But she had two decades of anger. Wanted to know why I never sent more money. Wanted to know if I ever loved her mom. Wanted to know why I left. I told her that what she was asking was complicated to explain. Love isn't a straight line. And it takes more than love to make a marriage work."

"It does. It really does."

"Everybody who is divorced used to be people in love, so love isn't the glue."

"Sounds like it was rough."

"I told her that she was my daughter and I loved her. Told her I wanted to walk with her at her wedding. I wanted to help her pay for the wedding, help make her day be the type of day that she wanted it to be, and walk with her. She told me that whenever she married, she'd walk alone. She said that all of her life she'd walked without me. She said that getting in contact with me was a fucking mistake. She cursed me just like that. Then she walked away."

"Did you go after her?"

"She's pregnant."

"Well, that could explain a lot, hormone wise."

"I didn't go after her, but when I left, she was still outside in the parking lot."

"You saw her."

"I went over to her and tried to calm her down. I held her in my arms and told her that I could be the best granddad in the world. Said that we could grow and get better at this father-daughter thing together. She asked me if a lousy dad equaled a wonderful grandfather. She pulled away, became real bitter and snarky. She is definitely her mother's daughter."

"Sorry to hear that."

"We cried for a while. I was a stranger to her. A stranger who used to sleep with her mother, nothing more. So I sat in her car and told her the truth. I didn't want to speak bad about her mother, but I told her the ugly truth. The drinking. The fighting. The other men. I guess I became as angry as she was. I thought that she would be mad or angered, but she cried and said that she already knew those things. She was angry because I had left her and she'd had to grow up with her mother. Her life had been hell. Then she told me that the wedding was off."

"You mean postponed?"

"It was off. She said that he left her. They're not getting married. I didn't ask her why. But if she was as rough with him as she was with me, she probably ran him away. She thinks that the man that she was going to marry left her the same way I had left her mom. She was afraid of being her mother. She has so much anger. And I'm afraid that she already is. They had put down money on this and that. Nonrefundable money, and he called and canceled it all."

I didn't say anything after that revelation.

He said, "So now she has nowhere to live. She's moving in with me."

"Okay."

"This one is my daughter. I won't feel like a fool if I take care of her from now until she can do better. The money that I had saved for her wedding, I'll use it to take care of her. I have close to forty thousand. Had almost forty-six, but Vera-Anne and her kids ate up some of it. Clothes for the kids. Pampers. Wipes. Milk. Vaseline. Powder. Soap. Lotion. Baby cups and spoons. I miss Vera-Anne, but she was a freeloader. I wanted to help her out, but I don't like feeling like I've been used. She was a freeloader. She used me for food and shelter. She won't get a job until she has to, and now she has to. Nothing in this world is free. When you're grown, you have to pull your own weight. She's not handicapped. She has to pull her own weight."

"I'll let you be the judge on that. What you're having to decide, it sounds tough."

"Love is always tough. Going against your heart is tougher."

"Sure is. It hasn't ever been easy."

He said, "Not in this jungle. Down here every day is a different battle."

"Not in my jungle either. It's just as rough. Love does us no special favors."

"I'll work and help my daughter get on her feet. She's my blood. She came from me."

"Redemption."

"Yeah. Redemption. I have twenty years of her rage and my guilt to work though."

"How do you think living with her is going to be?"

"Hell. It's going to be Hell. But it's a Hell that I created."

I handed him the key to the apartment that we were standing in.

I said, "I don't need it. No need letting it

go to waste. If your daughter wants to, if you want her to, she can just move up here and get her life back together. Or you can. Up to you."

"You're not coming back?"

"I'll go back to my jungle. This jungle is safer, but I'll go back to the backstabbing and ruthlessness that I've grown accustomed to. It's too kind over here."

He said, "I can sublet from you. I can pull a second job to pay you."

"I'm not doing this for money, Mr. Holder. When a man sees another man who needs help, he should help that man. That would make the world a much better place. A man never knows when the tides will turn and he'll be the one who will need help."

When I said that, he pulled his lips in. I'd fed him his own words and it hit home.

He said, "Look, I'm sorry about the things that I said. But when a man loves a woman, and that woman drives him crazy, when that woman that he loves just wants him for what he can do for her and not for love, it makes him want to act a fool. It didn't matter that she was younger than my daughter. We can't help who we fall in love with. We just wish that they fell in love with us the same way. I miss her. I miss her kids. But it is what it is, and that's all it is."

"Loving a woman makes a man do some crazy shit."

"You should know, James Thicke. We can agree on that, if nothing else."

I nodded. I wanted to ask where Vera-Anne had gone, but it wasn't for me to ask.

He said, "I was jealous of you. I was with a woman who didn't work and your wife made more money in weeks than I will make in a lifetime. And you make more than your wife makes. Maybe I felt like a fool. Like I had been tricked or something. After I had helped you move in, you told me who you were. That changed things for me, I guess. I thought you were a foolish man down on his luck and I came to help you move things from that U-Haul. You reminded me of my shortcomings. I saw you and I saw me sixteen years ago, unloading my furniture and moving here. But you could rent every apartment in this complex if you wanted. You could buy the complex, tear it down, and build a better one where we stand. I felt . . . that made me feel small."

I nodded. He'd never see me as a human being, not as a regular guy. He didn't know my family and me when were in the shadows of the Tottenham Hotspur Football Club. He didn't know me when my mother was a Chelsea girl. He didn't see us walking the cobbled roads of East London. Petticoat Lane. Brick Lane. The Indian shops. The smells. He didn't see that this place took me back to Hackney, back to Tottenham. I was home here. I grew up in this kind of poverty, so its people didn't scare me, and I didn't think that I was that different in character. In money yes, because money was a dividing line, but in the end, we all bled and died.

He asked, "Did you sleep with Vera-Anne?"

Compared to the things that had happened in my life, his problems were small, meant nothing, would all come to pass. Murder never came to pass. Still I gave him an audience and entertained his pain.

I said, "Nope."

"Did you kiss her?"

"She came to me crying about her life and when I consoled her, she kissed me, and that surprised me, but I pushed her away as soon as she did. So, no, I didn't reciprocate."

"She kissed you."

"Barely. Didn't last a second. I backed away from her, told her to respect you."

He nodded, then took a breath. "That's pretty much what Junkanoo said happened. He said that his momma went to you and she put her arms around you and kissed you."

"He told you."

"Because he knows right from wrong. Because I'm the only daddy he knows . . . he knew."

I nodded and realized that it was best that I said nothing else. Sometimes when a man's woman kissed another man, when she kissed him and meant it, when she kissed him and wanted him, the damage was done. He might as well have been taped fucking her three ways to heaven.

For a moment I had to breathe. Johnny Handsome had made my wife come.

He was dead but memories were eternal.

Mr. Holder said, "She lied. She stood in my face and lied on you. She has no character."

"She was scared. She knew what she had done was wrong. I told her that."

"But she spent my money then had the nerve to stand in my face and lie to me."

I nodded. His words were simple but blackness and pain resonated in every syllable.

I said, "She wanted to be out of poverty."

"We all do."

"She can't see that with you."

"She did nothing to help my situation.

And if she won the lottery tomorrow, despite all that I have done for her, despite how I feel about her, she would take her money and move on."

I let a moment go by. "How do you feel about her?"

"I love her. And right now, no matter what she did or said, that's the problem."

"Maybe what she was doing online was just flirting. People do that."

"She knew that you were my friend. Not some strange guy online. And she kissed you. She had no respect for me. You live one floor above me. And she kissed you."

He'd exhausted me with his pain. It was a bad time. My freedom was still at stake.

He shrugged. "If I take her back, I'll just be enabling her to be lazy and do nothing. When you take care of somebody, they get comfortable and think its their entitlement. It's like being lazy and on unemployment. Most of the people on unemployment don't look for jobs until the money runs out. Well, my days of socialism are over, so that means that her tax-free money just ran out. She kissed herself out of a free ride. Let's me know that I was really nothing to her. Nothing at all. I will no long enable her. So hopefully that poverty will motivate her."

He changed from speaking of Vera-Anne

in the tone of a lover to talking about her with the tone of a father who did what he had to do in order to make his child grow up.

I said, "You have a complicated life. As complicated as mine."

"But it's my life. It's ugly. I claim it. I'll never run from it, no matter how bad it gets."

"But you did run. It had become so ugly you had to run to keep from going crazy."

"I've never run."

"You made a choice. I never would have left my child. But it's easy for a man or woman to say what they would or wouldn't do when they're not wearing another man or woman's shoes."

"I didn't run. I did what I had to do."

"So did I, Mr. Holder. So did I. Nobody chased me. Sure, I didn't want to go to jail. No one does. But I didn't want to —" I paused, the memories from all that had happened almost to heavy to bear. "I didn't want to end up killing a man for sleeping with my wife."

"That boy killed a woman for making jokes about him and then he killed himself."

"I didn't run. I don't run. And maybe I should have run. But that's my problem to deal with. I'm going back home. Like a man. But it's not going to take me twenty years to do it. You left to keep from doing something unforgivable to your wife. I tried to do the same."

He nodded. That was my victory.

It was a bad week for him as well. Not on the same level as mine, but still horrific.

We all had bad weeks. We were all tested. We were all changed by events.

It just took him twenty years to make it back to the front of the line.

His bad season wasn't over. Mine hadn't ended. I had dead bodies behind me. There was a missing video recording in front of me. My bad season was a long way from being over.

"James Thicke."

"Yes, sir, Mr. Holder."

"Thanks for being my friend."

Not long after, Mr. Holder left. But his brokenhearted energy remained in the apartment. He left and I was back on task. I searched the apartment once more. I searched in vain.

When I went back inside the bathroom I looked down at the roll of toilet paper.

It hadn't been torn along the perforated edges.

CHAPTER 37

When he hit me, there was an explosion inside of my head.

The pain muffled his outburst. The blow from his fist had been as solid as it was abrupt. I staggered and I fell into my car, tried to grab the side view mirror to keep myself up. I was in the parking lot at The Apartments, at the side of my Maybach, and I had been attacked. It was Ted. It was Mrs. Patrice Evans's husband. Another man cuckolded. He had severe anger in his face and a tire iron in his hand. Tears in his eyes, jaw tight, he glowered at me the same way that I had glowered at Johnny Handsome in the rain. I fought to crawl away and the tire iron came down hard, struck me in the middle of my back. Bloodied and defenseless, I looked up at Ted Evans's wrath. That was when I saw her. Mrs. Patrice Evans. She was in the background, hysterical and crying. Her eyes were blackened, her lips swollen and bleeding profusely. She had on her panties and bra. She'd chased him after he had beaten her. She could barely stand up. My eyes met his. He drew the tire iron back, raised that metal high, spit flying with his every breath as he prepared to strike me in my head, gritted his teeth and prepared to send me to whatever existed on the other side of life. Then he screamed and brought the tire iron down.

Isabel was sleeping, her head resting on my chest when I jerked awake. My breathing was fast. It took moments to calm down and realize where I was. I was inside of Isabel's apartment. I'd come here after I'd collected the Post-its and left Mr. Holder. Ted's killing me had been a dream. A nightmare. Guilt. Fear. Isabel stirred, and then she shifted. She woke smiling. Her short dream had been peaceful. She adjusted her head on my chest as her fingers danced across my belly. Her hand touched me for a while and my mind let go of the nightmare. Isabel touched my penis, traced her finger along its length, and then she held its girth inside of her hand. The last of the nightmare abandoned me and I teased my fingers though her hair.

She said, "So you turned the apartment

over to Mr. Holder."

"His daughter is pregnant. And she's between jobs."

"So I heard. More than likely he'll forgive Vera-Anne and take her back at some point."

"He hacked her e-mails. He knows too much to ever feel comfortable with her. He knows the truth. He knows how she feels about him. And since he did that, she wouldn't trust him."

"When people no longer trust each other, it's a different ballgame."

In the background, from her record player, Bill Withers sang "Lean on Me."

Isabel whispered, "Tea?"

"In a moment. Your skin feels good next to mine. Let's enjoy being naked in your bed."

"Well, Varg, I'm glad you came to visit me."

"I was worried when I didn't see you, Sweet Isabel. I had looked for you in the crowd."

Isabel said, "Your wife. Stunning. She really made these flats a lively place for a while."

"Despite all that has happened, despite her dark clouds, she made the sun come out."

"Such a bloody scandal. Now the man she was with has killed a girl and killed himself."

"It will die down at some point. The public gets bored very easily. They will move on."

"You'll have to forgive your wife. In order to make your marriage work, as James Thicke, you will have to forgive your wife. We all make mistakes. That's why pencils have erasers."

"I know."

"Just don't forgive her too soon. Don't stop being Varg Veum too soon."

"Aren't you a tad bit selfish?"

She kissed my chest. "Just to let you know, I'll be here a while. Open invitation to you."

"A while? Going somewhere?"

"Soon I will put on my Union Jack T-shirt and travel back across the pond."

"Leaving America?"

"Yes. I should've returned home after my husband died, but I didn't. I thought that I'd become a teacher and change the Yanks. Well, I tried. Hopefully I made a difference. But I've overstayed my welcome here. I miss the dreariness of the UK. I miss all of my family as well. I miss the West End, Piccadilly Circus, riding the tube, the whole lot. My heart is in Great Britain."

"Sorry to hear that you're leaving."

"I'll be moving to Canvey Island. Would be nice to see you before I leave."

"That would be nice."

She said, "If only you were a tad bit younger. If only."

"And if only you were a tad bit older."

Sweet Isabel mounted me.

Soon I'd leave, not sure if I'd ever be able to become Varg Veum again. But for now, I clung to being Varg Veum. I clung to him the way I held onto Isabel.

Mrs. Patrice Evans lived in building K on the second floor, apartment K-269. I went to the apartment where she lived with her husband. There was a lot of foot traffic on her floor. And as people passed me and stared, I decorated her door with the hundred Post-its that she had put on my door. On the one right below the peephole I wrote one word in bold letters: GOODBYE.

That done, I put the Domino's hanger on the doorknob and headed toward my car.

Sometimes less was more.

But I knew that tonight there would be more, not less.

I tried calling my wife's assistant. I called her a dozen times before she answered.

She heard my voice and hung up on me.

I tried again and she did the same.

She knew too much.

She had been in the center of it all.

Anger simmering, stress rising, heart aching, I headed toward a confrontation that could rival my night with Bobby Holland. With Downey in my rearview mirror and the Hollywood sign growing larger with each passing second, I clenched my teeth and headed toward Los Feliz.

CHAPTER 38

When I made it back to my estate, I stood in the garage for a while. Each wall in the structure was a work of art, the building fit to be a wing inside of the Uffizi. The Bentley had been returned and rested comfortably with the rest of my fleet. Windshield and headlight had been replaced. Bullet holes mended. No traceable paperwork. As if there had never been a shootout on Skirball Center Drive. Regina hadn't been in the repaired car yet. I looked in the trunk and saw the computer that I had hidden there when I had left Bobby Holland's home a week ago.

Seated near the pool, surrounded by palm trees and waterfalls that defined our purlieu, my wife had a martini at her side. She was topless and had on a yellow bikini bottom. That meant that all of the staff was gone. Her hair was wet, slicked back into a ponytail. She'd been swimming. It had been a stressful day for her, a busy day for Hollywood. Johnny Bergs's memorial service had been held earlier. So had Bobby Holland's, only Holland's was smaller, quieter, with no hysterical fans lining the streets.

I didn't go to either. Regina didn't ask me to go. I doubt if I was missed.

One man had accidentally fucked my wife and I'd intentionally killed the other.

Regina sat up and as I approached, she said, "I fired my assistant."

Hands in my pockets, I stood in front of her. "Alice Ayres?"

"You know her name. I'm surprised."

I paused. "You fired her or she quit?"

"I realized, that after all of these years, I couldn't trust her."

"What did she do?"

"Don't play stupid, James."

"My psychic abilities are offline, so I won't know what you don't tell me."

She let a few dramatic seconds pass before she said, "Steve Martin."

As the lights in the back yard illuminated the moment, we stared at each other.

She said, "The iPhone that you're looking for."

"You have it."

"I have it."

"I figured that out while I was gone. Why

did you take it?"

"And you must remember to lock your phone. Always. You left it unlocked and sitting in the bathroom. If you had actually lost it, anyone could've found it. Do you have any idea what that would've cost us at this point? We would've lost everything two times over."

"I need that phone back from you, Regina."

"Well, I thought that it was the phone that you used to call that skank who came into your apartment. The one who came in like she was your whore. I was sitting on the bed and a naked woman ran in and jumped in the bed with me. Yeah, I looked for her number. I went through everything. I went through text messages. I went though e-mails. And none of it made any sense. I was wondering how your phone had e-mails that I had sent to my assistant and her e-mails to me. Then I realized that it wasn't your phone. It was hers. But you had it with you."

"Why would you do that?"

"I'm still a woman, James."

"I've never doubted that you were a woman, Regina. Not for one moment."

"I saw the videos. They were gruesome, but I watched them."

"Not as gruesome as having to watch you with Johnny Bergs."

"What I did wasn't criminal."

"By God's law."

She laughed. "When was the last time you heard about God putting somebody in jail? And if He did, there'd be nobody left to walk the streets. The 405 and the 10 would be wide open."

I took a breath. "Where is the phone now?"

"Did you pay my assistant to spy on me?"

"Of course not."

"She had the video of me. Of Bobby Holland. Of Johnny Bergs."

"She had the video of Holland supplying you, Bergs, and his date with blow and E."

"Bullshit. It's a video of us snorting blow. No one will care where it came from. No one would give a fuck. Why would you keep something like that? Were you going to hold that over my head and control me? Were you picking up where Bobby Holland left off?"

"I killed Bobby Holland for you."

"I'm flattered."

"Flattered."

"I am flattered. I really am. You killed a monster so you could take its place."

"I killed the Bergs because of you."

"Why would you keep something that could once again ruin us?"

"Why would I want to ruin us?"

"Or just ruin me? I wouldn't have had any idea that you had it."

"I killed for you. Wasn't that enough to show my level of fucking commitment?"

"Did you? Or did all of this come about because you can't handle your own damn jealousy? Seeing me with Johnny Bergs really got under your skin. It meant nothing to me. *Nothing.* And knowing that Bobby Holland was my ex probably bothered you just as much."

"Right. I'm going around Hollywood killing everyone you used to fuck."

"But the thing that happened with Johnny Bergs made you lose it."

"Was it intentional?"

"Would it matter?"

"Did you create another scandal? Was it fucking intentional?"

"Would it matter?"

"I guess it wouldn't."

"I'm tired of being manipulated."

"I've never manipulated you, Regina."

"The video of you and the Bergs. The shootout. I watched it all. Watched it a few times."

"I need that, Regina."

"It was amazing. I never would've guessed that you had that much rage inside you."

"I need that in my hands and I want it stored inside of my safe deposit box."

"No worries. I have already stored it inside of mine."

"It belongs to me, Regina. I want it stored inside of my safety deposit box, not yours."

"I'll keep it. Your wife will keep it for you."

"In case it ever comes back on me, I'll need that to show that it was self-defense."

She shook her head. "Wrong, James."

"It would help exonerate me."

"I told you that I was all the alibi that you needed. You should've destroyed it all."

"What am I missing?"

"The Bergs followed you and attacked you."

I nodded. "Five against one."

"I saw that."

"Self-defense."

"It plays out well on the video."

"They shot at me first and made threats."

"It was horrible, but you did what you had to do. However, it was hard to tell who had guns in that light. The problem was the gun that you used to shoot them with, James. You should've used your own gun. You used Bobby Holland's gun. And that traces back to Bobby Holland. Sure, it made it look like

Bobby was at the scene of the crime. Sure it led the police back to the man that you drowned. There would be only one question that they would need to ask you at this point. And it would be one question that you couldn't possibly answer. If you had to use that tape to defend yourself, it would do the opposite. How did you get a dead man's gun? I'm sure that the police are doing their best to make their theories work. Bobby killing the Bergs and then going home and slipping and bumping his head and drowning in his pool as his whore slept poolside. The video of the shootout would tie it all up. They'd know that you killed Bobby and stole his gun. I'm sure that the Hungarian claiming Bobby was there all evening added to the confusion, but they still know that something isn't right. Bobby killing five men before any of them had a chance to run more than a few feet? No way. He was a lousy shot with a gun. You've had professional training. You should've used your own gun, James."

When she had finished, all I could say was, "Something is always left behind."

She said, "And something is always done wrong."

"We can delete all of the videos together."

"Oh, I've already deleted mine. Mine is

already deleted. Only yours remain."

"Will you give me the iPhone so that I can delete the rest?"

"Of course I will. On our golden anniversary."

"Golden is fiftieth."

"I know."

"On our fiftieth wedding anniversary?"

"In a little over forty-seven years, it will be my gift to you."

I stared at her for a long while. The tension between us was disgusting.

In the end, I made the corners of my lips rise.

Her smile mirrored mine. "And one minor correction."

"Okay."

"It was four against one. The fifth one, you gunned him down like he was a dog."

"Bloodlust."

"The desire for extreme violence and carnage, often aroused in the heat of battle and leading to uncontrolled slaughter and torture. I think that's the proper definition of the word."

"Yes. Bloodlust."

She shook her head. "Should've used your own gun."

"Should've. But I had left it with you. Plus, a lot had happened that evening."

She reached for my hand and took the tips of the fingers on my left hand.

"You're mine, James. I told you how I felt about you from the start. I've admired you. I admired you long before you even knew that I was interested in you. All I want is you, James."

"You have me now."

"I own you."

"That you do."

"If I didn't have you before, I have you now."

We stared at each other a little while longer. My wife. Behind her that big swimming pool. Too much temptation. I left her, went back inside my office. I exploded and threw things.

When I was done destroying my office, my wife was in the doorway watching me.

"And by the way. I have five offers for movies. One by Spielberg. Two of the others are Oscar-worthy. And my office has messages from David Lynch, Martin Scorsese, Joel and Ethan Coen, Steven Soderbergh, Terrence Malick, Abbas Kiarostami, Ang Lee, and Hayao Miyazaki. A few others have called too. This is going to turn out to be a wonderfully busy season for me."

Sweat drained down my back. "That's great, Regina. Congratulations."

"My publicist and agent are begging to come back on board. They are kissing my ass like I'm Hazel Tamana Bijou. I'll take them back, but at a reduced fee, and they will work harder than slaves. I'm tired of them living off me. And my asking price just went up two mil. I'll be in front of Angelina Jolie and Sara Jessica Parker. I'm number one now. *I'm number one.*"

"Why so mean?"

"Being nice didn't work. Everyone treated me like shit and abandoned me."

"It's all working out in your favor."

"But no matter what I am offered, I want to star in *Boy Meets Girl* first."

"No problem. You own me. Your name will be above the title."

She stepped over the mess that I had made, and kissed me. When she was done, she went to my desk. She took a package out of her pocket, emptied medicinal powder, used her American Express Black card to make two white lines, rolled up a one-hundred-dollar bill, sniffed one line, then smiled at me. She wanted me to say something. She wanted a bigger fight.

She said, "You should try it."

"You're off the wagon."

"It's not as bad as you think. You should

573

snort some off my ass. Get a new perspective."

"So, you're not going to rehab."

She did the other line then reached inside her pocket and took out a watch. It was Bobby Holland's watch. She sat that timepiece on my desk as if that was now a gift from her to me.

She said, "I finally have control over my life. God's grace and mercy covers me."

A hint of benzoylmethylecgonine rested on the tip of her nose. Instinctively, I reached to her face and wiped away the product of the leaves of the coca plant. I stared at her as the nervous system stimulant took root. Her eyes lit up with the love for cocaine. I sat back down and watched her, then moved my eyes from her and faced my companion Underwood.

She asked, "What are you about to do?"

"I'm going to work on this script awhile."

"Almost done?"

"In the final pages of the third act. I have to write this final tragedy."

"I'm going to bathe. When you're done writing, come to bed."

"I'm going to be up a while."

"And, baby, this isn't a barn so please don't leave your clothes scattered everywhere."

Then she kissed me, eased her tongue inside of my mouth, and gave me so much passion. I held her and we kissed for as long as she wanted to, for minutes, but it felt like hours.

She whispered, "I do love you, James. I'm your number one fan. Always will be. But I have to protect myself the best way I know how."

"You don't trust me."

"I don't fucking trust you."

She left my destroyed office singing and headed for the main house, framed by extravagance. She was on top of the world. Or maybe she was floating on lavish clouds. She gazed back at me and smiled her flawless, smoldering billboard smile. I smiled a loving smile in return. She blew me a kiss. *I love you.* I blew her one in return. Then the woman with the perfect body, the perfect legs, the perfect breasts, the perfect ass, the prefect face, the woman from Montana, sashayed across our Ruritanian estate, a queen behind iron gates and high walls that surrounded her kingdom. She strolled across her land and went inside her eight-thousand-square foot castle.

Dead actor. Dead comedienne. Dead Bergs. Dead director.

Dying young had made many movie stars

permanent legends. They never had to age or fall from greatness. If Phoenix, Dean, or Belushi had lived, they'd have faded into oblivion in due time. Same for Amy Winehouse. If we lived long enough, we were well all tossed aside. Dying stopped the clock. A lot of clocks had stopped on behalf of Regina Baptiste.

I sat at my desk and stared at the residue from her medicinal powder. It was the same substance that I had wiped away from the bathroom counter back at the apartment in Downey. Her assistant had brought her clothing and some blow to powder her nervous little nose. Her assistant didn't have a choice. It was do it or lose her job. Regina Baptiste had done a line before she went to greet her crowd. Maybe that was when she had seen and stolen the iPhone.

My eyes went to Underwood, brain on fire, and fingers over the keys, but not moving.

And then I did type two words: *Red Rum.*

For a while I thought about Hazel Tamana Bijou. For a moment, again, I reached back.

I was angry with her for a while, again gnashing my teeth over what didn't happen in the past, vexed over the present that I owned now. Hazel had been the fork in the road. If only her text message had come through on that night two years ago. If only she had called me once over the next nine days. One phone call from Hazel could've changed the course of mighty rivers.

I looked at the photo of my wife that was on my desk.

Then I typed faster: *Red Rum Red Rum Red Rum.*

Bobby Holland's luxurious watch laughed in my face. Those chortles reminded me that his computer was still in the trunk of the Bentley.

I ran to the Bentley, removed the Mac, and rushed it to my office. For an hour I looked at Bobby Holland's archives, watched homemade videos that he had saved of my wife.

Something was always left behind.

Something wrong was always done.

In minutes I could upload the scandalous and career-ending videos he had of Regina Baptiste and show the world the superstar at her finest. I could upload everything that Bobby Holland had archived and send it from his e-mail accounts. He had been connected to a dozen social networking sites and his password had been stored on them all. Posthumous retribution was still vengeance. I could finish what Bobby Holland had started. I should. I really should.

I clicked an icon on the screen and the video of my wife with Johnny Handsome played.

I went to my file cabinet and opened the bottom drawer. Stored inside of that bottom drawer, beneath a pile of unsold scripts, was a wooden box. Inside that box was a bottle of 1978 Balvenie vintage cask single malt Scotch whiskey and a handwritten note from Bobby Holland.

THE COKE HEAD BITCH IS YOURS NOW. GOOD RIDDANCE AND GOOD LUCK YOU FUCKIN PRICK.

I opened the whiskey and poured three fingers worth inside of a Universal Studios coffee cup. When that was finished I wiped the powder away from the top of my desk with my dank finger, knew that it had stuck to my flesh as I stared at my wife's obsession.

Love was a beast that fueled anger. Only the pang in someone's heart could do him or her in. It was love, not its envoy, not a man and not a woman, that we fought and lost the battle with. Those had been the words of Isabel. The wisdom that had come from Sweet Isabel stayed with me for a moment. Then the echo from her words faded like a wisp of smoke in the wind.

I ran my finger over my gums, removed the residual blow that had been on my dank flesh, and then I backed away from Underwood. I vacated the well-decorated cottage that I used as my office, left the same furniture and artistic trappings that had decorated the life of Veum, the effects from the whiskey and the blow enlightening me, and moved across Spanish tile. I took a deep breath, and faced the pool. I'd drowned a man. I'd killed men. As the cool night air blew, I marched deeper into my lavish backyard and glowered toward the iconic HOLLYWOOD sign.

Filled with rage, each word seethed, "One text message, Hazel. One phone call."

I picked up my .38. Made sure it was loaded.

Once again it was time for us to make headlines.

CHAPTER 39

When I stepped inside, it was silent. She was there. My wife was standing at the opposite end of the long hallway, all of the lights dimmed, waiting on me, her body language harsh, her pose as if she were in search of aggression. She was ready for violence. She wore a long housecoat, her feet bare, faced me with her hands in both pockets.

She said, "I was waiting for you."

"I knew you would be."

We stared for a long moment before she said, "You look angry, James. Very angry."

"You look diabolical."

"I'm hurt."

"You fucked Johnny Handsome and now you're going to fuck me over."

She kept her eyes on mine. "What do you want me to do?"

"We are where we are. You got us here. Decide. This is your fork in the road."

She let a few seconds go by. "I wanted to be able to trust you."

"I wanted a wife who slept only with me."

She came to me and paused, her expression harsh, her hands moving inside of her pockets, her face telling me that she was making a life-changing decision. She swallowed, licked her lips, then she took out her left hand and gave me the iPhone that we had argued over.

With both hands, she wiped tears from her eyes and said, "Delete everything."

As she stood in front of me, I made sure it was the right iPhone and that she wasn't trying to pull a trick. It was the same iPhone. I deleted the videos of me murdering Bobby Holland, deleted the videos of me killing the Bergs. Then I reset the iPhone, wiped out everything.

She said, "Delete the photos on your Nikon too. I looked at them all. I saw them all."

"Okay."

"Naked women. I saw the photos of the girl on your bed. Photos of all those strangers. And the skinny girl with the dreadlocks. It was as if you ran off and had another life."

"You abandoned me. For a while, I did. I made friends. And I made enemies."

Her arrogance had waned, but she was

still angry. "Will you go back to that life?"

I hesitated. "Will you give me a reason to?"

She took a deep breath. "I guess we'd better pack. It's going to be a long trip."

"Where are we going?"

"Only a couple of places I can go from here."

"Which are?"

"Antigua or Australia, or an early grave."

"That's three places."

"Yeah. That was three. I'm buzzed, so let's just forget that I mentioned the third."

"So it's Crossroads Center or The Sanctuary."

"You can pick the facility. I won't argue. I won't fight. I want to be clean again."

"You could stay here and go to Promises. Or I could drive you to Passages."

"I want to be out of the country, away from lights, cameras, and the business. Away from all of the news about Bobby Holland and Johnny Bergs. I need to be away. Or if you want to visit England for a month, I can slip into The Priory in Roehampton. Doesn't matter. Just take me away from Hollywood and fix me. Fix me again. Can't let him win. Can't let Bobby Holland win."

I asked, "Why the sudden change? An hour ago, I was your worst enemy."

"I was watching the video again, just now. As angry as I was, as evil as I felt, one part got to me. It reminded me of something. That's why I was coming back out there to you."

"Which video?"

"Me. Bobby Holland. Johnny Bergs. In his trailer. Before all of this happened."

"Okay."

"I'm married to the best man in the world. Even if I never reach number one at the box office again, even if I never reach number three or five or seven, I'm number one in his heart and he is number one in mine. I know, that sounds corny. But being in love is corny. I'm from Montana. I was raised on corny. And hopefully I'll be corny until the day I die."

"You're quoting yourself."

She whispered, "In the end, we are all victims, not of each other, but of nature."

"Somebody should put that in a screenplay."

She put her arms around me and whispered, "Australia. I want to go back to Australia."

"Australia it is."

"Then I'll have my office call Spielberg and everyone else. I'll delay everything."

"Up to you. I'm your husband. But I'm

not the boss of your career."

"I have to listen to you. You're the only person in Hollywood who hasn't done me wrong."

"Hire your personal assistant back. And give her a raise."

She paused. "Can I think about it?"

"If you don't hire her, I'll hire her and let her work for me."

She pressed her lips against mine. "We should make a baby."

"For headlines."

"No. Because I love you. Because I really, really love you. I want to have your baby."

"We could get you well, practice, then practice some more, and see what happens over the next ten years or so."

The loaded .38 that was in the small of my back would remain unused.

So would the .22 that she had hidden inside the right pocket of her housecoat.

She was prepared to gun me down when I walked inside my house. She had calculated it all. She had read thousands of scripts and knew how to make this one end in her favor. She had the tape of me killing Bobby Holland. I was a jealous man, a murderer, a villian who had recorded his own wrongdoings. She could've shot me and as I lay dying, sipped wine, and dialed 9-1-1. All she had to do was show that to the police, then say that I came after her, and she was terrified, in fear of her life. She would've gotten away with it. Especially since I had my .38 in the small of my back. But she didn't gun me down. I don't know how close she was to becoming a widow.

I had been two seconds from being a widower.

Two seconds from having paparazzi and grieving fans outside my gates. Bloodlust lived.

I exhaled, swallowed, trembled, closed my eyes, happy that I didn't set my anger free and gun her down as she stood in the hallway.

Nobody would die tonight.

The mean streets of Tinseltown were filled with enough blood to last it for a while.

Being married was like a stagecoach ride in the old West.

When you started, you hoped for an enjoyable trip.

Before you reached the halfway point, you just hoped to live to tell the tale.

Tonight there would be no fireworks.

Tonight there would be no more headlines.

Tonight, in her eyes, I was more important than Hollywood.

Tonight she would be willing to drop the film for the guy.

I couldn't speak for tomorrow.

After all, tomorrow is another day.

¡BIENVENIDOS A LOS RECONOCIMIENTOS DE ESTE LIBRO!

O ye faithful reader, thanks for stepping inside the bookshop or mega-store or downloading or stopping by the library to pick up this copy of *An Accidental Affair.* I hope that you enjoyed the read from top to bottom. Pardon me for talking so fast. I just got off the phone with Gideon. There was a lot of noise and he yelled that he was in Uruguay, and then he shouted something about Midnight and The Four Horsemen before gunfire erupted and the call dropped. Now homie has me stressed out. He called me from an iPhone. Roaming charges are no joke. I hope his bill won't be as high as mine was.

The saga shall continue. In the meantime . . .

Thanks to all of the hardworking people at Dutton, the best publishing company from coast to coast. Brian Tart, once again, thanks a zillion for supporting my work and keeping me on the payroll. Denise Roy, my new editor, welcome aboard. Thanks for reading this when it was about 100,000 pages long. I brought the scissors and did a little redecorating. To Ava Kavyani and everyone working overtime in publicity, thanks. I've spent two seasons on the road and I'll do my best to stay home a while. Maybe. But I doubt it. Sara Camilli and everyone working at the Sara Camilli Agency, thanks for everything. I think I have eighty books to go. So, yeah, I better tell Ava that I'll need to return to the road. New places, new faces, new locations. Keeps it exciting para mí.

To Karl and Tammy at the Planer Group in Los Angeles, thanks for all of the hard work.

John Paine, de nuevo, thanks for all of your wonderful input.

Toni Goodwin, thanks for your assistance desde Inglaterra. Blimey! Brilliant!

Denea Marcel in Los Angeles. Muchas gracias, también!

George and Gladys, mis profesores de español en las Bahamas, Sonia Brown and Brown Entertainment, Dr. Myles Poitier, mi médico at Cable Beach, Robert and Carla Whitingham, many thanks for all of the support on the island of New

Providence.

Now, as usual, if I have omitted anyone, here's your chance to shine.

Saving the best for last, I want to thank _____ for all of their help while I was working on this novel. Ask 'em what they did. For many months I cracked a mean whip and they worked hard lifting these vowels and toting those verbs while trying not to dangle their participles. They will tell you what else they did to help. Wait. They signed a confidentiality agreement. They'll get sued if they tell. ☺ LOL!

Tuesday, July 26, 2011. 12:22 A.M.
 33. 65. 84. 42 75°F Humidity: 94%
 Current: Cloudy with scattered showers Wind: W at 2 mph

Cargo pants, polo, hair too long, y tengo mucho hambre. Voy a comer algo.
 Feel free to stop by www.cricjeromedickey .com. From there you can link to other sites, Facebook and Twitter. Oh, yeah. Stop by and join the fan page on Facebook.

E Jerome

ABOUT THE AUTHOR

Originally from Memphis, Tennessee, **Eric Jerome Dickey** is the *New York Times* bestselling author of nineteen novels. He is also the author of a six-issue miniseries of graphic novels for Marvel Enterprises featuring Storm (*X-Men*) and the Black Panther, and several short stories.